Parzival

A Journey of Initiation

2021
Innerwork Books
PO Box 1064
Mullumbimby NSW 2482
Australia

Innerwork Books

Hardcover ISBN: 978-0-6485789-3-2
Paperback ISBN: 978-0-6485789-4-9
Ebook ISBN: 978-0-6485789-5-6

Parzival

A Journey of Initiation

Adapted by Séamus Maynard
from Wolfram von Eschenbach's *Parzival* translated by A.T. Hatto

TABLE OF CONTENTS

Forward VII

Introduction XIII

Dedication 17

Prologue. 19

Part I- Youth 21

The Angevin 23

Soltane 42

Jeschute 51

Sigune The Sorrowful. 58

The Fisherman 62

Ither 65

Gurnemanz. 82

Condwiramurs 96

Part II- The Quest. 121

Munsalvaesche. 123

The Woeful Sigune 139

Jeschute & Orilus 146

The Three Drops of Blood 155

Part III- Initiation 177

The Sorceress & The Landgrave 179

Ascalun 194

The Anchoress & The Templar 217

Gabenis .225

Trevrizent 231

Orgeluse .250

Schastel Marveile 280

The Garland Tree 303

Clinschor .331

A Reckoning at Dawn 339

The Pagan Emperor 374

The Return 384

The Grail Castle 389

Epilogue 395

Appendix A- List of Characters 403

Appendix B- Extended Prologue 410

Appendix C- Notes on Iambic Pentameter   418

List of Illustrations:

The Dove and the Stone 18

Munsalvaesche 122

Gabenis 224

Trevrizent .234

The Grail Castle 388

FORWARD

Within this work we are invited to meet Wolfram von Eschenbach's Parzival through the ensouled process of artist Séamus Maynard. It is a gift and a necessity in this age to have the past work brought to the world in a renewed way that deepens the artistry. The arts are the gifted bridge to the spirit that feeds the longing soul, even when it is not aware of this longing. The path of initiation is not gifted, but must be won through our own efforts. In this incredible gifted bridge, we are instructed in the path of conscious initiation, shall we be willing to take it. The Parzival journey and the capacities that are developed on this journey are available to all, but only those with the will for the path may succeed in unfolding all its stages.

It may seem less relevant in this age of technology, to deepen our inner life and our inner capacities, but it is in fact a greater necessity. Through the arts we are adjusted from focusing on the outer being and who we are in our outer expression such as body type, gender, race, and sex, and focus instead on the inner being that is indeed shaped by the world and the circumstances of our life but is also beyond those earthly formative forces. The Parzival journey is a journey of developing inner capacity and as it is not the outer journey of one particular person, we can all enter the Parzival journey within.

Parzival is the story of an initiate's long journey to finding their own way into a conscious connection with the spiritual worlds. Parzival, like many, travels a solemn, individual path that is indicative of someone bringing into the earthly world a new way, the new age, the new method, the new way of seeing and perceiving that will be a way of the many in the future. This new way needs to be carved by the initiates, those that walk ahead of the group while serving the group's future.

Like all deep stories, this wonderful story is as complex as the human being, with so many aspects to unfold and understand that it can be entered into again and again. All inner aspects are given a symbol in the story, and so we cannot read it literally. Fortunately the artistic impulse of the work helps us to not dissect it in this manner, but the more we penetrate the work, the more it reveals. This is not a man doing outer battle with other men, it is an inner journey that can lead to deepening inner capacities. We are not told this is an initiate's journey; what we are told is that the Parzival archetype makes its way from dullness, to doubt, to blessedness. These are the three stages towards initiation through which all candidates for initiation must pass, but they are named differently according to different traditions. Dullness is an interesting expression in this story; in some Eastern traditions, it has been called ignorance, ignorance is the first call that leads us to enter life and gain knowledge through living. Dullness is represented in the story when the candidate leaves home and doesn't even know their own name and is dressed in fool's clothing. We repeatedly must leave the home of the spiritual world in order to awaken to the truth of who we are and why we are here. Within the Eastern traditions as well as many esoteric Western traditions, the human being does not only have one life but reincarnates. It is said that the rope of ignorance is the first rope that calls us into incarnation and the last to be cut through as through its fulfillment, it is not necessary to incarnate again.

Whether we recognise reincarnation or not, all as individuals move in life from not knowing to knowing in various ways, but the initiate does this in relationship to the spiritual realities and the spiritual world. In order to truly do this, many, very many forces must be slain: all the forces tied up in believing that only what the senses can tell us is real; all the powers that direct our lives according to a materialistic outlook on the world and on ourselves; all the enemies that want to keep us unfree. Parzival must learn to do battle within all that prevents the fullness of all knowledge, and the sword that is wielded is an esoteric symbol of clear thinking. We see the sword of the tarot and the myths, the must-have sword that has its place in the esoteric ritual work as a manifested talisman of clear precise thinking. All we have learnt to think in our youth is not enough to surmount the obstacles we now face within ourselves and those that come towards us from the common thought life of the community.

Many youth at 16 years of age awaken to their thinking in a new way, and with it they awaken to the restrictions that have been placed upon them and the enemies of the truth, beauty, and goodness of the life around them. They may awaken to realities beyond the conditions they find themselves born into and find an inner world that is unexplained by the thinking of materialism. However, they are still in a state of dullness, and even though they may be given entry into the castle, they are not awake enough to ask the question that would lead to greater knowledge, just as Parzival cannot, despite his youthful finding of the Grail Castle, Munsalvaesche. Parzival's finding is the beginning of his way out of the dullness as he learns to remain faithful to inner experiences. It is extraordinary that a story like this is not only an instruction of the inner journey of Parzival but at the same time can be the awakener to any individual that unites with it. It is a story that makes sense of our inner struggles and our inner displacement in life's outer presentations that seem erroneous to the awakening soul. The things that we are presented with as 'the way to be' are often in discord with the inner realms and can result in anxiety and depression if we are unable to reconcile the healthy inner responses to the injustices in the world that curb any human being from unfolding who they are and who they can be.

Parzival is assailed by the second stage of development, doubt, when leaving King Arthur's knights for the second time, after the shame precipitating tongue lashing by the monstrous Cundrie. All the thoughts that we must transform have a consciousness behind them that manifests to the initiate as a grotesque being. A being that all must meet as with it we meet what we have put out into the world. No one can help us here as we must all be responsible for our own shadow nature. It is here we see where we have contributed to the injustices in the world and wonder where the goodness of the spirit is. Who and what is behind all the errors of humanity, and why would the spiritual world allow this?

Parzival renounces the service towards the spiritual world, because within Parzival's eyes, God has failed their relationship. We may all have doubt in response to occurrences that we encounter inwardly on the inner development path, we may even reject them. We all meet doubt towards the spirit on the inner journey as we all meet fear of the spirit, although we may meet them to varying degrees. Fear can be projected as fear of rejection and can also be expressed in the force of rejecting others. How many times do we see the projection of what we most fear being placed outside ourselves. Through this rejection of the spirit without, the long lonely road begins, one where nothing but ourselves and the spirit within can get us through and overcome what we have met in ourselves, revealed by the encounter with the being, Cundrie, that acts as the catalyst for another stage of inner development.

Doubt can leave many unable to move, but Parzival continues to do battle with the foes of the inner path of development. It is not until after many jousts, none of them unseating the commitment to battle the untrue, and the breaking and mending of his sword, that on Good Friday, Parzival calls once again upon God to be a guide on the path that has been chosen and walked, out of his own free inner resources. The horse is given its own lead, and Parzival asks for it to take the best road that would lead to support. The horse takes Parzival to the hermit Trevizent.

Trevizent is a consciousness completely devoted to the path and tells Parzival of the spiritual evolution of the earth and of the burdens that are carried: failure to heal Anfortas, killing Ither in unchivalrous combat, and of the death of his mother, Herzeloyde. The weight of all this karma is too much for Parzival to bear. So Trevrizent offers to help carry it through the power of prayer until Parzival is ready to take on the full responsibility of this destiny. Once we have reached this stage the spirit is with us helping us in all we do, but we still need to meet what is ours to meet.

Now Gawain's adventures come to the fore, mainly his overcoming of Clinschor's Castle of Wonders. When Parzival and Gawain next meet, they fight each other without knowing whom it is they fight. Yet when realization sets in of whom they fight, each agrees it was as if they fought their own self. Each walks the path individually, but we gain collective capacities, and we can through these capacities recognize our true companions in the work. Within our being it is a great learning to recognise the foes, but also to not burn through all that is needed to continue to grow; not everything within is to be fought — some forces must be befriended.

— Lisa Romero, August 2021

Author, and founder of the Social Understanding, Gender, and Sexuality school and community programs (developingtheself.org)

INTRODUCTION

The inspiration for writing this piece arose out of a necessity, the necessity to uncover some aspect of the heart of the Parzival legend in order to give dramatic renderings of certain episodes that are depicted on his quest. These events as they are described through the imaginative pictures in the story provide an opportunity, not only for enjoying a good story, but also to come to a deeper understanding of the experiences that arise when an individual chooses to take up their own spiritual path of initiation.

As I worked to uncover these main events in the story, in order to portray them in simple dramatic renderings for groups of young people and adults, it became apparent that the translations of Eschenbach's Parzival that I was working with were cloaked in the literary and social conventions of the time in which the story was first written and later translated. The dense, academic, and literary cloak, which the story was wrapped in, obscured the imaginative and experiential impact of the events in the journey when it came to making a script for a dramatic telling of the story.

As an actor and storyteller, I had worked for many years with the texts of Shakespeare and other poets whose mastery encompassed the art of drama, and I missed the immediacy, imaginative power, and directness of such texts. In frustration, I was eventually led to creating my own script which would strive to emulate, in a modest way, the forms that those great masters of the word had employed to fashion their dramatic works.

The legend of Parzival is a living being which exists independent of its authors. It has been told many times by many different writers, and each time it is retold, new aspects of its nature are revealed while the heart of the legend remains authentic to itself.

The depth of experience which occurs when engaging with this tale on a deeper level than just the intellect is what has driven me to complete this project despite the obvious social challenges of offering a book which is currently being cut from the curriculum of many schools.

One of the glaring difficulties that I first encountered with writing the piece was the inherent patriarchal backdrop of the original tale. With a small team of committed editors, I have worked to recast all of the female roles in the story whose strong, clear voices, silent in Eschenbach's telling, rang clearly once they were somewhat unshackled from their prison of historical gender oppression.

It is of the utmost importance to grapple with these questions in our times. Having said that, it is also of the utmost importance not to do away with the deep wisdom and experience which lies within legends such as Parzival. It is crucial to approach a legend such as this one with the understanding that it is not at all meant to be understood as a literal representation of characters and events but as a dream-like depiction of inner soul experiences, all of which can be found in one human soul- regardless of their sex, gender, or nationality. The character of Parzival is a representative of an individual human being, the characters that he encounters depict the many varied, complex expressions of the human soul life and the events that occur are metaphors for the inner challenges and discoveries of a human soul on a spiritual journey. Though one can observe aspects of our individual nature which resemble one character or another character in the story, it is most important to understand that we each have the potential for all of the characters to live within our inner life of experience.

In order to truly understand the legend of Parzival, one must come to understand the language of soul pictures in which it speaks. Male and female characters do not need to be thought of as male and female in the way that we think of them but as representations of the eternal masculine and eternal feminine powers that make up the balance in every human being regardless of their sex and gender. Soul capacities have nothing to do with being male or female. One can understand this by the examples one finds not only in legends but also in everyday life. It is not only useful but also enjoyable and deeply fulfilling to approach the Parzival legend with this in mind.

Some helpful questions to ask when setting out on the Parzival journey could be: what qualities, capacities, or virtues do the characters express through actions and words? What virtues arise through the relationships between characters and from the unfolding events in the story?

In the realm of imagination, which is where the legend exists, we are not bound to our everyday materialistic sense of things but can be liberated to experience the beautiful language of soul in which such stories speak. When we set our literal mind aside, it becomes apparent that our own soul can recognize these deeper imaginative pictures that live in the story without the need to analyze or dissect the story with our intellects. The soul knows that the image of a sword is not a literal sword, but a picture of the mastered and clarified thought life. It can understand that a battle is not a literal battle where one would try to kill someone with the sword but a living image of the mastery we need to cultivate in order to navigate the treacherous inner realms of the soul. We must be able to have a sharpened and honed capacity for thinking and speaking our thoughts in order to navigate both the inner and the outer world of experience. That is what the mastery of knighthood symbolizes. The soul can understand that, but our dead, materialist, literal, and intellectual ways of thinking and understanding the world will never be able to comprehend the realms of soul that the legend of Parzival traverses.

XV

If one can truly enter the experience of the story, listening for the capacities of soul which speak through the characters, the door of experience will open and the deep wisdom and fructifying life within the imaginative pictures in the story will begin to nourish us, no matter what age, nationality, sex or gender we may be. The story then becomes a continuum of interacting virtues: strength consoles the loyal wounded heart, compassion listens to grief's deep understanding of life, steadfastness answers trepidation, faith holds out until the end of time, joy blesses faith, and love conquers all.

— Séamus Maynard, 2021

DEDICATION

In order for this story to be told,
A vessel 'round it needed fashioning,
Enough souls to contain it in the world.
The chalice has been formed and well upheld,
A few hands whose commitment, work, and lives
Have given space for it to be reborn.
To those souls who have striven for the Grail,
Both now, past, and in future times,
I dedicate this work in siblinghood.
To all those whom for love's benevolence
Now stand, whatever name you call upon
To aid you in your work, whate'er it be,
Be it to serve the good, in gratitude
And with companionship this labor comes.
Unto divinity I dedicate
The opportunity granted by grace:
The chance afforded to participate
In freedom with the greatest work of all.

PROLOGUE

Into our age, beings of eternity
Now manifest and herald forth this tale.
May primal wisdom, written in the stars,
Inscribed, safeguarded, be a healing balm
For ailments of the world's extremity.
Into the hands of honesty and truth,
Let fall these pictures of thy mighty works,
And thunder forth your epic messengers.
Begin now where a tale is best begun,
At its beginning; though were we to trace
All true things to their truest origin,
We'd find all roads lead to their truest source.
But getting there is how we learn to love,
Which is the worthiest of all the arts,
For journeying unfolds our humanness.
Thus, let us hear this epic tale of quest
And perseverance for the highest goal
Toward which a human life can ever strive-
As though it were the tale of each of us.
It's clothed in garments of another time,
Attired outwardly in foreign style,
Which might to some seem far from modern ways;
But, nonetheless, behind its ancient cloak
Resounds the very essence of our times.
May primal costumes make perspectives new,
Now hearing how the future sings its way
Through the characters of old into the present.

PARZIVAL

PART I

Youth

PARZIVAL

THE ANGEVIN

Now shall I tell you of bold Gahmuret,
The puissant prince of prosperous Anjou-
No knight excelled him on the battlefield.
He shattered countless lances while he lived
And was unconquerable in his day.
A man perfected in all knightly ways,
He was not known to boast and only sought
His goal of single and unwavering purpose:
The pursuit of honor through brave acts of knighthood.
His older brother was their father's heir,
And when the old king passed, his son was crowned.
This done, the young prince Gahmuret was free
To seek his worldly fortune how he chose.
He knew of no domain or monarchy
Where he cared to extend his services
Unless it be a one more powerful
Than any other kingdom on the earth-
Such was the wish of young prince Gahmuret-
And so he traveled far through distant lands
To serve the mighty Baruc[1] in Baghdad.
No powerful monarch ruled a greater army
Than that most puissant lord of pagandom[2].
Brave Gahmuret became his trusted man
And won the monarch many victories.

While serving him, Prince Gahmuret was sent
To lend aid to a queen of Zazamanc,

---

1   The term Baruc is generally thought by scholars to be a term
used in the Middle Ages which was synonymous with caliph. The
caliph was the chief Muslim civil and religious ruler in the Middle
Ages, regarded as the successor of Muhammed.
2   Non Christian civilization.

In Africa- the beautiful Belacane.
He came by ship, with his host, to her shores
And fought beside her till her foes were beaten
And driven back ne'er to return again.

Amid this war, Queen Belacane and he
Fell deeply in love, so the brave knight stayed.
Queen Belacane honored brave Gahmuret
And made him king of mighty Zazamanc:
To share the task of rulership with her.
He was lord of a beautiful domain
Upon the northern shores of Africa;
And there, for the remainder of his days,
He could have lived in quiet happiness
With his dear queen and their shared governance-
If he had been content to live in peace.
He had with the great might of his exploits
Thus raised himself from errant knight to king.
Yet having once achieved these victories,
His youthful restlessness returned again.
He yearned for further conquests of the shield.
He loved his Queen but could not bear to stay.
At last, he made his mind up to set forth
And laid plans for a swift departure hence.
Thus, unbeknownst to Belacane, that night
He sailed from Zazamanc. The queen awoke
To find a letter in her lover's hand:

"One heart salutes another, sending love.
In stealth, I've stolen from your side, dear one.
I go in secrecy to temper grief.
I will not now deny my love for you.
I am beset by thoughts of your embrace,
But I am called to acts of chivalry

24

And must pursue them though it cost me all.
I know not when I shall return again.
I leave my love with you and half my heart."

The queen was cut by grief to find him gone
And knew not how to remedy her plight,
For unbeknownst to Gahmuret, the queen
Was carrying their child in her womb
And had been waiting to reveal this news
Once she was certain it was as she hoped;
But now, she rued the secret she had kept
And yearned with all her heart for one more chance
To tell her Gahmuret of this new hope.
And more than that, she wished they had been wed.
But there was no way to send him the news,
For he had not revealed where he was bound.

When many months had lapsed from the event
Of Gahmuret's departure, Belacane
Was graced with the deliverance of a babe.
The child's eyes seemed like two starry portals
That opened to the wide breadth of the heavens,
And he was beautiful in all regards.
He bore the traits of his great lineage,
Two noble lines of mighty kings and queens.
His skin revealed his royal heritage,
For its soft surface was both dark and light.
These two skin tones were intermixed together:
A patterned patchwork rare and beautiful-
Just like his mother and his father's love
Which had merged from their two hearts into one.
When he was born, the queen held her son close
As though she clasped a treasure in her arms
And covered him from head to toe with kisses.
Queen Belacane named her son, Feirefiz,

Which means one of two skin tones from two lands.
He grew up to become a warrior
Of boundless strength and undefeated courage.
A clan of skillful craftsmen were employed
To keep the mighty Feirefiz supplied
With lances which he'd shatter in great jousts.
He was a powerful king and honored lord,
Whom many looked to with great admiration
For his nobility and leadership.

Now Gahmuret had voyaged for a year
And landed on the coast of southern Spain.
He made his way northward in quest of glory
Until his journey led him into Wales.
As he approached the city of Kanvoleis,
He saw the pennants of a multitude
Of warriors from many foreign lands,
All gathered for a mighty tournament.
The lovely Herzeloyde, who was the queen
Of two domains- those of Wales and Norgals,
Had sent word far and wide of this great match.
Whoever should prevail in the event
Would be her husband and king of her realms.
For having reached years of maturity,
She wished to find a suitable companion
To marry and share governance of lands.
The queen was well known for her radiance,
The power of which drew this throng of knights
From both near and far reaching realms abroad.
Brave Gahmuret inquired on his way,
Toward the host of pennants gathered there,
As to the cause of this royal event.
A squire told him of the circumstances
As Gahmuret approached the battleground.

Into the fray bold Gahmuret was seen
As he rode dauntlessly to meet the charge.
Whoever faced him was soon overthrown,
And as each lance was shattered, squires ran
To fetch the warrior another spear.
They were hard pressed to keep this knight supplied.
When no lance was on hand, he drew his sword
And fought with such unflinching strength, his foes
Were beaten back, were they one knight or ten.

His shield was blazoned with the house of Anjou-
His family's arms, the place of his upbringing-
And soon the whispers spread throughout the throng:
It was undoubtedly bold Gahmuret
Whose name, accompanied by tales of glory,
Had been flung far and wide throughout the world.
At one point, he drew rein and pulled aside
To catch his breath and briefly quench his thirst.
As he sat on his horse for this short space,
Now having loosened and removed his helm,
His eyes looked up to find Queen Herzeloyde,
Who sat beneath the awning of a tent,
Some distance off from where the battle was.
Her gaze shone back at him with radiance.
And for that moment, all the clash of war
And all the tumult of the tournament
Fell silent as they gazed on one another
And felt a bond of love between their hearts,
So recognizable and strong, it seemed
They knew the other from somewhere before
Though neither could have crossed the other's path
Before that blissful moment on the field.
If something had not come to intervene,
Who knows how long they would have stayed transfixed.

But while they were engrossed in this exchange,
A certain squire came to Gahmuret,
With lance in hand, replacing one he'd shattered.
This youth was not an ordinary squire,
It was Gawain, the son of bold King Lot.
He was too young to enter in the fray
Though he, with all his heart, yearned for the time
When he would be deemed old enough to joust.
He had been watching Gahmuret all day,
Observing the bravery and boundless strength
Of this exquisite master of the field.
The young boy felt his heart swell with excitement
And admiration, watching how he moved
And ducked and turned and charged relentlessly,
How he met every blow unflinchingly
And struck as though the gods were at his back.

"If only I could be like him someday,"
The boy mused to himself as he looked on,
"To learn such mastery would be a gift
Beyond all things that I could ever dream."

As Gahmuret was gazing at the queen,
King Lot and other knights were gathering
To make another foray on the field
And looked for Gahmuret to know his will.
They glanced around and saw him where he was
Beside the field upon his mighty horse.
Gawain then eagerly begged leave to go
And make this inquiry to Gahmuret.
King Lot agreed to give his son this charge,
And happily, the youth took up a lance-
The strongest he could find- and started off
Across the field toward noble Gahmuret.
Gawain was overjoyed to have this task,

For he was yearning to get near to him
And maybe even speak with Gahmuret.

"Most honorable knight," the squire said
Upon arriving next to mighty Gahmuret,
"I've brought this lance, for I saw yours was shattered.
I also bring word from Lot and his host
Who seek your aid to lead them in the charge."

The hero looked down at the eager youth,
Now broken from his rapture with the queen,
And saw the brave young squire, lance in hand,
Who looked up at the powerful champion
With awe-filled joy and heartfelt admiration.

"I thank you for this well-delivered message,"
Replied the gracious Gahmuret at this,
"And for the sturdy spear you've brought to me,
Good honest youth. Thou hast the look of kings.
I have no doubt, thou shalt be made a knight
Who in time will be known to do great things."
He smiled warmly at the happy youth,
Who smiled back and handed him the lance.

Just then a messenger approached the knight
And handed him a letter from the queen.

"I, whose heart has found its counterpart
In you, since first I saw you on the field,
Now send my love and salutation sir.
The inspiration you ignite in me
Is held fast unless you will set it free.
My longing for you has eclipsed my heart.
If thou wilt have me and return my love,
Take both my kingdoms and a crown withal."

Bold Gahmuret then laced his coif and helm[3]
And rode forth once again into the fray
To give expression to the love he felt
For Herzeloyde upon the battlefield.
His warrior blood was fired with such passion
That he became yet mightier than before.
All those who witnessed him in this event
Declared they'd seen what no one ere that day
Had yet beheld in any place on the earth.
It was a day whose happenings became
A legend chronicled down through the ages.
Such mastery in feats of chivalry
Has never to this day yet been outdone.
At times, he was seen charging forth headlong
Into a clan of several warriors
Who'd banded close to overwhelm the hero.
Straight toward just such a clan he would be seen
To thunder like a mighty god of war,
And when he struck, they'd break apart and scatter
Like pillars shattered by a catapult.
At other times, amid a cloud of splinters
From broken lances, Gahmuret was seen;
His foes would then descend on him in groups
To try to knock him from his sturdy seat
While he was unequipped and empty-handed.
Like a flash of light his sword would then be drawn,
And though they rushed upon him, he would fight
With such unstoppable courageousness
It seemed the might of his great heart would spread
Out to the farthest reaches of his limbs
And scatter them like leaves blown by a storm.
No other knight could match his mastery.

---

3   Chain mail head covering and helmet.

'Twas clear the victory that day was his.

As this great tournament came to an end,
A messenger was seen on the approach.
As he drew near, it was plain to behold
That he was from the French court of Anjou,
The home of noble Gahmuret's lineage.
This messenger brought news which cleaved the heart
Of the great hero who'd just won the joust.
The herald had got word of Gahmuret's
Return from the far east and Zazamanc
And followed Gahmuret unto that place
To bring him word of a sad turn of fate,
For Galoes, Gahmuret's beloved brother,
Had met his death upon the battlefield.

Bold Gahmuret's older brother had been king
Of prosperous Anjou, and with his death,
The crown was ordained for the next of kin.
Though devastated by this tragedy,
Bold Gahmuret was now king of Anjou.
And though he'd found love in Queen Herzeloyde,
He suffered greatly from this woeful news.

Despite the somberness which weighed on him
With the loss of his brother, King Galoes,
Brave Gahmuret and noble Herzeloyde
Were wed soon after that great tournament;
But ere they wed, they spent much time together
And spoke of many things close to their hearts.
One day as they sat close he said to her:
"Dear lady, ere we wed I must inform you
About my past and also of the future.
I have already once before this time

31

Found love with someone in a foreign land
Though I must also tell you that this love
Which we have found is of a different kind.
Though I did love before in all its fullness
And have born grief for leaving it behind,
I have not ever felt such happiness
And peace as we now share together here.
I do repent for lacking in steadfastness
And for deserting one who shared my love,
But I rejoice at having met you now
And wish to be unswerving in our bond."

To this, the Lady Herzeloyde replied:
"Thou hast my love forever, with my heart.
No truth or twist of fate will change love's course.
If you had done much worse than you have done,
My heart would still not change its steadfast course,
For though a storm hath struck or will strike yet,
The compass never wavers from the north-
And so my love for you will never cease.
I knew already of your history
And that you are the king of Zazamanc,
For word has traveled far from your exploits;
And though I knew these things, my heart still leapt
When you rode like a sign from God on high
Courageously into the thick battle
Before the gate of Kanvoleis that day-
You fought for our love with such strength and passion.
Let what has been rest in the peacefulness
Of our present love. So past heartache
By new love is redeemed forgivingly."

"Thou speaks into the center of my heart,"
Replied the knightly Gahmuret at this.

"And where there was a wound I now find peace.
But one thing further still besets my soul
And plagues me with anxiety, my love,
For though I know our love to be complete,
A haven for my lovesick restlessness,
I am in no way made for quiet life
And will not be content to stay at home
But must seek further exploits of the shield
And meet the mighty call of destiny.
I yearn to shatter many lances yet,
Ere I lay down the task of chivalry;
But this will not take my love from your side,
For I will fight with your love in my heart
And will leave mine to your care evermore."

"You make your own terms on that count my love,"
Replied the stalwart Herzeloyde to this.

"I love you as your nature doth instruct.
If I had wished to love another sort,
I would have chosen such a different one,
Possessed with other qualities than yours,
But I love Gahmuret the warrior,
Who rode before my gates of his accord
And chose to battle for the sake of love:
It's his love which I'll have, no other love.
Change not the slightest bit on my account,
For what love would it be if it were changed,
Not of its own accord, but by decree?
One might as well attempt to tame the sea
Or relegate the winds to thy own bidding
Or try to catch the sun's ray in a flask
To hide away from the world with lock and key.
Shine on, brave heart, to the wide earth's expanse,

Blow winds with thy great gusts of bravery,
And crash bold thunder of the ocean's glory."

"I will hold fast to our bond of love
Until my last breath has released me from this world.
And though I ride out past the farthest reaches
Of the great earth, my heart shall hold its course,"
Replied the brave, true-hearted Gahmuret.

Soon after this, these two beloved souls
Were joined in their great love for one another
With a joyful celebration of their marriage.
They were fulfilled in the happy embrace
Of their deep recognition and affection.
When he rode forth in quest of chivalry,
He bore the symbol of his father's line-
A sable[4] panther hammered on his shield.
Beneath the plate of steel upon his chest,
He carried his great love for Herzeloyde,
And on behalf of this love, he sought glory.
The queen gave her dear love a silken shift[5]
To wear beneath his armor o'er his mail-
A token of their love, for his protection.
And when he'd come home from his great exploits,
She'd put it on and see the many cuts
From sword blows and the tears of jousting thrusts
That had been hacked and rend into the fabric.

While journeying abroad, bold Gahmuret
Received word from the Baruc in Baghdad-
His old lord who by the Babylonians
Had in an uprising been overrun.

---

4   Pitch black.
5   A long, loose fitting undergarment.

So Gahmuret made for Baghdad to lend aid.
'Twas a sorry turn of fate that led him there
Though his arrival was met with great joy.

Queen Herzeloyde knew not of these events.
She, like the first blossom of the spring
Attended by prosperity and joy,
Was gentle in all aspects of her nature.
She was endowed with every attribute
That could be wished for in a head of state
And worked each day at serving goodliness,
Which strengthened the affection of her subjects.
She was now sovereign of three mighty realms:
Norgals, Anjou, and Wales. Her beloved,
Brave Gahmuret, was so dear to this queen
That she could not feel envy of another—
For their love gave her heart its completeness.

When six months had elapsed since Gahmuret
Had set out on his quest for chivalry,
She looked for his return with happiness
And sensed that he would soon turn his course
From conquest to the restfulness of home;
But all her joy was soon crushed with the weight
Of heavy grief and drowned in bitter woe;
Such can be the way with earthly life:
Joy one day, and the next day, tragedy.

One afternoon, the lady took her rest
And fell into a deep and troubled slumber.
It seemed to her as though she stood alone
Upon the high plain of a tall plateau,
And all around her shooting stars fell fast
Until one swung too close and caught her up

And swept her upwards to the lofty heights,
Where lightning bolts assailed her from all sides
So that her tresses hissed and burned with sparks.
The thunder crashed and peeled with deafening claps
And showered down hot tears of scourging fire;
Then as she writhed and turned to free herself,
She thought she broke herself out of the dream,
But when she turned, she found a horrid beast
Part lion and part bird which grasped her hand
At which point it seemed everything was changed
Forevermore, ne'er to return to joy.
She found that she was carrying a serpent
That grew within her where a babe should grow.
This beast then to her terror tore from her,
And when she looked down, she beheld a dragon
That, to her horror, suckled at her breast.
The dragon then flew swiftly from her sight
And bore her heart, torn from her, in its grasp.

No sooner had she woken from this dream,
Then suddenly her love's most trusted knight
Was seen on the approach before her gates.
He was accompanied by several more,
All with the look of sorrow in their eyes.

The brave queen rose and entered the great hall
To hear whatever news these messengers
Now brought before her with the weight of doom.

"Why dost thou come here unaccompanied
By any but yourselves?" the good queen asked.
"Where is thy master? Is he following?
It is not customarily his way

To send his vassals[6] in place of himself.
Instead of him you are accompanied
By the presence of unhappiness.
Speak now, what news, for I can wait no longer."

Then weeping till they almost could not speak,
They told her of the death of Gahmuret.

The queen stood still and silent listening
Though grief cut to the core of her brave soul
And rattled the foundations of her heart,
Yet still she stood and heard their every word
And grappled her brave heart up to the task
Of facing what she knew to be her fate
With Gahmuret. It was as though the words
Brought by these woeful messengers
Spoke something that she'd always recognized
But never understood until that day.
The terror of her dream not long before,
Though horrifying, had prepared her soul
With just enough endurance to withstand
The overwhelming shock of this great loss.
The battle in her heart was racking her
So that her bright complexion lost its lustre.
Her body felt faint and began to tremble,
But still she wrestled to remain upright
And fought with all the strength within her soul
To overcome the shaking of her grief
In order to speak what she yearned to ask,
The question that was burning in her heart
Like fire: "How did my beloved die?"

---

6   A high ranking knight under the protection of a feudal king to
whom they had pledged loyalty and service and from whom they
had received land. Vassals were often princes, dukes, earls, or barons.

Gahmuret's most loved and trusted knight
Approached and knelt before the steadfast queen
Then rose to take her hand and meet her gaze.
And though tears ran like fountains from his eyes,
He told her the sad sequence of events:

"Alas, long life did not attend my lord.
The dauntless man was leading a great host
Into a mighty battle in Baghdad
Where he had journeyed to lend the Baruc
His aid, for they were badly overrun.
Plagued by the onslaught of the merciless heat,
He bade his troup pause to collect themselves
And take refreshment ere they made for war.
He'd taken off his helm while they were stopped-
Which planted his demise- alas, this fate.
His enemies knew that his presence there
Would mark the swift demise of their success.
They also knew he could not be defeated
And lacking the integrity of knighthood-
Ah, who could live with such an ugly stain
Emblazoned by their hand into the book
Of deeds to the destruction of honor-
The enemy spies made entry to our camp
Beneath the seemly guise of an alliance.
They smashed a flask filled with a wicked potion
Upon my master's helm without his knowing.
This potion was designed by sorcery
To soften through the metal of the helm
Until 'twas rendered to a fragile state.
If only you could have been witness there
When they rode forth in company to war-
So many shields were broken on that field
As they raced to the fray on Baghdad's plains.

The squadrons charged together which such force-
It was as though two mighty ocean waves
Collided and breached through the other's walls
To wind around commingled in the tide.
The pennants from both sides were billowing
Above the press of grappling warriors.
Many valiant knights fell on that field,
Yet next to the great feats of Gahmuret,
The glory of all others shrank to nothing.
He struck with a godlike strength upon the field
The like of which has never yet been seen,
Nor will again in any future age.
At times, he was beset by several knights,
And at such moments was our hero seen
To battle on with such a boundless courage,
It seemed as though the force of his great heart
Was like to burst forth from his armored frame
And scatter all who came into his path.
He gave all that he had up to the task,
And when he'd given all, he gave yet more.
But then the cruel fates took their ruthless toll.
As my true-hearted lord thus battled on,
Straight through the very thick of that fierce war,
A king named Impomidon rode toward him.
This king was driven by a vengeful aim,
For Gahmuret had thrust him from his horse
Before the gates of Alexandria
With thousands looking on some years before.
My brave stouthearted lord tried with his strength
To knock those who assailed him back in time
In order to engage this evil king
Who rode him down while he was thus beset-
Such is the way with lowly treachery-
But as my dear lord swerved to meet the charge,

His foe struck home a devastating blow.
The lance pierced cleanly through my master's helm,
And there a splinter from the shaft was lodged.
But did our good courageous lord then fall?
No, he did not. But with a will of iron,
He steered his horse forth from the battlefield
As his life swiftly ebbed and death approached;
They were the last steps he would ever ride.
We helped him from his horse onto the ground.
The chaplain came and knelt down at his side.
He made his last confession ere he died
And sent this shift and the lance that severed him
From us, and this life then drew his last breath
And crossed out of this world into the next.

The Baruc spared no cost for our lord's tomb.
It is bedecked with gold and precious stones.
His body was embalmed amid much grief.
The stone above his grave is a great ruby
Through which his youthful body can be seen.
Our wishes were respected and a cross
Was set above his grave to signify
The crucifixion as Christ, by his death,
Redeemed us through his loving sacrifice.
Upon his helm, they carved an epitaph
And fixed it to the cross above his grave.
These are the words of the inscription:

Through his helm a lance thrust struck this hero,
Lord Gahmuret by name, a mighty king.
He ruled three lands and was born of Anjou.
He lost his life in Baghdad on the plains
Defending the cause of his friend the Baruc.
The glory of his life was so exalted

That it shall never be eclipsed hereafter.
No one from him has ever won surrender.
He lent aid and good counsel to his friends,
And while he lived, he suffered pangs of love.
He was loved by not only Christian folk
But those as well from many other faiths.
This hero strove for love and honor only
And so dies a renowned and honored knight.
He is victorious over perfidy[7].
We ask God's mercy for him who lies here."

7   Untruthfulness.

SOLTANE

There was a queen who suffered poverty
For sake of loyalty so that the gift
Might, having been surrendered thus by choice,
Renew itself in spirit bountifully.
'Tis but a few alive upon the earth
Who'd give up earthly riches for heavenly glory.
Nevertheless, the Lady Herzeloyde
From her three kingdoms did estrange herself.
She bore a burden of sorrow so great
The day and night were ever one to her.
Thus set on grief, she fled all worldly joys,
Withdrawing to the wilds of Soltane,
A wilderness set far from lands well known
To even the most adventurous traveler.

She took her child with her, the one heir
Of her beloved Gahmuret, whose death
In battle by the hand of mortal foe,
Abrupt and tragic, was her sorrow's source.
Were it not for her beloved child,
Death might have put an end to all her woes.
Her son was her one salvaged heart's delight.
He was the raft by which she kept afloat
Upon the floods of overwhelming grief.
And when she held him in her arms, it seemed
As though her dear beloved Gahmuret
Was there with her again as in a dream
Where what has been blurs with the present hour
In shadowed silhouettes of what's to be.

She was as kind a queen as ever lived,
But in her human frailty and her grief,

42

Queen Herzeloyde held from the world her son.
She cosseted[8] the child and clung to him
In isolation as the healing salve
To her cracked open soul, hoping the youth-
In ignorance of his great lineage,
All unaware of his inheritance,
And uninformed by aspects of the world-
Would stay as solace for her love bereft
And purpose seeking heart. Queen Herzeloyde
Was fearful- having lost one love to war-
She'd lose her most dear son to such a death,
Were he to ever learn of chivalry.
She could not bear that thought, and so she vowed
To keep the greater portion of her heart
Intact by sheltering her only child.

When he was still quite young and unaware,
She called her people to her in Soltane
And with severity gave stringent orders:

"You'll breathe no word of knights around my son,
For if my child learns of chivalry",
I would be grieved and very heavyhearted.
So keep your wits about you when you speak,
And keep him in the dark concerning knights
And all that has to do with chivalry."

The child was reared in the wilds of Soltane.
He had his bow and arrows which he'd cut
And fashioned from the woodland underbrush.
With this, he'd shoot his arrows at the birds.
But when he'd shot a bird that had been singing
With full throat but a moment earlier,

---

8   Coddled, indulged, or overprotected.

He'd burst straight into tears and grasped his hair
And wreak cruel vengeance upon his own head.

He bathed each morning in the meadow creek,
Surrounded by wild flowers and tall grasses.
No cares had he, besides the singing birds
Whose sweet songs brought a tightness to his chest
And seemed to pierce his heart. Then all in tears,
He'd run back to his mother, who'd exclaim:
"Now who's been vexing you, sweet child? Who?
You went out to the meadow, did you not?"
But he'd be lost for words and wouldn't speak.
So she pursued this in her thoughts awhile.
One day she saw him gaping at the trees
To see the happy clamor of the birds.
She realized then it was their piping songs
That brought the twinge of tightness to his breast.
So she then turned her hatred on the birds.
But why? For all her wisdom, she knew not.
She wished to put an end to all their singing
And ordered that the birds be captured
And taken from the wilds of soltane.
The youth observed the servants of the queen
Ensnaring the birds with nets and was alarmed.

"Now why are they so angry at the birds?"
Exclaimed the youth. "They are not causing harm."

He begged the queen to put an end to this.
And as she watched and heard her child's cries,
She uttered softly: "Why did I forget
And vainly intervene with God's design?
Shall birds withhold their happiness for me?"

"Oh mother, what is God?" replied the child.

"I will tell you who God is my son.
'Twas He who came in shape alike to us
And who is brighter than the sun itself.
My child, take this saying to thy heart:
Pray to Him when you find yourself in need.
His steadfast love has never failed the world."

She told her son of how things of the world
Had come to be through God's creation.
This done, the spry and agile lad dashed off
Into the hills and through the mountain streams.
He learned to throw a javelin with skill
With which he'd hunt the nimble-footed deer,
Who never heard his tread, so soft he ran.
He had a lethal aim and rarely missed.
Around the turning seasons, with the years,
He grew up tall and handsome, strong and proud.
He bore the look of mighty kings and queens-
The line from which he was the living heir,
Though his appearance matched that of a serf,
A country peasant lad, or shepherd youth.

One day as he was hunting down a slope,
He heard ahead strong hoofbeats on the path.
He raised his spear and like a wild cat,
Prepared to spring and waited the approach
Of what his destiny had sent his way,
Now thundering toward him down the woodland path.

"What's this I hear?" the youth thought to himself.

Three knights rode at a gallop into view.
Their armor glinted, blinding in the sun,

As they rode toward the petrified young boy.

"God help!" he cried in fear as they approached.
At this, the foremost knight became enraged
And lost his temper at the sight of him-
The young boy trembling on the ground mid path.

"This stupid whelp will slow us down!" he growled.

But at that very moment, toward them rode
A fourth knight at an elegant full tilt.
And beautifully attired he was indeed.
He rode a warhorse equally bedecked
As he in finery- a princely sight.

"Two knights we now pursue in haste," he said.
"Have you just seen two knights ride by this way?
They are deceitful wreckers of the good
And violators of the knightly code-
Devoid of honor- who have sought by force
Their fortunes, harvesting from passers by.
They are not truly knights of chivalry
But masquerade as members of the code."

Yet as he spoke, the youth could only think
That it was God before him, whom his mother
Had often spoke of, so he cried in fear:

"Now help me, most helpful God! Your help, I beg!"

"I am not God," replied the knight, amused,
"Though I do gladly aim to serve His will.
If you had eyes within your head, you'd see
Four knights before you."
                                    "Nights?" replied the boy.
"Did you say nights? What is a night besides

The absent day? If you lack godlike power,
Then tell me who it is makes you a night?"

"King Arthur is the one who gave the grace
Of knighthood to our thankful services,
Which we repay with deeds of chivalry,
In honor of his name and company-
The mighty Table Round- to bring the good
To all the lands who thrive beneath his reign,"
Replied the knight who was himself a prince.
"Were you to find your way into his halls
You need not be ashamed of what a knight
He'd make you, for your features do bely
That regal blood doth course throughout your veins,
Your garments but a decoy to this truth.
My first glance tells me you're of noble stock."

"Oh good sir God, what makes you look so bright?"
Replied the naive and bewildered youth.
"I see so many rings upon you tied,
Up here, and also there, and under here!"

The child tugged the knight's shirt of chain mail
And on the many surfaces of steel
In which the dapper knight was now encased.

"What are these rings tied up so close together
That you are wearing like a metal shirt?
I've seen the rings my mother's ladies wear,
But they wear them on ribbons 'round their necks.
And what is this that you wear o'er the rings
So bright and stronger than a tortoise shell?
Why won't it come off when I pull at it?"

"Now look," the knight said, holding up his sword,

"If I'm attacked by foes, I fight with this
And ward them off by striking them with blows,
And I protect myself by using this
To stop their blows from cutting into me."

"If deer wore hides like that," the youth replied,
"My javelin would never do them harm.
But many deer fall dead before my feet."

The other three were angry with their lord
That he, their prince, stood talking with this fool-
In their eyes but a ragged shepherd's son.

"May God protect you," said the gracious prince.
"If only you had some common sense in you,
You'd have the makings of a well-bred knight.
The power of God keep harm from you, sweet youth."

With that, he and his knights then galloped off.

The queen's field workers were in deep despair
When they beheld the four knights thundering past.
"How did it come to this?" they asked themselves.
"If our young master's seen those warriors,
Our lady's trust in us has been betrayed!
Harsh words we'll surely have from her for this."

And true enough, the lad lost interest
In hunting for deer with his javelin.
He went straight to the queen and told a tale
That sent her reeling. In her shock, she swooned
And lay before his feet for quite some time.
Once she'd regained her senses, she then asked:
"My son, who told you of the knightly order?
How did you come to hear of chivalry?"

"I saw four knights, dear mother, bright as God!
They told of knighthood. Arthur's kingliness
Must guide me to the office of the shield
And knightly deeds."
                              This gave new rise to grief.
The lady found herself at her wits' end
To glean a way to woo him from this aim.
But the simple lad kept asking for a horse.

"I cannot now deny him," Herzeloyde
Regretfully considered in her heart.
"But it will have to be the poorest nag
That I can find which I'll bequeath to him.
In fool's clothes, I'll adorn him, innocent.
If he is handled roughly for these things,
He'll surely then come back to me again."

Next morning, when the sun peaked o'er the hills,
The youth, in the ragged garments of a fool,
Was eager to set off upon his search
For Arthur's court and acts of chivalry.
Queen Herzeloyde embraced and kissed her son
With an ache unfathomable in her heart
As thus to him she spoke her parting words:
"Before you go, I must teach you some sense:
When riding over murky fords, take heed.
Where they are clear and shallow, trot in brisk.
It must become your custom to greet all
Upon your journey, be they glad or woeful.
If a grey-haired man to you bestows his grace
And teaches you good manners, to his words
Give all of your attention, do his will,
And do not be enraged at what he says."

49

She paused with hesitation and then said:
"There is another thing which you must know,
The cruel and arrogant King Lahelin
Hath stolen from our family two domains
O'er which you rightfully should rule as king."

"I'll be revenged on him!" the youth replied,
Brimming with hubris and naivety.

Good Herzeloyde looked deeply at the youth:
"Now lastly, let me give you this advice
Before I say farewell to you my son:
Whenever you can win a lady's ring,
Then take it. Waste no time, but kiss, embrace,
And take her ring, for it will bring good fortune
And with that will your spirits be raised high
If she is true and good of heart that is."

Once more she kissed her only living joy
And followed running as he rode away
With eagerness toward his destiny.
When she could see her dearest son no more,
She fell down to the earth where to her heart,
Grief gave her such a cut it beat its last,
And death drew from her lips her final breath,
Which sighed away unto her sorrow's end.
Without a reason for which to exist,
Her death preserved her from a life's travail,
Which lived, to grief would have brought no avail.

JESCHUTE

So forth the young lad rode upon his nag,
In flapping skins and sackcloth, like a fool.
But knowing only what his mother said,
He brimmed as though bedecked in finery.
Thus joyfully toward the world he sauntered forth.
At length, he came upon a rippling brook.
A chicken could have crossed it without fuss,
So shallow ran its course. On either side,
The flowers blooming with the grasses swayed
Upon the early summer's gentle breeze,
But dark appeared the water to the youth.
Recalling now his mother's words, he paused
And after careful contemplation chose
To wait until he found a ford to cross.
He followed the stream's course throughout the day.
Beneath the moon of pearl, he slept that night
And with the early dawn, resumed his way.
The sun was barely cresting through the wood,
With orange angled rays that reached through trees
Like the golden arms of God to hug the world,
When lo, he came upon a shimmering ford.
And there he crossed as had his mother urged.
He found a meadow on the farther side,
And there, a fine pavilion had been pitched
With many colored, silken, samite cloth
And ribbons fine that fluttered in the wind.
'Twas quite a stately sight for any eyes,
But even more so for our sheltered lad.
This tent belonged to Duke Orilus de Lalant,
Whose wife the simple youth found fast asleep
Within that wondrous tent, for as it happened,
The duke was out, and the beautiful Jeschute

There rested as she waited for her love.
So sweetly she did slumber there before him.
Upon her hand, the youth beheld a ring.
Bedecked with gems, the band of gold did glint
Which caught his eye as he observed her there.
His mother's words to him again returned.
Seeing the ring, he sprang onto the couch.
She woke in terror with the youth upon her.
Enraged with horror and astonishment,
The duchess thence to him exclaimed aloud:
"Who does me this outrage? you make yourself
Too free. Be off with you, unruly youth!"

He took no heed to what she said, instead,
He pressed his mouth to hers and took a kiss,
For thus his mother's words he took to heart,
And wasting not a moment, as she fought,
He seized and pulled the ring from off her hand.
This done, he spied a brooch upon her wrist
And took the golden band from her as well.

Once he'd retrieved the ring and brooch, he whined,
Complaining to the lady of his hunger.

"Don't eat me!" The disheveled lady cried.
"The foolish boy complains to me of hunger!
If you had any sense, some other food
Would be your choice! There is some bread and wine.
Go eat and drink of them, and leave me be!"

How little he cared what all his hostess said,
Or where she sat. He ate his belly full
And drank some heavy draughts to wash it down.

"Young man," she caught her breath enough to say,

"I must ask you to leave my ring behind.
My brooch as well, and take yourself off now,
For if my husband comes to find you here
When he returns, you'll have to face such wrath
As you will after wish to have avoided,
For you have sorely trespassed 'gainst my honor."

"Why should your husband's rage make me afraid?"
Replied the youth naively as a child.
"But if my presence does your honor harm,
I'll gladly go away."
      Up to the couch
Again he went and took another kiss
Before he rode away without her leave;
Though he did say, "God be with you, my lady-
That's what my mother told me I should say."
He left a lady who would thence endure
Much hardship from his reckless ignorance.
Bereft of ring and brooch, she- tousled thus-
Exemplified the quintessential picture
Of infidelity and could not hide
Appearances of guilt from the jealous eye
Of her proud husband, who on coming home
Was seized with wrath by what her visage showed.
And for this, she withstood neglect and shame.

The duke, soon after, to his tent returned.
As he approached, the traces in the dew
Revealed the tussle that had there ensued.
Some ropes had been torn out in the exchange,
And someone had been trampling the grass.
He found his wife in quite a wretched state.

"Alas, madam," said prideful Orilus,

"Is it for this that I have done you service?
My glorious exploits are all disgraced!
You've clearly found yourself another lover!"

"My lord it is not so!" the lady wept.
"You are the only one I've ever loved.
I'll love you now until my dying day!
Alas, that this appearance looks not so."

"If you think I'll believe a word of this,
Then you're the more deceived; don't waste your breath!"
Replied the furious Duke Orilus.

"A mad fool rode this way," the lady ventured,
"How strangely he behaved! He was quite mad
And was attired in a peasant's garb
Haphazardly, with furs and ragged cloth,
And yet he bore the look of kings and queens
About him in his features and his gaze.
I wonder who his parents could have been
That he should bear the look of both a fool
And someone of a noble lineage?"
The lady paused in ponderance as she spoke,
Struck by the strange remembrance of the youth,
Despite the urgency and immediacy
Of the exchange in which she found herself.
This was too much for her hot-tempered husband.

"You liked his looks! You made a pair with him!"

Orilus, now enraged unto the brink
Of boiling o'er all limits of restraint,
Spake, seething through his teeth, his face quite red.

"No! God forbid," she cried "he was a fool!

If you had seen his buskins and his furs,
His utter disregard for decorum,
You'd be ashamed of what you're saying now!"

"Alas, madam, I've never done you wrong
Unless it's but one thing that angers you:
That for my sake, you did renounce the rank
Of queen and took the humble name of "Duchess."
But I'm the one whose rank is lowered now,
Demoted when I wed a wanton duchess!
When all is said my mettle is so keen,
Your brother now has cause to hate you for it.
Except he once o'erthrew me at Purin,
But later I threw him down at Karnant;
My stout lance ran your favour through his shield
And thrust him off his crupper in your name.
Yet I have failed to reap fruits from these feats-
As this most deep disgrace informs me now.
I beg you now to credit this, madam,
I slew the brother of Lord Gahmuret,
Famed as the mightiest that ever lived!
On countless occasions have I won you glory
And brought down many of the fiercest knights.
The knights of the Round Table hate my name,
For eight of them have been unhorsed by me;
I won the sparrow hawk that day for you.
And watching with you sat the king himself,
Who had my sister, Cunneware, with him,
For she attends his court with Guinevere.
Until she sees the most courageous knight,
She'll never let a laugh come from her lips.
How little did I dream that you would take
Another lover, my dear Lady Jeschute!
If only that fool would come back this way-

There'd surely then be fighting to be had,
In much the way there was just now this morn;
I fought a prince and did him some mischief:
My lance thrust stretched him dead upon the ground!
If still you think I owe you anything,
You'll have to learn to make your way without.
I shall not warm to your embrace again
Where I have lain enamoured in the past.
I'll make your red lips fade. I'll teach their hue
Unto your eyes and rob your happiness!"

The princess looked up at her vengeful husband
And spoke with earnest sorrow in her voice:
"Show now, by how you treat me, your respect
And honor for the code of chivalry.
You are a knight, to knighthood's oath hath sworn.
You are good, true, honest, and well discerning.
But you now hold me fast within your power.
You can inflict through what you now decide
Much suffering and sorrow on my life,
So listen first to my defense, I beg.
There will be time enough for punishment
Once you have heard my story to its end.
In faith, if I should die at someone's hand,
However soon, I'd take that moment gladly
As consolation for my grieving heart,
Now that I am the object of your hatred!"

"You've grown too proud my lady, for my liking,"
Replied the duke to sorrowful Jeschute.
"I'll put an end to this where you're concerned.
We shall not eat nor drink together more;
Our sharing of one bed is at an end.

56

Your bridle will now be of ragged bast.[9]
Your palfrey[10] shall go hungry evermore.
Your pretty saddle shall be cut to shreds-
And shall most surely have the worst of it!"

He ripped and tore the samite off the saddle
And smashed the seat she used to sit upon.
The modest woman had a heart of gold
And suffered greatly from his spiteful wrath.
His fit of rage was all too sudden for her.

He then re-tied that saddle with the rope.
"Now let us ride, madam" he said to her.
"Perchance we'll find the man you know so well,
He who enjoyed your favors here today-
How I would relish it! I'd try my hand
Though he breathed fire like a raging dragon!"

All thoughts of hope and laughter gone from her,
In tears, the lady set out dolefully.
Whatever she endured she did not mind
But only that her husband suffered so.
His desperation gave her such distress,
She would have rather chosen death than this.
Her faithful love deserved heartfelt compassion
For all her suffering and tribulation.
And thus, they rode off following the steps,
Which the naive and careless youth had left.

---

9   A frayed rope.
10   A mare.

SIGUNE THE SORROWFUL

The simple youth rode on, while in his wake,
Between the hapless duchess and the duke,
Turmoil ensued, caused by his blundering.
To everyone he met, he said the same:
"Good day! That's what my mother said to say,"
Or "God be with you on this happy day-
That's what my mother told me I should say."

Thus he rode down a wooded mountainside
And heard from forth a patch of rocks, a sound.
It was a woman weeping, rend with grief.
As he approached, he saw she'd torn her garments
In heartfelt lamentation for her loss:
There, in her arms, a prince, her love, lay dead.

The youth then spoke to her amid her woes:
"Downcast or joyful I must greet them all,
For thus my mother has instructed me.
God keep you, lady. It's a sorrowful sight
I see there in your lap. A wounded knight.
Who gave him to you thus?" he asked her plainly.

The lady only wept without reply.
Though she spake not, he still pressed her for answers:

"Who shot him?
Was it a javelin?
It looks as if he might be dead, madam.
If you will tell me where your foes have fled-
They cannot have gone far- I'll ride them down
And gladly fight them with my javelin."

At length her sighs of woe found breath enough

To speak an answer through her blinding tears.
"You are a courteous youth, all hail to thee,
Your innocence and beauty be thy grace,
And bléssed be the path on which you tread.
No javelin hath pierced this noble prince.
In a fierce joust was he slain by the hand
Of a mortal foe which brings this grief on me.
The compassion that you've shown me signifies
An honest heart, born of nobility."

But fearing the unseasoned, headstrong youth,
Who was no match for her fierce enemy,
Would seek a battle with proud Orilus
And sacrifice himself on her behalf,
Instead of answering the youth's appeal,
She turned the topic with an inquiry:

"What is your name, dear youth? Where is your home
From which you've ridden now to find me here?"

"They call me Bonfit Cherfilsy Beau Fits
Back home, which is a two days' ride from here."

Through grief, her eyes lit up with recognition.

"Why you are Parzival!" The lady said.
She knew him by the title that he gave,
For she had once been in his mother's care.
"Your name means *pierced through the heart*.
Your mother's faithful heart by grief was torn
When death took her dear love from her in battle.
Your father's death brought deep grief to her soul.
She is my aunt which makes you and I cousins.
I am Sigune, your mother's sister's daughter.
I'll tell thee, cousin, of thy lineage.

You are born of a race of kings and queens:
An Angevin[11] was your father, Gahmuret;
Your mother was a noble queen in Wales.
Kanvoleis was the city of your birth,
A fact that I know surely to be true.
There, had things not gone tragically, you'd reign.
King Lahelin hath wrested from your possession
Two kingdoms which by rights belong to you:
Wales and Norgals- your father's lands,
To which by blood you are the rightful heir.
My love, now lying here slain in my arms,
Fought valiantly to keep your throne intact.
The brother of the ruthless Lahelin,
Known as Duke Orilus, hath slain this man.
He was one of your subjects ere his death.
His service has but brought his early end,
And my e'erlasting unrequited grief.
A life of woe will be my destiny;
From henceforth must I bear this heavy sorrow."

"I must now mourn this woe and bitter wrong!"
Sincerely spake the outraged, wide-eyed youth.
"That this knight died not only for your love
But also while protecting my domains
Means that I must now battle with the knight
Who did these wrong deeds to both you, my cousin,
And me- my mother and my father too!
It is sad how I never knew that man-
The one you told me of, who was my father.
I am so sorry that he had to die.
If he were living, he would not stand by
And watch his lands be stolen idly.

---

11   A person from Anjou.

I'm certain that he would have fought for them.
In truth, I will avenge this sabotage.
Is he close by? The foe that did you wrong?
I must pursue him and avenge your love!"
And nothing she could say would hold him back,
So ready was the youth to gallop forth
To seek revenge for her amid the fray.
But knowing it would only bring more grief
Were he to die, she then informed the lad
About a road that led away from foes
And into Britain, reassuring him
That he would find her enemies that way.
So off he toppled on his dingy mare,
Upon a broad and even thoroughfare.
To everyone he met along his way,
No matter if they sat astride a steed
Or trudged on foot, the youth gave a cordial greeting
Just as his mother had instructed him:
"God be with you! That's what my mother said."

THE FISHERMAN

But weariness beset him as the dark
With eventide drew on. And so, the youth,
Without a sense for quality in things,
Discovered, indiscriminately, a house
That sorely left some room for want indeed-
It would have spooked the average passer by:
Unkempt and dreary, in the dwindling light,
It seemed to creep with shadows into view,
Untended, drab, and neglected like a shrub,
Abandoned on an old forgotten plot.
A churlish fisherman belonged to it.
Discourteous was he to blood and bone,
With low comportment in his marrow steeped.

The fisherman was entering the house
When drawing rein the youth called out to him
Requesting shelter and a bed that night.
The fisherman paused to take in the lad
And spat his surly answer with a growl:
"I'd not give you e'en half a loaf," he said.
"If someone thinks I'll give them what is mine
With generosity for no return,
Well mark my words, they'd just be wasting time.
See I don't fend for any but myself.
You can wait all day, you won't get in here,
That is unless you have something to pawn,
In which case I'd be sure to take you in."

But when the boy held forth the golden brooch,
The fisherman's dour face cracked with a grin.

"If you'll stay with us here, this night, young lad,
Then we'll be sure to treat you with respect."

"Tomorrow morning I'll seek Arthur's Court.
If you'll feed me tonight, and in the morn
You'll lead me to the king, the gold is yours,"
Replied the youth.
                              "Now that, I'll gladly do!
I'll take you anywhere you'd like, my lad,"
Replied the fisherman with glinting eyes.

And so, the youth stayed with the angler.
When morning broke, he rose from sleep refreshed
And eager to be off to Arthur's court.

They set forth in the gentle light of dawn
And journeyed many miles as the sun
Arose and made its way toward mid-morn.
They rode at quite a clip despite their steeds,
Which in both cases were a sorry sight.
Together those two made a ragged pair:
A boy dressed like a fool in furs and rags,
Led by the grim and greedy fisherman.
They had just crested a steep wooded hill
And were descending down the farther side
When all at once the trees came to an end,
And spread before them was a gentle vale,
All swathed in mist and dappled with the sun.
And there, they saw before them Carleon,
The stronghold of King Arthur and his host.
Its many pinnacles and mighty towers,
Bedecked with battlements and stately archways,
All gleamed, ablaze beneath the morning sky.
The fisherman drew rein and hailed the lad:
"If further you would venture from this spot,
You'll have to be your own guide to the gate.
The common folk of my sort wouldn't mix

With courtly types. I would not e'er be caught
Setting foot beyond those city gates.
They have a kind of air about them, sure,
Those courtly folk. A kind of haughtiness.
It makes my hair stand up and sets my teeth.
Were I a dog, you can be sure of it,
I'd nip at royalty for wearing airs.
You wouldn't find me there without a brawl.
And I would be the one who's worse for that-
So I'm off ere the nobles know I'm here."

And off he slyly slinked as doth a hound,
Who's snagged the meat from off the countertop,
When from the block and toward to pot, the cook
Has turned their back to stir the stock for stew.

So onward rode the lad upon his nag.
To either side the flowers were in bloom,
Amid the gentle, genuflecting grasses
That offered homage to the summer's breath,
Their soft caress ruffling his locks.
His knotted reins of twisted hemp hung slack,
For weakly did his beast plod, stumbling on,
And dumbly held its course along the road.
No leather sleek upon that mount was seen,
No samite fair or ermine mantle clasp,
'Twas not a blazon surcoat that he wore,
His javelin and furs were all he bore.

ITHER

As he proceeded toward the city gates,
Within the meadow decked by blossoms fair,
He came upon a most exquisite sight,
So rare it stopped the young lad in his tracks.
A knight armed head to toe in red was sat
Astride his russet charger, also clad
Magnificently crimson in its dress.
'Twas something to behold this warlike[12] pair.

"God keep you. Thus my mother bade me speak
To everyone I meet!" the youth called out.

"May God reward you lad and thy good mother,"
The striking knight replied without a pause.
This knight was born of a noble lineage.
He was a nephew of King Uther Pendragon[13]
Which made him a cousin of King Arthur's.
The knight had been raised at King Uther's court,
And Uther had been like a father to him.
The knight was more than an ordinary lord,
He was a king himself in his own right
And ruled the neighboring land of Cumberland.
His name was Ither, but this well known lord
Was called throughout those lands, the Red Knight.
His armor burned as crimson as a flame,
As did his horse, swift-footed, with its plume
And covering of scarlet samite bold.
His surcoat too matched red, the spear he held-

---

12   Fierce, courageous, skilled and unafraid of battle.
13   King Arthur's father. Legend has it that Arthur and his father
Uther never would have met. In some legends, Uther died while
Arthur was still an infant.

Both shaft and iron point- and as he wished,
His hefty sword glowed red gold on its hilt,
Whose blade of steel like coal gleamed crimson fire.
This King of Cumberland held in his hand
A cup of skillfully engraved red gold
Which he had taken from the Round Table.
His red locks by the sun were set ablaze
As fair in speech he met the simple youth:

"Now hail to thee young lad and to thy mother
Who bore thee well. All blessings on her heart,
For never saw I one so royally made
Who bore the look of kings so thoroughly
Without the aid of finery or class.
I see nobility beneath those rags
That seems to shine through outward poverty
As doth the sun gleam through the ragged clouds
Which though they seek to stop its radiance
At last must part before its luminance
And let their tattered cloak be pierced with rays.
The light within thine eye is born of love,
And love in thee shall be the champion.
Now do me this kind favor if you will:
Bear greeting from me to King Arthur thence
And to his mighty company renowned.
Say unto them that I be not a vision
Who's come to haunt them once and disappear.
Here I abide and wait against their honor
Until one of them comes to joust with me,
And thereby keep intact their reputation,
Which seems to have departed from their midst
With this red cup of gold that came with me,
For I have poured its contents on the queen
And red the stain upon her ivory cloak.

Such is the custom when a king claims lands
That rightfully belongs to his estate.
And so, this insult I have placed on them,
The famous and renowned company,
Has stated by action what discourse would lame:
That I may claim what blood and lineage
Have made me heir to this kingdom's crown.
Doth not the king hold value for his name?
Has honor taken wing from all his knights?
What secret do they hold so carefully
And close within the comfort of their walls?
Or do they fear to settle this account?
Unto the queen speak fair and say the drops
That I spilled on her fell against my will.
I did not mean to lay offense on her
But slipped upon the flagstone of my name
By which I came for what is rightly owed.
And thus, the wine did spill upon her lap
While docile her lord and company
Did look askance and stand on ceremony-
What is their answer to my challenge?
That I would know. If you will thence and back
And bring me word from them, you'd have my thanks."

"Right gladly will I do this office for thee,"
The eager lad replied, and off he went.

The youth then made his way up to the gate,
As he drew near it towered ever higher,
And as rays of the sun shot through the mist,
The gate shone forth with a striking radiance.
As has been told, the keystone of the arch
Which vaulted o'er the formidable gate
Was carved into the likeness of a lady
Whose striking gaze seemed lifelike to behold

As though this goddess saw into the hearts
Of those who passed beneath her watchful eyes.
It was the empress of the mystic lake,
The mighty Nymue[14] who stood on guard-
Protector of King Arthur and his people.
Her tresses and her garments circled her
And merged into the ripples of the lake
Which swept away to either side of her
And stretched wave-like across the mighty arch.
In the center like a crucifix
She stood, arms spread wide with an upward lift,
As though she held the lintel in its place.
To either side of her were Arthur's wars,
Delineated in strange mystic signs
And symbols, woven like a tapestry
Of past and future ages mingling
With present life as though time had departed
And left a dizzying patchwork of events,
All joined together closely in one place.
The bottom of each pillar was a dragon-
King Arthur's coat of arms and lineage,
The noble line of mighty Pendragons.
Upon each pillar were the warriors
Of Arthur's host each conquering a beast
Or wrathful dragon with a sword of flame.
Around the upper sections of the posts
Were all the star signs of the zodiac
In symbols of King Arthur's company
And fixed atop one pillar was the sun
And on the other was the waxing moon.

---

14   Nymue is often depicted in the Arthurian legend as the Lady
of the Lake who gave the magic sword Excalibur
to King Arthur.

The youth stood gazing spellbound at the sight
Of all the pictures on the mighty gate
Until he utterly forgot himself,
For every image seemed as if it moved
And breathed in animated harmony.
Each aspect living in its rightful place,
Orchestrated by a lawful order
As though it was a complete universe.
Though he knew nothing of this ordered way,
He could not take his eyes off the gate.

Who knows how long he'd have remained transfixed
Had not a sound disturbed his reverie.
It was a trumpet blast heard from within
Announcing a new matter of import
Which was to be voiced to the king and council.
This brought the youth out from his ponderance.
With awe and wonder, he stepped toward the gate
And passed beneath the watchful Nymue.

Once he had entered through that mighty arch,
A throng of people gathered 'round the youth,
All pressing close to see the strangely dressed,
Young stranger, who despite his ragged garb
Walked with an air of grace attending him-
Uncanny and yet undeniable
As though great kings and queens stood at his back
And gazed from far horizons, through his eyes.

To the youth, each person who was gathered there
Appeared so royal and so elegant
He could have mistaken a great many of them
To be the king or queen of Carleon.
His glance alighted on the gentle gaze

Of a page amid the throng, and when their eyes
Had met, the page then smiled at the youth.
This page's name was Iwanet, a prince
And nephew of the Lady Guinevere.
To him the simple youth said- "God keep you,
That's what my mother always said to say.
I see so many Guineveres and Arthurs.
Which one of them makes people into knights?
I've come, because I wish to be a knight."
At this, the friendly page began to laugh,
"You'll never find the right ones out here sir!
But if you follow me inside the castle,
I can assure you, you'll soon find them there.
Are you of age to swear the code of honor?
You are not far off by the looks of it.
But you have not become a squire yet?
I am a page and soon will be a squire.
Perhaps we will two be squires together
And may in time be siblings of the code."

The simple youth stared back without reply,
He comprehended little what was said.

"But come," said Iwanet after a pause,
"You wish to see the king and queen,
And here I stand delaying what you seek-
Come follow me, I'll bring you unto them."

The page then led him up the great stone steps,
Through the archway of the open doors,
And into Arthur's mighty palace hall.
The great Round Table was placed at the center
Before the great thrones of the king and queen.
Upon each seat positioned at the table,

Engraved in gold and silver letterings,
The name of each knight shimmered radiant.
Sir Kay the seneschal[15] stood near the king,
Above the king's throne was a golden sun
Bejeweled with many precious gems of ruby,
Amber, emerald diamond, and sapphire
So that it danced and flickered like a flame.
Beside King Arthur, Lady Guinevere
Sat under a symbol of the silver moon
Which also was bedecked with the rarest gems
Of pearl, topaze, diamonds, and amethysts
That glimmered like soft moonlight over water.
Before this council matters of the land
Were brought to be weighed and determined.
The seats placed at the great round wooden slab,
In rightful order of the zodiac,
Were empty, for it was not time to feast.
The mighty warriors of Arthur's host
Were standing in two flanks beside the thrones
To hear each matter as it was announced,
All ready to receive a knightly quest
Or offer any service to their king.
Beside these warriors were many people,
All noble members of the monarch's court:
Lords, princes, royal ladies, pages, squires,
Dukes and barons and queens from near and far.

At that same moment that the youth was led
Into the palace hall by Iwanet,
The page, Bold Kay the royal seneschal
Was strategizing, as he often did,

---

15   A high ranking knight or lord in charge of administrative
affairs in a royal, medieval company.

With Arthur on an issue of import.
It was the Red Knight they were speaking of.
While noble Kay and Arthur were in council
And all awaited Arthur's final word,
There was discussion among those of the court
With murmuring throughout the spacious hall
Upon the pressing topic there at hand.
The hubbub slowly grew into a clamor
As many voices spoke of this issue,
And some small factions of the court then turned
To other topics as the time wore on.

Above this din, impatiently, the lad,
Dressed like a fool, raised up his youthful voice
And called out loud enough to stop the throng
And catch the ears of Arthur and the queen:

"God keep you all of Arthur's company,
Especially King Arthur and the queen.
I had strict orders when I left my mother
To give them a special greeting from us both.
A knight that I saw shining all in red
Gave me a message for the king and queen.
I think he wants to fight. He also said
He's sorry that he spilt wine on the queen.
So wondrously bright and red he looks-
His armor and his trappings with his horse.
Oh, if I only could have those things!
If I could have all that is his to wear,
So happy I would be, it looks so fine.
If it were mine, I'm sure I'd be a knight!"

And all who stood within that stately hall
Broke off their discourse and took in the youth,

For never had they seen so strange a sight:
A shepherd's son, dressed like a lunatic,
Who yet at closer glance bore the strange air
Of regal purity and kingliness.

"May God reward you for your greeting sir,"
The king replied as he beheld the youth
Who stood naive before his noble gaze.
"The man this armor sits on is not weak
Or lacking in the skills of war. In fact,
So formidable a warrior is he,
I dare not gift you with his red trappings.
No fault of mine has kept me from his favor,
But his ill will towards me brings us grief.
For that, my joy is shattered by this man-
Known by the name Ither- the Red Knight."

Sir Kay stepped forward then and intervened,
For he was dubious of anything
Unusual that came before his king.
The youth's appearance was not ordinary,
And as protector to his majesty,
Kay was on guard for trickery and craft
And wicked sorcery which in the past
Had been aimed at both king and company.

"A mean king you'd be to hold back this gift,"
Sir Kay the seneschal advised his king.
"Why don't you grant the little brat his wish.
Unleash him on the Red Knight- what is lost?
This youth must face fierce odds ere he be knighted,
And Ither's presence nags us like a pest!
There's naught to lose whichever one prevails;
I'm not concerned for either contestant."

"I'm sorry to deny him," said the king,
"But I fear he'll be killed ere he's been trained,
For he could make a worthy knight some day.
I'll wager he has never held a sword;
He is young and has barely come of age.
He's scarcely ready to be sent to fight.
He must be rightly schooled in chivalry,
Not offered to the dogs before he's seasoned:
The lad's no match for such a one as Ither.
I cannot in good conscience send him forth."

To the youth he then turned and kindly spoke:
"Young sir, I cannot grant you your request.
If I could bestow this gift, I surely would.
The Red Knight is a formidable foe,
Well seasoned by the heavy blows of war.
In time, with patience, you'll be made a knight,
And then such challenges will be your charge.
Till then, the gift requested must wait."
At this, much to the shock of everyone,
The boy began to stamp and shake his fists.
He gnashed his teeth and tore the air with rage.

"The armor's mine!" He shouted without shame-
Embarrassed though those in the hall became.
"That you deny me is not as I wish!
Now grant it me: it's mine, and I will have it!"

And thus he stamped and puffed before his liege.

So when at last it was made plain to Arthur
That there was no way to dissuade the lad,
He gave leave for the youth to claim the armor
From Ither, the Red Knight of Cumberland.
The sovereign prayed that by some stroke of grace

The boy would not be slain in the attempt.

So off the young lad raced to claim his prize.
As he made haste to exit through the hall,
A throng of nobles pressed to follow him-
Among them Kay the trusted seneschal.
The page then led him past a gallery,
And there, he watched a scene which caused him grief.
The queen was sitting there with knights and ladies,
And all observed him as he hurried by.
The proud and radiant Lady Cunneware-
Related by blood to Duke Orilus-
His sister and a princess of high birth-
Was there amongst the nobles looking on.
She had not once been known to laugh or smile.
This was a gift and curse which she endured,
For only when she had beheld a knight
Whose heart was most pure and courageous
And strongest of all knights within the world
Would loyal hearted Lady Cunneware
Permit herself to let her laugh come forth.
It was as though part of her was concealed,
Locked away and withheld from the world.
Steadfast and true for many hopeful years,
She waited for the day when joy would come
And elevate her heart from somberness,
For from that moment forward she would be
At liberty to laugh as others did.
The recognition of the truest heart
Would lift the curse and bless her life with joy.

Now as the youth, dressed like a ragged fool,
With flapping skins and sackcloth, hurried past
To hasten to his mangy toppling mare,

A laugh burst from the lips of Cunneware,
Thus breaking the long curse of melancholy
Which had reigned o'er her heart until that moment.

Surprised and outraged that this simple fool
Could, after such long years of tribulation,
Awaken mirth in Lady Cunneware
Without exerting any courtliness
Or effort to obtain her joyfulness
And further that this one who made her laugh
Was so crude in appearance, comportment,
And so unruly in the way he spoke
Was more than Arthur's seneschal could bear.
Sir Kay began to rage within himself
With such ferocity that he was up
And on his feet before he'd paused to think.
His hand flew to a cudgel at his side
And gripped it tightly as he faced the youth,
Prepared to raise it and exact his wrath.
The youth looked back at him without a flinch,
And Kay was stopped in his career of rage.

Impatiently Kay let go of the cudgel
And turned his wrath on Lady Cunneware.

"Have some respect, madam," he snapped to her.
"You've smeared your good name with unseemliness."
This unjust outburst of rage so abrupt
Was met with disapproval by those near,
Which only made the vassal boil more;
Kay seethed, now quite beside himself with wrath.
"Now I shall be the net to catch your honor
And strike it back again with vengeful words.
Perhaps you'll not forsake your manners then.

You've sworn your oath and held it over us
And made claims of the bravest knight of all-
That you'd not laugh till you saw such a one.
So many worthy knights have to these halls
Been honored as our most esteemed guests.
Not one of them have you graced with your laughter,
And now you waste mirth on one without worth?
You laugh for one who's lower than a page-
Who has no notion of the knightly code!
This is a shameful thing that you have done!"

His vindication towards this honest lady,
Whose friends were very sorry for her plight,
Would not have stood before an emperor.
She was a noble princess of high rank,
And had her brothers, Lahelin and Orilus,
Been looking on, she would not have been wronged.

The helpless youth stood by consumed with rage
At witnessing these cruel admonishments
And wished that he'd known how to intervene.
But having never learned of courtly discourse,
He knew not how to stop the ruthless Kay.
And when he was about to interject,
Kind Iwanet, who stood beside the youth,
Reached out and clasped his hand to lead him forth.

Out through the archway of the lofty doors
Along the street and to the castle gate,
The youth then toppled on his ragged steed.
Good Iwanet the page ran just behind.
They passed back through the city's mighty gate
And approached the field toward the Red Knight.

"King Arthur has bestowed a gift on me!"

77

The eager youth heaved when he had arrived
Before fierce Ither, who awaited him.

"I told him as you'd asked that you spilt wine
Upon the queen and were annoyed at this,
For having been so clumsy in this way.
Not one of them had stomach for a fight.
But you must give that armor sir, to me;
Additionally, what you're riding on
Has been by King Arthur bequeathed to me.
'Twas made my gift at yonder palace sir.
I'm to be made a knight in it today.
If you begrudge me, I'll take back my greeting,
So if you're wise, you'll straight bestow it to me.

"If Arthur gave away my armor thus,"
Replied the bold Red Knight unflinchingly,
"You'll have to take my life to obtain it.
So this is how King Arthur treats his friends.
He sends a youth to settle his accounts!"

"I dare to see what's due to me fulfilled!"
The prideful youth unto the knight exclaimed.
"Now stop your wrangling and hand it over!
To be a meager page is not for me,
I will pursue the calling of the shield!
You must be Lahelin, my mother's foe,
The one she told me of who took my lands!"

He snatched the bridle of fierce Ither's steed
And began to pull on the bridle with all his strength.

The knight reversed his lance and thrust the boy
With such strength that he and his wretched nag
Were toppled down amid the bowing blossoms.

The warrior was quick to flare to blows,
And once ignited, his hot temper seared
Like a wild fire and would not abate.
He beat the boy until blood like a fount
Sprung from his pores and sprayed forth in a cloud.
The boy stood shaking, enraged with pain and shame.
His hand flew quickly to his javelin
And gripped it wrathfully as from its sheath
He hurled the lethal spear against his foe.
It shot with deadly aim and hit its mark.
Within the narrow space between the helm
And where the breastplate came up to the throat,
The seam where Ither's shirt of mail was tied
Was where the spear's point found an opening.
The noble knight swooned backward in his saddle
And toppled to the ground, killed instantly.

But now the naive youth could not discern
In what way to remove his new won prize.
He turned the body over and over again
And tugged at all the clasps to no avail.
He'd never seen how armor was put on
Or how to take it off. Kind Iwanet,
Who'd stood by and observed this tragedy,
Was sorry for the king of Cumberland,
But he took pity on the naive youth
And showed him how the clasps could be undone.
Once off of Ither's body, Iwanet
Then helped the youth to put the armor on.
In order to begin, the page attempted
To take some of the thick skins off the boy.
The stubborn lad refused to leave his furs,
Insisting that they stay beneath the armor,
Which was a challenge for the goodly page,

Who struggled to contain the bulky skins
Within the tight clasps of the rigid steel.

But when he gently offered to remove
The sheepskins from the young boy's tawny calves,
The lad again began to cause a fuss
And stamp his legs and shout until the page
Chose acquiescence as the fastest way.
At length, the lad was armed and set astride
His new won steed, magnificently raised
From lowly nag to a wondrous stallion.
He was then seized with fervor for adventure
And wishing to attain the greatest heights
That feats of arms could win by daring acts-
Without returning to King Arthur's court
To claim his gift and tell of Ither's fate-
He took leave of the page who'd helped him so
And rode off bouncing like a sack of wheat
Upon his wondrous mount. His shield hung limp
And dangled loose, flopping against his side,
Like a songbird bird hopping with a broken wing,
Attempting to take flight and keep aloft.
So well bedecked was he but had no skill,
And thus, he made quite a perplexing sight
As he rode dazzling red but cocked askew,
So uncoordinated and untrained.
Confusing at its best this must have looked.
He left a good knight slain in woeful state,
Amid the flowers, stripped of everything.
But those who loved proud Ither buried him
With many tears to water his sad grave.
They made a headstone with these words inscribed:

"Here lies Ither, king of Cumberland,
  Slain by a javelin"

The youth, now clad from head to toe in red,
Knew not the sad import of what he did.
He gave no thought but only sought his goal-
To be what he knew little of: a knight.
In later years when he'd learned honor's code
And had sworn to the law of chivalry,
He burned with shame and sorrowful remorse
And mourned to think what he'd in ignorance,
And what selfishness reeked on his goodly foe.

Proud Ither's armor had proved to be his ruin.
The youth's wish for it ended that king's life.

GURNEMANZ

Now on he rode astride his new won steed,
Which had the unusual trait that neither hill
Nor sloping valley hindered its momentum.
The stallion never seemed to break a sweat.
No rock or fallen tree e'er checked its speed
As deftly it sure footedly progressed.
Its rider having no experience,
Knew no commands by which to change its pace,
So he left it to gallop through the day.

"This horse is very different than the one
I rode before," pondered the youth. The trees
And hills and fields go by so speedily,
And when I look down, the grass is all a blur."

The youth had no means of determining
How many miles they were covering.
In truth, he rode the same space in one sun
As what a seasoned rider would in two.
Now as that globe of russet gold sank low
And gloaming westerly toward earth's rim,
A castle roof rose mid the evening gleam.
And as the turrets climbed into his view,
Naively Parzival could only think
That they'd from seeds been planted and grew there
Like sprouts from out the earth before his gaze
As he drew ever nearer to the fortress.
And thinking that King Arthur planted them
Amazedly he marveled to himself:
"Not once have I e'er seen such mighty crops.
My mother's workers never grew the like;
What farmers Arthur and his knights must be

To plant fields such as those I see ahead,
There sprouting up and growing before my eyes!"
He made his way toward the silhouettes,
Where he would lay his weary head that night.
This land, known as Graharz, was governed
By Gurnemanz, a mighty prince of state,
Who at the moment of our youth's approach,
Stood at a doorway hung with linen swaths.
High on a castle wall, the linens wafted
And playfully caressed the evening air.
He stood o'erlooking all that heavenly land
Like Eden's garden, gilded soft with sun.
So beautiful it was, one might've thought
It was enchanted.
                        As the unschooled youth
On horseback jostled toward the castle gates,
Across the verdant summer sward, he lurched
And listed side to side with shield hung limp.
His arms, fatigued, were bouncing 'gainst his leg.
A strange unruly sight was this approach,
Such fine apparel with no hint of poise.
His sad comportment savored not of strength
Or bravery but signified a fool.

As Parzival approached the castle gate,
The bridge was lowered, and in rode the youth.
Gurnemanz the prince was standing by
Beneath the reaching shade of linden boughs
That stretched across walls. Lord Gurnemanz,
A courteous lord, who was from falsehood free,
Gave Parzival a welcome, face-to-face-
(No knight or squire had been sent ahead
To bear this greeting for him to the youth):

"Good evening sir," he said, "God rest ye well."

To him, the unrefined youth bluntly spake:
"God be with you. That's what my mother said.
So that's what I tell everyone I meet.
She also said that if I found a man
Whose hair was grey- his council I should seek."

"If you have come for council," said the prince,
"And aid from me, then you must now agree
That you will heed my words whate'er they be
And to them give all your attention fully."

Then from his hand, he cast a fledgling falcon
Which straight flew upwards and into the castle
And disappeared amid the roofs and towers.
Its feet were decked with bells which softly rang.
It was a messenger, for shortly after,
A group of well-clad pages came to them.
Prince Gurnemanz then bade his host of servants
See to it that their guest was given ease.

At this, the naive boy piped up again:
"My mother spoke aright. An old man's words
Are surely to be trusted without doubt."

They led him presently into a courtyard.
A clan of knights there hailed him courteously
And bade him to come down from off his steed.

"No knight would I be were I to dismount,"
Replied the earnest youth. "I'll not come down.
Whatever happens next I'll keep my seat;
And also, as my mother said to say,
God be with you, to each and everyone."

They thanked him and his goodly mother too
And urged him to come down from off his horse.
It took them many tries and urgent coaxing
Ere they succeeded in convincing him.
Eventually however he conceded.
They led him to a chamber to disarm.
The lad staunchly refused. They had no end
Of aggravation with that chore. At last,
They took his armor off despite his threats,
For whether he would or not, it was removed.
Once it was off, they were aghast to find
A lad appareled like a fool in rags,
With buckskins flapping at his tawny sides.
They gasped and gaped and knew not what to do
Till finally an aged knight cleared his throat
And said: "In all my days, I've never seen
Such noble progeny. I do declare
He has the mark and look of kings indeed."
Then heartily they all joined in, affirmed
And vouched agreeably he surely had
The look of regal bearing about his nature
Despite the unruly state of his attire.

At seeing the bruises on the young boy's frame,
Prince Gurnemanz now graciously spoke up:
"These wounds speak of some cruel and arduous fight.
Perhaps he earned them on behalf of love."
"I think not so," replied the aged knight.
"No one would have him dressed so like a fool.
He must have had those wounds some other way."

Gurnemanz then washed and dressed the wounds
With such care as a father gives his son.
He gently coaxed the youth out of his rags

85

And into finery brought by a squire.
Once this was done they led him off to dine.
The stranger was in desperate need of it.
He'd ridden from the fisherman's that morn
And hadn't eaten once, which left him famished.
He dug in like a boar before a trough
And hogged through piles of provender ravenously
While those around him gaped and looked aghast.
The host assumed the youth did this in jest.

"Don't wait on ceremony! Dive right in!"
He said. "Don't let restraint get in the way!"

The boy did not look up but kept devouring
Until he'd stuffed his gullet to its brim.

"You must be tired" said the kindly host.
"Were you up early?"
                              "Heaven knows I was,"
Replied the boy. "Each morning I arise
Before the sun has come over the hills.
My mother's always sleeping when I wake.
She usually does not rise so early."

Good Gurnemanz laughed heartily at this
And led him to a chamber with a bed.
'Twas o'erlaid with a silk embroidered quilt.
The boy had no sooner climbed beneath the sheets
And laid his head against the downy cushion
When sleep caressed his heavy eyelids closed
And o'er his senses draped soft slumber's veil.
He slept so soundly that he hardly moved
Or shifted through the night but lay quite still
Until the morning light crept with the dawn
And gently pulled the blinds of night away.

Some servants were at work within the room
As silent as the coming of the morn;
But nonetheless, the motions of their task,
Though soundless, stirred the youth to wakefulness.
The prince had sent them to prepare a bath
For the young lad without disturbing him
That he might wake to find it all in order.
They set it by the bed upon the rug,
Strewn 'round with rose petals awaiting him,
And left the room as soon as this was done.
So up he got and climbed into the tub.
Once he had bathed, he rose and left the tub
And made his way back to the splendid bed,
Where they had left him finery to wear,
Which next he donned before his host appeared
And gave him morning's greeting graciously.
A company of knights attended him.
He took the boy in hand to lead him out
And asked the youth how he had slept that night.

"If mother hadn't told me to come here,"
Replied the boy, "I wouldn't have survived."

"May God reward you both," returned the prince.
Our simple warrior then went to Mass
As Gurnemanz encouraged him to do.
And there, the prince informed him of religion:
To sign the cross and ward the devil off.
And after this, they went into the palace.
Once there, they found a table ready laid.

"Where have you ridden from?" the host inquired.
The youth then told him everything he'd done:
The taking of Jeschute's wrist brooch and ring

And how he won his splendid scarlet armor.
Lord Gurnemanz sighed at this sad account,
For Ither's tragic death disheartened him.
He looked compassionately at the boy,
And though he was dismayed by Ither's death,
Kind Gurnemanz saw promise in the youth
Who sat before him. It was ignorance
That had won the armor so disgracefully,
And Gurnemanz knew that with tutelage
The unschooled youth would be an honest knight
And so determined that his guest be dubbed
"The Red Knight" for this future hope.

"You speak like a child," the prince informed his guest.
"Why do you not stop talking of your mother
And turn your mind to things more relevant?
If you'll permit me now, let us begin.
Firstly, never lose your sense of shame.
If one is past all shame, then hope is gone.
One then lives like a bird who's always moulting
And shedding its good qualities like plumes,
Descending downward slipping toward demise.
You have the bearing of nobility
And may in time be looked to as a ruler.
Now if you are indeed of kingly blood,
Remain compassionate to those in need,
And kindly strive to ward off their distress.
Be generous and practice modesty.
Someone of standing who's fallen on tough times
Must wrestle with their pride- a bitter fight.
You should assist a person such as this.
If you relieve them, God's reward will come.
Such people have it worse than those with naught,
Who've always begged at windows their whole life.

A nobleman who squanders property
Does not display a noble spirit thus,
And if he hoards his wealth excessively,
He'll bring dishonor down upon himself.
Give moderation its due course and measure.
Do not ask many questions. Eyes, ears, taste,
Smell, touch, these basic senses reveal more
And teach one more than prying with inquiry.
However, if someone seeks words with you,
Then you should speak to them and not withhold
Considered answers that are to the point.
Accompany bravery with gentle mercy.
Now show me you have followed my advice.
When you have won submission from a foe,
Let live unless they've done you mortal wrong.
You'll oft bare arms in life, but when you're through
Then always be sure to wash your face and hands:
When the iron from your armor leaves its stain
Of rust upon your skin from a long day
Of toiling in battle, you must wash
And carefully tend your body's welfare
Then will your freshness and nobility
Be restored from the grime of laboring,
And people will behold your princeliness
And treat you with the honor you have earned.
Be brave and cheerful, humble, strong, and kind,
For this will bring you standing in the world.
Hold others in esteem; this elevates
A person's worth. Do not forsake their cause.
Thoughts such as these should give strength to a person.
If you choose lying, you may for a time
Deceive another, but eventually
The dry wood in the thicket snaps and warns
The watchmen of the prowler hidden by.

And so it is with love. Dishonor not
Another's love. Be upright with their heart
And honorable, or else, love's honesty
Will by its shear benevolence reveal
Its remedy for cunning and deceit,
And you will surely be disgraced in shame
And suffer pain and endless torment thus.
Take this to heart, for I have more to say.
In love, two people are much like the sun
And what we call the day, for they are one,
And neither can be parted from the other.
They blossom from the very self-same source.
There's more for you to learn of knightly ways.
Just think how you approached me on your horse.
On many a wall that I have seen ere now
Are shields slung better than the one you wore.
It's not too late; let us go to the field
And give attention to your education
By training expertise in all these things."

And so, the prince rode out onto the meadow
And trained his guest in feats of horsemanship.
He taught him how to charge up to full tilt
With a touch of the spur against his horse's flanks
And how to place and aim his lance correctly
While covering with his shield against his foe.
This done, he asked some rugged knights to joust
And urged his guest to face off against them.
The lad delivered his first thrust on point
And swung a sturdy knight clean o'er his crupper,
Much to the shock of all assembled there,
For his opponent was formidable.
A jouster there was born before their eyes.
Urged by the blood that flowed within his veins

And courage from the line of kings and queens
That he was heir to, Gahmuret's young son,
A beardless youth, threw down five more stout knights,
All in a row, as he had done the first.
And all did marvel at his native skill,
Combined with his extraordinary strength
And boldness- which had greatly exceeded
Their prospects for his first day on the field.
Prince Gurnemanz then led him home again.
Young Parzival had had good sport that day,
But in the days succeeding, he would grow
To be most expert in the craft of war.
The tried hands that observed him there declared,
'For one who had so recently been trained,
His strength and skill were quite remarkable.'
That evening he sat with the prince's daughter,
The beautiful Laize, who dined with him.
In this way, for two weeks, they served their guest,
And after supper she withdrew at once.
But one thing nagged at the young knight's conscience.
Before he sought a lover's company,
He yearned to venture out into the world
And test himself with exploits of the shield.
He felt the triumphs of this world's adventures
That lead toward the next enticing him
With greater strength each day until at last,
One morning, he begged leave to venture forth
Away from fair Graharz where he had received
His mentorship from noble Gurnemanz.

The prince rode out with him to open country,
And there, beset by heartache, he revealed
His bitter sorrows to his young apprentice:

"In you, I lose my fourth son" said the prince.
"I thought my tale of woe had reached its end
In three sad acts, but now, it seems a fourth
Must add its mournful dole ere I find rest.
Oh, if my heart were torn in four parts
And born away in four directions
'Twould be more comfort than to bear the grief
I bear for having it be torn apart
And still remain as one within my breast:
One part for you, who rides away, three more
For my dear sons, who died most gallantly.
The death of Schenteflurs, my eldest son,
Destroyed my happiness. He lost his life
Attempting to assist Condwiramurs
In Belrepeire, which is a citadel
Within the mighty kingdom of Brobarz.
There dwells this good, kindhearted empress
Who refuses to marry King Clamide.
When this brave queen did not requite his wish,
Cruel King Clamide laid siege to Belrepeire.
My Schenteflurs fought on the queen's behalf
And strove against Clamide with all his strength.
He would have conquered the unruly king
Had not Sir Kingrun the vassal of Clamide,
Then ambushed my dear son. On that sad day,
My foremost heir, brave Schenteflurs was slain.
My second son Count Lascoyt met his death
Competing for a sparrowhawk. And there
Every shred of joy was stripped from me.
Though how 'twas possible that any joy
Was left to wring out of my soul astounds me.
The dear, good Gurzgri was my third and last.
He wed the beautiful Mahaute. The pair
Had journeyed forth after their union

In quest of fortune and adventure. Alas,
When they came to the land of Brandigun,
He met his death upon the battlefield.
A knight named Mabonagrin slew him there.
My dear wife swooned and died at this sad news.
It was more grief than her poor heart could hold,
And stricken thus by grief, it ceased to pulse.
My heart's still sinking with this tide of sorrow,
And now, you ride away from me so soon!
Wretch that I am! Oh why can I not die?
Since not my noble daughter nor my lands
Have met your liking well enough to stay?"

The promising youth to his host's sore plight
Was now made 'ware and knew not what to do
Or what words he could speak to Gurnemanz.
He had to go but felt the pangs of loss
That wrung his mentor's sorrow-ridden heart,
For Gurnemanz had made it all so plain.

"My lord," he said "I have not yet reached years
Of understanding or discretion. Yet,
If ever I can win renown enough
To warrant love's pursuit, I'll ask Liaze
For her most dear and worthy hand in marriage.
You have here told me of a heavy grief,
But once time and adventure ripen me,
Then, being able, I'll rid you of woe."

The youth then took his leave while faithfully
The good Prince watched him go as his last hope
Departed hence, toward the wilderness.
Both knew within, he would not come again.
Both knew no choice of theirs had made it thus,

And both were truly sorry this was so;
But nonetheless, the voice of destiny
Was softly murmuring within their hearts,
Whose cry of wisdom cannot be denied,
For no amount of reasoning can still
The soft persistence of her influence.
Though she may be ignored, her echo stays
And lingers till she's given audience.
If she be stalled too long, her tune may shift,
But her determined countenance remains.
Indeed, sometimes to great extremes must she,
High Destiny, resort to waken us.
But in the end, though she calls on the fates
To shake the earth and summon fell events,
Conspiring to rouse us from our beds,
Where blissfully in ignorance we dream-
So married to our slumbering are we-
This Empress of action's patient invitation
Steadfastly awaits us to participate.

Awakening won't forever be with pain,
For though our stirring may be turbulent
And may indeed arise from suffering,
When mighty destiny is given ear,
She comes accompanied by gentle peace,
Who brings acceptance as a healing balm-
With which to soothe and tend a broken heart.

And so it was, with noble Gurnemanz,
The goodly prince, who gave young Parzival
The training needed to begin his life.
Parzival set forth prepared for chivalry,
With education and maturity.
For this good Gurnemanz received no pay,

But peace came with acceptance to remend
His tattered, grief worn heart, before the end.

CONDWIRAMURS

The youthful warrior rode on equipped
With all the noble traits that make a knight
Well suited for the task of chivalry.
No longer did he lurch from side to side
With shield hung limp and bouncing 'gainst his leg.
Now thanks to Gurnemanz, the poise he held
Astride his steed possessed the mastery
To match the young knight's regal lineage.
Adorned by young adulthood's hopeful bloom-
Amid the dawn, through dissipating mists,
He roamed. The early morning freshly rose
With the promise of another rising sun.

But now he was beleaguered by remorse
At having left his mentor, Gurnemanz.
Not only this, but thoughts of dear Liaze,
The noble princess, both gentle and kind,
Who had to him been loyal as a friend
Now also gave him angst as he rode forth
Away from fair Graharz, toward his future.
So wrapped in his thoughts was young Parzival
That he cared not what pace his stallion set
But let it go and never curbed its speed.
The powerful horse seemed naturally inclined
To run for many hours at a stretch
Without the slightest sign of tiring
Or slackening momentum from a gallop.
And rarely did they pass by furrowed lands
Or well-tilled country, but rode over hills,
And wild, untilled, grassy plains, unknown
To any but the most adventurous;
And through the woodland valleys too they plunged,

Where many logs had been by axes felled.
He held his course, passed mountains high and wild,
Until he reached the kingdom of Brobarz.
As afternoon began to tilt its light
Toward evening on the looming mountain peaks,
He came upon a torrent[16] raging fierce,
Whose sound was made known long before 'twas seen,
As it hurled and churned against its mighty rocks.
Across this swirling gorge lay Belrepaire,
A city in the kingdom of Brobarz.

The river thundered, veering steeply downward,
Impetuously rushing to the sea.
A bridge hung spanned across the pitching gorge,
And far below the river met the sea,
Churning in a vat of foam and spray.
'Twas well positioned for defense, this city.
The bridge swung fiercely in the gusting wind.
Young Parzival moved toward the narrow pass
But when they reached the bridge his horse shied back.
So he dismounted fearlessly and led
The steed with care across the perilous bridge.
He had to take great pains to mind his horse
And keep the beast from slipping off the edge.
It took some time to make their way across.
Each step had to be placed attentively
While blasts of wind whipped 'round them howling
And moaning balefully beneath the bridge-
Which lurched and listed,[17] threatening to send
Both horse and master to the swirling flood.
When they had reached the middle of the pass

---

16   A river with turbulent rapids.
17   To tilt to one side.

Where it became most treacherous and limber,
The horse was spooked by a sudden burst of wind,
Which sent the giddy bridge into a dance
Above the churning cauldron far below,
And whinnying, it drew back on its reins.
The young knight without hesitation turned
And gently placed his hand upon the bridle.
His grip held firm with inner steadiness,
And his voice never wavered as he spoke
To soothe the great beast in its nervousness.
With this, trust came back to the mighty stallion
Enough to press on toward the farther side.
The bridge grew sturdier with every step
As they came closer to the river bank.
At last, they reached the far side of the pass
And stood once more upon the solid ground.
There, they found a meadow spread before them
Where many fearsome battles had been fought.
The ground was charred and blackened underfoot;
A mighty siege had laid waste to that field.
It was deserted but where grass still clung
It had been churned by hooves and well trampled.
This battleground stretched from the swinging bridge
Up to the stately gates of Belrepeire.
Toward this gate the young knight made his way
Until he stood beneath the outer walls.
He found an iron ring hung on the gate
And with strength swung it 'gainst the wooden door
So that the sound rang, echoing within.
A silence followed; all remained quite still.
At length, a solitary servant answered.
He looked out of a window high above
And said, "if you've come as an enemy,
You're wasting time; we've suffered ills enough

From heartless foes without you joining in."

"Here stands a knight who offers help to you,"
Replied the dauntless youth up to the window,
"If I can be of service in your need."

At this, the thoughtful page went to the queen
Then brought the youth within the city walls.
The people of the city flanked the street.
Great catapults crept forward, pushed by ranks,
Behind which stood a hoard of vile archers
And men-at-arms with great spears on the march.
Not only this but merchants also stood
With javelins and sturdy battle axes,
According to the order of their guild.
But everyone inside the city's gates
Looked gaunt with hunger and fatigued by war.

The marshall[18] to the queen had much ado
To lead the young knight through this well-armed mass
Into a courtyard, well-equipped for war
With turrets above chambers, barbicans,
High angled towers, dark tunnels, and causeways.
From all sides, knights approached by foot and steed
To welcome Parzival within their walls.
This company was also weak and pale;
A long siege had reduced them to starvation.
Their bellies were sunken; their hips were gaunt and lean;
Their skin lay shrunken and stretched across their ribs,
For thieving famine robbed them of their flesh.
The king of Brandigun brought this to pass.
This monarch was at war with Belrepeire,

---

18   High ranking officer of the queen and overseer of her military
and administrative affairs.

Because the queen would not requite his wish.
This King Clamide was set on marrying her
And would not cease until she acquiesced.
For this, her subjects gave their sacrifice
Of suffering out of the loyalty
They bore for her as queen and sovereign.

"If you wish sir, we'll take you to our queen,"
Said the queen's lord to the young Parzival.
He was ashamed the princely warrior
Should be received amid their sorrowful plight.

"I'd gladly take that honor," he replied.
And so they climbed the lengthy flight of stairs
Up to the entrance of the stately palace.

The lovely radiance of the queen's good heart
And the kindly beauty of her gentle eyes
Preceded the sovereign of Belrepeire
In a blaze of light before the two had met.

Her uncles escorted her on either side:
Two kind dukes who had renounced their swords
To live a life of devotion unto God.
These uncles were indeed a noble pair,
Two grey-haired, handsome princes, as they paced
And with great ceremony led the queen
Towards the stairs to meet her honored guest.
And there she met the noble warrior
Then led him to a hall to take his seat.
Her company of knights and noble ladies
Had lost a great deal of their health and strength.
This queen had taken leave of happiness,
But the beauty of her spirit still shone through.

"Liaze is here before my very eyes,
The daughter of my teacher, Gurnemanz.
How can she be here and also with her father?"
Thought youthful Parzival unto himself
Inwardly riddled with confusion.
"My sadness has become more bearable
Now that I find her here with me again,"
He then concluded musing to himself.
But though he wondered thus, this queen surpassed
In beauty anyone he'd ever seen.
Now his self command was so complete,
Since Gurnemanz had taught him etiquette
And bade him to refrain from asking questions,
He could sit by the queen without a word.

But now the queen was thinking to herself:
"Perhaps this man is looking down on me,
Because my flesh from hunger is reduced.
No! Surely he does not pass judgement here.
He is my guest, and I will be his host.
Since I'm his host, perhaps I should begin
The conversation. Then the queen spoke gently:
"I heard you sent your pledge of aid to us.
So one of my young pages has informed me.
To my deep sorrow, we have not had guests
For quite some time because of our sad state.
But tell me sir, where have you journeyed from?"

"This morning I rode from a gentleman
Of flawless loyalty named Gurnemanz,
Who rules the stately kingdom of Graharz.
From there, I rode until I reached this land."

"If any other told me this," she said,
"I'd not believe they did it in one day,

For when my messenger has ridden it,
He has not covered that distance in two.
The sister of your host was my dear mother.
I and my cousin good Liaze have wept
For many long and sorrow-ridden days.
If you hold Gurnemanz in high regard,
Accept our hospitality tonight.
I will now tell you of our troubles sir.
A famine grips us caused by siege and war."

At this, her two kind uncles intervened,
For they could see the suffering of the queen.
Her uncle Kyot was the first to speak:
"Dear lady, we must honor our new guest
And share what portions we have left in store."

Then Manpfilyot spoke with encouragement:
"What need we ration with so little left?"

"Dear uncles, I thank you with all my heart,"
Replied the gentle queen to her two uncles.
"A crew of hands was sent to fetch these things
And soon returned with the few victuals,
Which yet remained of their provisions,
And the enfeebled people were revived."

The queen gave word to share it amongst her folk.
At this, they all were happily fulfilled.
She then gave orders to prepare a bed
In order that her guest might take his rest.
'Twas not a bed of poverty that night
On which the noble youth laid down his limbs.
'Twas soft and plush as any bed could be.
He did not keep the knights attending him
But sent them hence and soon was fast asleep.

He had not slumbered for more than an hour
When as he slept, a rain began to fall
And mingled with his dreams to stir his rest.
This rain continued as he dreamt aloft
Until at last it roused him from his sleep.
As he awoke with bleary sleep still clinging
Around his eyes, he hazily beheld
The figure of a woman by his bed,
Weeping bitter tears which fell upon him,
For war and death of all her champions
Had wracked her heart; no sleep relieved her eyes.

Condwiramurs had left her bed that night
To seek the counsel of this youth as a friend.
As she approached the young knight's room, she saw
The candles by his bed were bright as day.
She knelt by him and could not help but weep.
She was so utterly wretched that the tears
Rained down on Parzival where he lay sleeping,
And though she strove to keep her sobs from sounding,
There was no stopping them till they were out.
And this at length awoke the sleeping youth.
The lady asked him if he'd hear her woes,
And he quite gladly said he'd lend his ear.
He rose, and they at length sat side by side.
Condwiramurs recounted all her woes:
"I fear that it shall rob you of your sleep-
The heavy grief I bear upon my heart.
A king known as Clamide and his vassal
Have laid my lands and castles all to waste.
Aside from Belrepeire, they've all been plundered.
My father died and left me ill-prepared
To face the fearful dangers that have come.
I was the ruler of a mighty host:

103

Courageous kinsmen, princes, vassals, dukes,
Both humble and renowned, all valorous.
But more than half have died in my defense.
How can one in this wretched state be glad?
I've reached the point where I would rather die
Than be the wife of this most cruel Clamide,
For it was he who slew dear Schenteflurs,
My cousin, so valiant, chivalrous, and bold
In the youthful flowering of knightly ways.
He was the son of good Prince Gurnemanz
Who is my uncle and Lord of Graharz."

At hearing his friend's name, the youth was sad.
His spirits fell as he came to his mind.
"Could anything be done to help you madam?"

"Yes," said the queen, "Kingrun, the seneschal
Of ruthless King Clamide, were he subdued,
Much respite would I have from his advances.
He's thrust down many courageous knights of mine
And slain a goodly some in his assaults.
He comes again tomorrow and is driven
By visions of me in his master's arms.
You've seen my palace sir? Its walls are high.
I'd pitch from them headlong into the sea
Before Clamide should ever marry me.
That's how I'd cheat him of his craven boasts!"

"If Kingrun be of French or English stock,"
Replied the honest youth to the sad queen,
"Or what'er land from which he may descend,
Tomorrow, by my oath, you'll be defended.
My utmost power is at your command."

As far as lovers go, these two were green.

104

So sweet and innocent, they made a truce:
That she would lay with him beneath the quilt,
But they'd refrain from kissing or embracing.
In truth, they gave scant thought to that at all.
She climbed into the bed next to the youth,
And there they lay, close in the sheets together.
The night was silent, soft and deeply still.
No sound announced itself to break the calm
Besides the gentle sighing of their breath.

The night's soft stillness faded into dawn.
At daybreak, she arose and took her leave.
Inclining her head, she thanked him gratefully
And went out without waking anyone.

The warrior did not sleep that early morn
But lay awake preparing for the day,
And as the sun made haste to climb its heights
And burst through shimmering clouds, the knight arose.
He heard Mass which his lady's chaplain sang
But rarely moved his gaze off of the queen.
However much the chaplain sang his chants,
The young knight only had eyes for the queen.
Once they had broken their fast, he called for arms,
For he was well-prepared to face his foe
Before he rode forth from the palace gates.
Sir Kingrun's entourage stood by the field.
And there, the seneschal awaited him
With upraised lance amid the grassy plane
On which he'd thrown down many warriors.
The son of Gahmuret rode forth alone,
The prayers of those behind him at his back;
This was his first encounter with a foe
Since he had been trained by Prince Gurnemanz.

He took a wide sweep for his headlong charge
And galloped toward the ruthless seneschal.
The seneschal had urged his steed to gallop,
Accelerating gradually in pace
Toward the youth until he reached full tilt.
The shock of their attack ungirthed both steeds
So that they staggered back onto their haunches;
Their belly girths were snapped in the collision.
But both knights took the blow and found their feet
Beneath their reeling beasts upon the ground.
Now neither knight paused to regain their breath
But found their blades awaiting in their sheaths
And drew them forth advancing toward each other.
The seneschal was wounded in his chest;
His arm was also injured from the charge.
Never before had Kingrun's strength been matched,
Nor had he once sustained an injury
Of any weight before facing the youth.
The dauntless young knight's sword arm took its toll
Upon the battle seasoned seneschal.
He answered blow for blow with such account
That Kingrun had the strange impression
That catapults were hurling boulders down.
It was no catapult that brought him low
But a sword blow through his helm from Parzival;
It clashed down like a stroke of lightning
And smote him to the core of his proud soul.
The youth then hurled him down into the dust
And thrust his knee against his armored chest.
The vassal offered him what no one else
Had e'er received from him until that day,
His unequivocal and plain defeat.

"Surrender is of no avail to you,"

Replied the dauntless Parzival to him,
"Unless you offer homage to Gurnemanz!"

"Oh no, my lord! I'd rather choose my death,"
Replied the vanquished vassal of Clamide.
"I took the life of his son, Schenteflurs.
God's graced your hand with strength and fearlessness.
Whatever comes, your strength is proved on me;
My life is at your mercy which will reap
Much glory. Your fame and your reputation
Will be increased- you will gain much success."

"I will allow one other choice for you,"
Replied stout-hearted Parzival to him.
"Acknowledge your submission to the queen
On whom your lord has wreaked much suffering."

"If I do that, I'll surely meet my death,"
Replied the downcast Kingrun to his foe.
"If I were brought within those city walls,
They'd mince me with their sharp swords into shreds.
I've mortified all their best warriors
Upon this field before their wrathful eyes."

To this replied the steadfast Parzival:
"Then take yourself into the land of Britain,
And bring your homage unto Arthur's court.
Give Arthur and the queen my compliments,
Include in this all of their company.
Among those in the royal entourage
Of noble Guinevere, there is a princess
Who is known by the name of Cunnaware.
This princess was disgraced on my account
And ruthlessly shamed before the eyes of all
Who had assembled there simply because

She laughed when she beheld me as I passed.
I owe her my condolences and my honor.
Instead of taking your life from you sir,
I charge you to serve Lady Cunnaware.
Indebt your knightly service to her charge,
And tell her that I too am at her service."

"This I will do, brave sir," replied Kingrun,
"And follow your instructions to the word."

This done, they took their leave of one another.
On foot, young Parzival reclaimed his horse,
Who had recovered from the hefty charge
And now awaited him some distance off.
From there, he made his way to Belrepeire
With rein in hand, on foot, up to the gates.
This victory against the seneschal
Astounded all the citizens inside;
So long had they endured this man's oppression,
They knew not if the good news could be true.
Young Parzival was brought before the queen;
She did not stand on ceremony now.
She wrapped her arms around the warrior
And held him as though they would merge to one.
A change had dawned in noble Parzival
And the steadfast and good Condwiramurs
As though a spark had caught between their hearts
And softly grown into a gentle flame.
The two then went with other courtiers
To dine in honor of the victory
And liberation of fair Belrepiere.
The food was brought before them, and they supped.
The people in the city flocked to them

And hurried to swear fealty[19] to the hero
And urged him to become their honored lord.

And now, what blessed fortune blew their way-
Two gleaming sails beneath the sun were seen
Upon the rolling sea against the sky.
The sails belonged to vessels which had blown
Straight into Belrepeire, sent from a gale,
Which drove them off their course.
The bottoms of these crafts were laden full
With cargo that could not but bring them joy,
For they were packed to the gills with food!
God in His wisdom had ordained it thus.
The famished crowd poured down toward the port
That was positioned well against their foes;
No enemy had any vantage there.
The starving mob might very well have sped
Straight down to the ships and pillaged them
Had not the queen's stout marshal placed the ship
Beneath the protection of his majesty.
'Twas for their good that he laid down the law
And warned them to forbear on pain of death.
He had their health in mind when he did this,
For they'd have gorged themselves to their demise,
So famished were the people of that city.
He led the captains of the merchant ships
Up from the cove in through the castle walls
And brought them to the presence of the queen,
Who waited with her beloved Parzival.
The two kind rulers who were of one mind
Gave orders for the merchants to be paid
And doubled the amount of what they'd asked;

---

19 A formal pledge of loyalty to a ruler.

Though food was scant, there was no lack of wealth.
Once more in Belrepeire, the plates were full,
And fat dripped on the coals as they once had.
Good Parzival and the lady that he served
Proceeded faultlessly in rulership;
They organized that people should be fed
With wise restraint. A mighty feast was held.
Each citizen was given small amounts
Until their bellies regained tolerance
For larger quantities of nourishment.
Once this had been accomplished in due course,
The portions were doled out without restraint.
No matter what their rank within that land,
The dwellers of that city had their fill.

And would the prince and queen of Belrepeire
Now celebrate their nuptials as well?
Both answered "yes" to that expectant question.
Soon after, they were wed with quiet joy
And deep fulfillment in their happiness.
A joyful celebration then ensued
With song and feasting throughout Belrepeire.
Then on the third night after they were married,
They found each other in love's close exchange.
In this, their joy was evermore increased,
For as the day and sunlight live
Together, joined in singularity
Like two aspects of one divinity
That lend a birthplace for the happiness
Of human beings, beasts, all living things,
So does one love that lives within two hearts
Create a third love born out of the two.
This third love is most beautiful of all,
For it encompases all of the loves

And is not only three, but also one:
Three loves combined is one love's unity.

But this sweet respite from the strain of war
Was only to last the span of several days,
For restless King Clamide still sought his goal.
He, with his army, was on the approach
At having heard the news that starvation
Was forcing Belrepeire toward its demise.
So on he came, intent to storm its gates
With sword and fire, till he grasped his queen.
But not long after Kingrun was defeated,
A page rode towards Clamide as he advanced.
The steed's flanks had been torn by this man's spurs:
So furiously he rode toward his king.
As he came near the king, he spoke the news
Quite out of breath, with no formality:

"Upon the plain in front of Belrepeire,
A fierce encounter has just taken place.
The seneschal has been defeated there;
A knight has bravely smote him to the earth.
Kingrun, commander of our host, is gone;
He's on his way to Arthur's court in Britain.
The mercenaries have maintained their posts
At his command, before he headed forth.
You'll find the city well defended sir.
Within a fearsome warrior awaits
Who has no other wish than battling.
Your soldiers say that Queen Condwiramurs
Has sent for Ither, King of Cumberland,
The Red Knight to defend her city gates.
He is a member of the Table Round;
His blazon was identified by them

When he came out to joust most valiantly."

"Condwiramurs shall have me as her lord,
And I shall have both her and all her lands!"
The wrathful Clamide bellowed at the page.
"My seneschal, Sir Kingrun, sent me news
That soon they will be forced to yield the city
And that the queen would have to yield to me!"

The king rode on, but now a knight approached
Who also galloped at an urgent pace,
And he attested to the same events.
At this, the king's high spirits were deflated.
But then one of his entourage spoke up:
"My lord, we must proceed with the attack.
We must now claim revenge for Sir Kingrun.
Send forward your whole force against the gates,
For surely with our numbers, it will fall.
This found good favor with the covetous king,
And so he gave word for a full attack.

But Parzival, Condwiramurs, and those
Who dwelt within the walls of Belrepeire
Were well aware of the strong likelihood
That vengeful King Clamide would lead his host
And try to storm the city in his wrath.

When that proud king arrived before the gates,
He found the army of Belrepeire waiting
Outside the stronghold's walls upon the field.
Clamide gave orders for a swift attack.
They drove together in a great assault.
The ones besieged resisted their assailants
With courage and did not yield any ground,
For they were stout of heart, repaired to health.

Their sovereign Parzival fought out in front
And battled as though angels fought through him.
He struck down many knights upon that field
And unrelentingly forced back his foes,
For all he met were thrown down by his sword.
The flashing of his blade was ever seen
Above the sea of soldiers, cleaving helms
And hurling back the press as they attacked-
Like a hurricane of fire in a storm.
Brave Parzival's armor glowed red like hot coals
As rays of sunlight caught its scarlet gleam,
For this he became known as the Red Knight.
His courage seemed to spread throughout his ranks
And every soldier felt within their heart
A flame ignite so that they fought like gods.
The army's power was increased tenfold
As dauntlessly they fought their adversaries.

Now as he fought, the young prince grew aware
That King Clamide had chosen somewhere else
Away from where he fought before the gates
To do his fighting, far from Parzival.
And so, the Red Knight looked for Clamide's pennant.
He saw it with Clamide some distance off,
Surrounded by his stately entourage.
Towards the flag the Red Knight turned his steed
And made his way to rougher country.
He thundered through the ranks of enemies
And struck down every foe who crossed his path.
The Red Knight's blows rained with an army's strength
And cut his swath through the wall of Clamide's host
Relentlessly until he'd made his way
Out to the battle's rim to meet his foe,
Who'd perpetrated his queen's suffering.

At length he found the pennant of Clamide
And took a wide sweep for his fearless charge.
And on he came as though fresh to the fight
And hurtled down one of the entourage.
Once more he wheeled his beast of war around
And turned back towards Clamide's protective clan.
It was magnificent and terrible,
Beholding these intrepid feats of arms:
The bold red warrior upon the field
Who struck as though the gods were at his back.
No force like that had e'er been seen before.
Meanwhile Parzival's army had pressed hard
And steadily drove back their enemies.
Clamide's close entourage was dwindling
As several had been struck down at his side.
The king now found himself to be at risk
And called off the attack before defeat.

Young Parzival gave word that the prisoners,
Which Belrepeire had taken in as captives,
Be well provided for within its gates,
And for three days he entertained these guests.
The army of Clamide, outside the walls,
Assumed they'd never see their comrades more,
And with anxiety they thus awaited.
But on the third morn of captivity,
They looked and saw those from their company
Returning to their ranks quite happily.
They did not break a sweat or hurry back
But walked a pace of leisure and contentment
And seemed to stumble slightly as they ambled,
For Parzival and good Condwiramurs
Had filled them to the gills with food and drink.

"You must be famished," said some worried friends
Who greeted them as they returned to camp.

"Don't waste your pity on the likes of us,"
The captives chuckled back, well satisfied.
"There are such quantities of food inside
That if you stayed encamped here for a year,
They'd keep you and themselves both well maintained!
The queen has found a handsome prince to wed,
Who has the marks of royal lineage.
He is a picture of nobility,
And honor, chivalry and courtesy."

                    "Be silent!"
Snapped Clamide angrily when he heard this,
Quite tortured with regret for all his toil.
He sent an entourage to Belrepeire;
They bore a message for the queen's new prince.
"To he who now defends the queen," it read:
"If eligible for a single match
Should he that has been recognized by her
Still dare defend her and her lands from me,
Then let there be a truce between the hosts
And let us meet upon the dueling ground,
One knight against the other, till one falls."

The youth was gladdened by the embassy.

"Tell him," he told the entourage of knights,
"My honor stands as pledge that not one soul,
No matter how endangered I become,
Shall take the field to bring me any aid."

Each warrior that morning cased themselves
In shimmering steel and made fast every clasp

Then girt on their great swords and headed forth
To face each other on the battlefield.
There was no more to say; it was to deeds
They turned to learn what daring destiny
Now held in store for dauntless Parzival,
Condwiramurs, and the fierce King Clamide.
They said no word as they approached the field
But urged their powerful stallions to full tilt.
Clamide's horse was a gift that he had won:
With feats of arms he'd claimed that mighty steed.
It leapt headlong towards the fell attack.
Brave Parzival's steed was also set for war,
Well armed against the worst, with metal plates
And housings of red samite o'er the steel,
Which fluttered in the wind and whipped the air
Like flames raised by the billows heaving breath.
They set their lances as they reached full tilt
And came together like a burst of storm
That cracks the heavens open with its bolts.
The joust was well matched; neither missed their mark,
And neither from their saddles were displaced.
They drew their swords and fought astride their beasts,
Both exercising deftness in their blows
And in their footwork with their stallions.
They fought until their mounts could do no more;
Exhausted, both steeds dripped with perspiration.
The knights dropped from their chargers to the ground
And met each other blow for blow on foot,
Each striking fire from the other's helm
While lightning sparked between their flashing blades.
Their wooden shields were whittled down to chips
As though they both tossed feathers at the wind;
But nonetheless, the son of Gahmuret
Remained unwearied in his dauntless limbs.

And suddenly, it seemed to bold Clamide
The truce had been forsaken, for he swore
That stones from mangonels[20] were being hurled
By catapults from forth the city's walls,
For mighty blows were raining down on him.

"You ought to mind your honor, sir!" he cried.
"You swore an oath you'd use no allied help,
But here I'm being battered by great stones!"

"I do not think you're getting hit by stones,"
The lord of the land said to fraught Clamide.
"There's no bombardment from the city gates.
I gave my word against that, I assure you."

Clamide was weary; though he liked it not,
The battle's outcome was not far away.
But he fought on until he could no more,
For blood streamed from his nose and stained the earth,
And Parzival grasped hold and threw him down
And quickly bared Clamide's head of its helm.
The vanquished king lay waiting for his death.

"My wife is free of all your mistreatment,"
Exclaimed the victor to his fallen foe.
"Prepare yourself for death, or beg for mercy."
"No, no, most gallant knight!" replied Clamide.
"Your honor has been proven many times
Upon my now defeated personage.
How could you gain more honor sir than this?
Your queen can dub me now a luckless man
While your good fortunes have been raised by this.
Your country has been well and squarely saved.

---

20   Catapults.

But as a ship unloaded from its freight
Is all the lighter for it and floats loose
Upon the tides of fortune, thus am I.
My power has become a shallow draft,
And all my knightly zest is at an ebb.
What need is there to do more harm to me?
I suffer living death since I am torn
From her who has encompassed my desires
To which my heart and mind have been a slave,
And for all this, I have reaped no return.
What worth is there in killing me then sir?
As a result, I must then yield her lands
And her to you without a question.
Unfortunate as I am, it must be so."

The victor paused and thought of Gurnemanz,
Who taught him of all noble knightly ways.
A brave and gallant knight should be prepared
To show his mercy to a pleading foe.
"I will not make exceptions for you sir,"
He said to sad Clamide upon the ground,
"From taking your submission to Liaze
And to her noble father Gurnemanz."

"Oh no, I cannot sir," replied Clamide,
"For I have done that family mortal wrong!
I killed his son. You must be softer, sir:
His Schenteflurs too, for Condwiramurs
Went head to head with me and would have won
Had not my seneschal come to my aid
And laid him in the dust before my feet.
Had not that happened I would now be slain.
I've lost so many of my knights since then;
I've now become a beggar for my life.
What more do you want from my wretched life?"

"I will abate your fears," said Parzival.
"Go to the land of Britain, sir, from here,
Where Kingrun has since gone ahead of you.
Seek out the court of Arthur and his queen.
Convey my blessing to the goodly pair,
And ask their sympathy on my behalf
For the offense that I brought hence from there.
A lady laughed when she encountered me
And was then shamed on my account for this.
It grieves me that she suffered so for me.
Recount to her how much it disturbs me;
Surrender your submission to her sir;
And do whatever she may ask of you,
Or else now meet your death upon this field."

"If that's your offer, I'll not pause to question,"
Replied Clamide to noble Parzival.
"I'll undergo that journey as you bid."

And after he had sworn his oath, he left
To set forth for the land of Arthur's court.

The beautiful city of Belrepeire
As well as the great kingdom of Brobarz
O'er which young Parizval now reigned as king
Was now restored to health and nourishment.
Great joy and happiness were seen once more.
The father of his queen had left great wealth,
Bright jewelry, precious stones, silver and gold;
They doled these out with magnanimity,
Which won the hearts of those beneath their rule.
Their land was decked with many colored pennants,
And bright new shields adorned the city's walls.
He and his knights held mighty tournaments;

And fearlessly, the young king showed his worth
Along the kingdom's border 'gainst its foes.
Condwiramurs had never wished for more;
The sweet young lady had her heart's desire.
Her love was strong, and his as strong as hers.
He was as dear to her as she to him.
She knew that he was trustworthy and true
Unto his very core unflinchingly.

One morning he spoke softly to his wife:
"My lady, I must ask your leave to go.
I wish to find out how my mother fares,
For I know not if she be well or ill.
I'd like to go there for a little while
And also seek out chivalric encounters.
Whatever I achieve will be in service
Of our love and our companionship."

In such terms did he ask his leave to go.
She loved him so, as doth the story tell,
That there was nothing she would hold from him.
He rode forth from the gates of Belrepeire
With solitude from his companion.

As green turned scarlet, amber, gold and brown
And meadows lay draped with a cloak of frost,
The young knight set forth on his lonesome quest.
The crisp air was warmed by the autumn sun
Whose gentle rays embraced the mellow earth.
It was the festival of Michael-
The warrior archangel of the heavens
Who slays the dragon with a sword of flame.

PART II

The Quest

MUNSALVAESCHE

There is a love that hovers o'er our souls,
Like wings of angels poised upon a breath,
Awaiting recognition from our eyes.
And when we see within each other's gaze
The stars alight and feel the warming band,
Uniting in a sunlit ring of grace-
Like home forgotten but returned anew
Within a waking moment like a dream-
Then masters of winged servants weave aloft,
And 'round our wavering hearts, a vessel forms
Well fortified with both strength and courage,
Past earthly means, to catch of wisdom's light
One hallowed drop, from far beyond the reaches,
Which may fall to the cup we hold between.
And nothing of this world or of the next
Can breach its solid rim or shake its base-
This sturdy vessel linked betwixt the lives
Of all who see their part and hold their piece
Within the chain of spirit bridging worlds:
Strong enough to stand through any siege,
Light enough t'illume the darkest night,
And warm enough to thaw the coldest heart.
Then through this causeway built between our souls
As though from heaven itself pours alchemy-
A fiery liquid gold- into the world,
Which burns away impurities and lifts
Our eyes up to the heights as though the sun
Had given each of us one of its rays
To carry through the world.
                                        So was the love
That hovered o'er two noble souls who lived.
Between their royal hearts a third ideal

Was born in purity and innocence,
Perfected in potential. Had they been
Inhabitants of heaven, it would have stayed
A shimmering perfection, unrealized;
A bright and hopeful promise, unsullied
By pangs and longings of this world's constraints.
A love like that is not a thing of earth.
Yet, born into this world, accompanied
By labor's cries and given for no gain,
It may be freed. Thus love fulfills its aim
And so begins the struggle and the pain.

So Parzival and Condwiramurs his queen
Were crowned with grace yet set before the trial
Of testing life for all whose hearts seek truth.
Their kingdom, once depleted by war and siege,
Now flourished forth abundance like a fount
Of endless bounty, bottomless, unstopped
By drought whose every draft brought youthful strength.
The harvest yield spilled o'er the brimming lid
For all who dwelt within the happy walls
Of that fair city, ruled by the gentle pair.
Set by the sea, into its nestled cove
Came merchants from afar with spices fine;
Exotic fabrics and jewels from distant lands
And riches beyond measure found their way
Into the royal port of fair Brobarz.
Their love so true and good could only grow.
And as it grew, it seemed to pour and reach
To every corner of the land in rays
Of sustenance to nourish everyone.
But destiny doth not wait for comfort's sake
Or swaddle in complacency. Each step,
Hard earned though it may be, leads to the next.

And those who wake will hear its call or feel
It pulling them softly out of quiet lives.
But hearing that call brings no peace of mind,
Nor doth it place us on the horse, hold reigns,
And tell us "all is well" and "we'll arrive,"
With reassuring consolations of soft
Encouragement. Only one's own bold legs
Can mount the treacherous steed, one's own true heart
Alone will know the way, and only one's
Clear, honest mind can choose to chart the course.
The torch's light, once lit, can dawn with dread
In soul for what will next be called upon
To serve the beckoning future's mystery;
While bleak, the altar begs its sacrifice
From seeking souls on destiny's behalf,
Who stone-like, statuesque, and silent waits
Fulfillment from courage, trust, and willingness
To step into a God willed task for love.

'Twas yearning for adventure that consumed
Young Parzival's brave heart and gave no rest.
He, torn by love for his dear wife, was called
To deeds of chivalry in feats of arms
And from that call was never given peace.
It was as though they held each other green
Before life's journey had yet seasoned them
To be at rest within a settled life.
Thus, old love in young hearts on lovers' souls
Hath oft and doth oft take its troublesome toll.
At last, he had no choice but to tell her
And set his compass towards- he knew not where.
And though it gave them both no end of heartache,
The steadfast queen heard truth in what he spoke
And was united with him in his quest.

Her love that for him was so absolute
Could not keep him away from what he loved
And where a quest called beckoning to him.
She was the very wind that filled his sail
And urged him on where'er his compass led.
Hot tears rained down the day they took their leave
And parted ways from one another so-
Parzival and Condwiramurs his queen.
But forth he rode despite their shared distress.
Salt rivers flooded from his burning eyes,
The fount of which sprung from an aching chest.

He rode a greater distance than one day
Allows the average rider to achieve.
Through wilds and over rocky fords, he ranged
Where trails nor roads defined his reckless course.
He did not steer the beast on which he rode.
The warrior's head drooped on his chest while thoughts
Of his dear love beset his weighing heart.
His reigns dragged careless in the underbrush,
And oft he moaned at what he'd left behind
Till dusk poured through the chilling air to kiss
His tear-stained cheek and rouse him from his thoughts.
He looked and saw he'd come up on a lake.
Some anglers had moored their fishing boats,
And one of them was wearing clothes so fine,
A quality that were he lord of all,
They could not have been made more royally.
He wore a hat of peacock feathers, lined
With silk so rare it looked not of this world.
Parzival addressed this fisherman:

"Kind sir, do you know of a place close by
Where I could knock for shelter and a bed?"

The angler looked pale as he responded.
It was the tipping point of day and night
When forms begin to fade from lucid sight
As though the air were swallowing earth's lines
In shadowy liquid shapes that trick the eye.
From out of the dwindling light, mixed pale with shadows,
His voice rang stark and hollow as he spoke:

"I know no habitation for thirty miles
Around this lake but for one mansion lone
Which stands nearby. I strongly urge you now
To make that house your place of rest tonight,
For nowhere else will you attain by dark.
Once you have ridden past the rocks, turn right,
But from there, you must follow on with care.
Some tracks may lead to unknown country-
You could miss your path on the mountainside;
A fate sir that I would not wish on you.
If you succeed and find the right way there,
Then I shall be your host this evening."

Young Parzival set off along the path.
He passed the rocks, turned on the path with care,
And followed it until he saw the castle.
The mighty fortress like an apparition
Before him loomed. Nothing had been spared
To make impregnable that stronghold there.
Smooth and round it stood as though great lathes
Had formed and shaped its walled perimeter.
Unless attackers were to come by wings
Or be blown there upon the winds, assault
Could never harm it. Clustered towers climbed,
With great embattled turrets, towards the heights.
Had all the armies of the world laid siege,

The hurt imposed would not have ruffled once
That fortress' defenders. Long before,
Their foes, exhausted by their own attack
Thrown futile 'gainst a wall impenetrable,
Would've quit the field ashamed in their defeat.

As Parzival approached, the drawbridge lowered,
And the bold knight rode in through the fortress gates.
Inside there was a smooth and untouched lawn.
No sport had churned that grass with trampling.
At his approach, a company of knights
Awaited his arrival on the green
And welcomed him to follow through the doors.
The mighty archways reached majestically,
Carved masterfully with many signs and scenes,
Which seemed as she stole from swift night's approach
To catch fair twilight's hem. Mysterious
Were they- these symbols- wonderfully profound,
But only a person who was versed in magic
Could read their sacred meaning. Nonetheless,
They spoke a language to the depths of soul,
Resounding with a formidable awe.

The knights then led him to a chamber
To help disarm and wash the stains of rust
Left by his armor. When they saw the youth,
They treated him with grace, esteem, and honor.
Once bathed, he was adorned in finery
Provided by the hostess of the house;
From her own wardrobe were the garments brought.
Then to the palace hall they led him next.
A hundred splendid chandeliers were hung
With many candles set on high aglow
Above the heads of the gathering company.

Set elegantly on the massive walls
In a gradient sweep from straight to curve aloft-
The mighty roof arch scooped toward the heavens,
And not a seam or joint was visible.
Below this point, fine tapestries were draped
With colors soft yet bright that seemed to glow
With more light than a taper gave alone.
Beneath these, set in each of the four walls
Built masterfully with strength and elegance,
Surpassing far the most exalted craft,
Stood marble fireplaces radiant:
A sunlike warmth burned east, south, west, and north,
And logs of lignum aloe from each hearth
Bedecked the air with a fine exotic scent,
Which taught the soul of new experience
And wondrous, far off, unfamiliar lands.
Four hundred couches lay upon the floor.
Embroidered cushions spoke of untold wealth
As did the carpets spanning between each perch.

The master of the house sat on a bed
Set up against the northern fireplace.
He looked more dead than living.

Parzival

Stepped into the great hall, and his kind host
Bade him approach to claim a seat beside him.

"Were I to sit thee farther off," he said,
"'Twould be to treat thee as a stranger here."

Great sorrow in his voice bespoke a heart
That was oppressed by devastating grief.
'Twas sickness made him crave great roaring fires
And woolen robes to ward the wracking chills.

Rich robes these were for they were sable lined,
Both long and wide, with hues of black and grey.
A cap of similar fashion on his head
Was bound with bands of fine Arabian gold,
And flashing in the center shone a ruby.

The company had gathered by this time
Where they were shown a spectacle of grief.
A page ran through the doorway with a lance.
From the lance's point blood issued forth
And ran down the shaft till it almost touched his sleeve.
At this, great lamentation filled the hall.
The folk of thirty lands could not have wrung
Such woeful torrents from their flooding eyes.
The page then bore the lance around the room
To each of the four walls and back out the door
Through which he'd entered, whereupon the pain,
Thus prompted by this sorrow, was assuaged.

Then two steel doors at one end of the hall
Swung open as two noble maidens entered.
So pure in gait and feature- their approach-
It was as though the very air itself
Was changed and filled with gentle majesty.
Each bore a candelabra filled and lit
With tapers to illume their presences.
Fair blossoms bound with silk adorned their heads.
Their robes of finest cloth were scarlet brown.
Next came a duchess with her lady fair;
Two stools of ivory white they brought with them.
Their vestures were as well of russet hue.
All four bowed low to greet their royal lord.
The two who bore the stools then set them down
Before him and his guest. Then both pairs stood

And waited close at hand as through the door
Another eight maids came, dressed all in green,
Their robes of samite verdant as the grass.
And four of them held tapers tall and bright
Which cast their light upon a precious stone,
Cut broad and flat- held by the other four-
To make a table as with steady steps,
They came up to their lord, bowed reverently,
And set it gently on the ivory stools.
It was a jacinth stone which drank the sun
So that its colors shone back full by night
As though that source of light was on it still.
Two princesses came shortly after them.
Each bore a keen, white, silver knife like snow-
Blades sharp enough to cut through tempered steel.
In front of them, four ladies bore four lights
That gleaming shone upon the exquisite knives,
Which after gracious bows were then laid down
Upon the jacinth table. Then they turned
To join the other twelve; all gathered there,
The group together made eighteen. Then
Six more maidens- wearing robes of light
With interwoven fabrics crosswise cut,
Half golden samite, half a silk brocade-
Came shimmering luminescent through the room.
And last of all that royal train- the queen
Of that fair castle entered the great hall.
Her presence shed such brilliant radiance
All imagined that the sun was rising
Despite the fact that night's engulfing dark
Had by that hour cloaked the sleeping land.
She was as modest, pure, and good of heart
As any living soul could ever be.
Not one thing false or impure could entice,

Enforce, or woo a way into her heart,
Well fortified by fiery devotion.
For tirelessly, day and night, she worked
To fashion herself worthy of her task.
She bore with her the very consummation
Of heart's desire, its root and blossoming,
A thing which human beings call the Grail.
'Twas paradisal, transcending all things
Of earthly perfection. Lights encircled
The Holy Grail: six finely wrought, tall viles,
Transparent glass, each burning balsams[21] brightly.
With measured steps, these servants of the Grail
Approached like messengers sent from on high.
The queen bowed low as did the other maids
Who bore the flame. Then she- whose office highest,
Most holy, chosen by the Grail itself
To serve its hallowed cause, denying all
The wayward falsehoods of the earthly world-
Upon the jacinth table placed the Grail.

Then with the six accompanying her,
She joined the other eighteen gathered there.
They stood together with their holy queen,
And she stood in the center of the group
With twelve and twelve to either side of her,
The Grail before their lord and Parzival.
It was the very essence of true bliss,
An endless cornucopia of gifts,
Such that it scarce fell short of what is said
Of the heavenly kingdom. Such a bounty there
Was given with a limitless supply

---

21   A resinous pitchy substance extracted from a variety of trees
and shrubs to be used for its aromatic and medicinal purposes.

That nothing in this world alone could match.
The frugal and the glutton equally
Were served their fill, for any longing true,
From honest heart, with one word was fulfilled.
And furthermore, whatever kind of drink
A soul could name, by virtue of the Grail,
They'd see it there within their golden cup.
Elixirs as though from the fount of life.
And all the opulence and finery
That'd come in preparation, all the knights,
And holy maidens, all the trimmings rich,
The carvings, tapestries, exotic scents
Upon the gentle air to say no word
Of the mighty castle in whose very hall
Majestic they did sit and dine- all these
Combined- though nothing of this world has seen
Their like- paled before the presence of the Grail.
'Twas not of earth but brought to mortal life
Sustaining sustenance: a bounteous
And endless source of divine nourishment.

Now Parzival did well observe these things,
Magnificent and wondrous. But held back
By the dictates of decorum, he refrained
From asking any questions. Honoring
The tutelage he'd had from Gurnemanz,
His mentor in the code of chivalry,
He hesitated, thinking to himself:
"My teacher Gurnemanz advised me 'gainst
All questionings that could be understood
With patient observation and restraint.
What if I stay as long here as I stayed
With Gurnemanz when he taught me of knighthood?
I'll surely learn how matters stand that way

Without even a single question asked.
Though there is much to learn about this house,
It must be gleaned without an inquiry."

While he was musing thus, a page appeared.
This page was carrying a splendid sword
Whose sheath alone was worth a thousand marks,
And when the blade was drawn from forth its scabbard,
One could not help but wonder at its gleam.
The noble host bestowed this splendid gift
Upon young Parzival.
                              "Kind sir," he said,
"I took this sword into the thick of battle
On many fields before I was reduced
To this infirmity which I now bear.
Now may it make amends for any lack
Of hospitality you've suffered here.
Whene'er you put it to the test in war,
You can be sure it stands you in good stead."

Now unbeknownst to youthful Parzival,
This gift was given as a prompt for him
To ask a certain question of his host.
But still the knightly code of etiquette
Held sway, and he did not ask anything
Of his kind host or of the company.

But squires and pages then appeared and began
To set to work removing banquet settings
And tables. And the queen, exuding grace-
The same grace as when first into the hall
She'd come with balsam flames around the Grail-
Then took it up again with reverence pure,
And hallowing its path, the others joined

In holy train; when exiting the hall,
Each servant performed their reverent office
Obeying the lawful order of their entrance
And followed, trailing in its luminance.

"A bed has been prepared for you by now,"
The host said to his guest. "If you are weary,
Then my suggestion is to go to bed."

Young Parzival arose from where he sat;
The host then bade his guest good evening.
The knights leapt to their feet and led him forth
Out of the great hall and into a room
Magnificently furnished with a bed
O'er which a costly silken quilt was laid.
When Parzival sat down, a swarm of pages
Rushed in to help him with his boots and clothes
And brought a bed shirt of the finest cloth.
No sooner did he put the tunic on
And lay his wearied limbs upon the bed,
Then slumber's potion wafted o'er his sense
And lifted his soul to the arms of sleep.

But as he slept, he was accompanied
By darkness and grim toil till the dawn,
For sorrows to come sent him their harbingers
Where he lay sleeping, wracked with restless dreams.
He was beset on every side by war
With crushing sword blows raining down on him
And charges thundering toward him from the dark.
In all directions, shadowed hosts arose
In ranks like waves upon a phantom sea
Enraged with torment as breathless he fought
To keep from being pummeled to the earth.

And ne'er a space of rest could he but catch
As ruthlessly the wrath of war did press
Around him like a vice until the dawn.
At daybreak, wrung out by these bleak events,
He woke with sweat soaked through his clinging sheets.
He looked around to find he was alone.

"Good morrow!" he called, hopeful that a voice
With cheering reassurance would reply
To banish the misgiving in his soul
That clung there stonelike, cold, and stubbornly.
No voice replied. The silence echoed back.

"Oh," he thought, "where have the pages gone?"
He looked and saw his armor by the bed,
Upon the carpet, laid out with two swords.
The one was his, the other was the gift
His host had given him the night before.

"Alas," he thought, "what is the meaning of this?"
"Well, clearly I must up and arm myself.
 Such anguish did I suffer in my sleep
That I can only think there must be toil
Which fortune holds in store for me today.
But if the lord of this dominion
Has been attacked, I'll gladly lend my sword
And do whatever bidding he commands."

The warrior rose and armed himself
From heel to crown and girt on both his swords.
Once fully armed, the young knight sallied forth.
Outside he found his warhorse at the stair
Already bridled, groomed, and saddled up.
Against his horse, his shield and lance were propped.
But ere he took the saddle, he turned back

And ran throughout the echoing palace,
Bowling open many mighty doors
Of chambers, calling out for anyone
To answer him, but to his deep chagrin,
And indignation, not a soul replied.
Now roused into a fury, he ran back
To where the night before he'd from his horse
Dismounted on the smooth and untouched lawn.
But here, he found the grass had all been churned
By the trampling of many horses' hooves
And scattered lay the morning dew, thus marred.
Enraged, he ran back to his stallion;
And yelling at a fevered, angry pitch,
He leapt into his saddle recklessly.
The castle gate had been left open wide
And through it ran the tracks of many hooves.
As from the castle walls, he galloped forth
In hot pursuit upon the trail of tracks.
A page who had till then remained concealed
Then suddenly appeared, accosting him.

"Damn you where'er the sun now lights your path!
You foolish goose! Why didn't you open your mouth
And ask the question? You refused the gift!
A prize of heavenly magnificence
Beyond the most exalted of all dreams!"

As Parzival drew on his charger's reins
To ask the page what he meant by this rant,
The page behaved as if he was sleepwalking
And slammed the gate shut tightly. Trouble now
Was rousing Parzival to wakefulness.
Until this point, he had not known much sorrow
And was unused to suffering or pain.

He set off in pursuit along the tracks.

"I imagine those who've ridden out ahead
Are fighting bravely on their lord's behalf,"
He thought. "But if they had only asked me,
Their ranks would be no worse for my inclusion.
I would not quit the field but would stand by-
Right through the thick of it and so repay
Their noble lord for his most precious gift:
This splendid sword he gave to me! Perhaps
They think I am a coward."
                              He rode on
And followed the trail, but it began to fade.
Those riding out in front had splintered off
In all directions as the path grew faint
And narrowed to the width a deer might wend,
And then at last, he lost it all together.

THE WOEFUL SIGUNE

Thus onward through the thicket rode the youth
Of purpose reft and to direction lost,
Beset by gnarled undergrowth and brush.
Twisted bracken cowering beneath
The stark and lonesome trees like withered witches
Sighed, dryly rattling their bone dead leaves
Against the thin and creeping morning chill.
In all directions spread the wilderness
With labyrinths of tangled paths entwined
Upon themselves- they held no steady course.
No sooner did one start, than it would end
Or merge into another which would steer
Away from the direction of the last;
But nonetheless, the warrior progressed
And held his course led by the lamp of heaven
That tilted through a shrouded veil of clouds.
The soft grey lantern through the canopy
Still cast its beam despite its dismal cloak.
But as he persevered with grappling
His ragged course amid the ravelled paths,
He thought he heard the cadence of a voice.
So soft and mournful was the pitch, he guessed
It must've been the discontented wind
Tormenting anguished boughs to moan their dirge.
But just as it was banished from his mind,
It came again, this time distinctly human.
And yet again, the lamentation rang.
He made his way toward the haunting sound
Through thickets, fallen limbs, and scattered rocks
Until at last he came upon a clearing.
The grass amid the clearing shimmered clean
With morning dew, and on a linden bough,

A maiden wept as though grief's plunging depths
Would purge themselves down to their last fathom.
Yet nothing of that well's base was in sight,
For as each sob was like a bucket drawn
And emptied out upon the woeful ground,
Another flooded in with her next breath.
So wretchedly she wept, the sight would draw
Out mercy from the most unflinching heart.
Reclining in her arms, her love, a knight,
Lay slain. His body now embalmed, she held
The object of her grief close to her heart.
Not recognizing her, young Parzival
Rode toward her through the clearing unaware
She was his cousin on his mother's side.
He greeted her with gentle courtesy:

"It is a sorry sight to see thee thus,
My lady; if my help could bring you aid
In your distress, I'm readily at your service."

To this the woeful maiden then replied:
"I thank you for your thoughtful kindness sir.
What brings you to this lonesome wilderness?
It is not safe to travel in these parts-
Harm easily befalls the unschooled here.
I've heard and also seen with my own eyes
That many lose their lives amid this wood.
Turn back if you wish to preserve your life.
But where was it that you found rest last night?"

"A mile or more back there is a castle,"
Said Parzival. "I rested there last night.
Indeed it is magnificent to see.
I witnessed it in all its varied splendor
And rode out from its gates a short while hence."

To this the lady answered doubtfully:
"You should not be so ready to deceive
When someone freely gives their trust to you.
Your shield descries[22] that you're a stranger here.
Have you traversed the forest all this way
And ridden to this clearing from the ploughlands?
This surely would have been too much for you.
No limb or stone has e'er been hewn or moved
To make a dwelling for thirty miles around.
There is alone one solitary castle,
Magnificent and rich in heavenly splendor.
If any seek it out intentionally,
Search as they may, they will not find it sir.
Despite that, one encounters many folks
Who place themselves into this deadly peril.
Were someone ever meant to see the castle,
They must discover it unwittingly.
Presumably you've heard of it before.
It's known as Munsalvaesche, and all the realm
Surrounding it is called Terre de Salvaesche.
The ancient Titurel bequeathed the fortress
Unto his noble son, King Frimutel-
Such was the warrior's name and many laurels
Were won by his strong hand ere in a joust-
Impelled by passion, he rode to his death.
This Frimutel, the son of Titurel,
Had left three noble daughters and two sons.
Four siblings from this family yet survive,
But now they live in abject misery
Despite their rank. One of them, Trevrizent,
Lives penitent in humble poverty.
His brother Anfortas cannot sit, nor stand,

---

22   To determine, identify or distinguish by sight.

Nor lie, but he can only lean with pain.
He's Lord of Munsalvaesche- cursed by misfortune.
Had you gone there and done the task ordained
By God the wounded king would now be free
From the grief and agony that he endures."

"I saw great marvels there" said Parzival,
"And many wondrous things." As he said this,
The lady on a sudden knew his voice:
"I know your voice, why you are Parzival!"
She said.
      "Now tell me, did you see the Grail-
His lordship separated from his joy?
Speak! Tell me the glad tidings- is he healed?
If so, an end has come to his sad plight,
And heaven blessed your destiny shall be!"

"How did you recognize me?" said the knight.

"You've seen me grieve my sorrows once before,"
Replied Sigune. "I told you who you are.
Your mother is my aunt, my mother's sister.
She is a pinnacle of loyalty,
And may high God also requite your goodness.
You showed compassion for me and my friend
Who met his death before our love could live.
I hold him here. The torment of his death
Stays with me everywhere and does not fade
But grows so that each day I learn new grief."

"Alas, dear cousin, the virtuous Sigune?"
Replied young Parzival amazedly.
"Can it be you who told me truthfully
Of who I am and of my lineage?
You are so pale. Where is your youthful spirit?

The radiance that shone so beautifully?
Come, has it fled dear cousin? Your head is bare.
It grieves my heart to see thee full of woe.
Come, we must now bury this dead man here."

To this the sorrowful Sigune replied:
"If anything can ever give me joy,
It is but one thing and that is to hear
The good news of the man of suffering.
If you have helped him, you have earned high praise.
I see his sword is clasped around your waist.
If you know of its powers, you will fight
With fearlessness. Its edge is tempered well.
For a time it will hold true. And then one day
The blade will shatter. But beside Karnant,
There is a spring whose name is known as Lac.
If fragments of the sword have not been lost,
Then take them to this stream when it is broken.
It must be brought to where the water leaps
From forth the rock before the light of dawn.
There you must carefully replace the shards
And wet them with the water from this spring.
At this, the shattered pieces will rejoin
As one again far stronger than before.
Dear cousin, listen to me, all these things
And all the marvels you have wondered at
Will be at your command, and evermore
You'll wear a crown of bliss and majesty
Above all other earthly royalty.
All that can be wished for belongs to you—
If only you have asked the question."

"I did not ask it," said young Parzival.

"Alas, that I now have you in my sight,"
Replied the sorrowful maiden, "since you failed
So utterly and contemptibly to ask-
You saw such wondrous things at Munsalvaesche!
To think that you could not be moved enough
To find it in yourself to ask the question
While you sat in the presence of the Grail!
You saw the maids who gave their life to serve-
Who give their lives each day to purity
In order that they carry unbesmirched
The mission of the Grail within the world!
You looked with those two eyes upon the lance!
And yet, you stand and gaze upon me now
With those selfsame, compassionless eyes. O
What prompted you to come and find me here?
I would have thought that you could only act
In obedience with the high nobility
And purity from which you have descended.
You have been graced with heavenly qualities
And have been guided by the hand of God
Into the presence of the Holy Grail!
Yet there in the place of most divine hope
As all the hosts of angels held their breath
Awaiting one small question from your lips-
The balm, the healing salve to suffering-
Your selfishness and ugly wolfish fangs
Revealed themselves: for you denied your task!
But can it be that you were unaware,
And wilt thou still remain so even now?
Oh do not look to me, look back within-
You'll never find it here- accursed man!
Dishonorable wretch, why do you gape?
You should have had compassion on your host!
You should have asked about his suffering!

You live, but as for what the spirit sees,
You are as dead as this man in my arms."

"Dear cousin," said bewildered Parzival,
"Do be a little kinder, I beseech you.
  If I have done amiss, I'll make amends."

"You are exempted from making your amends,"
She answered, "since I'm well aware that grace
And honor left your side at Munsalvaesche.
You fool. I'll speak no further with you sir.
This is the last word that you'll have from me."

Distraught, the youth protested but in vain.
Naught that he said could move the maid to speak.
She turned back to her well of grief again
As though the burden of another loss
Had doubled the weight of her injury.
And so in this sad state, he turned from her
Amid the dewy glade, drenched in her woes,
And rode away greatly distraught at heart.

JESCHUTE & ORILUS

It was a source of great remorse for him-
Young Parzival- that he'd not asked the question
As he sat by the ailing fisher king.
Now thanks to these harsh self admonishments
As well as the increasing temperature,
Which elevated with the climbing day,
The warrior was soon bathed in perspiration.
He untied the laces of his helm and rode
While carrying it underneath his arm.
At length he found a trail and followed it.
It plainly had been travelled recently.
The tracks depicted that a well-shod steed
Had been attended by a shoeless mare.
The latter was that of a lady's mount
Who he then came upon in front of him.

Her mare was given up to misery:
One could behold each rib through its sad hide.
Its halter had a rope attached to it.
Its mane unkempt swept almost to its hooves.
Its eyes were sunk deep in their hollow sockets.
The nag had been neglected altogether.
The lady was herself thin with neglect.
Her scant clothes were mere rags and worn tatters.

When Parzival addressed her, recognition
Came to her eyes. He was the wild youth
Who'd torn her ring and brooch from her before.

"I've seen you once before to my great sorrow,"
She said to Parzival, "and since that time,
My clothes are rendered poorer than they were
Much thanks to your encounter with me sir.

If you had not approached me on that day,
My reputation would not have been stained."

"Please reconsider madam," said the knight,
"Since I took up the shield and learned its office,
Not you nor any other have I shamed.
In truth I'd rather dishonor myself!
But otherwise, you have my sympathy."

The lady wept, and in her wretched state,
He could not help but feel compassion for her.
She wept so bitterly it pained his heart.
He knew not what to do to comfort her.

"Come put my surcoat 'round you in God's name,"
He said. "It's offered with heartfelt respect."

"If all my happiness depended on it,
I would not dare to touch your surcoat, sir.
If you wish to ensure that we're not killed,
I urge you now, please ride some distance off.
I'd not be sorry if I die myself,
But that it might not go so well for you."

"Why who should take our lives?" said Parzival.
"They're given by God, and if an army came,
I'd stand my ground to fight for both of us."

"A noble warrior would seek our lives,"
She said, "so full of fight that six of you
Would surely have your hands entirely full.
I was that knight's wife once, but now alas,
I feel below that of a serving maid,
For he, in this way, ruthlessly doth vent
His unrelenting wrath upon my soul."

"Who else is with your husband?" asked the knight.
"I'll gladly die the day I learn to flee."

"There's no one with him but myself," she said.

The warrior retied his ventail across
And firmly set his helm back on its perch,
Adjusting it until the sight was right.
As he prepared himself to joust, his charger
Lowered its head towards the lady's palfrey
And whinnied loudly. The warrior riding ahead
At hearing this turned 'round to see his foe.
Then angrily the duke wheeled his horse 'round
And set himself to battle Parzival.
The shield of Orilus was emblazoned
With a vivid image of a lifelike dragon.
Upon his helm another dragon reared,
And on his armor, there were numerous
Small dragons fashioned out of richest gold.
Each dragon had two rubies for their eyes
Which glimmered darkly from their metal sockets.

The two intrepid heroes took wide sweeps
And thundered toward each other like two storms
Advancing from the edges of the sky.
Bold Parzival moved like a wildfire
Ignited from a bed of scarlet coals
Now set ablaze as he rushed toward his foe.
Proud Orilus with the dragon on his shield,
The emblem of his family's lineage,
Lunged forward with an equal surge of force.
Both lances shattered in a cloud of chips,
But both held fast- unshaken in their saddles.
They drew their blades and fought ferociously,

Striking at each other from their seats.
Such skill and strength each warrior possessed,
It seemed as though two gods were battling.
And ever did they hack and lunge and turn,
Maneuvering their horses masterfully.
The blades clashed fiercely with each crushing blow
And grounded against each other grittily.
Each warrior threw every ounce of strength
Against the other unrelentingly.
Both shields were hacked and cleaved with battering.
Orilus reared and ducked with mastery,
But Parzival met each blow with another
And hacked the dragon on the duke's high crest
Down from a menacing fiend to a meager stub.
The dragons on the duke's helm, shield, and armor,
All set with ruby gems for glinting eyes,
Were battered by the Red Knight's swordsmanship.
It was as though he fought a host of dragons
And slashed their ruby eyes out of their sockets.
If one had witnessed this, one would incline
To boast of having seen so fell a match.

Jeschute vouched to herself she'd not seen better.
She stood by wringing both her worried hands-
The honest lady wished no harm to either.
Both chargers were now dripping perspiration
From the exertion. Both knights sought renown.
The clashing of their swords made blinding sparks
That leapt like lightning between their flashing blades
And off their battered helms as these two strove-
Which cast a haunting light upon the scene.
The clash of battle echoed through the wood
As the assault rose with intensity.
The duke was using all his skill and strength.

He was possessed of both great expertise
And physical prowess when it came to war.
This won him victories on many fields.
Relying on this power in his limbs,
He grasped his arms 'round sturdy Parzival,
Intending to eclipse him with his strength.
The Red Knight met him in the deadly grip
And ripped proud Orilus clean out of his saddle
Then swung the duke beneath one of his arms,
Leapt down from off his horse, and braced his foe
Across a trunk that lay close by their steeds.
Thus pinned securely, Parzival then spoke:
"It's time for you to take back the disgrace
This lady suffers under your displeasure.
Unless you take her back into your favor,
Your life is lost."
                          "Nay," replied Duke Orilus,
"That will not happen quickly! I'll not yield,
For I've not yet been pushed to that extreme!"

Then Parzival increased his strong embrace,
And blood ran from the vizor of the duke.

"Alas, bold knight," he gasped to Parzival,
"How have I ever come to this strange fate
That I should end up dead before your feet?

"I'll gladly grant you life," said Parzival,
"If you'll return your favor to this lady."

"That I shall not!" replied Duke Orilus,
"For she has wronged me far too grievously.
She once was rich in noble qualities,
But she has since diminished them and plunged
Me to disaster. I am otherwise

Amenable to do whate'er you wish,
If you will give me life. God gave it me,
But now your sword hand is his angel sir;
I'll owe it to your glory from now on.
Come shall I buy my life back royally?
My puissant brother wears a mighty crown.
He governs two great kingdoms- one is yours.
If you will have it, he will buy my ransom
Quite handsomely, be well assured, brave sir.
I'll furthermore attribute my dukedom
To your name, sir. Your glorious renown
Will gain much merit from me. But brave knight,
Exempt me from rejoining with this woman.
Command me to whatever else you'll have:
I cannot mend with a dishonored duchess."

"Possessions, peoples, and lands will not avail you,"
Said Parzival, "Unless you pledge your word
That you will hie thee straight to Arthur's court
And offer homage to the king and queen.
There is a maiden who dwells at their court;
She was shamed by one whom vengeance awaits
Unless she herself bids me otherwise.
You must surrender yourself to her sir.
Beyond that, I intend to see this lady
Restored and reconciled to thy favor.
But if you cross me, you shall ride from here
A corpse upon a bier, mark my words.
So let me have your word upon it straight."

"If my life won't be bought from you with gifts,"
Said Orilus, "I will do as you bid,
For I wish to continue living, sir."

Since he had promised to be reconciled
With his Jeschute, the Red Knight let him rise.

"My lady," said the duke as he arose,
"My loss in battle has been brought about
On your behalf. Come to my arms again.
My reputation suffered much from you.
But what of that? It now must be forgiven."

Without delay, she leapt down from her mare
And ran straight to his arms; she was so kind.
The blood had dried and caked around his mouth,
But this did not deter her lips from his.
She'd never wavered in her love for him
And in God's eyes had never done him wrong.

Then they all mounted and rode through the wood.
At length they came upon a hermit's cell.
This cell was hollowed in a rock alcove;
There was a reliquary on a plinth
And propped against the rock, a painted lance.

When Parzival beheld the holy relic,
He was so filled with sorrow and remorse
That he was promoted by humility
To action on behalf of kind Jeschute.
"If I have any worth at all," he said,
"May I forever be disgraced and barred
From glory in this life, and may my fame
Be brought to naught in this life and the next;
And that these words are fact let my soul's worth
Stand sure in the eyes of Him whose hand is highest-
Let me be mocked and damned throughout the world,
If ever this good lady did amiss
When I tore her gold brooch and ring from her!

I was a foolish youth- no knight- not grown
To understanding. Weeping copiously,
She suffered at my hand. Much she bore
In wretchedness on my account. I tell you
She is an innocent woman. There is nothing
That I will gain from speaking this true vow.
May honor and my word be pledge enough.
I give her ring back with this solemn oath.
Thanks to my youthful ignorance, her brooch
Was thrown away, for I knew not its worth."

The good, kindhearted lady then received
The ring back to her care as from his lips
Orilus wiped the blood to kiss once more-
The darling of his heart- steadfast Jeschute.
Then tenderly he wrapped her rag clothed body
Within his cloak. Once this was done, he turned,
And with clear eyes, he spoke to Parzival:
"Your oath so freely offered to my heart
Doth bring great joy. My wrath, grief, bitterness,
And sorrow have been banished by your words.
Defeat in battle, which I've rarely known,
Restored me back to happiness again.
Now I can make amends with my beloved.
I left her unaccompanied that day.
What could she do to prove herself to me?
She mentioned your good looks, so I believed
You'd tussled with her in a love affair.
But now, may God reward you! She is cleared
Of infidelity! No gentleman
Was I when I rode forth from her that day."

"Good sir," said kind Jeschute to Parzival,
"All that I've suffered is now turned to joy.

So long it's been since I've felt happiness,
But then I knew it not as I do now.
No soul can know true joy until it's filled,
Eclipsed, and tipping o'er its very brink
With happiness as we now find ourselves.
May God reward the goodness of your heart."

The duke and duchess begged their newfound friend
To join them in their royal camp nearby,
But their persuasions were of no avail.
Good Parzival took up the painted lance,
Took leave of the duke and duchess, and rode forth.

THE THREE DROPS OF BLOOD

By this time Parzival's renown had spread
Throughout Great Britain. Many worthy knights
Had come to Arthur's court to pay homage
Unto the king at Parzival's behest,
All having been surrendered to his sword.
So regularly did these messengers
Of Parzival's brave prowess arrive at court,
The king began to long to meet this knight,
Who thus, mysterious and from afar, had been
So loyal to his majesty. The king
Now wished to invite the champion to join
His ranks as member of the Table Round.
And so King Arthur with his company
Set off upon a journey o'er the land
To find the hero whom so many'd praised.
And after eight days riding, crossing through
A great many territories, fierce and wild,
They set up camp as evening draped its silk,
Transparent veil across the fateful land,
Near Parzival, who unbeknownst to them,
Lay close at hand, for things must run their course.
And fortune with her servants there at work
Was weaving destined threads together as
Perpetually she does by God's command.
Chance at her side was busy hatching plots,
For never is an opportunity
Forgone when the divine can set the stage
To weave God's lessons into mortal ways.

As camp was being pitched by many hands
And evening's richest colors decked the sky,
King Arthur's falconers rode out to scout

155

The area surrounding them and catch
What game they could before the night closed in.

But 'gainst them, ill luck had a stroke to play,
Which deft it did, for they lost on their way
Their best falcon- just as the dark drew on.
And heedless to their calls, that night she lodged
Near Parzival where neither knew the forest,
And both were freezing cold, for as they slept,
A heavy snow upon them gently fell.

When Parzival awoke, he saw his path
Was covered o'er ahead with a heavy snow.
From there, he made way out through rough lands,
With boulders toppled round and fallen trees.
As he progressed, the bright gold yellow orb
Of fiery warmth, which kindles each new day
Since first the world was born, began its climb
Aloft the morning's pristine blue expanse.

The forest thinned out as the burgeoning day
Reached with its rays through tree limbs cloaked in snow.
The rays of sunlight, fractured by the bows,
Sent scattered shafts of light into the gloom:
Bright heralds sent from the beacon of the world
To cheer the darkened corners of the earth.

At length our hero, trailed by Arthur's falcon,
Proceeded to the snowy, open fields.
A lonesome tree was stretched upon the ground:
Felled there by mighty gusts. The god of winds
Had laid that lengthy trunk out long and low
Where gathered now some thousand flocking geese;
And suddenly, the watchful bird of prey
Was in amongst them; fierce, she plummeted

With deadly speed and struck one of the geese,
Who barely got away beneath a branch
Spread from the fallen tree. Three tears of blood
Fell from its wound upon the pure white snow.

When Parzival drew near and there beheld
Those scarlet drops against the canvassed snow,
Love's longing struck him, aching through his heart.
A feathered bolt well aimed had found its mark,
Loosed from the string of love's winged messenger.
He said aloud: "Who might this artist be
That moves my heart with three dabs of a brush?
Three drops upon the snow laid masterfully
In truly the depiction of my love.
My dear Condwiramurs! Blessed by God's hand,
How I rejoice to find your countenance
Here imaged for my eyes. My love, here lies
Your picture fair: two drops against your cheeks,
The third against your chin as blessed they fell.
How close your presence hovers 'round me now
Like a visitation o'er my questing soul;
While on the wind, it seems I almost hear
Melodic cadences in fragment strains
Of your sweet voice, resounding in my heart:
The words we'd share were we with waking sight
Made manifest to see each other's eyes!
Long have I ridden since we last embraced
The day I left your side in Belrepeire.
Alas, my love! Would you were with me now.
In this way, he became lost in his thoughts
Until he fell spellbound into a trance,
For love enthralled him there with such a power
That he sat in his saddle motionless
As though asleep upon his stallion.

But meanwhile, the bold Sir Segramors
Of Arthur's troup had grown impatient
And restless in the royal camp that morn.
And as the sun ascended through the sky,
He felt the broadening day to be a curse,
A tedium that he could not endure.

The king gave word at dawn to stay encamped
While he deliberated carefully
On where to move to next. He'd warned his knights
Their camp was placed precariously near
The territory in which Munsalvaesche-
The castle of the Grail- was said to be.
"Most worthy company," he said, "beware
Of skirmishes within this wilderness
Or jousting to enhance your reputation.
Take heed of any challenge in these lands.
This territory borders on a forest
Patrolled and guarded by a brotherhood
More fierce and more warlike than any other
To walk the earth. This fellowship protects
The sacred Grail, kept in a fortress known
As Munsalvaesche. For this, they bear a strength
Unequalled by the standards of this world.
And though the way unto this fort be barred
By a magic force- which keeps its presence hid
With paths that tangle o'er themselves in knots
To steer the unschooled soul out of its way
And into deadly peril- the brotherhood
Additionally guard this jewel of heaven
Ferociously and won't hold back if crossed.
If everyone rides forth like scattered leaves
Upon the winds of whim, engaging these
Fell Templar knights, our ranks could be o'erwhelmed,

And our position bordering the Grail,
Now tenuous, would then be compromised.
Do not with haste accept such challenges,
But exercise restraint, and come to me.
We'll weigh the risk of sending forth a knight
Alone into the fray to win renown
With fortifying our strength in numbers.
Band close our company. Though by the same,
We'll not hold back if battle to us calls.
Discernment here with us shall be our friend
As we now chart our course."

       Sir Segramors
Would never walk but always ran in leaps
And mighty bounds wherever he would go.
And wherever fighting was to be had,
He had to be shackled, or he'd mix straight in.
Impatient as a bull held behind bars
Before a fight, he paced the camp that morn.
When suddenly into the camp, a lad,
Who on a scouting errand had been sent,
Ran shouting that a knight in full panache
Was halted close at hand with upraised lance,
Set poised and ready, waiting for a joust.

Her majesty, the Lady Guinevere,
Whose countenance of gentle dignity
Was said to be a paragon of grace,
Lay at that very moment fast asleep
Upon her bed, within her tent. The queen-
So soft at rest with morning's gentle birth
She seemed to drink the heavens with each breath-
Was wearied by the eight days' ride and took
The moment's gift bestowed by Arthur's choice
To pause and consider before he moved,

159

With gratitude. And as though draped on clouds,
She rode the blissful currents of the heights,
Restored by remedy of needed sleep.

But with a sudden stir, her rest was wrought
In reckless fashion from her by the door
Of her pavilion as it open flew;
She thought a storm had hit the camp- so fierce
And ruthless was the whirling gust that came
With thoughtless Segramors into her tent,
For he had bulled his way past both her guards
And barged into her tent as doth the sea
Which forces 'round the feet of surdy cliffs
And rages in the pools who tranquilly
Have sat in stillness since the tide last came.
Thus did this headstrong knight audaciously
Careen into her tent to seek her favor.
"My dearest Queen!" he bellowed like the wind,
"A favor I'm compelled to beg of thee!
A knight doth wait outside our camp bedecked
In full panache inciting us to joust.
I fear that in obedience to the king
We will be cowards and not sally forth
To keep intact the mighty reputation
This glorious company maintains and thus
Will let our names be sullied by this fool-
Who thinks he can with his display of strength
Outdo us- where with one turn of my lance,
I'd throw him down and win instead renown
For all who serve our king. The longer now
We stand here idle with our swords all sheathed
And lances laid to rest, the more will shame
Be heaped upon us like a vile plague.
On bended knee I do beseech you now

To put a word for me into the nearest
And closest chamber of your husband's heart.
Use all your graciousness to sway his liege
On my behalf and strongly urge him there
To make exemption from his word this once-
That I, without a fuss, may quickly snuff
The flame before it even sparks, for thus
With single hand will I bestill the frenzy
That could break among our ranks, save other knights
Less seasoned than myself and far less skilled
From catching shame, which would besmirch the name
Of this great host, and thereby win acclaim
Instead, for all. Beseech you, go to him,
For as I have just spoken only now,
To wait is only to increase our loss;
We must act soon to gain the surer foot.

And thus he spoke, impelled by his intent,
Reckless as a gale among the trees.
The queen, a pillar of tranquillity,
Did rouse herself and blink to overcome
The clinging swaths of cloud around her head
As ruthless from her sleep she thus was rend.
And as he spoke with flashing eyes and face,
A dawning crimson, she, who loved all knights
Of Arthur's company for both their strengths
And human foible, was so much a friend
To every loyal knight of that great host
That even in such disregard as this-
She could not help but love the knight who knelt
Before her like a boiling cauldron now
For all his brazen and headstrong nature which
Had served her Lord in many a circumstance.
So good and gracious was this gentle queen

That she would never make her knights feel shame
For what they couldn't help but heard them out
With patient strength, compassionate accord,
And thoughtful contemplation when they spoke.

So as into the clear and waking day,
She climbed from sleep where some would be annoyed
By Segramors' insensitivity-
Her only thought was of how good it was
They had within their midst committed knights
As bold as he, who now had turned a hue
Of crimson there before her very eyes.
Had she not been the Lady Guinevere,
Not known him closely as a lifelong friend,
This may have caused alarm in her. Instead,
The corners of her mouth began to lift
Into a smile which as he evermore
With fervor waxed then spilled into a laugh.
Sir Segramors, perplexed and at a loss,
Then caught the spark of knowing twinkling
Behind her eyes and recognizing now
The brashness of his entrance- rude, abrupt,
And blunt as blocks- he too began to laugh
Through his ambition, despite his urgency,
At the absurdness of the scene he'd made
Though still he hoped the queen would hear his plea.

"Dear Segramors," she said as their shared mirth
Subsided, "it does not surprise me now
That you have come to ask this boon of me.
The king has given word here to remain
And practice with restraint when feats of arms
Present themselves. Your tendency to rush
And entrance to my tent, you must admit

is not the custom. Are you quite sure
That recklessness be not the helmsman here?
'Tis good that you have come before you went
Straight to the fight, abrupt as may have been
Your entrance. Do not flare to blows with haste.
You must in truth agree, you've oft been known
To tangle where a patient word could mend."

Then, seeing him turn from red, to purple, blue,
And though it may have been a trick of vision,
She could have sworn she caught the hint of steam
Ascending from his ears. "Lord bless his heart,"
She thought to herself, "if I do not take heed,
He will ignite and burn to ash and cinders
Before my eyes." And so to Segramors
She smiled and gently said: "But very well,
I know thy purpose has a good intent,
And could I read thy heart, though it be hasty
And sometimes overzealous, it would scan
True to the king and loyal to his cause.
I will go unto him on your behalf
And put an urgent word into his ear,
Which may if you are fortunate strike a chord
Persuasively and turn his heart to look
With kindly favor on your worthy cause."

And thus assuring him he had her word
That she would to the king with urgency
And ask this boon on Segramors' behalf,
The queen did as she'd promised then sent word
To Segramors the king did grant him leave
To tourney[23] with the unknown challenger,
Awaiting at the border of their camp.

---

23   Joust.

Sir Segramors then quickly armed himself.
And fighting with the buckles as he moved
In reckless motion toward his horse, before
The clasps around his calves were fully fast,
He- shouting at his squire who, stumbling, came
With shield and lance- then leapt astride his steed,
And grasping his jousting equipment from the squire,
He lunged into a gallop eagerly
Intent on being first into the fray
To test his metal 'gainst the mysterious
Opponent at the camp's perimeter.

He found young Parzival there where he was sat,
Still as a statue, gazing at the drops
And thinking of his dear Condwiramurs.

Segramors challenged him before he struck.
"Sir knight!" he said, "You have chosen a place
To make your stand which you will now regret,
For here your challenge must contend with me.
Unless you give yourself to me in peace,
I'll be constrained to settle this by force,
Which probably will not end well for you!
Now will you render yourself up or no?
Consider yourself warned, for with no word,
Your silence will for me suffice enough
As answer to my challenge, and I'll not
Hold back!"
                But Parzival remained stock still,
Lost to the world- thanks to those drops of blood
And fervent love. Finding no answer there,
Bold Segramors then wheeled his charger 'round
To deal a joust his foe would not forget.
The beast on which young Parzival was sat,

With this, urged on by instinct, also turned,
Responding to the suddenness of the move,
And with that turn, the young knight lost from view
Those scarlet drops upon the snow. At this,
Clear reason gave him back his waking sense.
But Segramors was bearing down now hard
At full tilt on him. So brave Parzival
Spurred on his horse to a gallop; taking aim,
He took the mighty blow of Segramors'
Straight through his shield but held his sturdy seat
As calmly as a swan o'er glassy lakes
Who glides serene while Parzival struck home:
An answering stroke that sent his challenger
On a hurtling flight, headlong through the air
And crashing with an unforgiving force
Onto the cold, hard ground where like a heap,
He lay still, stunned for quite some time. This done,
Brave Parzival then turned his steed around
Without discovering his rival's name
Or whom he served and rode to where the drops
Lay waiting for him on the patient snow.
No sooner did his eyes alight on them,
Then love again did wind him in its toil.
Not one word did he utter, only gazed,
For he at once was reft of common sense.

At length the stunned Sir Segramors came to
And roused himself and stumbled back to camp.
The prompt Sir Kay straight brought the king the news
That bold Sir Segramors had been unhorsed
And that a tough knight stood by, eagerly
Awaiting one of them to joust with him.
The king then gave Sir Kay his leave to go
Avenge the honor lost by Segramors,

So valorous Sir Kay then sallied forth,
Decked fully in his knightly panoply.
He hailed the statuesque knight on his horse,
Perched still as a lake, protected from the wind.

"Grave sir," said Kay "since it befell you here
To insult the king, if you'll be ruled by me-
And as I see it, it will serve you best,
If that is what you do- you'll don a leash
And let yourself be led into the king's
High presence, there for him to judge your fate
As consequence to this offense you've made.
If not, there's nothing you can do to escape
My ruthless vengeance, which I'll not hold back,
Unless you peaceably comply with me.
If you forgo my offer now, grave sir,
You'll soon regret your snub and hubris,
For this, once forgone, cannot be taken back,
And by your choice, you will be roughly handled,
Roughly received, and roughly subdued sir."

But Parzival, a captive to desire,
Remained still, silent, and transfixed. Then Kay
Raised up his lance and gave young Parzival's head
A mighty thwack, so hard his helmet rang.

"Wake up!" said Kay. "Your sleeping arrangements here
Are without bedlinen! I have other things
In mind for you- I'll bed you in the snow.
If the beast that bears sacks to the mill was thrashed
As I'll thrash you, it would rue its sloth
And sluggishness!"
                    Then Kay lunged at him hard,
And Parzival's steed was forced to turn around,

Resulting in the fate that he again
Lost sight of his sweet heartache long enough
For reason to return a second time
And give him back his senses- and none too soon,
For Kay was putting his horse to a gallop.
So Parzival again spurred on his horse.
They leveled their lances as they reached full tilt.
Exactly where his eye had measured it,
Sir Kay delivered his mighty joust clean through
Young Parzival's shield, punching a hole in it,
A veritable window. But before
His pride could slake its thirst with vindication,
The blow from Parzival struck like a storm
And thundered home, as Kay, the seneschal
Of mighty Arthur's court, was flung headlong
And hurtled through the air, down on the tree
Felled there, beneath whose limbs the injured goose
Had from the falcon fled. The wounded knight
Lay stunned and motionless, pinned by his horse-
Killed by the charge. Now wedged between his saddle
And a boulder, Kay's right arm and left leg both
Were broken. Girth, bell harness, and his saddle
All snapped under the impact of the charge.

A word about Sir Kay before proceeding:
Of all the knights from Arthur's company,
Bold Kay has always been the one to get
The most unflattering legacy proclaimed.
His name in many tales told of the knights
Has oft been sung in wavering tones that scarce
E'er reach the pitch yearned for by hopeful ears;
But nonetheless, we must recall to mind
His loyalty, forever laid before
His royal leader's feet, which never budged.

He was the king's stepbrother and had fought
Beside him from the first through all the wars.
Great battles had Kay for the king withstood.
And as the mighty ruler's seneschal,
It was his task to keep out treachery
And crooked aims from entering their ranks,
Which oft found homes in wayward hearts who strove
Persistently to find a means to poison
Or pull apart the powerful Round Table,
For in those days, as in our day, not all
Committed themselves unto the path of good.
And many such sought out false ways to breach
The strong walls of that goodly company.
Those spurred by goals of harm and hate's intent
Were often guised in seemly appearances-
Like venomous snakes laid in a flower bed.
For these good reasons, Kay was said to have
A sharper edge than others of that host.
His prowess with the sword and lance was less
Than warriors such as Gawain or Lancelot,
The bold Sir Bedivere, Bors, or Pellenor.
Their prowess seemed to grow unendingly
In strength and mastery upon the field.
They were the first to ride into the fray,
And god-like might stood at their backs in war.
They struck like thunder with angelic force.
And Kay could not contend with them in valor,
For he, though trained for war, had other work.
He rode throughout the ranks amid the clash,
Maintaining order, passing Arthur's word
Among the company. He organized
Supplies, provisions, arms, and weaponry
And strategized logistics with the king.
His work as seneschal kept him afoot

And edgily alert to miss no trick:
Taking orders, giving audience,
Condemning falseness, offering council.
He organized and buffered that whole host-
Alleviating practical detail.
Though some might call it "thankless," 'twas a task
That earned its weight in gold to say the least.
Without him, order would have all been lost.
The company would have been spread too thin
With running here and there confusedly,
And all their power would have been dispersed.
Instead their strong hearts were all strung together
And held united within a sun-like force:
And that, they'd wield into the world for good.
'Twas Kay, the spark, who wove the flame between,
And thus was he a gift for all the knights-
Protector to the king and company.
And when he spied a viper in the grass,
Woe to that serpent, for the wrath of Kay,
I'd not wish on a friend or enemy.
His rage was fierce as lacerations slung
From bull whips, leaving welts upon the soul-
Reminders to those who might use deceit
As means to gain access unto the king.
And that is why he seems unsavory
In all the tales of old. 'Tis true sometimes
His wrath fell on the innocent misplaced,
For humanly, too eagerly sometimes,
He indiscriminately doled out his dish.
But at his core, though sharp-tongued, he was good.
His temper had not served him in this case
However, as he lay thus, stunned and tangled,
With broken limbs, snapped gear, and a dead horse.

But now, young Parzival was by his love
For his beloved queen Condwiramurs
Compelled to forgo any pleasantries
Or claiming of his foe's allegiance
Or staking Kay's surrender for the sake
Of building his renown and turned again
To find the drops of blood laid with his love
Upon earth's alabaster cloak of snow-
Which once again did rob him of his wits.
He was beset by thoughts of both the Grail
And his Condwiramurs, but now, 'twas love
That in the scales was weighing heaviest.

The wounded Kay was fetched away at once
To Arthur's tent where noble Sir Gawain-
Who, known to be the gentlest of knights,
Though masterful in battle, both to foes
A threat and yet the most gracious of lords-
At seeing his fellow Kay in such a plight
Was pained at heart, and though his rank surpassed
The level at which there was any need
To tangle in such matters trite as these,
He called for his horse and without spurs or sword
Rode out to meet the knight whose heart was still
A captive to almighty love.
                                                And so,
Gawain did smoothly canter towards the knight,
Not charging, for the gentle warrior
Wished peaceably to find out who it was
Had overthrown two of his company.
He spoke kindly in greeting Parzival,
But his words passed by the spellbound warrior.

"My lord," said Sir Gawain after a space,
"Since you refuse my greeting, it would seem

170

You mean for this exchange to come to blows.
But I am not so faint of heart brave sir,
And once I've armed and turn toward the fight,
I'll not then stop to question otherwise:
We will be forced to reckon with each other
Amid the unforgiving pitch of battle.
You have now thrown the vassal of the king
And his good kinsman down and shamed them both
As well as his own royal personage
And brought disgrace upon our company.
Yet if you'll follow my advice, bold sir,
Accompany me to my sovereign's presence.
I'll win good favor from him on your behalf
To overlook these insults to his name."

But no amount of reasoning or threats
Or coaxing forth could bring young Parzival
Out from his trance of spellbound reverie.
Gawain, however– the glory of his realm–
To love's sweet pang, was not a foreigner.
He had been held by its dominion,
Had felt its stab, and understood the sway
It measured over unsuspecting hearts.

"What could it be?" he pondered to himself,
"Would render someone speechless in this way
So that all words and common turns of phrase,
All practiced modes of everyday exchange,
Would be thus lost to the average expectation?
It is not average for one to be mute
When fully armed for battle on a horse.
And yet, it smacks of something I have known,
For surely when a soul by love's sweet pang
Is overcome, then one is often reft
Of common speech– for nothing can compare

With such a power of benevolence.
What if it's love that now oppresses him?
For what besides love could cause such effect?"
He took note of where Parzival was looking,
Observing he did not gaze back at him
But held his vision downward at a slant
Toward the ground. And thus by following
The direction of young Parzival's rapt gaze,
He saw the drops of blood upon the snow.
"Ah," he mused "three scarlet drops of blood
Upon the smooth untarnished cloak of snow.
This is indeed a very striking sight.
And were a heart beset by love's sweet ache,
This could most surely hold a soul bewitched
So that one's ears might render themselves deaf
To customary terms in just this way."

He flung his cape of Syrian silk, lined
With golden fabric, o'er the crimson tears,
And when the drops were hidden from his view,
And Parzival could see them there no more,
His senses were restored to him again,
Though love for his queen stayed within his heart.

"My dearest love," he said, "where have you gone?
A mist has come and robbed me of your presence?
You're stolen from my sight in broad daylight
Before my eyes though how, I do not know.
Oh, where's the lance I brought with me today?"

To him the gentle Lord Gawain replied:
"It shattered in two mighty jousts."
                              "On whom?"
Replied the bewildered Parzival. "No shield

Have you, or sword: how could you joust with me?
Though now I must endure your mockery-
You may perhaps show more respect hereafter;
I've kept my seat when jousting more than once."

"The words I spoke to you," replied Gawain,
"Were friendly and transparent, not double-tongued.
A king with all his knights is close at hand;
If you will ride with me into his presence,
I'll see you're not attacked by anyone."

"My thanks to you, kind sir," said Parzival.
"You speak fair, and I'll try to deserve it.
Since you have offered company, good sir,
Will you please tell me who it is you serve,
And also who you are most gracious knight?"

"The king I serve," said gentle Lord Gawain,
"Is one from whose nobility and love
I have received much generosity.
Whatever God's bestowed on me, I place
In dedication to his worthy cause.
King Arthur is his name. I am Gawain."

"You are Gawain?" replied young Parzival,
Unable to contain astonishment
At being close to so renowned a knight,
A warrior who demonstrated mastery
In every aspect of the knightly code,
For all the virtues of nobility
Informed his character to such degree
That he was thought to be a pinnacle
Of chivalric attainment- unrivaled
Throughout the world and famed for those high traits.

"What scanty credit sir," said Parzival.
"Shall I gain being well received by you,
For I have always heard it said of you
That you receive all whom you meet this way!"

"Be that as it may," said Sir Gawain,
"May this, our good exchange, be but the sign
Of future friendship. Now if you'll concede
And let me give my word on your behalf,
The king will welcome you into our midst.
Right glad I'd be for your good company,
For thou hast shown thy prowess twice this morn.
For this, my brethren groan but will amend,
And if it be as I suspect, the aim
And purpose of our quest has been attained.
For though I hardly dare to guess at it,
I ween thy bearing speaks nobility
Beyond the pall of ordinary knighthood,
So let us put this guesswork to the test
And see if things be as I now predict."

Young Parzival was overjoyed to meet
The noteworthy Gawain, whose wide renown
As Arthur's nephew and the champion
Of the Round Table was unparalleled.

"But tell me Sir Gawain," said Parzival,
"Are those tents pitched by Arthur's company?
For I cannot return into his presence
Until I have avenged a lady there.
When last I was at court, she laughed at me,
And the seneschal then shamed her with his words.
I cannot meet the king till she's avenged,
For I have sworn to win her honor back;

And therefore, I'm ashamed to see the king
Before I have put these things back to rights."

And gentle Sir Gawain to him replied:
"This deed by you has justly now been served;
You threw him down upon that fallen tree.
He broke his right arm and his left leg sir.
Come see where lies his horse, killed by the charge,
And there, the shivers of your lance are strewn-
The one that you were wondering about."

"I must take thee at thy word, friend Gawain,"
Said doubtful Parzival to his companion,
"That this be the same man who shamed the lady.
If so, I'll ride wherever you may please."

Gawain laughed heartily at this reply:
"What sir, shall I now treat my guest to lies?
Bold Segramors too was unhorsed by you,
A strong knight, well known for his feats of arms.
He was the first to fall, and Kay was next.
You have achieved much honor from them both."

The two companions rode to Arthur's camp
Amid the happy dawn of early friendship,
Acquainting one another in the other on their way,
Where they, by everyone, were well received,
And Arthur was most joyful of them all,
For it was as Gawain had almost guessed:
They'd found the one whom they had come to fetch.

The Lady Cunnaware whom he'd avenged
Was overjoyed to meet good Parzival;
Gawain sent word ahead, and forth she came,
Accompanied by beautiful Jeschute.

These two rejoiced when they heard he was near
And walked to him; each held the other's hand.

"I had refrained from laughter till we met:
The day that my heart told me who you were.
And then Sir Kay undid my happiness,
But now it has been put to right again."

Sir Kingrun and Clamide attended her
As well as her brother, the brave Duke Orilus.
He stood beside his dear beloved duchess.

"No knight has ever sent me greater honor,"
Said Arthur when the two had finally met.
"That you restored Jeschute back to good favor
Would have been praise enough to join our ranks;
Kay's misdemeanour too is put to rights
And would have been before if we had spoken.
Good fortune is however with us now,
For we have ridden forth with this intent:
To find your whereabouts and welcome you
To be a member of our company."

The invitation was not turned away,
For Parzival was overjoyed at this.
Sir Segramors and Kay begrudgingly
Forgave their new companion for their pain
And vouched his skill was great, commending him
A knight unparalleled in strength and vim.

PART III

Initiation

THE SORCERESS & THE LANDGRAVE

A jubilant festivity ensued
In Arthur's camp. So many gracious lords
And noble ladies gathered in one place,
All feasting and dancing together joyfully
To welcome Pazival in company-
A member of the mighty Round Table,
For ceremony's due solemnity
Once taken- with bold oaths of siblinghood-
Then turned to merriment with their shared mirth
In celebration of the coming spring.

But through their midst, a maiden rode abruptly.
So sudden was this entrance, it 'scaped not
The observation of a single soul;
Her mount stood high as would a stallion,
But at a closer glance, one plainly saw
A mule whose nostrils had been sliced.
The beast was marked with many searing irons.
This hellish creature bore its burden on.
And she herself did not look like a lady
Or any average person of this world.
A pair of tusks thrust, jutting from her jaws.
Her nose was like a dog's. Upon her head
Her ears appeared to be that of a bear's.
And from her fingers, talon-like, her nails,
Resembled lion's claws. Her name was Cundrie,
And she was known to be a sorceress.
She rode to where the king sat in high state
And paused before him to address his presence.

"Lord Arthur Pendragon, what you have done
Has here besmirched the names of all your knights

As well as you. A sickly shame has poisoned
The lot of those who would in high degree
And honor now be sat. For perfidy
Has joined your ranks and weakens their esteem.
King Arthur you once stood above your peers
For glory and integrity, but now,
Your fame on its ascent has toppled down.
Your prowess, once above all other people,
Now lags and hobbles, stumbling behind.
The might of the Round Table is destroyed
By welcoming Lord Parzival amid
Its shining and untarnished company."

Then wheeling round, she turned to Parzival:

"Cursed be your outward beauty and your strength!"

She, spitting venomously, directed all
Her horrifying force at Parzival.

"It may be that you think me monstrous,
But I am far less monstrous than you!
Explain to me now, Lord Parzival,
How did it come to pass when you were sat
Before the sick, grief-stricken, fisher king
That from his sorrow-ridden sighs, you failed
To free him? Plain to see, his agony
Was made apparent for your callous gaze.
'Twas plain as day- clear as a cloudless sky!
You ought to have had more compassion
Upon his suffering! Oh heartless guest!
I swear upon your head, there never lived
A person of such stature, so bereft
Of commonsense and goodliness! You fraud!
Did not your host present you with a sword

That you in your unworthiness received?
You serpent's fang, you poisoned feather hook!
You are a man devoid of decency
And reft of any honor, Parzival!
With your own eyes, you gazed upon the Grail!
If you had thought to ask your question there
At Munsalvaesche, it would have brought you more
Than all the wealth in Trabonit- the most
Renowned and bounteous city in Pagandom!
Brave Feirefiz, whose courage never fails,
With his fierce deeds was made lord of that land-
For Tribonit's great queen sought an alliance
With Feirefiz when she heard of his strength.
He was already king of two domains.
So many hold him in such high esteem
And seek to emulate his qualities.
Those from all lands and cultures flock to him
For council and advice in rulership.
His strength and courage is inherited
From him who was a father to you both.
Great Feirefiz, like you, is son to him
Who was known for his magnanimity,
His noble spirit, and his warrior heart:
Bold Gahmuret, the king of three great lands.
Your brother in all ways upholds these traits
And is magnificent to gaze upon.
His beauty is reflected by his skin
Which is both dark and light all intermixed
As were the loves from the two mighty hearts
Of noble Belacane and Gahmuret.

In Feirefiz lives another Gahmuret
Who like you has not ever been excelled.
Your father bore the fruits of mastery.

All perfidy was weeded from his soul
Ere that most noble of all knights met death.
There is one name beside bold Feirefiz
And his brave mother, mighty Belacane,
Who holds an equal and untarnished rank
Before the eyes of both God and the world,
And that is Lady Herzeloyde, the queen
And wife of Gahmuret, your good mother.
The qualities she bore hold ill accord
With your false deeds which have cut glory off!
You must believe good things of Herzeloyde
And that your father was born of great worth.
His soul was stamped by honor's coat of arms
And unbesmirched by falseness or deceit.
The heart within his breast was truly great!
Had Herzeloyde e'er strayed in constancy
Or fallen to the hands of disrepute,
Then I might possibly have been convinced
That you were not the son of Gahmuret;
But no, your mother is made of the same
True stock as was her love. Her constancy
Has been the cause of her great suffering.
Alas that it to me was e'er made known
That Herzeloyde's child had strayed from the path
Of righteousness and fallen to disgrace."

The maiden then surrendered to her grief
And wrung her hands and wept with bitter tears
That flooded from a well of sorrow deep.
'Twas the goodness of her heart which brought this sadness
Upwelling from her soul and down her cheeks.
And now, she turned back to their lord the king
To address other matters of import:
"Is there a worthy knight among this host

Whose noble heart yearns to pursue a quest
For a love most rare and most glorious?
Four queens I know of with four hundred maidens
Are captives in a castle of enchantment.
This dire fortress where they now reside
Is called Schastel Marveile, found in the land
Known by the same name as this famous fortress:
Terre Marveile. The way is treacherous,
But all achievements next to those attained
By undertaking this intrepid quest
Would pale to nothing if success be won."

Then off she rode with many a backward glance
And wringing of her hands as she departed.
And heartfelt woe throughout that goodly crowd
Brought tears to the eyes of many gathered there.

Now barely had the space of one breath lapsed
Upon the heels of Cundrie's departure,
Which left a doleful silence in its wake
To those of Arthur's host assembled there,
When in the distance was heard on the approach
The thundering of mighty horses' hooves.
Then into their view rode a warrior
Of powerful stature. And onward he came
Until he'd reached the outskirts of the throng.

"I seek the king and his nephew Gawain.
Where are they? My business is with them,"
The warrior proclaimed as he drew near.

This newcomer's appearance was exquisite.
He was from foot to crest decked splendidly.
He held his sword in hand within its sheath
And removed not his helm as he approached.

These gestures showed the tenor of his message:
The execution of justice was his aim.

"Fair greetings to the king and all his host."
He then continued upon being led
Before the king and those assembled there.
"From only one here I'll withhold my greeting,
For he has made himself my enemy
And shall now answer for his erring ways
With blows if he would still maintain his honor.
Oh where is Lord Gawain, for he it is
Hath robbed me of my joy and happiness.
Alas that he has now brought injury
Upon my heart, for he once knew esteem
And high honor but now must be my foe.
Untarnished was his name until the day
He let ambition guide his noble hand
To slay my kinsmen in the act of greeting.
The curse of this foul deed rests on his head!
If Lord Gawain denies this treachery,
Let him make good against the accusation
By reckoning with me in single combat,
Forty days from this day in Schanpfanzun,
The city capital of Ascalun.
Within the presence of that country's king,
May there his innocence or guilt be judged
In God's eyes with his death or victory."

At this, soft sighs of discord and unease
Spread with a murmur through the goodly throng.

"Bold sir," replied the brave and just King Arthur,
Arising from his seat and stepping forth,
"No one surpasses our Gawain in strength,

Gentility, grace, honor, and esteem.
He is my nephew and second to none.
If his name has been slandered, it will be
My sword that you will have to reckon with,
For he's outranked by no one but myself,
And for him I would lay down life and limb-
Though such an act be viewed as threatening
Unto the safety of my dominion;
Yet doth such claims, ill founded as the one
You now cast like a gauntlet at my feet,
Call forth the full extent of my wrath."

Then recklessly up leapt dashing Beacurs,
The brother of Gawain, and bravely cried:

"Lord Arthur, let me stand in for Gawain
And settle this account on his behalf.
I cannot sit by while my brother's name
Is slandered wantonly for all to hear.
My blood is pulsing at the boiling point-
That this brash man should sit upon his horse
And casually rake Gawain's esteem
Across the smoldering ashes of hearsay
Is not the least bit to my liking, sire.
In forty days I'll ride forth and reclaim
My brother's honor- needlessly undone
By this misconduct and this injustice!"

Courageous Beacurs then went to Gawain,
Knelt down before him, and appealed to him:
"Remember brother how you've always helped
And guided me to lay by all that's false,
To strive for honor only, and to seek
The true path on behalf of goodliness.

185

Now let me spare you this ill-placed misfortune
And be your proud and grateful champion.
If I survive this ordeal, the renown
And glory will be yours- I'll give it all
To you and hold back none upon myself."

To this replied thoughtful Gawain, "Dear brother,
I've sense enough not to grant this request
Though it springs from the noblest of hearts.
I know not why I must face this encounter,
Nor do I care much for this kind of fight.
I would be glad to take up thy kind offer
If it did not place thy young life at risk.
To let thee fight for me would never suit,
For wert thou then to fall, how would I live?
The reckonings called forth by destiny
Must be faced down upon their first approach."

Beacurs persisted, pleading with Gawain,
But nothing he said changed his brother's mind.

The guest who had thus far remained quite still
Throughout this discourse now interposed:
"I have not come to seek the exchange of blows
With someone whose name I have never heard of.
He may be brave and noble, strong and loyal-
In those things let him rest his self-assurance;
Nonetheless, I have no quarrel with him.
The one I've come for I've already named:
Gawain- it's him if he would keep his honor,
Or no one else. I guarantee Gawain
Safe passage on his journey through our land.
Until the day appointed for the match,
May you sir, travel safely and in peace.

You may count on my word, for it is good.
I am a prince of Ascalun, Landgrave
Of Schanpfanzun- Kingrimursel my name."

And with those words, this Lord of Ascalun
Then turned his horse and rode forth from their midst.

More murmurs of unease spread through the throng
When Kingrimursel had spoken his name,
For he was known to be a champion
Of undefeated courage and great strength,
And many feared for noble Gawain's life.
The incidents which had occurred left much
To understand and much to talk about.

There was discussion of the lineage
Of Parzival, for Cundrie had proclaimed
He was born of a royal king and queen.
A number of that host recalled the day
When Gahmuret and Herzeloyde had met-
The day that Gahmuret the Angevin
Had won the heart of noble Herzeloyde
Before the mighty gates of Kanvoleis.
Many of King Arthur's company
Were present at that fateful tournament
And had witnessed the feats of Gahmuret.
They spoke and gazed with awe at Parzival,
But Parzival was not aware of them.
He sat with his gaze averted toward the ground,
Afflicted by the war within his soul
That now raged in him like a wildfire.
How could his great strength, mastery of the sword,
Or the well-trained etiquette of chivalry
Bring aid to Parzival now? But one grace

He had still, one remaining quality:
A sense of remorse, which stood the test of time.
For at its core, his heart was always free
From all that can by wickedness be claimed
And like a captive held for evermore.
But now a darkness overwhelmed his mind.

There was a noble lady in the throng
Who had come from the kingdom of Janfuse,
A pagan region close to Zazamanc
Along the northern coast of Africa.
This gracious lady rose from where she sat
And gently spoke to downcast Parzival:
"There was a man of whom Cundrie told us
Who is well known to me- brave Feirefiz,
Your brother. He is king of Zazamanc
And Azagouc, two mighty dominions
As well as the great city of Tribonit.
Your brother is blessed with prosperity
And wondrous beauty which is most unique:
His skin is both dark and light intermixed
Like a tapestry of his great lineage.
He is known for his magnanimity,
His eloquence, his strength, and gracefulness.
As Cundrie spoke, his name is Feirefiz.
He is a monarch of such high esteem
That he is sought out from far reaching lands
By those in quest of counsel and protection,
And many swear allegiance to his rule.
He is a master of diplomacy.
When it comes to war, no one can contend
With his unequaled strength and boundless courage.
He is a revelation on the field,
And not a soul can stand up against him.

I am a cousin of Queen Belecane
Who is the mother of brave Feirefiz.
Now sir, I see that you are much like him
And bear the same marks of nobility,
Stamped with the seal of heaven on your soul.
Do not lose heart for bearing this sad blow.
In time you will learn to conduct yourself
In all that you endeavor to achieve
With that nobility which lies within your nature."

"I thank you lady for this consolation,"
Said Parzival, "Yet I am still not free
From the oppression of these doleful feelings.
The pain I bear is too great to express
When I am subject to humiliation
And mockery before the eyes of all.
I will not ever be returned to joy
Until I have once more beheld the Grail.
However long or short the time may be,
I will not ever waver from my goal
Though it stretch till the end of my existence.
I have obeyed the precepts of my schooling
Administered by noble Gurnemanz,
But now these teachings are the very things
That have undone my purpose in the world,
For the kindhearted man who was my tutor
Instructed me to forbear from asking questionings
And to guard against all unmannerliness.
I see before me many worthy knights
Who stand and gaze at me in my distress.
Come noble ones, advise me what to do!
How can I gain good favor from you now?
I am in great haste to take leave of you.
Whilst my repute still flourished in your eyes,

You gave me company. I now declare
That you are free from having to endure
The stain inflicted by my presence here
Until I have gained that which I have lost!
Great sorrow will attend me on my quest
Such as draws water from the heart's deep well
Up to the eyes, and I can feel no bottom.
Oh, alas! So many I have left
At Munsalvaesche- so many noble maidens!
And thus I was cast from true happiness,
For any marvels of which people speak
Are nothing compared to the Grail!
Its king is subject to a wretched life.
Ah, sad Anfortas, what joy did I bring you?
No joy, but only pain for suffering!"

So great his shame, he could not bear to stay.
And so from Arthur's court, he took his leave.
This found no favor with the goodly king,
For Arthur was compassionate and sad
At Parzival departing from their midst.
And everyone in that good company
Was saddened by this turn of destiny.

Gawain arose and went to Parzival,
Embracing his distraught friend with compassion
And spoke with brotherly companionship:
"There will be fighting on the quest you face.
The Grail path is known to be treacherous.
May God watch over you in your endeavor,
And may his hosts protect and guide your way."

"My thanks to you, friend," answered Parzival.
"I hope for you that your great strength and skill

Will aid you on the journey that you face.
But alas, does God Almighty live?
Were He the power that He's said to be-
If he were active and omnipotent,
He would not let such shame be heaped on me.
Since I was taught of grace, I've served his name
With duty and obedience. But now,
I'll quit His service, and if God knows of wrath,
I'll don it like an emblem on my heart.
By anger's force will I be recognized
From this day forward- and we'll see if God
Knows rage enough to find me in the world."

And thoughtfully Gawain replied to him:
"The riddles of God's teachings could confound
The wisest and the bravest of this world,
But there is solace on the path of goodness
And purpose in the task of brotherhood.
May truth become the north star of our quests.
May love and faith be our swords and shields,
And may hope bear us upwards in our hearts
And towards the calling of our destinies."

The two friends took their leave of one another,
And both made ready- each for a lonesome quest
Which would put both their spirits to the test.

The lady Cunnaware helped Parzival
To arm, and when his horse had been prepared,
She walked with him to where the steed awaited.
The lady was as grieved as any there
For Parzival. She bade the knight farewell
With gentle kindness and compassion.

The warrior- now clad from head to toe
In shimmering steel, all of the highest grade,

With tabard and surcoat bedecked with gems-
Though heavy-hearted was by strings of fate
Then urged to mount his steed and ride away.
The image of Condwiramurs his queen
Would stay with him upon his lonely quest,
And marvelous exploits before her feet
Would thence be laid like heralds of his strength
To honor her in reverence of their love.
But more than that, his goal of singular aim,
The quest to which he'd turn unflinchingly,
Expending all his prowess as a knight,
Unswerving in endeavor, would now be
At any cost of life and limb to seek
Through treacherous and unforgiving toil
What but a few e'er reach: the Holy Grail.

Gawain too had prepared himself to ride.
He set forth toward the intrepid reckoning
Awaiting him and fortified his heart
To face the fearsome duel that was to come.

The two great heroes left a somber crowd
Sobered by the weight of these events
Which had robbed Arthur and his company
Of its two most distinguished champions.

Then there was talk among those of that host
About the strange and haunting mysteries
Of sinister enchantment in the land
Known by the name of Terre Marveile
Which Cundrie had referred to when she spoke
About the four queens who were captive there.
One member of the company spoke out
And told them of a mighty warrior

Whom he'd encountered when he'd tried his hand
With rescuing the captives in that land.

"I was thrown down by a most fearsome knight
Who is known by the name of the Turkyot,
For so he's called by all who know of him.
He is formidable amid the joust."

Many of King Arthur's company
Set forth to undertake this mighty quest
Of rescuing the queens in Terre Marveile,
But not one knight succeeded in their goal.
They were all barred from finding any path
Which could lead them into that haunted land.

ASCALUN

'Twas many weeks of battling and toil
Ere dauntlessly Gawain toward Ascalun
Made his approach. His journey was waylaid
By many skirmishes and mighty jousts
From which, had honor bade him, he'd have steered;
But though these fierce encounters tested him,
They, in the end, brought him only more glory.
Proud fortune was Gawain's love and protector,
And though she rarely let him taste defeat,
She rarely gave him rest from honor's toils.

The time appointed for the fateful duel
Was now at hand. Gawain, though innocent,
Now turned his course toward his reckoning.

The forest that he had now to traverse
Would be enough to dissuade many folks-
Were they in search of reasons to desist
From heading toward a fell match such as this.
The ground was gnarled and very uneven
Caused by coppices, stumps and fallen trees,
Rocks, boulders, and great nets of twisted roots
And gullies that plunged down on either side-
With steep ravines and treacherous inclines.
As he progressed, he kept a watchful eye
For signs of Ascalun while making sure
That Gringuljete, his great warhorse, was safe
From faulty footing and the snares of roots.
In many places, he walked by the steed
On foot to guide it through the wooded gauntlet.

At length he glimpse the cultivated land
Of Ascalun, and toward it he made his way.

Once out in open country he made haste
To find his way to the city of Schanpfanzun.
Some people that he passed told him the way.
It led across vast, hilly, open ranges
With rolling, grassy plains and open skies.
At last, he saw a fortress in the distance.
Bright it shone against the tilting sun
He made his way toward the gleaming walls
Of this castle resplendent in the morn.

Before the gate was spread a spacious plain,
And as Gawain made for the castle gate,
He saw five hundred knights approaching him.
This mighty entourage was out for sport-
And many birds of prey flew with that host.
King Vergulaht was riding out in front-
'Twas said he was of a fairy lineage.
In any case he bore the look of kings-
Gawain thought him a second Parzival.
Just then, a heron veered into a swamp
To flee its fierce aggressors in pursuit.
The group of royal falcons followed suit
And headed straight toward the tangled swamp.
To rescue his fair hawks King Vergulaht
Lunged to their aid but failed to clear the swamp,
Resulting in him taking a wet fall
Into the shallow waters of the mire.
The rescue was successful for the hawks
However- though he got a dunking.

It was to this scene that Gawain approached,
Where Vergulaht, despite the compromise
Of his position, gave Gawain a good welcome.

"I think it best for you to find your way
    Up to the castle on your own," he said.
"You are now at the gates of Schanpfunzan.
    I will be with you shortly but must first
    Make sure my business here has been resolved.
    At which point I will follow thitherward.
    My sister is at home in yonder palace
    And will be hostess until I arrive.
    If this does not suit your appraisal sir,
    I'll make arrangements to come with you now.
    But if you are content with her welcome,
    I'll stay to put my falcons back in order.
    My sister is well praised throughout the land
    For her charms and rare beauty, which you'll see."

"I see lord," said Gawain, "that you must tend
    To your affairs. I shall be well content
    To find your sister as you have suggested.
    I will go in and introduce myself
    While you complete your business in the field."

"I'll send a knight ahead of you good sir,"
    Said Vergulaht, "to give her word of you
    And your approach- that she may make you welcome."

"My thanks to you kind sir," said Sir Gawain,
    And headed along the road toward the palace.
    As he passed through the mighty castle gate,
    He took note of the stoutness of the fort
    That he was entering. It was well made
    And sturdy as a stronghold ever was
    With elegant ramparts and lofty towers,
    Beautiful causeways and vaulting arches.

He rode into the courtyard where a knight

Met him and led him into the palace.
On their way in, the knight requested leave
To relieve Sir Gawain of shield and sword.
Without a challenge this request was granted.
What need was there for weapons in this instance?
Gawain had been pledged word of safe conduct.

Inside he found the princess Antikonie.
The two paused to take stock of one another.
At this, both of their pulses were increased,
And both felt fire burning on their cheeks.
As they stood and looked, one upon the other,
A messenger approached and gave account
Of Vergulaht's request to host their guest.
She listened, then dismissed the messenger.

"My lord," the princess said to Sir Gawain,
"My brother has commended you to me
And has requested that I be your host.
It is the custom to receive a guest
Of high esteem and honor with a kiss.
I do not wish to impose such a custom
Were it in opposition to your liking.
I will admit to liking you enough
To seal our first encounter with a kiss.
Come sir, what say you to this offering?
Now bid me kiss you if you deem it right,
Or otherwise forbid us this exchange."

"Madam," replied Gawain, "so apt your lips
Appear for kissing that it seems I must
Be welcomed with a kiss if you're inclined
And equally obliged to such a greeting."

They had now drawn quite close as though a tide

Had swept them toward each other in the current.
And there, a kiss was shared such as is not
So customary when two strangers meet.

The noble guest now sat beside his host.
There was no lack of spirited conversation
From either side of this giddy exchange.
As soon as food and drink were brought, the maid
Who'd brought it to them quickly made her exit.
The other serving maids recalled to mind
Activities that took them from the room.
Now how would these two thrive left on their own?
How would they manage the unwieldy pull
Of their desire. The answer? They would not!
The torture of restraint was far too much.
The space between them shrank with every breath.
They merged together like two tributaries
That join each other and become one river.
The river in which they now swam together
Was flowing till it almost burst its banks.
The current was the flow of their passion.
So hard pressed were they by this magnetism
That barring the swift moment's intervention
They'd surely have forgotten their surroundings
And lost all sense of time, place, and the world.
But suddenly a doddering old knight
Came stumbling in to their heartfelt dismay.
He, having lost his humor years before,
Now grumbled in. His old heart nearly stopped
When he found those two so passionately met.
There was a silent moment where it seemed
The old man had been turned to solid stone.
But with a start, he then regained his wits.

"Alas!" he cried. "Was it not enough sir
To slay my lord and bring grief on our house
For which reason you have come to Schanpfunzan,
But now will you have your way with his daughter?"

The old man then began to shout and call
Thus, sounding the alarm for all to hear.

"Madam," then said Gawain, "what shall we do?
We have no weapons to defend ourselves.
Oh that I had my sword here with me now!"

"Let us take refuge outside my bedchamber
Atop that lofty turret over there,"
Resourcefully the young lady replied.
"We'll have the upper hand from that vantage
And will be able to defend ourselves.
Perhaps things will then take a better turn!"

She took her friend Gawain up to the turret
While on their heels, up from the city center,
An angry mob approaching could be heard.
And as the press swarmed 'round the turret's base,
Antikonei tried to appeal to them.
The fierce mob paid no heed to her appeals;
The angry din drowned out the voice of reason,
For they were fixed on the exchange of blows.

By now Gawain had grasped an iron bolt
Which normally was used to bar the door
That entered to Antikonie's bedchamber.
With this, he took his stand against the mob.
Each stroke sent his assailants reeling back.
The princess now sought out another weapon
And found a chessboard which she brought to him,

And this he made good use of as a shield.
She, in the meantime, hurled the heavy pieces
Down on the mob with strength and accuracy.
Those kings and rooks[24] defended well their queen,
For those they hit were toppled without fail.
She wept as she stood bravely by her love,
For she was quite beside herself with rage
Brought on by this public indignity-
Whose plain intent was to humiliate.
She, nonetheless, did not desert her love
But fought beside Gawain courageously.
Her tears were not enough to blind her aim,
For she struck down as many as her friend.
And when there were no longer pieces left,
She grasped an iron sconce from where it stood
And set to work again upon her foes.
She fought as fiercely as her dauntless friend
And struck her enemies with strength and skill.
Gawain for his part smiled thankfully
That he had such a worthy companion
Amid this scandalous catastrophe.
In many circumstances ere that day,
He'd gladly have accepted her assistance
And would have chosen it o'er many others.
Not only this, but when he glanced at her-
So beautiful and wild next to him,
Her fierce eyes glinting from behind her tears,
Her hair undone, and fighting with abandon-
His heart would swell with such intensity
That he became like several warriors
And filled with such a limitless power
That it would seem to spill out all around him

---

24   A chess piece.

So that as he advanced the crowd fell back
As though an ocean surge had driven them.
These two now came on like a force of nature,
Striking with the rage of hurricanes.
They were indeed a force to reckon with,
And many fell before their hefty strokes.
The mob, now not so prideful as before,
Came flinching toward them, ducking from their blows.

Now as this scene unraveled, Vergulaht,
Having attended to his hawks, appeared.
He, without taking time for better judgment,
Assumed Gawain must surely have done wrong
And joined the mob. Gawain was forced to wait
Until King Vergulaht had armed himself.
This done, he set on Sir Gawain with blows.
Armed only with the door bolt and chessboard
Against the fully armed King Vergulaht,
Gawain gave his good name greater increase,
For he fought well despite the ill-stacked odds;
But nonetheless, he was forced to give ground
Unless he wished to sacrifice his life-
Though this ground was hard won by Vergulaht.
At last, Gawain, despite his valiant efforts,
Was slowly forced back up against the wall.
His situation was precarious
To say the least, the well-armed Vergulaht,
Backed by the wrathful crowd, was pinning him.
But just when bold Gawain thought all was lost,
The man who'd challenged him at Arthur's court,
Kingrimursel, the kingdom's mighty landgrave,
Arrived and to his outrage and dismay
Beheld his brave opponent in this state.
He wrung his hands and pulled his hair with rage

And dug his fingernails into his scalp
When his eyes took in this catastrophe.

"I gave my word that this man would be safe
Within our kingdom's walls until the day
Appointed for the duel, and on that day,
The only sword that would be raised toward him
Was to be mine and mine alone! By God!
Have all of you gone mad and lost your wits?
There is no one more noble than Gawain
Besides his uncle- the king of all Great Britain!"

He charged into the fray to help Gawain,
And any hapless soul who blocked his path
Was laid out long upon the stony ground.
It was not long before he'd reached his guest.
The landgrave was not one to hesitate-
He pressed in with Gawain against the wall,
And with great thrusts and blows, he set work.
For honor's sake he put his life at risk;
He battled back that mob and his own king,
For he would have no life if not with honor.

The crowd and Vergulaht could not contend
With the ferocity and strength of Kingrimursel,
Gawain, and the good Princess Antikonie.
They were all driven back by these brave three
Until a path was broken through the mass,
And the warrior trio hastened to their safety.
Out in the open, they regrouped and made their stand.
But many of their foes were now disheartened.
The landgrave was a well-respected lord
And loved by all his subjects who now faced him.
They were ashamed to battle with their master

And wary of his deftness with the sword.
Their siege upon the three was now half-hearted.

"What?" said Vergulaht. "Are you all cowards?
Will you, the many, cower before these three?
If Sir Gawain has done me an offense
And trespassed in my house, he must be served!
Have at them, you fools, and bring Gawain to me!"

Some knights amid the throng protested this,
"Sire," they said, "please do not make us fight
With our dear lord the landgrave over there,
He is well loved by us his loyal subjects.
Not only this but we wish to preserve
Your reputation and renown, great King.
Were you to slay your noble guest Gawain,
Unarmed as he is in his present state-
Whom Kingrimursel promised safe passage-
You'd only bring disgrace upon your name
Which would stick fast there like a vile stain.
Think better Lord, and call off this attack."

On hearing this sage council, Vergulaht
Was well advised and called off the assault
While he thought more on how best to avenge
His father's death. Gawain was innocent;
It was another knight named Ehkunat
Who'd slain the prior king of Ascalun.
But rumors had been spread about Gawain.
A messenger thought it was Sir Gawain
That he had seen nearby the battlefield
Where stealthy Ehkunat had done this deed.
Gawain was in the skirmish on that day,
But at the moment of the tragic death,

He was elsewhere engaged upon the field.
Gawain knew he had been falsely accused-
In truth he was grieved on his foe's behalf,
For having lost their king and father thus,
But being made of true nobility,
He'd chosen honor of the knightly code
In answering the summons to the duel
Instead of trying to avoid the match.
Gawain placed all his trust in his Creator,
Knowing that no words could change a truth.
And that is why he'd journeyed many miles
To find himself entangled in these matters.
Sir Ehkunat not only slew a king
To bring a kingdom and its people grief,
But he had also caused Gawain great strife
With his ambitious, cruel, and thoughtless act.

The truce now having been agreed upon,
Gawain and Kingrimursel quickly departed
And caught their breath away from all the throng.
"Lord Vergulaht," now spake Antikonie,
"Had it pleased God that I were made a knight,
You would have lost your urge for fighting here.
But though I am a princess and unarmed,
I bear a shield that in your negligence
You fail to recognize, which I will name.
Do not avert your gaze while I speak brother.
You were content to meet me in the fray
Where I, though never taught the tricks of war,
Defended our guest with what I could find
At my disposal. Now do me the grace
Of meeting the cuts and parrys of my words
With the dignity and plain dealing they deserve.
The shield I carry is invisible

To those who lack the eyes to see its nature.
It is emblazoned with nobility
Steadfastness, constancy, and seemliness.
We come from the same royal lineage,
And yet, you treat me as your property.
I interposed to guard my noble knight
Whom you sent up to meet me as my guest.
Now were the tables turned and had I sent
A princess up to you to entertain,
You'd have been free to meet her as you saw fit.
No crime has been committed here, and yet,
You now side with the rabble against me
Without so much as a moment's hesitation.
Do not, sir, underestimate your sister.
You'll make a foe who you'd wish was a friend.
The flight of our guest to my protection
Where he was forced to battle for his life
While I, unarmed, could only do the same,
Will bring disgrace upon your reputation."

Kingrimursel now having caught his breath
Returned and spoke his mind as he approached:
"When I gave Sir Gawain safe conduct here,
I placed my trust in you, my lord and king.
Your word was pledged that were Gawain to journey
To Ascalun, then I, on your behalf,
 Should guarantee that one man and no other
Would offer him a duel upon the day
Appointed. Now my lord, I call my peers
To witness that your actions have reduced
And undermined my reputation.
If you do not know how to treat your lords,
Then we, your lords, will undercut the crown.
If you have any decency, you'll own

That we share a close line of royal blood.
If I were merely kin by distant bonds-
Rash man, this reckless trespass would be still
Far past the bounds of chivalry and honor!
Wherever it is rumored that the nephew
Of mighty Arthur under the safeguard
Of my word made the journey to our lands
And there, was ambushed ere the sun went down
In a most disgraceful and unseemly manor,
My infamy will perish instantly!
Fool of a king, he was not even armed!
He had to wait for you to arm yourself!
Heaven forbid you suffer the faintest scratch
By facing your foe with an ounce of courage!
Had you attacked him with a kitchen knife,
The odds would still have been stacked in your favor,
For you fought with the rabble at your back
While your opponent showed his wholesome mettle,
Pressed against the unforgiving wall
With what rude implements were lying by.
His desperate battle will undo my fame
And cut my happiness off at the root!"

At this forth one of the king's men- Liddamus-
Stepped and spoke: "What is this man Gawain-
Who slew my sovereign's father and just now
So nearly dishonored my noble lord
By being so familiar with his sister-
Doing so in his palace? Is he yet living?
If the landgrave is truly a nobleman,
He will avenge the death of my lord's father
Without more posturing and lofty words.
The one life will requite the other fairly."

Gawain was in more peril than before,
If these words held sway o'er the king's persuasions.

"Those quick with threats should hasten to the fight!"
Kingrimursel retorted heatedly.
"It makes no difference where you choose to fight,
Sir Liddamus; at close range or far off
You are one who is easily thrown back.
I'll wager that I'll save this man from you,
And even if he'd done you mortal wrong,
You would still have to leave it unavenged!
When one has shared the battlefield with you,
One becomes most acquainted with your absence-
Your utter lack of presence in fray.
One learns to give attention to one's back,
For where thou wouldst have been, one finds a gap
Deserted, unprotected, and exposed.
With my own eyes, I've seen your cowardice
Enough times to prove that you'll never stand
Behind the words you speak so brashly now.
You've always been the first to fly the field.
The crown of any king would sit askew
If your advice were taken for the truth.
I myself would have faced brave Gawain
Within the dueling ring had Vergulaht
Not now eroded the integrity
Of our pact. He now must bear my wrath
Along with the weight of his own misdeed.
I must say I had higher hopes for him!
My lord, Gawain, wilt thou agree to duel
With me in one year's time from now
If my lord will agree to spare your life?
I offer you my hand now in good faith."

Gawain politely offered his assurance
And met the landgrave's offer with a handshake.

"Kingrimursel," said Liddamus at this,
"I care not how I stand in your esteem.
Though you outrank me, I too govern lands.
Wherever I may go to war or not
If there I choose to fight or flee the field
Is up to me and quite beside the point.
I am well situated without your approval
And do not need your praise for self-assurance.
Were you or any Briton to wish harm
Upon my personage or on my lands,
I would not bring one hen into the coop
For fear of prowling foxes in the night.
I merely asked, as reason prompted me,
A question in regards to my lord's business.
A man from Briton who is our foe
Was challenged by you sir to fight a duel.
And being summoned here for this event,
That man has now arrived. Avenge your lord,
But bring me not into your quarrel sir!
If someone slew my royal sovereign's father
Whose vassal sir you were then, settle it,
And settle it with him who did the deed!
I have done no harm to my sovereign's father.
And I am reconciled by his loss-
His heir now wears the crown. I am content,
For his nobility is high enough
To make him worthy as my overlord.
Let those who wish to fight display their valor;
I will be glad to hear news of the outcome.
And let the victor receive all due praise.
For my part, I will not let love or honor

Delude me into forfeiting my life.
I battle from behind the moated walls
Of fortresses and hunt my prey disguised."

"You speak in much the way," said Kingrimursel,
"That many of us have become accustomed
To hear when you're around Sir Liddamus.
You now advise me to the very thing
That I am set on. I shall teach Gawain
Revenge, or else he must slay me instead."

"I quite agree," said crafty Liddamus,
"But even if I owned as many lands
As Gawain's uncle Arthur Pendragon,
I'd give them up before I drew my sword
To fight. You, sir, may keep your precious glory.
As for myself, I am no Segramores,
Who must be bound, so keen is he to fight,
For there are those of us who ne'er draw sword
And ever are found with those who seek flight,
Who nonetheless attain such stately power
That many come to us with caps in hand.
Though I may never hack my way to honor
With sword and shield and glorious feats of arms,
I will assume great power and take gifts
Of wealth from those of lesser wit and thrift.
Rest 'surredly, my skin will ne'er be marred
On your behalf, Sir Landgrave Kingrimursel."

"Desist with this unruly wrangling!"
King Vergulaht impatiently broke in.
"It is not to my liking in the least
That you are both so free with your tongues here
And blatantly uncensored in my presence.

I am too near for you to raise your voices;
It does not beseem either you or me!
Now sister, take your companion with you
And the landgrave as well, and leave us here.
Those who wish me well come speak with me
And help me weigh what best is to be done."

"Be sure to add your false word to the scales!"
Antikonie retorted to her brother
As she, with brave Gawain and Kingrimursel,
Withdrew to await the verdict in her quarters.
The princess now took her guest by the hand,
And Kingrimursel followed to her chambers.
The three friends had now to await the verdict.
The princess had a third for company:
This was anxiety for Sir Gawain.
She fretted silently all through the day.
A meal was served, and they ate heartily,
For those three had worked up an appetite
While battling for their lives not long before.

Meanwhile Vergulaht was holding council.
He had called thither many noble subjects
Well suited for debate and stately council
For issues of such fraught complexity,
Concerning matters of integrity
With reputation and renown at stake.

"Confound this muddled turn of destiny!"
Said Vergulaht once he had heard from all.
Some had said one thing; some said quite another.
And each lord seemed to argue with the last,
All angling for Vergulaht's approval
In hopes of gaining favor from the king-
Which could lead to more power and possessions."

The king's outburst brought silence to the room.
"It's gone from bad to worse," he then continued,
"For not a week past I had ridden hence
To find adventure, and there met a knight
Who without pausing threw me o'er my crupper!
He made me promise then to win the Grail
On his behalf though it cost me my life!
This was the promise that he forced from me.
And if within a year's time, I had failed
To win the Grail, and if I was still living,
I must then journey unto Belrepiere
And lay myself before Condwiramurs,
The queen of Belrepiere, and be her captive.
He said he had a message for this queen-
That I should say I had been sent to her
By him who had freed her from King Clamide
And that he, her servant, would be o'rejoyed
If he, my victor, still lived in her thoughts."

"Lord, if I may," now spoke Sir Liddamus,
"Let Lord Gawain stand in for what this man
Hath wrung from you, and like a puffing rooster
Doth now insist that you must honor him
In these absurd acts of humility.
Now let Gawain ride forth, freed from his bond,
To duel with the landgrave, and let him quest
On your behalf to find the Holy Grail,
For were he slain beneath your roof, then shame
Would be this kingdom's close companion.
So pardon his misdeed, and win the love
Of your dear sister back, then, let him ride.
He has endured great hardship in these walls
And will most surely meet his death ere long,
For never was a house more fiercely guarded

Than is the deadly fortress of the Grail.
Leave him at ease tonight, and in the morn,
Inform him of your generous decision."

The group assembled all agreed to this,
And so Gawain's unerring life was spared.

Next morn, the handsome Princess Antikonie
Led her dear friend Gawain before the king.

"My brother," she said when they stood before him,
"I bring the knight whom you yourself hath sent
Into my care. For my sake, treat him well.
Do not begrudge nor shirk this fair request,
It will raise your worth and integrity
And will become you better than my hatred,
Which coupled with the disapproving world
Will not sit well on you, as you I'm sure
Have understood by now- if common sense
Had anything to offer you in council."

"I shall oblige you sister," said the king.
"You think wrongdoing has now severed me
From virtue and nobility and slain
My reputation and integrity?
If that were so, how could I be your brother?
For were all lands in Christendom[25] to praise me
And pledge their fealty to my governance,
I would renounce them, were that your command.
I'll have no happiness or public stature
Unless it is accorded with your favor.
To bear your hatred would be my undoing.
My noble Lord Gawain, hear my request.

---

25   Christian civilization.

You've ridden hither on behalf of honor,
Now for that honor, help me win the pardon
Of my good sister in lieu of my fault,
For rather than lose her affection sir,
I would now overlook the mortal wrong
You have inflicted on me- if you'll pledge
That from this day onward, your goal shall be
To win the Holy Grail on my behalf."

Ne'er yet had bold Gawain been known to flee
Or dodge the treacherous call of destiny.
This new intrepid summons to the fray
Was no exception, for he graciously
Obliged the challenge without wavering.
Those of the company assembled there
Who stood or sat in near proximity
Took close stock of Gawain, observing him.
They could not help but feel love's admiration
And yearned within their hearts to emulate
His dauntless courage and gentility.

Kingrimursel too then forgave the king
Who'd lost the mighty landgrave's allegiance
By disregarding his word of safe passage.

The bold landgrave then spoke to Sir Gawain:
"Right glad am I good sir to call you friend,
For though the code had pinned me as your foe,
To battle with you was not to my liking.
What happiness to part in brotherhood
And carry each the other's memory
In the allegiance and esteem of friendship!
I will be joyful when I hear your name."

"Good sir," said kind and courteous Gawain,
"I must admit that for my part I too
Was never happy with our enmity.
In equal turn I rejoice in our friendship."

The time had come to set forth on his quest
To seek the Grail though death await him there.
Gawain made ready with the kindly help
Of his dear friend, the brave Antikonie.
They shared a final meal before he parted,
And sorrow joined them for their last exchange.

"Alas that I must part from you so quickly,"
Said gentle Sir Gawain as they sat close.
"So short a span of time to share in love
Before cruel destiny bids me depart."

"Never have I known heartache and joy
To share so intimate a dwelling place
As they do now entwined within my bosom,"
Replied the thoughtful princess Antikonie.
"For while I mourn the haste of your departure
And dread lest I shall love the bright world less
Without the sweet gift of your presence near,
I yet rejoice that our love was discovered
In this short breath of time and would not wish
For such a thing to have been overlooked
Or never for our paths to have been joined.
What boundless joy to once have known this love!
And though the pang of parting cleave our hearts
Into a thousand glorious and shimmering pieces,
Let them be like the scattered stars on high
That ornament the mighty dome of heaven:
One sky illumined by the many flames

Of lovers' hearts all lit from one same source.
Far greater would the tragedy have been
Had our meeting never come to pass-
For were two bright lamps of the midnight sky
Such as these which we carry in our hearts
Left aimlessly to wander through the night,
Never once to share in happiness,
Not once to swing from the arc of our orbit
Into each other's bountiful embrace
Or find the heaven of the other's gaze-
Oh such would be the greater tragedy!
Let us not mourn what cannot come to pass,
But rather let us rejoice in our love.
No better terms could come for your acquittal,
And so we must put faith in destiny.
There is one more thing that I wish to say
To you, dearest of friends, ere you depart.
I ask that you believe what I now speak:
Whenever you are hard pressed in a battle,
If e'er your knightly task has cast you down
Among the bitter hosts of care and grief,
Think of me now before you as I am
And know that ever in my heart of hearts
Through victory and in direst defeat,
The love I bear will always be with you."

"My dear and loyal-hearted friend," he answered,
"We are like one mind placed inside two bodies.
It was indeed a happy day that fate
Coordinated our distant steps
To carry us into the other's presence.
I will devote my knightly aspirations
To serve the love that lives between our hearts.
A joyful destiny has given you

Such virtues that free you from falsity
So that your honor is second to none.
May fortune ever grant you her protection!"

The noble princess then kissed her companion,
And they both felt the strength of their affection.
Although it was a struggle to depart,
Gawain at last said farewell to his friend
And turned to where his warhorse Gringujlete
Awaited him. He then climbed to his seat
And turned the steed away from Ascalun
Toward what fortune held in store for him.

THE ANCHORESS & THE TEMPLAR

The ruthless words of Cundrie, having struck
A warlike chord in Parzival's brave heart,
Awoke within his soul unwavering
Determination for the Holy Grail,
A quest from which he could not be deterred.
The hero ranged vast distances on horseback
And o'er the waves in ships. No one who dared
By joust to challenge him e'er kept their seat;
With such unflinching courage did he thrive
Against whatever odds were thrown at him.
And downward plunged the glory of his foes
While upwards his renown made its ascent
Relentlessly. He fought through many wars,
Expending all his strength to such degree
That all who strove against him to build fame
Could only do so, trembling in fear.
And nothing of the day or year he knew
Besides the season, which he only guessed,
As recklessly he rode his rugged course.
And rumbling in the thundering of hooves,
His name with tremors rolled across the land.

The great sword gifted to him by Anfortas-
When Parzival sat by the wounded king
Before the presence of the Holy Grail-
Was broken into shards in a fierce duel.
But by the powers of the magic spring
That his good cousin told him of, named Lac,
The mighty blade was rendered whole again.

Our story finds him now upon his quest
Amid a vast expanse of wilderness.

217

One day as he rode searching for adventure,
He came upon a newly built cell through which
A swift stream flowed. The dwelling at one end
Was raised above the water. An anchoress
Was master of this humble house of prayer.
The seed of sorrow fed from love of old:
Each day would blossom in her heart anew.
It was Sigune with her beloved knight
Or rather the embalmed corpse of her love.
Her life was spent on bended knee in prayer.
The joys of this world had deserted her;
Her lamentations needed solitude.

Brave Parzival rode over fallen trees
Up to her window and called out to her.
"Is anyone inside?"
                    "Yes!" said Sigune.

Then Parzival dismounted from his horse
And turned the beast onto a patch of grass.
He then ungirt his sword and went to ask
About their whereabouts in that great wood.
He looked in at the window. It was bare.
The cell within was reft of any joy.
He asked her if she'd come and speak to him.
The pale young woman courteously rose
And left her prayers to meet him at the window.
Upon her hand, he saw a precious ring,
Yet still he did not recognize his cousin;
So pale and wan with grief was dear Sigune.
Beneath her cloak against her skin, she wore
A sackcloth shirt, for sorrow was her lover
And laid down gaiety from her sad heart.

"There is a bench outside the window there,"
The lady said, "if you have time and leisure.
Pray sit there, and we two can hold discourse."

The warrior accepted her invitation.

"It's inconceivable to me," he said,
"How you can lodge here in this wilderness
So far from any road. Where is your source
Of nourishment? I see no crops nearby."

"My nourishment is brought to me," she said
"By Cundrie from the Grail each Saturday."

At this the knight assumed that she was lying,
And fancying she might deceive him more,
He asked her banteringly through the window,
"For whose sake do you wear that precious ring?
I've always heard it said that an anchoress
Restrains herself from having love affairs!"

"Your words would make me out to be a fraud,"
Replied the good and sorrowful Sigune.
"By God, I say I'm free of all deceit.
I wear this ring for love of a dear soul,
Whose love I never took possession of
With any human deed. My unwed heart
Impels me still to love him nonetheless.
For here inside with me, I have the man
Whose ring I've worn since Duke Orilus slew him,
And I shall love him through the joyless days
That yet remain for me. It is true love
I shall bestow on him, for he strove hard
To win it honestly with shield and lance
In chivalric style. He died serving me."

219

At hearing this, good Parzival realized
It was his cousin, Sigune. He bared his head,
Removing his mail coif, and she knew him.

"Why you are Parzival!" Sigune exclaimed.
"Now tell me how you're faring with the Grail.
Have you yet come to understand its nature?
Or what direction has your quest now taken?"

"I have forfeited all my happiness
In that endeavor," said the warrior.
"The Grail gives me no lack of weighty cares.
I left a land o'er which I wore a crown
And a most loving wife. I long for her,
Her modest, courteous ways and often pine
For her- yet even more, for that high goal,
To see great Munsaelvache and look upon
The Holy Grail which has not come to pass.
My cousin Sigune, acquainted as you are
With all my sorrow, it seems so unjust
That you should treat me like an enemy,
The way you did that day when we last met."

To this the good Sigune to him replied:
"All cause I had to censure you," she said,
"Will be forgiven. You have suffered greatly
And forfeited much happiness indeed
When you neglected to make inquiry
As to the anguish of the kind Anfortas.
A question would have won you everything
A heart can wish for. It's no wonder cares
Have made themselves your quest's companions
And pushed your happiness away from you.
But may the hand of Him, who succors all

And knows all suffering, bring aid to you.
What if you prove so lucky that a track
Should lead you to behold great Munsalvaesche?
For Cundrie rode away a short while hence;
I'm sorry I did not ask if she went
To Munsalvaesche from here or somewhere else.
Each time she comes, her mule stands over there
Where water from the spring pours o'er the rock.
Most likely she will not be far ahead.
If you ride after her, you may catch up,
And she could guide you to the Holy Grail."

The warrior at once bade her farewell
And set out on the sorceress' trail.

The mule had gone that way, but tangled growth
Encroached upon the path and barred the way.
And so, the Grail was lost a second time.
His happiness was once more dashed to pieces.
Had he discovered Munsalvaesche again,
He would have surely done much better there
With asking the ailing king about his sorrows.
The disappointed knight continued on.
He knew of nothing else that could be done
But to ride aimlessly amid the wilderness.

But as he rode, a knight approached him swiftly.
"It gives me great displeasure that you beat
Your track through my lord's forest in this fashion.
I'll give you a reminder you'll regret,
For Munsalvaesche is surely not accustomed
To having anyone ride close to it
Without a desperate battle, offering
What those outside our forest would call 'death.'"

The Templar then tied fast his coif and helm;
Brave Parzival too made ready for the joust.
When they were set, both gave full rein to charge
And drove their spurs into their stallions' flanks
And lunged toward full tilt; intrepidly
They aimed their lances as their pace increased,
And neither missed their mark. Bold Parzival
Withstood the blow against his plated chest
And firmly gripped his seat while with deft skill,
His blow went clean and accurately past
The shield of his opponent, guided smoothly
To where the other's helmet lace was knotted.
He struck his foe so squarely that the Templar
From Munsalvaesche was rolled out of his seat
And down a gully in the mountainside,
So far his tumble never seemed to end.
But Parzival raced forward on his horse
To follow his joust through so that the beast
Pitched downward off the gully's rocky edge
And hurtled to its death. But as it fell,
Skilled Parzival had grasped hold of a branch
With both hands as downward his steed fell
So that when all was said and done, he hung,
Suspended in the air with hands and arms
Wrapped 'round the bough of a great cedar tree.
His horse lay dead below amid the brush.
He found a rock lay close enough beneath
To set his feet down on it easily.
The other knight was making haste to safety
By scrambling up the gully's farther side.
If he was wondering about the state
Of Parzival's victory, it seemed the Grail
Had more to offer him. At any rate,
He wasn't looking back but towards escape.

Brave Parzival found this knight's horse unscathed
With dangling reins amid the tangled bracken.
It stood there waiting for him as though told
To do so. Parzival approached the steed;
He gently spoke to it and set his foot
To stirrup, swinging upwards to the saddle.

He'd lost his lance in that fell jousting match
But gained a powerful steed in place of it.
The joust he'd undergone against the Templar
Would've won the praise of any had they seen.

And off he rode upon his newly won steed.
The honor that he bore- a hollow trophy-
Would ride on with him over many miles
Amid the vast and barren wilderness.
And onward pressed his journey dauntlessly,
Toward what destiny next held in store.

GABENIS

The warrior then rode for countless days;
No notion had he of his whereabouts.
But destiny steered him upon a course
Away from fierce encounters with the Templars
Who guarded Terre de Salvaesche and the Grail.
But he was grieved the Grail was kept aloof
As aimlessly he ranged the wilderness.

One morning close to Easter, though the year
And day were to him ever then unknown,
As he rode through a great forest where a light
Soft cloak of snow lay nestled on the ground,
An aged knight approached him through the wood
Whose grizzled beard and silver hair did frame
A face with youthful skin that shone out clear.
His wife like him was grey haired and smooth skinned
Though it was evident that youthful days
For these two were but distant memories.
Their bodies were bare but for rough cloaks of sackcloth
With which they'd wrapped themselves against the cold
Upon their humble pilgrimage to prayer.
Two daughters, dressed in similar attire,
Accompanied the pair. So beautiful
Were they that their soft radiance could not
Conceal itself beneath their humble garb.
All wandered barefoot- though 'twas bitter cold.
A throng of others followed them attired
In similar rags of sackcloth, all unshod:
Ladies with their lapdogs, knights and lords,
Squires and young pages, all in train.
And all progressed in silent reverence,
Displaying meekness and humility;

Their pride subdued. In contrast, Parzival
Had taken such good care of his appearance
That his magnificent caparison[26]
Displayed him as a most prestigious knight.
His lavish armor quite outshone that train
Of silent pilgrims on their sacred errand.
He deftly tugged the reins and turned his horse
In order that this company could pass.
Then Parzival saluted the grey pair
Who despite the appearance of their garb
Possessed the regal qualities of lordship:

"Good morrow friends and all your company.
I do not wish to keep you from your quest-
Whate'er it be. But I have wandered far
And wonder if you know what land this is?"

To Parzival, the grey-haired lord replied:
"Good morrow to you sir, God keep you well.
This territory's called Terre de Salvaesche.
A vast and boundless wilderness, it spreads
In all directions for many a mile.
But why art thou bedecked in full apparel?
Has not the Holy season given cause
To forgo opulence and choose a shift
More humble, true, and in obedience
With such a blessed time? This day of all
Is not befitting for such decadence."

"My Lord," replied brave Parzival, "the day,
The year, and season are unknown to me.
Good sir, I know not when the year begins,

---

26   The decorative trappings of a knight and their horse which
were often of the same design.

Nor do I ever count the passing weeks.
I used to serve one who is known as God
Until it pleased Him to ordain such shame
Upon me that I chose to quit His service.
Till then, I'd never failed Him in devotion,
And many have told me I should seek His aid,
But all that's come of this is misery."

"Do you mean God, born of the Virgin Mary?"
replied the grey-haired knight. "If you believe
In His incarnation and His passion for us,
Upon this day which we are now observing,
That armor ill beseems you. For this day
Is called Good Friday in which all the world
May both rejoice and mourn with suffering.
For where has greater loyalty been shown
For us by God than when upon the cross
He died? If you are of the Christian faith,
Then let this company here afflict you:
He bartered his life to redeem our debt,
For humankind was bound for devastation,
A world devoid of goodness, truth, and love.
His sacrifice brought spirit into matter
So that the world may be redeemed again.
And thus, all gifts and graces we enjoy
As human beings and benevolence
Within the world are owed in full to Him.
But this was given at great cost and grief.
Unless you do not think of this as true,
Remember sir, what day it is. Ride on,
Not far ahead along our tracks, there sits
A holy man. He can bring aid to you
And teach you of these things if you so wish.
If you have aptness and humility,

He'll help you free yourself to find new hope."

"Why are you being so unfriendly, father?"
One daughter asked. "This weather's bitter cold.
How can you give him this stringent advice?"

At this the second daughter spoke her mind:
"Why don't you offer him a place to rest
And warm himself out of the frigid weather?
However splendid he may look, encased
In shimmering steel, he must be very cold!
You have rough woolen tents set up nearby,
And if King Arthur were to call on you,
You'd keep him well supplied with victuals.
Be kind, and take this knight away with you!"

"Good sir," he said, "my daughters speak aright.
At this time every year, despite the cold,
I set out from a place not far from here.
I'd gladly share with you what food I've brought
To aid me on this humble pilgrimage."

"These people are so lovely," thought Parzival.
"I'll not ride on beside them while they walk
With nothing on their feet. And if we stopped,
I don't think I would join them in their prayer.
It would be best for me to leave them now-
Since I'm at odds with one they love so well."

"Dear friends," he said, "please give me leave to go.
I wish you all prosperity and joy.
May happiness abundantly attend
And duly nourish you throughout your lives.
And may your courtesy attain reward
To match the generosity and grace

You give in trying to make me comfortable,
But I must go."
                    He then inclined his head,
And they in turn tipped theirs regretfully.

And so, the son of Herzeloyde rode on;
His steadfast discipline commingled in him
Humility with strength and compassion.
Because he had a loyal heart, remorse
Began to stir in it, for only now
Did he begin to wonder at the world
And ponder how it may have come to be.
Just then did he think of his Creator,
How mighty a being, such a one must be.
"I wonder if God doth possess a power
So great as to be able to overcome
And succor as would overcome my grief?"
He asked himself. "If He e'er loved a knight,
If any knight has ever earned reward
With shield and sword from Him, or if it be
That knightly ardour can e'er be so worthy
To gain His aid such that could rescue me
From care, and if this be His day of help,
Then I say, let Him help if help He can!"

He turned 'round to look back from whence he'd come,
And they still stood there saddened by his absence.
In truth, those were good, loyal-hearted people.

"If God is so omnipotent and mighty
That He can guide a horse and other beasts
And people too, then I will praise His power.
If in His wisdom, He can guide my horse
So that success accompanies my quest,

229

Then in His goodness, may He bring me aid.
Now go wherever God may choose to lead!"
He laid the reins down on his horse's back,
And with his spurs, he urged the beast onward.

TREVRIZENT

The stallion continued through the forest
And made for the abode of Trevrizent,
A holy man. Following the path,
The horse was guided by an unseen hand
To wend its way through the wilderness
Until they came upon the humble dwelling.
The hermit sat quite still as they approached.

Bold Parzival soon recognized the place,
For he'd passed by there several years before.
He'd sworn an oath in this place on that day
And found a lance, the which he'd taken up
To carry on his quest. The hermit spake:

"Were you impelled by some extreme encounter
To deck yourself with this extravagance
Upon this Holy day? Or was there war
That forced you 'gainst your will into this armor?
If not, some other garb would suit you more.
I hope you'll tell me of some desperate
Adventure that has driven you to don
This most immoderate apparel here
Upon this glorious and sacred day.
But pray, dismount beside this fire; sit
And warm yourself."
                        The warrior alighted
And courteously stood beside the man.
"Kind sir," he said, "please give me your guidance.
I wish to find new hope, for I am lost."

"My guidance you shall have," replied the man.
"But tell me, who has sent you hitherward?"

"As I rode through the wood," said Parzival,
"A grey-haired man approached me with his host,
All dressed in rags. He kindly greeted me
And sent me unto you to seek your aid."

"Ah, that was Gabenis," replied the host.
"He is perfected in all noble ways
And is descended from a royal line.
On this day every year he visits me."

"When you saw me approaching your abode,
Were you at all afraid? Was it irksome?"
Said Parzival.
     "Believe me sir," replied
The hermit, "bears and stags have irked me more
Than human beings. Truly will I say
That human nature is well known to me.
I've never fled the field in all my days.
While I bore arms, I strove and fought for love
As you do now. From time to time, I've paired
The more pure thoughts with the more tarnished ones.
I lived in dazzling style to win the favor
Of those I served. But all this is forgotten;
I think no more on any of these things.
Give me your bridle, and your horse shall rest.
I have no fodder, but some ferns and bracken
Should keep him in good fettle for a while."

He rose and led the steed to a rock alcove
Beside a waterfall. They gave the beast
A mound of ferns and wild vegetation
To keep it well contented for a time.

The host then led the young knight to a grotto.
And there, a fire burned. The holy man

Then lit a taper, and the warrior
Removed his armor to recline upon
A bed of ferns. The warmth spread through his limbs.
As he lay there, he saw a reliquary.
And as he looked, he slowly recognized
It was the one he'd sworn on for Jeschute.
At length the knight spoke in the quiet stillness.

"I recognize this reliquary sir,
For I once travelled through this very place.
'Twas several years ago by now I think-
Though what the time of year was I know not-
All sense of time for me is fully lost.
It must not have been in the wintertime,
For I remember dazzling flowers there.
That day when I was here I found a lance
Which I took with me on my journey thence.
Did you at that time dwell within this wood?
Do you remember if you saw that lance?
If so, may I respectfully inquire
As to how long it's been since I was here,
The day I stopped and took that sturdy lance?
The days, the weeks, the seasons, e'en the years
Have merged, entangled in my clouded mind."

"'Twas Turrian, my friend, who left it there,"
Replied the holy man to Parzival.

"He said he missed it later, but 'tis now
Gone four and a half years and three days
Since last you came and took it as you said.
If you should care to listen while I read,
I'll calculate the passing years for you."

And from his book he read to Parzival
The full account of all the passing years

That had elapsed since Parzival swore his oath
For beautiful Jeschute and Duke Orilus.

"And only now do I become aware,"
 replied the heartsore Parzival at this,
"How long I've ridden with no sense of joy
 Or purpose. Joy to me is but a dream.
And though I know not why, I'll tell you more:
For all this time that I have wandered lost,
I never have been seen to cross the threshold
Of a church or ministry of holy prayer.
All I've sought is battle till this day.
I am deeply resentful to the one called God,
For he is godfather to all my troubles!
He has raised them up and crushed my happiness.
If only God would ease my suffering
And comfort me as people say he does!
What solid ground would happiness provide
Beneath my toiling steps were it returned:
A salve to soothe the aching of my soul.
If my heart has been wounded in this way,
How can it merge with joy and be made whole
When sorrow ever sets her thorny crown
On glory, won by deeds of arms, in acts
Of chivalry 'gainst formidable foes?
The fault lies at the feet of him who's said
To have all succor in His power then.
If God were truly great and wholly good,
He would by now have eased my wretched soul.
For if he's prompt to help as people say,
He surely has not brought his help to me,
For all the help such people tell of Him!"

The hermit sat in silence for sometime
Till Parzival was driven to suspect

235

His humble host had either lost his wits
Or gone to sleep or was bereft of words
With which to give an answer. "Very well,"
He thought, "'tis no surprise to me this man
Has nothing in reply to say to this."
But all at once, the hermit spoke his mind:
"If you have any sense, then you will trust
In God. He will help you- since He must help.
May God help both of us. Yet kindly sit,
And give me a full account of all your woes.
Come, tell me how it came to pass that God
Became the object of your wrath. Yet first,
With patience, hear while I his innocence
Proclaim. You must with fullest constancy
Hold fast to mighty God unswervingly,
For God himself is perfect constancy.
And known in essence by the name of truth
Has God to falseness ever been a foe.
By nature it is not in God to play
At falsity, deceit, or negligence.
Additionally, nothing can be gained
By rage or hatred from Almighty God.
I urge you to forbear from all loose speech.
Do not be careless with your words or deeds.
Hear what then is reaped by wreaking vengeance
With careless words and wrathful utterance.
One by their own mouth thus condemns themselves,
And by their own tongue cuts from under foot
Their one hope of receiving help from God,
For thoughts without the light of the Creator
Are darkness with no beam by which to see.
Locked up without a key to set them free,
They keep the sun's rays out from inner realms.
But of its nature is the Godhead pure,

For it shines through the wall of darkness.
And when a thought springs from within one's heart,
Before it pass the skin, it will be scanned,
And if it be a pure thought, only then
Does God accept it. And since God scans thoughts
So well, how our frail deeds must surely pain him.
When someone forfeits God's benevolence
In shame and rage, so God must turn away:
To whose care then shall human schooling turn?
Where shall a soul then turn to find refuge?
If you are going to turn and battle God,
Who always stands with love and wrath in hand,
Both at the ready, you're the one who suffers.
Now school your thoughts so that the light of God
Shall soon requite the goodness in your heart."

To this young Parzival then did reply:
"I've spent my youth in care and anxiety
And suffered much travail for loyalty
With hardship as my sole companion
Until this day."

To this then spoke the hermit:
"I would like to hear of your travails
Unless you do not wish to share them, sir."

"My deepest and most difficult distress
Is for the Grail," said noble Parzival.
"Though for my dearest wife and queen, I yearn
Perpetually as well, a ceaseless ache
That torments me continually on my quest."

Perplexedly the holy man replied:

"That you do long for your dear wife is good
And justly as it should be. But you say

That you are searching for the Holy Grail?
No one can win the Grail besides a one
Acknowledged by heaven as destined for it.
This much I have to say about the Grail,
For I know it and have seen it with my eyes."

"Were you there, sir?" said Parzival.
                                    "Indeed,"
Replied the wise and honest Trevrizent.
"It is a fierce and warlike company
That dwell within the walls of Munsalvaesche.
I'll tell you how they take their nourishment.
They live by a stone whose essence is most pure.
If you've not heard of it, I'll name it here;
It's known as Lapsit Exillis.
By virtue of this stone, the Phoenix burns
And from its ashes is reborn again.
Thus does the Phoenix molt its sacred feathers;
When done, it shineth out all dazzling bright
And lovely as before. And furthermore,
However ill a mortal soul may be,
The day on which a person such as this
Has gazed upon the stone, for seven days
They cannot die. Such power does the stone
Confer on mortals that their flesh and bone
To youth is all restored though hair remains
Its aged grey. This stone is called the Grail.
Today a message lights upon the Grail,
Governing its highest properties,
For today is Good Friday when infallibly
A dove from heaven wings its way to earth.
It brings a small white wafer to the stone.
The dove all dazzling white then flies aloft
Back up to heaven. And with every year,

Good Friday brings the dove unto the stone
From which the stone can give all that is good
Of healthy nourishment. Such benefit
The stone bestows upon its brotherhood."

To this the earnest Parzival replied:
"If brave acts win not only fame on earth
But can as well unlock the door to heaven
By fighting to protect the Holy Grail,
Then I must tell you that my one desire
Has been to lead a life of chivalry.
I've fought wherever fighting came my way;
I've never fled from any battleground;
My warlike hand holds glory in its grasp.
If God is any judge of skill and strength,
He will appoint me to that company
So that the brotherhood will know me there:
A warrior who will not desert the field."

"There, you would have to guard against arrogance
By cultivating humbleness of spirit,"
Said steadfast Trevrizent to Parzival.
"You could be misled by youth into breaches
Of self-control, and pride goes before the fall."

The old man's eyes began to fill with tears,
Recalling now the tale he was to tell.
"There is a king, sir, who is known as Anfortas.
This king is lord protector of the Grail,
And as it happens, he is also kin-
In that he is my brother. But the pain
And agony with which his punishment
Was reaped upon him for his youthful pride
Should move us both to never-ending pity.

His youth, wealth, and pursuit of his own goals,
Outside those ordained by the sacred Grail,
Pursuing love not written on the stone,
Brought harm through his actions into the world.
Such ways are not permitted by the Grail.
All knights and squires of that company
Must guard 'gainst self-gain, pride, and indulgence.
This purity the brotherhood protects.
By force of arms, they hold off every foe
From coming uninvited to the Grail.
And thus, its miracles are only seen
By those who have been summoned to the castle
To join the holy company of the Grail.
And only one e'er came to Munsalvaesche
Without first being by the Grail assigned.
He had not reached years of maturity!
He rode thence saddled by his own misdeed
In that he said no word to his kindly host
About the sorrowful plight he found him in.
It is not mine to lay blame on anyone,
But he'll be bound to pay for his misdeed,
For Anfortas bore a load of suffering,
The like of which has never yet been seen.
Before this man had come to Munsalvaesche,
One of the Templars of the Holy Grail
Had ridden out to face King Lahelin,
For Lahelin had challenged him to joust.
And there the Templar met his early death.
King Lahelin led the Templar's horse away.
When you arrived sir, I observed your horse.
It is marked with the Grail insignia.
The turtle dove is branded on its forearm.
Good sir, are you Lahelin? Or have you slain
King Lahelin and thus obtained his steed?

For in my makeshift stable stands the horse
Whose mantle also bears the Grail's emblem.
The horse doth plainly come from Munsalvaesche,
Because the saddle shows the turtledove,
An emblem which the kind Anfortas gave
For horses when his happiness still lived.
Their shields have alway borne the same device.
'Twas passed down from our grandfather, Titurel,
Whose son, our father, was King Frimutel.
King Frimutel was wearing that device
The day he lost his life in a great joust.
No one has loved their spouse as much as he;
I mean with such undying devotion.
You should renew his ways and love your spouse
With all your heart. Follow his example-
You bear a strange resemblance to him.
He was Lord of the Grail while he yet lived.
Ah, sir, where have you journeyed from?
Please kindly say from whom you are descended."

They each then looked into the other's eyes.

And Parzival replied to his kind host:
"Sir, I am the son of Gahmuret
Who ere my mother bore me met his death
Impelled by knightly ardor in a joust.
I am not Lahelin, nor have I slain him.
The only corpse that I have ever stripped
Was pilfered by me in dull ignorance.
Guilty am I of this shameful crime,
For I slew Ither, King of Cumberland.
My sinful hands stretched him dead on the grass
And took from him all that there was to take."

241

"Alas, dark wicked world, why are you so?"
Replied the hermit, saddened by this news.
"Instead of joy you've brought me only pain!
So this is the reward you offer now?
Such is the doleful end of your sad song?
It is your own flesh and blood that you've slain!
How will you honor Ither of Cumberland?
He bore the fruits of true nobility.
How will you make amends for slaying him?
May God have pity on you for this act!
And add to that, my sister Herzeloyde,
Your mother died from grief on your account
In great distress and sorrowful agony!"

"What's this that you are saying to me now?
Cried noble Parzival. "Oh no my lord!
This direful news doth strike into my heart
 And cleaves it down unto its very root.
Alack the day that I was ever born
To live to be the cursed wretch that I am.
If this is true, were I lord of the Grail,
It would not give me any consolation.
Do as good people do and truthfully
Recount it plainly- deal justly with me sir:
Are these things true that you have said to me?
Are you my uncle? Is my mother dead?"

"It is not in me to deceive you nephew,"
Replied good Trevrizent to Parzival.

"As soon as you had left your mother's side,
She fell, struck by the weight of all her woe,
And there upon that ground, she breathed her last.
You were the beast she suckled, the dragon

242

That flew away from her. It came to her
Once as she slept, before you were yet born.
I have a brother and a sister living.
My sister Schoysiane bore a child
And died while she was bearing that sweet babe.
Her little daughter was known as Sigune,
Who was entrusted to your mother's care.
One of my sisters lives and is unwed.
She is Repanse de Schoye, Queen of the Grail,
And is the most powerful priestess of its order,
For she has trained herself to serve its cause.
Only those who've purified themselves
Have strength enough to lift the sacred stone.
 Our brother is Anfortas of the Grail,
The lord protector of its company.
Alas, that joy is so far from reach.
These things all came to pass in such a way
That one must marvel at the strange events.
I'll tell you, nephew, of these wondrous things.
Your kind heart will be moved to pity him.

The day my father died, my brother Anfortas
Was summoned to be the keeper of the Grail.
Now at that time, we were both still quite small.
But when my brother reached the tender age
That brought the first few bristles to his chin,
He was assailed by love as is love's way
With striplings when youth blossoms and comes of age.
But any keeper of the Holy Grail,
Any Templar warrior who serves its name,
Or any squire who accompanies
One of these Templar knights amid the fray-
Anointed with its power and endowed
With a godlike strength far past the average

Of human limitation- at its feet,
Must lay their talents, gifts, and all their aims.
Ambition to its cause must be surrendered.
And unknown to the world in earthly ways,
This warlike host must tread invisibly
With only its endeavor to defend:
To bring its light through all its messengers
To things devoid of spirit and redeem
The matter laden and self-serving world.
And any lord protector of the Grail,
Who uses this heavenly force in any way
For other things or follows their own goals
While bearing its bright light, will have to pay
Inevitably with great pain and loss.
As his endeavor, Anfortas chose a lady
Whom he judged to be of a noble line
Though not within the ordinance of the Grail.
He strove to build his title for her love,
Attaining her affection with his prowess
With shield and sword upon the battlefield.
He served her boldly with unflinching courage,
And many shields were riddled by his hand.
As errant knight, the youth won such renown,
It ran no risk of ever being rivaled.
Amid the clash, his battle cry rang out: "Amour!"
But the power of that shout was not quite right
In its alignment with humility.

One day adventure urged him out alone
Drawn by his fervor toward a wretched fate.
While jousting, he was wounded by a lance
That had been infused with lethal poison.
The man who fought him there and rode that joust
Was raised on greed and fostered with ambition

And taught to bend the world to his own aims.
This villain gave no thought to godliness
Or love of fellow siblings of the earth.
He only thought of how to reach his goal.
He was convinced he'd win the Grail by force.
He sought out many chivalric encounters
In distant countries, crossing land and sea
With one thought in his mind: to win the Grail.
His prowess robbed us of our happiness.
Anfortas though must be commended too.
He'd slain that villain there upon the field
But carried off the lance head in his body.

When the king returned to us so pale
And drained of all his wholesomeness and strength,
A physician probed the wound to find the lance head.
I fell upon my knees and vowed to God
That I would practice chivalry no more
In hopes he'd help my brother in his need.
I also swore to give up meat and bread
And wine- to never relish anything
Possessing blood or flesh of any kind.
We carried him before the potent Grail
In hopes of any aid that it might give.
But seeing it came as a second wound
In that its power would not let him die.
Nor was it right for his young life to end
Since I had chosen this life of sacrifice,
And our bright lineage had been reduced
Down to a vestige of its former strength.

The sorrowful king's wound began to fester.
All the various books of medicine
That we consulted failed to furnish us

With any remedy to heal the wound.
All the wide array of antidotes:
Vicious serpents that carry their venom hot
And other poisonous reptiles we found,
All that the doctors by the art of physic
Suggested to us were of no avail.

At last, we fell to our knees before the Grail
Where suddenly we saw its prophecy:
A knight would come to us before too long
And were he heard to ask a certain question,
Our sorrows would be at an end forever.
But if someone were to alert the knight
Of the question, it would fail in its effects;
The injury would stay as it had been
And give rise to an even deeper pain.
'Now understand,' the writing testified,
'If on the first night he omits the question,
Its power will pass into nothingness.
But if he asks the question in its season,
The kingdom shall be rendered unto him,
And by God's will, the sorrow shall be over.
Anfortas will be healed but king no more.'
We anointed his wound with whatever we could find
To soothe it, but his pain gave him no peace.
He took to fishing on a nearby lake,
Because the fresh air eased his suffering.
It cooled the fever from the burning wound
And gave some respite from its foul odor.

I then withdrew to this place, and scant joy
Is all these passing years have offered me.
Since then, a knight has ridden to that place.
But it would have been much better had he not.

That was the knight I told you of before.
The only thing he took from there was shame,
For he beheld the marks of suffering
But failed to ask his host any question.
Since youthful inexperience ordained
That he did not inquire about his host,
He missed a golden opportunity."

"My dearest uncle," said good Parzival,
"If shame would let me now reveal it here,
I'd tell you a misfortune that befell.
Alas! I beg of you your courtesy
And pardon for the misdeeds I have lived.
I fear from sorrow I shall ne'er be freed.
I beg you now, deplore my youthful folly
But give me loyal aid. The one who rode
To Munsalvaesche and saw the marks of woe
And who did nonetheless not ask a question
Was I, unhappy wretch. Such was my error."

"What are you saying?" replied the holy man.
"Your five God-given senses cut off their aid
From you. How cold and unfeelingly you blocked
Compassion from your heart when it was faced
With the kind Anfortas in his agony!
Yet I will not deny you my advice.
Sometimes one's youth can hinder wisdom's light.
And on the other hand, if age persists
In folly, you could say that purity
Has then been sullied, and the youthful green
Has wilted that would bear you noble fruit.
Could I restore your youth and nerve your heart
So that you would once more attain great honor
And not despair of God, then your achievement,

So glorious, would rate as full amends,
Redeemed, fulfilled, complete and heaven blessed.
But God himself will not abandon you,
And I now council you in His good name.
Give me your sins; your penitence I'll vouch
Before Almighty God. Then do his will
As I shall now instruct you, and let nothing
Hereafter daunt you in this worthy task."

There Parzival stayed with the holy man
A fortnight's interim while his kind host
Looked after him and helped him face these things-
The errors of his past. They slept upon
The cold hard ground and ate the roots and herbs
They foraged from the forest floor. But moved
By the loyal love he felt for his new friend,
Good Parzival did shrewdly there observe
That he slept better on the cold hard ground
Than anywhere before- though there, at times,
Had in his past, been spread before his whim,
All delicacies that a soul could crave.
This new contentment settled in his heart,
Rejuvenating and restoring strength
To set off on his journey once again.

Through their discourse which spanned across the days,
Much was revealed between them. Mysteries
Of their shared lineage uncannily
Now drawn together by the strings of fate.

When two weeks reached their end, he then took leave
Of Trevrizent his uncle and set his course
Toward new horizons of untold portend.
His sorrow's tribulation he had faced

In reckonings that inwardly bore shifts
To liberate his heart from error's burden.
The future held out open hands, the which
He felt without ambition as he placed
All outcomes, all woes, all hopes, and all his strength
In the hands of his Creator, turning his heart
Toward serving that benevolence in the world.

ORGELUSE

Twelve cycles of the night sky's pearly sphere
Had wound themselves once 'round the turning seasons:
Once had the royal sun bestowed his bounty,
And once the brimming harvest had been stashed.
One time beneath her snowy blanket slept
The good earth and now stirred she in her rest
And shifted in her slumber as the spring,
Like morning's gentle summons, called her softly,
Though buds had not burst fully into bloom-
Ere steadfastly Gawain had made his way
To where our tale rejoins him on his quest.
Behold him now before you in your mind.
Draw slowly from the broad expanse of space
In toward his distant image, once a spec
Now growing by degrees in your mind's eye
Out from the landscape. See him moving.
Fly on the bird's wing from afar, in close
Swoop down, and see the saddle buckle's grip
Around the horse's girth; see mane and bit[27].
Watch as the strength of the intelligent beast
Works with nobility to conquer distance.
Behold the hooves of mighty Gringuljete
As they churn up the earth beneath Gawain.
And there he sits- the graceful warrior
Astride his steed. They're heading toward adventure.
They move and think in motion like one mind
With two aspects: the master and his horse.
The day on which we now encounter him
Finds him as he rides on a level plain.

---

27 The piece of metal which rests in the horse's mouth that the
reins are fastened to.

A tree stood at the far end of the field,
And there, he came upon a lady's palfrey.
Upon the tree he saw a battered shield
Through which a lance had punched an opening.

"I wonder," thought Gawain, "who I shall meet
Upon the other side of this great tree?
It seems I've stumbled on the resting place
Of a great and fearsome warrior princess.
Though guessing by the damage of her shield,
She has been recently engaged with battling.
I hope I will not find her badly wounded!
If she be friend or foe or needing aid,
I am prepared to fight, help, or console."

The mighty tree had such a stalky trunk
That he had to ride all the way around
Before he came upon the palfrey's master.
And there she sat, abandoned to her grief,
For joy and happiness had left her there,
And lying on the ground in front of her,
A knight, her love, lay wounded mortally.

"Dear madam," said Gawain gently to her,
"I'm sorry to find you in this sorrowful state.
Forgive my asking what I now must ask
While you are in the throes of heavy grief.
I would not dream of interposing here
Except that there may be a way to help.
May I inquire if this man yet lives,
Or has he now departed from this world?"

"He lives," replied the maiden in her grief,
"But he will not live for much longer now.
He was pierced by the cruel thrust of a lance,

251

And now he'll bleed to death internally.
Oh, tell me sir, what can be done for him!
I guess by your comportment and your voice
That you have seen more suffering than I.
Please give me any guidance you may have."

"I will do what I can," replied Gawain.
"I've seen wounds of this nature ere this day,
And if I had a tube to give to you,
We could now undertake to save his life.
If only I had something of this sort."
He quickly took a branch from off the tree
And peeled the bark to fashion her a tube.

When it was ready, he then said to her:
"Fear not, his wound is not a fatal one.
The blood is simply pressing on his heart."
He then instructed her to use the tube
To siphon from the wound the excess blood
Which then relieved pressure on the heart.
Her wounded love then soon regained his senses
And was revived so that his speech returned.
He saw the warrior and spoke to him:
"My thanks to you, kind sir, for lending aid.
I think I may have passed forth from this world
Had you not stopped and given us your help.
Have you come in pursuit of chivalry
Unto the mighty kingdom of Logroys?"

"I have indeed," replied gentle Gawain,
"Though I was not sure of my whereabouts
Until I heard you mention them just now."

"I too came hither searching for adventure,"
Replied the wounded knight, "though I regret

That I dared come so near this kingdom's borders.
If you have common sense, you'll now depart
Before you meet a fate akin to mine.
I never dreamt that it would come to this.
A knight known as Lischois has wounded me.
He cast me ruthlessly down to the earth:
A joust that went clean through my sturdy shield
And through my body. This kind lady here
Then placed me on her palfrey from the field
And brought me hither to this resting place.
Pray won't you tarry with us for a while?
Beseech you sir, stay for our company."

"Were I to stay, who would avenge you sir?"
Replied Gawain, determined to depart.
"I must go find the one who laid you low
And offer him the answer he deserves."

"Do nothing of the sort-" replied the man,
"It is no child's outing that you'll find
By riding off in that direction sir."

Gawain bound the knight's wound with a scarf-
The maiden lent her garment to this end-
And prayed for both the wounded and his love
Then set off following the bloody trail
Which in retreat they'd followed to that place.
Not far along the path he saw Logroys.
'Twas not for nothing that realm was well praised!
It was magnificently placed into the land
With a splendid fortress, elegant and strong,
Whose rampart wound around a mountainside,
Ascending in a spiral toward the top
Where sat the mighty structure like a crown,
Perched high upon its lofty earthen dome.

Gawain had journeyed almost all the way
Up to the castle on this winding path
When his eyes came to rest upon a sight
Which brought him both joy and the pang of heartache.

Forth from a rock there flowed a little spring,
And by the spring, there stood a striking lady.
Her beauty shone forth with a radiance
And power like a bright ray of the sun.
She was the noble duchess of Logroys,
And many folks were smitten with the strength
And the power of her presence and her beauty.

"If I may dismount by your leave, madam,
And if you'll have me in your company,
My sorrows will be transformed into joy.
No knight will ever have been happier
Than I if you will have me in your presence."

"What of it?" said the lady to Gawain.
"This is not news to me. Don't lavish me
With praises, or you may yet reap disgrace.
I don't wish to hear all your platitudes.
If I accepted praise from everyone
Without discernment or integrity,
How would I know truehearted declarations
From feigned devotion, cunning, and deceit?
I must guard 'gainst praise so that only one
Who is most trusted will have my acceptance.
I don't have any idea who you are.
It's time you left me though you'll not escape
My judgement sir: you are near to my heart,
But you are on the outside- not in!
Many people open up their eyes

So wildy to see what wounds their heart
And gape so unabashed at their desire
That they might just as well hurl both their eyes
Forth from a slingshot straight at what they see!
Now trundle your unwanted platitudes
And your wretched desire somewhere else-
At someone else's love other than mine.
If you sir are a man who sues for love,
If thirst for quest has brought you hitherward
In search of deeds of arms and chivalry
To win a lady's favor, no reward
Will you receive from me sir, I assure you.
You will only achieve dishonor here
If I tell you the truth, fool that you are."

"Madam," replied Gawain, "you speak the truth.
My eyes indeed have put my heart at risk,
For now that they have come to rest on you,
I must declare myself your prisoner!
Please treat me gently, for I'm smitten with you.
However much it irks you, I am locked
Within your heart! So loosen or bind me there.
You'll find my mind is set on our union
To such degree that if even a chance
Of this outcome were possible, my yearning
Will never lose sight of that happy hope."

"I do not recommend you serving me,"
Replied the stoic maiden to her suitor,
"For if you wish to gain reward by this,
Your efforts will lead only to disgrace;
But since I see your mind will not be changed,
I order you to take me with you now.
I'd like to see if you will fight for me,

255

Though if you care for honor, you'll refrain.
Depart now while you still can with your life,
For at a certain point you'll wish you had,
And then, there will be no more turning back.
So seek another's love now if you're wise,
Or be a fool and take me with you sir.
But if you take me with you, be assured
Great trouble will be your companion later."

"How would I be entitled to your love
If I had never proven my devotion,"
Unwaveringly answered Sir Gawain.
"Wert thou to take me now without a test,
I would not be deserving of your love.
When one longs keenly as I do for love,
They must prepare themselves to serve it first
Ere they expect their love to be requited."

"If you insist on serving me," she said,
"Be ready for a life of battling.
And for this, you will only reap dishonor.
I do not need the service of a coward.
Go follow yonder path across the bridge:
That path will lead you to an orchard lawn.
You'll find my tethered palfrey waiting there
Among a merry throng of revelers.
They will be singing and playing their lutes,
And they will try to steer you from your course.
Pay them no heed, but untether my horse.
Once she's untied, the mare will follow you,
Then lead her here to me where I will wait."

Gawain leapt down from trusty Gringuljete
And looked for somewhere to secure the steed,

But nowhere could he find to tie the reins.
He contemplated asking if the lady
Would hold his horse while he performed her bidding
But wondered if it would be unseemly
For him to ask for her assistance thus.

"I know what's troubling you," the lady said.
"Give me your horse. I'll hold him while you're gone.
This favor though, will do you little good."

"My thanks to you, my lady," said Gawain
And reached to hand the reins to her.
                                        "I see,"
The lady said, "you are indeed a fool,
For you expect me to clasp what you've touched."

"I never lay hold of the lower part,"
Replied Gawain. She took hold of the reins
Below the place where Sir Gawain had touched.

"Make haste," she said, "and bring my mare to me.
As for our traveling in company,
Your wish is granted, you may ride with me."

This was a happy outcome for Gawain.
He left her and made haste across the bridge
Into the orchard filled with revelers.
When they beheld the noble Sir Gawain,
They were dismayed that such a worthy soul
Should be subjected to their lady's ways.
Many noble knights came up to him
And made him welcome with heartfelt embraces.

"Alas," they said, "our lady lures you sir
Into great peril, which cannot end well.

It's a sorry sight to see so fine a knight,
Consenting to her cruel and thoughtless bidding."

Gawain paid them no heed as she had asked
And found her palfrey tethered to a tree.
Beside the palfrey stood a grey-haired knight
Whose long beard had been braided carefully.
He met Gawain with kindness and distress
And was greatly perturbed on his behalf.

"If you are open to suggestions sir,
You'll leave this palfrey and depart from here.
No one will stand between you and the mare,
But if you've always done what's good for you,
You'll choose what's best and leave this horse alone.
A curse upon my lady for her malice!
So many fine knights have died for her cause."

"Kind sir," replied Gawian, "mourn not for me.
Were I to die while serving your good duchess,
I would consider it a happy death
Since living somewhere else away from her
Would be a sad life I'd not wish to live.
If danger waits upon my path ahead,
Why should I fly from what God has ordained?
I am not wiser than my Creator-
The outcome of my life is in His hands.
I'll ride the path he has provided me,
For fleeing danger is no way to live,
And life is made most poignant when it's taken
In all its fullness without cowardice."

"Then woe to what will follow," said the knight
And untethered the palfrey for Gawain.
Gawain then said farewell to those nearby

And walked forth from the orchard toward the bridge.
The palfrey followed though she was not led
Upon the narrow path across the bridge
Until they came to where the lady stood
With Gringuljete, awaiting their approach.

Gawain once more was smitten with her beauty
As he walked towards her, for her radiance
Seemed ever new to his fresh adoration.

"Welcome back, you goose!" the lady said.
"If you are still determined to serve me,
Then you will surely prove yourself a fool,
For you will be the master of your folly!
What great cause you have now to not do so!"

"Though you are angry with me now," he said,
"I trust in time you will join me in love.
Meanwhile, I will render you my service
Until you feel inclined to honor me.
But first shall I now help you to your horse?"

"I have not asked you to," the lady said.
"Let your untested hand do no such thing!"

She then leapt with both mastery and strength
From where she stood amid the fresh spring flowers
Onto her palfrey's back. "How pitiful
It would be to lose so esteemable [28]
A companion. Now may God lay you low!"

This powerful duchess, known as Orgeluse,
Was in no way a generous companion.

---

28   Worthy of admiration.

She ordered Sir Gawain to ride in front,
And when he did as she had bidden him,
She rode hard on the heels of Gringuljete
Which forced Gawain to keep his lady's pace
In order to stay out in front of her.
And if he slackened, she would urge him on.
Now as they made their way across a field,
Gawain there spied an herb which he knew well
To be a remedy for curing wounds.
The nobleman swerved therefore from the path
And dropped down from his steed to harvest it.
This done, he mounted Gringuljete once more
And rejoined Orgeluse upon the trail.

"I see my new companion is adept
In medicine as well as chivalry.
If you can hawk pills and sell boxes sir
As well as pluck roots out of the earth,
You'll make a good wage with your haggling."

"As I rode toward your castle," said Gawain,
"I passed a wounded knight beneath a tree.
If we ride by that tree and find him there,
This herb will heal him and restore his strength."

"Well that sounds entertaining," said the duchess.
"Perhaps I too will learn of medicine
And hawk my craft as my companion does."

Just then, a squire made his way to them.
He came to give a message to his lady.
Gawain now stopped to wait for his approach,
And as he did so, he was struck with awe
At the appearance of the lady's squire,
For he was truly monstrous to behold.

His name was Malcreatiure. He was the brother
Of Cundrie La Surziere the sorceress
And was the spit of her in most regards.
Like hers, two boar's fangs jutted from his jaws,
But unlike Cundrie whose hair dangled long,
His hair was short and sharp as a hedgehog's coat.
He rode a wretched nag that limped and lurched
Beneath its master's weight. From time to time,
It lost its footing so entirely
As it came onward stumbling over stones
That its weak knees would buckle to the ground
And lurch back up to hobble toward Gawain.
The squire did not wait to greet Gawain
As he approached but started shouting at him
Before he'd made his way up to his guest.

"Sir!" he shouted rudely at Gawain,
"You strike me as a fool, trying to woo
And serve my lady in this fashion!
If you by some strange chance were to survive
The fierce correction that awaits you now,
Your glory then would be unparalleled;
But if you are an average knight at arms,
Your punishment will be so unforgiving
That you will wish you'd chosen otherwise.
You will be beaten till your hide is tanned,
And you will beg for mercy ere the end!"

"Never in my days have I endured
Such blatant rudeness and indecency,"
Replied Gawain to this unruly greeting.
"It is not I who should receive these threats
Or fear the dangers held in store for me.
It's those who've joined the throng of recreants

Who live by trickery and laziness.
They are deserving of your ill-placed words
And punishment by law of destiny.
Until now I've lived free of such corrections;
However, if you and your lady here
Should wish to persist in your mockery,
You are the one who will enjoy the taste
Of what you'll soon refer to as my wrath,
Once you've become acquainted with it sir.
However frightful your appearance is,
It will not stop me from ending your threats!"

Gawain then seized the squire by the hair
And hurled him from his nag onto the ground.
There, on his back, the squire timidly
Looked up toward the wrathful Sir Gawain.
His hedgehog bristles had avenged him though,
For they had cut Gawain's hand till it bled.
So deeply they had pierced the brave knight's flesh
That blood was running very visibly.
The lady laughed to see this wretched sight.

"I love to see you quarreling!" she said.

They set out with the squire and his nag,
Hobbling and stumbling beside them
Until they came upon the wounded knight.
Gawain then loyally bound up the wound,
Administering the herb as he did so.

"How have you fared since you rode hence from me?"
The wounded knight inquired of Gawain,
"I see you've brought the lady who is bent
On harming you. It is her doing sir
That I have come so close to meeting death,

262

For she involved me in a deadly joust
Which put my life and property at risk.
If you desire to maintain your life,
Let this deceitful woman ride away
And henceforth have no more to do with her.
Judge from my state where her advice will lead!
If I could find a place where I could rest,
I think I will recover fully there.
Will you please help me to that end good sir?"

"Ask any help you wish for, it is granted,"
Replied the bold and courteous Gawain.

"Not far from here, there is a sanctuary,"
The wounded knight appealed to Sir Gawain.
"If I were there, I could rest for a while.
We have my dear companion's sturdy mount.
Please help her up, and place me at her back."

The noble warrior untied the mare
From where she'd left it tethered to a branch.
As he was in the act of leading her,
The wounded knight abruptly yelled- "Keep back!
Why are you in such haste to trample me?"

At this, Gawain politely turned his steps
And led the horse around the other way.
And at a slight hint from the wounded man,
The lady followed Gawain around the tree
Unassumingly and at a gentle pace.
Gawain then hoisted her onto her steed.
At that instant, the wounded man leapt up
And vaulted onto mighty Gringuljete.
Then off the injured knight rode with his lady
Before Gawain had time to intervene.

Again the duchess laughed at this afront:
"I took you for a knight!" she taunted him,
"Soon after that, you turned into a surgeon,
And now you are demoted to a footman!
If anyone can make a thrifty wage,
You certainly can trust your tradesman's wits!
Foolish man, do you still seek my love?"

"I do my lady," answered Lord Gawain.
"Your love to me would be the dearest thing
That I could ever dream of honoring.
There is no one upon this earth I'd take
Instead of you. Were I offered the wealth
Of seven kingdoms and the love of all
Who dwelt within them in contest with you,
I'd leave them to their riches and choose you.
Your love is what I seek and your love only.
If I cannot attain it, may I die
A bitter death in the fruitless attempt.
Now whether you call me a squire, knight,
A peasant, or a footman, the insults
And mockeries that you inflict on me
Will harm you more than they have wounded me;
The errors in your words will stick to you.
Though they have not vexed me, they lower you."

The wounded man returned on Gringujlete.

"Are you Gawain?" he asked the warrior,
"If so, you have been paid back now in full!
Remember when you overpowered me
And took me prisoner in single combat
And brought me to your Uncle Arthur's court?
He saw to it that I ate from a trough
With dogs for an entire month on end!"

"Are you Ujurns?" Gawain replied unmoved.
"I don't deserve the harm you wish me now,
For I won you the pardon of the king.
They were ignoble thoughts you acted on
For which you were excluded from the fold
Of chivalry and there declared an outlaw.
You violated a defenseless maid
And took your pleasure at honor's expense.
King Arthur would have punished you with death
Had I not said a word on your behalf."

"Whatever happened there, you are here now,"
Replied Ujurns. "Have you not heard the saying
That if a person saves another's life,
The one they saved will be their enemy?
I've acted as one with their wits about them,
And for that, I have won a goodly steed."

He dug his spurs into the horse's flanks
And once more rode away on Gringuljete.
Consumed with anger and robbed of his steed,
Gawain was forced to watch his foe depart.

"His vengeance will be thwarted," said the duchess.
"It is unlikely that you'll win my love,
But he'll be so rewarded for his deeds
That he will be ashamed he kept his life
When he left Arthur's court to make his way
Into the jurisdiction of my lands.
He will be brought down for the lady's sake,
Not yours. Gross misdemeanors should be punished."

Gawain went over to Malcreatiure's nag.
The lady told the squire in his tongue
All that she wanted done up at the castle,
And he departed to enact her bidding.

Gawain inspected his new ragged steed,
And he surmised it was not fit for fighting.

The duchess spoke, "Tell me you'll not ride on."

"I will do," said Gawain, "what you desire."

"You'll wait a long time to discover that!"
Replied the lady.

        "Until doomsday then,"
Gawain steadfastly answered, "I will wait."

"I think you are a fool for doing that,"
She said. "Unless you give it up and leave,
You will be turned forever to a mope
And will need to avoid all jolly folk,
For you will always have fresh tribulations."

"I am content with serving you madam,"
He answered, "whether I have joy or grief,
For my love told me I should wait for you."

He turned once more to find his wretched steed.
It was indeed a very sorry sight.
Its stirrups were made of the poorest bast;
He feared they would not hold up in a joust.
In all his days, Gawain had never seen
A poorer saddle laid upon a horse.
He did not mount for fear of tearing it.
The horse's back was sagged and hollowed out.
Were he to leap on it, it might cave in.
Gawain in times past may have balked at this
Procedure, but he now set forth on foot
And led the horse while carrying his lance.
Proud Orgeluse laughed heartily at this:

"Have you brought merchandise to sell here sir?
Whom shall I thank for sending unto me
A doctor and a marketeer in one?
Be mindful of my tax collectors sir,
For they may strip your good humor from you!"

He found her jibing so acceptable
That he did not mind anything she said.
Discomfort vanished when he looked at her.
To him, she was the fresh bloom of the spring
That in his eyes was placed with all things bright.
She brought such sweetness to his happy gaze
And pangs of longing to his aching heart.

At length the duchess and the warrior
Came to a forest through which they progressed.
Gawain then led his steed up to a stump.
He took his shield which he'd placed on the horse
And slung it round his neck then used the stump
To gently climb onto the horse's back.
The nag could barely haul him from the wood
Out to the ploughlands. There he saw a castle
The like of which he'd never seen before.
Its whole circumference was magnificent
With lofty turrets, elegant archways,
And pinnacles that seemed to pierce the sky.
He also noticed many noble ladies,
Seen through the windows of the mighty palace.
There were at least four hundred at a glance.
The castle's causeway reached down to a river
Whose current, though fast, was navigable.
Upon the far side from the castle's causeway,
A landing for a ferry could be seen.
To reach the fort the duchess and Gawain

Would have to cross the river swift and wide.
The two made their way toward the ferry quay.
 Beside the landing spread a jousting field
Over which the mighty fortress loomed,
And there, Gawain beheld a warrior
Who was not one to hold back from a fight.

"I've told you many times of the disgrace
That you would reap here in my servitude,"
The haughty duchess chastised brave Gawain.
"Defend yourself as best you can, you fool.
You've come here now, and nothing will aid you.
This knight here will most surely throw you down.
And if your breeches get torn in the tussle,
The ladies in the castle over yonder
Will be your witnesses. They'll see the shame
Of your disgrace and pitiful downfall.
Imagine that while you ride to your doom,
You goose. Make ready to taste your defeat!"

The master of the ferry crossed the water
At the command of mighty Orgeluse,
And much to the bereavement of Gawain,
She went aboard and hurled one last assault:
"You will not be joining me on board!
You stay there as a sacrifice to fortune!"

"Why are you in such haste to leave me here?"
 Gawain called back to her despondently.
"Is this the last that I shall see of you?"

"The honor of you seeing me again
 May yet befall you, but it won't be soon!"
Such were the lady's parting words to him.

And now, Lischois Gwelijus galloped on
Toward the stalwart warrior Gawain.
To say he flew would be impossible,
But short of that he moved at such a pace,
One could imagine he might leave the ground.
This was a testament to his great steed!

"How shall I meet this charge," thought brave Gawain,
"Would it be more advisable on foot
Or on the back of this weak, wretched nag?
If he plans to attack me at full tilt,
Not reining in his charge, he'll ride me down.
His steed will have to stumble o'er my nag,
And he will then be flung out of his seat.
I'll meet him then on foot, once he is down."

Gawain prepared himself to face the joust
As his opponent thundered on toward him.
He urged the wretched nag straight at his foe
As best he could and leveled his stout lance.
Both thrusts were aimed with expertise and strength
So that both spears were shattered in the joust,
And both knights were laid out upon the ground.
Just as he'd planned, Gawain's foe had been flung
Out of his saddle as his mighty horse
Was tripped off balance by the wretched nag.
They both leapt up from where they lay stretched out
Amid the meadow's early springtime flowers,
Drew forth their swords, both set on battling,
And set to work with mighty thrusts and blows.
Their shields were hacked and battered down to blocks
In very little time as those two fought,
And sparks flew from their helms and flashing blades.
They answered blow for blow for such a span

Of time that were they two smiths they'd have tired.
Gawain had learned the skill of wrestling.
He knew the way to get beneath the sword
Of his foes, grab a hold, and hurl them down.
So when he'd worn down his opponent's strength
With masterful sword work, he ducked beneath
The great sweep of a wide blow from his foe,
Caught brave Lischios around his armored waist,
Then hurled him to the earth and pinned him there.

"You must surrender to me now," said Arthur's nephew.

Lischios, now lying pinned beneath Gawain,
Was unaccustomed to surrendering.
It seemed so strange to him that anyone
Could have the strength to wrestle forth from him
What had not been exacted from him yet:
An oath exhorted in his own defeat.
He in the past had been the one to claim
A great many victories over his foes.
He was not now inclined to trade them in,
And so, he offered up his life instead.
"Does victory rest with you now?" he said.
"She was mine for as long as God had willed,
And I was given all the glory from her.
Now let your noble hand make a swift end.
When knights and ladies learn of my defeat
It would be better if they also hear
Of my swift death upon my vanquishment!"

Gawain again demanded his surrender,
But Lischios' only wish was now to die.
"Why should I kill this worthy knight?"
Gawain inquired inwardly. "Would he

Now follow reason and obey my word,
I'd let him go without inflicting harm."

He tried again but still to no avail.
Gawain then let the warrior arise
Without giving his pledge of surrender.
And now, each of them sat amid the flowers.

It then dawned on Gawain, who'd not forgotten
His plight of having such a wretched nag,
That he should mount the steed of his opponent
And set spurs to the mighty charger's flanks.
The horse was well caparisoned for war.
It had a coat of mail and plates of steel
O'er which was draped a samite covering.
As he ran toward the beautiful warhorse,
It turned to him and whinnied in a way
Which sounded so familiar to Gawain
That his heart leapt for joy within his breast,
And with a burst, he vaulted to its back.
The graceful steed leapt forward powerfully
At feeling his master in his rightful seat.
Gawain's soul filled to the brim with happiness
As the beast's long leaps began to gather pace.

"Can it be you, dear Gringuljete my friend?
Have we two been united once again?"
Delightfully Gawain cried to his steed.
The beast gave answer with his mighty hooves
That rumbled on the ground like steady thunder
And tossed his graceful mane as if to say
"You are the master I serve willingly."

"Perfidious Urjans stole you from me,
Yet now by God's grace, I find you again!"

Gawain continued, still in disbelief.
"But who has decked you out so splendidly?
If it is really you, God, who is known
To be the the one to bring an end to grief,
Has sent you back to me most graciously!"

The good Gawain who'd been close to despair
Now felt his spirits rising up once more
At finding steadfast Gringuljete again.
He was still pained by thoughts of Orgeluse
Who had heaped so much sorrow on his heart,
But Gringuljete brought wind back to his sails
And placed his watchful mind back in its seat.
Meanwhile, proud Lischios leapt up and dashed
To where his sword was lying in the grass,
Torn from his grip by dauntless Sir Gawain.
Their shields had both been whittled to their grips,
So both knights left them lying where they were
And made toward each other, once again-
Determined to give fierce proof of their worth.
Each was of such a noble lineage
That neither was content to take defeat.
Their armor, swords, and helms were now their shields
To ward off death since both shields were now spent,
All which received the brunt of this fierce clash.
They fought with such strength, skill, and abandon
That anyone who watched this reckoning
Would have been both afraid and struck with awe
By the deadly beauty of this deft encounter.
Such mastery with the sword had ne'er been seen.
Lischios now wary of Gawain's swift strength and skill,
Time and again leapt back from his advances
And then again pressed in upon his foe
With battering blows in quick succession.

Gawain turned every stroke from his opponent
And answered with unflinching mastery.
Had anyone e'er doubted who he was
And seen him there, they'd know he was indeed
King Arthur's kin and from that glorious
And mighty company, the Round Table.
From time to time between their blows were seen
Bright flashes of fire and then again
Swords raised upwards on high by valiant hands.
Though Lischios dodged, Gawain pressed doggedly
And strove to close the distance from his foe.
They ducked and turned with deft maneuvering,
Attacking from the side and from the back
Then lunging forward, and wheeling round the other
As though they stepped the paces of a dance-
A graced and deadly choreography.
At last, once more Gawian ducked through the blows
As though he saw a path between the blades
And seized Lischios, now gripped in his embrace.
With great strength, he then hurled his foe beneath
And once again pinned Lischios to the ground.
Once more Gawain demanded his surrender,
But Lischios was unwilling as before.

"You waste your time with seeking my surrender!"
The sad and twice defeated Lischios cried.
"Rather than surrender, take my life!
Now let your noble hand make a swift end
To all the fame and glory that I've known.
I am now cursed before the eyes of God
Who has thus vanquished me of happiness.
It was for love of mighty Orgeluse
That many knights have had to yield to me.
By slaying me, you will attain the glory

That I have won from all those worthy knights."

"Now truly," thought Gawain, "I'll not do so,
For were I to slay such a valiant knight,
God and the world would cease to smile down.
It was his love for mighty Orgeluse,
The same that has been fired in my heart,
Which drove him to attack me in this way.
Why should I not let him live for her sake?
If she is destined to return my love,
He will be powerless to change what fate
Will then have given to my happiness.
If she had been here and witnessed our fight,
I am quite certain she would have to give
Her credit to me for earning her love.

"For the sake of Orgeluse, I'll spare your life,"
Steadfast Gawain declared to bold Lischios.
The two now were aware of their fatigue.
Gawain then helped Lischios up from the ground,
And they sat down apart from one another.
The master of the ferry came ashore,
And on his arm was perched a moulted merlin.
It was the law that when a joust was held
Upon that meadow, he should claim the horse
Of whoever had been defeated there
And bow to him who claimed the victory.
Thus from the field he drew his revenue.
The meadow was the only land he owned.
He had descended from a royal line,
But he was well content to earn his living.
He made his way to where Gawain had sat
And courteously asked to claim his due.

"I am not one inclined to trading sir,
   But perhaps you'd be inclined to spare your toll,"
   Said bold Gawain on hearing this request.
"My lord," the ferry master answered him,
"There are so many witnesses up there
   Within the castle who just watched you win
   A splendid victory upon this field,
   So you will have to offer me what's due.
   Did you not win this horse in a fair joust?
   You overcame a mighty warrior
   Who was quite undefeated till this day.
   Your victory- for him a heavy blow-
   Has thwarted him of all his happiness
   While fortune has bestowed her grace on you."

"He thrust me down," replied bold Sir Gawain,
"Though I repaid him for it afterwards.
   Since someone must pay taxes here to joust,
   Let him discharge it. There's his little nag
   Which he won from me when he thrust me down.
   Take his horse if you wish to, noble sir.
   The person who shall claim this warhorse here
   Will be myself, for I'll not part with him.
   You talk of right. If you knew the half of it,
   You'd not agree to me leaving on foot.
   This morning that great steed belonged to me.
   'Twas given to me by the duke Orilus,
   But Prince Urjans usurped it for a while.
   You'd sooner get a mule's foal than this horse.
   But I can offer you another prize
   If you will have it. Since you value him
   Who rode this horse against me earlier
   So highly, in place of this horse, take him.
   You may be glad to have his knightly service."

275

The ferryman was happy with this offer.
"I've never seen so rich a gift!" he said,
Amused. "If it is fitting for someone
To claim so fine a prize, then I'll accept.
If you can guarantee this splendid gift,
Then my demand shall be greatly exceeded!
For truthfully, this man has always been
Of such a worth that if you gave me now
Five hundred swift warhorses, I'd take him
Before I took them from you, noble sir."

"I will deliver him," replied Gawain.

"Then here's my thanks to you, most noble sir,"
Replied the ferryman. "My gracious Lord,
He then continued, "will you honor me
Yet one step further and reside this night
Beneath my roof in comfort as my guest?
'Twould be a most felicitous event
For me to entertain one of such worth."

"I ought to ask you for what you've requested,"
Replied Gawain, "For I am overcome
With weariness and will require rest.
It is the way of her at whose command
I suffer hardship, to turn sweet to bitter.
Alas, cruel loss weighs heavy on my chest
Which always was uplifted by God's joy!
My heart beneath this weight seems to be crushed.
Where shall I turn to look for solace now?
Must I endure such grief for love unmet?
A person with the power that she has
Should treat another's suffering with care."

Now hearing that Gawain was suffering

The ferryman addressed his new companion:
"Sad today, glad tomorrow sir-
That's the rule both in the meadow here
And in the forest, everywhere amid
This land of marvels o'er which Clinschor reigns.
No cowardice or courage will change that.
You may be unaware of this fact sir,
But this land is held by the spell of Clinschor
Whose magic holds its sway both night and day.
If one has courage, luck may come for aid.
But sir, the sun is sinking very low,
And you should come aboard while there is light."

Lischois accepted the terms of his surrender
And gladly pledged to serve the ferryman.
Gawain and Lischois stepped aboard the ferry,
And the ferryman followed leading Gringuljete.
They crossed the river ere the sun had set
And entered the kind ferryman's abode.
It was as fine a house as ever stood.
The most grand of King Arthur's royal houses
Were no more elegant than was this dwelling.
Gawain was soon disarmed and dressed to dine
With fine and fresh new garments from his host.
These well-cut items were to him delivered
Directly by the daughter of the host.
Her name was Bene who greeted Gawain
With courtesy and kind gentility.
Gawain returned her greeting happily,
For these two took a liking to each other.
She then withdrew as water was brought in
For him to wash before he dressed himself.
This done, a couch was made upon the bed
Within the chamber where he had been led

To disarm, wash, and thus refresh himself,
By draping a fine coverlet of silk
Across the wide span of the goodly bunk.
A table was then placed before the bed
On which was laid a spread of victuals.
Bene then entered with the host and hostess-
The master and the mistress of the house.
The lovely Bene sat with Sir Gawain
Upon the bed, and opposite these two,
Her mother and the ferryman were sat.
A pleasant evening was by these four
Passed gaily while they broke bread and shared tales.
The ferryman and his family had heard tell
Of noble Sir Gawain from Arthur's court
And were o'erjoyed to host him as their guest.
He was in turn glad for their company
And lightened by their hospitality.

At length their happy meal drew to its end.
The settings and the table were withdrawn.
The coverlet was taken from the bed.
The host and hostess wished their guest goodnight
And withdrew leaving Bene with Gawain.
The two then spoke together for a while,
Each happy with the other's company.
But weariness now lulled Gawain to sleep
As he reclined while speaking with Bene,
His newfound friend upon the downy bed.
They were still speaking when he drifted off.
She called to him and saw he was asleep.
Not wishing to disturb the warrior,
She made him comfortable as best she could
And gently placed a pillow for his head
Then drew some of the blankets over him.

Through all of this, he did not even stir.
There were a great many pillows mounded up
Upon the bed and coverlets aplenty.
Sweet Bene then selected some of these
And made herself a bed upon the floor.
She wished to keep her new friend company
As he slept in her house so far from home
In case he woke to find himself alone.

SCHASTEL MARVEILE

Gawain, beset with weariness, slept deeply
And woke as night slipped into early dawn.
He rose to find sweet Bene where she lay
Still tranquilly at rest in soft repose.
He felt a bite of chill upon the air,
And so he pulled a quilt from off the bed
And gently draped it o'er her as she slept.
One wall of this fine chamber where he'd rest
Had French doors set with many panes of glass.
Outside these doors, he saw an orchard lawn.
So through the door he stepped to take the air
And listen to the birds sing their first notes.
He had not stood there long when he beheld
The castle he'd observed the eve before
While facing his adventures on the field.
He wondered at the many noble ladies
Who could be seen behind the great glass panes
Of the casements[29] in the stately stronghold's walls.
He was surprised that they were all awake,
For it as yet was only early dawn;
The sun had not yet crested o'er the hills.
He felt the weariness still hovering
Around his eyes and thought: "I'll sleep again."
And so, he wandered back into the room.
He drew the lady's cloak from where it lay
Draped o'er a silken cushion on a couch
To wrap himself against the morning chill
And once again lay down upon the bed.
At length the maiden awoke from her slumber
And rose to find her guest there where he now lay

---

29   Windows.

In light repose wrapped in her silken cloak.
Not wishing to disturb her friend at rest,
She sat down quietly beside the bed.
Gawain soon shifted and broke from his sleep
To find his patient friend awaiting him.

"Good morrow lady," Gawain said to her.
"How kind of you to wait so quietly
While I slept here. Have you been waiting long?"

"Good sir," she said, "my waiting is no burden
Since it be one so kind and generous
For whom I wait, and though it be no chore,
I have not been awaiting you here long."

"Had I known you were here," replied Gawain,
"I would assuredly have woken sooner,
For I have questions which I'd like to ask
About the castle I have seen close by.
Within its walls I saw so many maidens.
Who are they? And why do they dwell there?"

Kind Bene looked as though she had been startled.
"Please do not ask me those things sir!" she said.
"I beg you, cease this line of questioning.
I cannot tell you anything about them;
I know but am forsworn to secrecy.
Please do not be offended by this sir,
But on this topic I'll not answer you."

Gawain persisted in his inquiry,
But loyal Bene only wept at this
With bitter tears and showed great signs of woe.

While they sat thus, the master of the house
Came in to bid good morrow to his guest.
He was surprised to find his daughter weeping
So bitterly, and so he said to her:
"How fare thee child? Why art thou so grieved?
Is it for love that you do weep this way?
Perhaps I have now interrupted you
Amid the discourse of a new fledged affection!"

"Nay father, 'tis not so! Speak not of this
With such unmitigated presumption
Before our courteous and noble guest!"

"Forgive me daughter," said the ferryman.

"Good sir," Gawain now gently interposed,
"It was a question which I asked Bene
That gave rise to her sorrow in this way."

"Ask not again!" replied steadfast Bene.

"What question was it?" said the ferryman.

"'Twas merely in regard to what I've seen
In the fair castle filled with noble maidens,"
Replied Gawain, "for I am set on knowing
Who they might be and why they dwell up there."

"Desist from following this inquiry!"
The ferryman now pleaded with Gawain.
"In God's name do not ask these questions sir,
For there is only anguish on that path."

"Then I have reason to avail their plight,"
Steadfast Gawain replied to his kind host,
"From what you say I gather they are captives?

Why does my questioning displease you so?"

"Alas," the host said, "'tis your courage sir
And your good heart which drives you to insist
On following this trail of inquiry
Toward a path of unforgiving peril.
I only pray to God that your brave soul
Can bear you through the gauntlet of demise
Which you will face if you pursue the quest
That will be brought to you if you persist."

"You must inform me," said noble Gawain,
"How matters stand in yonder castle there.
If you deny me, I'll pursue my quest
By other means."

        "I cannot help but feel
Regret that you insist on asking sir,"
Reluctantly replied the kindly host.
"Hold close your shield and gird yourself for war.
You are in Terre Marveile, and Lit Marveile
Is there- a fell and treacherous adventure.
My lord, the perils in Schastel Marveile-
The castle about which you have inquired-
Have never as of now yet been attempted.
By uttering these words, I sound the knell
That summons you toward impending doom.
If you have sought adventures in the past
And won acclaim, however great the glory
Attained from them, they were but child's play
Compared with what is now awaiting you."

"I should be very sorry to depart
From here without exerting myself first,"
The resolute Gawain said to the host,

"In service of those who have been detained
In yonder castle. It would be a shame
To not learn more about those prisoners.
I've heard of them before, and having come
So near to them, I'll not now shirk the challenge."

"No hardship can compare with that of one
Who must withstand the perils of this quest,"
The host informed his guest with heartfelt grief.
"For it is sharp and terrible indeed.
Believe me sir, I'm not one to deceive."

Gawain courageously ignored these fears.
"Now tell me how I best can face this challenge,"
He said, "I shall be glad of your advice."

"If God ordains success for you, brave sir,"
Replied the thoughtful ferryman at this,
"You will be lord of this dominion.
If your Creator graces you with strength
Enough to free the captives held up there
As well as men at arms and nobles too,
You will attain unparalleled acclaim
Such that no other has e'er yet achieved.
But as it stands, you do not lack in glory,
For only yestereve the bold Lischios
Surrendered his exalted fame to you.
Sweet youth, you hold so high a reputation
Within your grasp, its sheen would not be tarnished
If you were now to ride away from here
And save your young life from the grip of death."

Gawain declined this courteous advice,
For he was now determined for the quest.
A morning meal was brought into the room.

The three then sat and broke their fast together.
Not much was spoken during this exchange
Though they strove to maintain their cheerfulness.
When they had finished, all the plates were cleared.

"Bring my equipment to me," said Gawain.

The host himself brought these things to his guests,
And courteous Bene then helped him arm.
This done, the ferryman fetched Gringuljete
And brought a tough shield for his honored guest
Which he bequeathed to him for his protection.

"I'll tell you how you must comport yourself
When faced with all the perils of this quest.
You must at all times keep my shield with you
Which has not ever yet been hacked or pierced-
For I have never fought. When you arrive
Up at the castle sir, before the gate
You'll find a huckster[30]. Leave your mount with him.
Be sure to purchase something from his wares,
And he will guard your horse with earnestness.
If you withstand the perils in the castle,
When done, you will be glad to have your horse."

"Shall I not ride my horse into the castle?"
Gawain then asked.
                    "No sir, you certainly
Must not," replied the ferryman to this.
"The ladies who you've seen inside the stronghold
Will all remain quite hidden from your sight
When you have entered, for the hour then,
When you must face your peril, lies at hand.

---

30   Vendor or retailer at a stall.

You'll find the palace utterly deserted.
May God's grace stay close by you at this point,
For you must enter the enchanted room
Where Lit Marveile resides! Heaven protect you!
When you lie on the bed, 'twill be your fate
To suffer what God has in store for you.
May he bear your stout heart through the ordeal
And manifest a joyful outcome for you!
Now if you are a worthy knight, young sir,
Remember, keep this shield close at the ready
And never part with it whate'er occurs!
The same is true when it comes to your sword,
For just when you think that the trail's done,
Then it will turn to battling in earnest!
You must keep your wits sharpened at all times."

Gawain then mounted trusty Gringuljete,
And as he did so, good truehearted Bene
Could not conceal her spirits faltering.
The ferryman's eyes also could be seen
To glisten with tears of paternal care.

"God willing," said Gawain, "I'll not be long
Rewarding you for your kind harborage
And your most gracious hospitality."

He then set forth toward the ominous
Schastel Marveile and his uncertain fate,
Awaiting him inside the fortress walls.

He found the huckster at the castle gate
And there dismounted to inspect his wares.
Gawain had never seen so many riches
Laid in a merchant stall before his eyes!
Magnificent gems and dazzling jewelry

All glinted there and glistened in the light
Of early morning. 'Twas almost too bright
To look upon. The Baruc of Baghdad,
The richest emperor in all the world,
Whom noble Gahmuret had served before he died,
Would have been glad to visit that grand booth
And trade some of his boundless wealth to own
A few rare pieces from that splendid trove.

Gawain politely gave the huckster greeting
And asked to see some modest articles,
Small, simple, and not made beyond his means.

"In truth," the huckster said, "for all the years
That I have been here, no one else has come
To look upon these wares and purchase them.
No one till now has yet been bold enough
To face the perils held within these walls
Nor yet has anyone come to this place:
You are the only customer I've seen.
If you are built with a stout heart, kind sir,
Then all these goods will soon belong to you;
They have been brought here from far reaching lands.
If you are bent on winning great acclaim
And have come here in quest of adventure
And if success attends your brave attempt,
Then you can settle with me afterwards,
For truly then will all of this be yours!
Continue on and may God's will be done!
If you should like to leave your horse with me,
I'll gladly tend to him while you are gone.
You need not worry, I will treat him well."

"I should be glad to leave him with you sir,"

Replied Gawain, "if it's not too much trouble.
But truly sir I must admit to you,
I've never before seen such opulence
Held in one merchant stall in all my days."

"Sir," the huckster answered pleasantly,
"What can I say? Myself and all my wares
Will be yours if you make it through alive.
Who else would have more right to my allegiance?
May God stand by you in your bold assay."

Gawain's intrepid heart now prompted him
To walk on foot in through the fortress gates.
The stronghold that he saw in front of him
Was vast with each flank stoutly fortified.
Enclosed within its walls he found a field
With many towers looming o'er the ramparts.
The palace roofs resembled peacock's plumes-
So brilliantly arrayed were they with hues;
No snow or rain could ever dull their sheen.
He climbed the great steps of the palace hall.
The door was open. He stepped beneath the archway
Of the great vaulting doorway to the castle.

Inside, the palace was finely adorned
With window shafts that vaulted loftily,
Well-fluted, through which rays of daylight reached.
In alcoves lay a number of fine couches,
And here and there upon them costly quilts
Of many kinds, both rare and beautiful,
Were draped. Upon these seats of opulence
Some ladies had been perched not long before
And had now taken care to leave the room.
Gawain walked through the spacious palace hall,

Alert and watchful, poised in mind and limb.
When he had crossed the hall, he saw a door
That stood ajar which led into the room
Where he was to find glory or meet death.

He entered. The pavement on the floor
Was smooth and clear as spotless panes of glass.
Upon it stood the famed bed: Lit Marveile!
Each post of this bed rested on a sphere
Of glowing ruby: polished, round, and sleek.
The dark magician who had made this bed
Had with his trickery charmed it with spells.
Additionally, with his strange concoctions,
This witch had made that pavement surface slick
So that when brave Gawain walked boldly in
He soon discovered himself struggling
To keep his footing as he made his way
Steadfastly toward the bed. With every step
He could make little progress toward his goal.
He moved as though upon a sheet of ice.
Additionally, every time he stepped
Toward the bed, it moved away from him.
The weighty shield he bore now hindered him
And added aggravation to his efforts.

"Witchcraft or no, I'll get to you," he thought.
"You think you can outdo me with your tricks
And sorcery? Well I am here to prove
That dark arts are no match for a stout heart.
I promise whoe'er rigged this sorcery
That I'll win through, come hell or high water,
And show that goodness is the way to glory!
If I can but get close enough to leap,
I'll pounce once and for all onto that bed!"

Just then the bed stood still in front of him.
He gathered all his strength, and with a leap
He landed in the center of the bed.
No sooner did he touch down on the mattress
Than the enchanted bed began to lurch
And hurtle itself fast and forcefully
From side to side and hard against the walls.
In all directions it careened itself
Without once leveling in its breakneck pace.
Each time it hit against the stony walls,
There was a crash as deafening as a clap
Of thunder when it breaks straight overhead.
Relentlessly the bed flew back and forth,
Continually slamming to the walls.
The clamor was increased to such a pitch
That had all of the thunder in the world
Been in that room, with all the trumpeters
Who ever lived, playing with all their might,
It would not have been heard above the din
Caused by that haunted bed smashing the walls.

Gawain had found a perch not made for rest,
For though he lay there, he was wide awake.
So overwhelming was this turbulence,
He held his shield braced close against his frame
And left his fate with Him who never tires
Of helping those in need who seek His aid,
For that is what a wise and brave heart does
When faced with such a dire circumstance:
Appeal unto the grace of the Almighty
And lay the outcome at the feet of God.
He then asked Him whose power and goodness
Had been at work in all Gawain's achievements
To now watch over him in this assault.

Then all at once the bed came to a halt
And was still in the center of the room.
This was a signal for what was to come,
A peril even greater than the last.
Five hundred sling stones had been primed to launch
By subtle witchcraft, and they were all aimed
Directly at the center of the bed.
And so began a battering indeed
As all five hundred stones were slung at him
With deadly accuracy and at great speed.
Gawain was pummeled by this hefty hail,
But thankfully the tough shield from his host
Withstood this onslaught and protected him
From mortal harm though there were holes in places.
At last, the battering came to an end,
And for a moment, he breathed thankfully.

But on the heels of this fierce pummeling,
Five hundred gruesome crossbows then appeared,
Each taut with lethal bolts upon the string,
All mercilessly aimed toward the bed!
Then with a frightening whir, the bolts released
And shot like deadly lightning at their mark.
The cruel bolts whined and hissed maliciously,
All thudding as they stuck into the shield.
It was not long before this volley ceased.
The whining and the thudding died away.

If there was someone who sought comfort out,
I would not recommend that bed to them.
Gawain could now attest that on this couch
The hues of youth could quickly turn to grey.
But his stout heart and hand held steadily
And did not tremble under the duress.

The bolts and stones had far from missed their mark.
Gawain was cut and bruised through his chain mail.
He hoped to God his troubles were complete,
But now he had to battle for his life.
A door at one end of the chamber opened
And through it walked a hulking ruffian,
Unpleasant to behold, clad in a smock,
With tangled oily hair on which a cap
Made from the leathery skins of water beasts
Was perched. His baggy breeches had as well
Been fashioned from the hides of water snakes.
In hand he bore a club set with a spike
Whose bulge was thicker than a water pot.
This bulky roughneck made for Sir Gawain,
Which was not much to noble Gawain's liking;
He was put out by the discourtesy.
"This fellow is not armed," thought brave Gawain.
"He won't be able to defend himself
Against me fully, clad as I now am."

Gawain sat up as if he were not hurt.
His wounds gave answer to this sudden move.
At this, the ruffian retreated back
One step and roughly growled at bold Gawain:
"You need not fear me fool, but all the same,
I will see to it that a thing occurs
By which means you'll be forced to lose your life.
That you are still alive is only due
To Satan's power. Till now he has saved you,
But from here, nothing can prevent your death.
This I'll deliver to you once I've gone."

The roughneck then walked back out through the door
From which he'd entered and passed out of sight.

Gawain rose to his feet and drew his sword.
He cut the bolts shot from the many bows
Which had embedded themselves in his shield.
They'd forced their way clean through and struck his mail,
Each with a clang as mettle answered metal.

Then suddenly he heard a mighty roar
That rumbled in the floor against the walls
And boomed up to the roof as though great drums
Were being sounded in the castle's depths.
Gawain whose courage and integrity
Had never once been shaken from its footing
Now for the first time pondered to himself:
"I wonder what will happen to me now?
Have I not had my share of tribulations
For one bleak day of trails as it is?
Is there yet more fate holds in store for me?
I must prepare myself to make a stand.
Come, dauntless courage, fortify my heart,
Breathe fire through my limbs, and steel my grip!
Rally spirit upwards to the charge.
Come soul, brace thyself toward the blows of war:
Whatever devilry comes through that door,
I will not buckle now or bow to fear!
Come heart, good heart, hold fast and do not budge!"

He held his gaze toward the roughneck's door,
And out from it a mighty lion leapt,
Tall as a horse, whose fierceness was increased
By hunger, for the beast had not been fed.
Gawain increased his grip around the strap,
Which held his shield as well as his stout hilt[31],

---

31 The handle of a sword.

And leapt down from the mattress to the floor.
The massive lion in its wrath of hunger
Began to lunge and swipe at Sir Gawain
With bared fangs, all the while snarling
And growling viciously with deadly claws
Like menacing knives splayed out as it struck.
The beast paced, prowling and encircling
Around the warrior relentlessly,
With lowered head and limbs poised for the leap.
Gawain maintained his ground as best he could,
Applying sword and shield to fend it off.
But now the lion increased in its wrath
And strove to leap upon the warrior.
Gawain was battling the beast in earnest,
Fending off each onslaught with his shield
And swiping with his sword to drive it back.
The great cat smote the shield hard with its claws
And broke clean through the sturdy barrier.
It then began to wrench upon the shield
And nearly tore it from the brave knight's grip!
The beast was snarling and grappling.
Gawain held onto his shield and raised his sword.
He smote the great beast's leg with all his might
And hacked off the lion's gruesome paw;
The beast was left to move on only three.
The fourth paw had remained wedged in the shield.
At this, the beast's blood gushed forth copiously
And made the slippery ground more treacherous-
Gawain was hard pressed to maintain his stance.
The fearsome lion was continuing
To leap upon Gawain, baring its fangs
And snarling wildly with each attempt.
The chamber swam with blood poured from its wound.
At last, it leapt with all its strength and wrath

Upon the warrior with the intent
To crush Gawain beneath its body weight
And snap the knight's neck with its mighty jaws.
Gawain went straight toward the lion's leap,
And summoning the last dregs of his strength
And all his courage into one great blow,
He struck and drove his sword up to the hilt
Until it pierced the mighty lion's heart.
The huge cat fell back from the warrior,
And he ducked swiftly out from under it.
The beast's rage then immediately ebbed;
It stumbled for a few steps haltingly
And fell dead to the ground, motionless.
And there, the gruesome lion lay outstretched
Encircled by a pool of its own blood.

Gawain now felt compassion for the beast-
A pang of sorrow for its wretched death
As it lay there before him on the ground.
But he had won through and endured the test.

"Now what is best for me to do?" he thought.
"I do not want to sit here in its blood;
This bed too dashes 'round so maddeningly
That if I have much sense, I'll not lie down."

The world began to spin before his eyes.
His head swam in a whirl from all the stones
And bolts which had been slung and shot at him.
His many wounds were bleeding copiously,
And all his gallant strength ebbed from his limbs.
He swooned and fell down to the bloody floor:
The lion was a pillow for his head,
And underneath his body lay his shield.

Now all was still and quiet in the room.
The battering and sorcery had ceased.
Enchantment had been lifted from those halls.
Gawain's stout heart had withstood all the trials
And borne the light of goodness like a torch
Through all the baleful shades of sorcery:
The dark spells on that stronghold were dispersed.

The spectacle was now by unseen eyes
Viewed from a window high above the scene.
A gentle face peered from a lofty casement
Upon the bleak display laid in that room.
It was a youthful maiden who looked down
And there beheld the spectacle beneath.
She was so stricken by the deathly scene
That when she told the lady whom she served-
Who was the goodly empress, Queen Arnive,
King Arthur's mother- what she had observed,
The kind Arnive shed tears of compassion.
So fraught the maiden was who brought this news.
They feared the knight she saw had not survived.
Arnive went to observe the scene herself,
And when she saw the knight upon the ground,
She too could not discern if he was living.

"I shall be mortified if your great courage
Has brought your noble life to such an end,"
Arnive thought to herself. "If you've been claimed
By death here fighting bravely for our cause,
Your goodness shall forever bring me sorrow
Since such a loyal heart has prompted you."

She sent her maidens to attend to him
And bring her news of hope or words of grief.

They entered and moved softly through the room
To find him lying there in his sad plight-
The shield on which he lay washed with his blood.
They moved close to discover if he lived,
And were both brought to tears as they did so.

One of them gently unlaced and removed
His helmet, marked by many hefty blows.
She then untied his ventail to reveal
His face. Some flecks of foam lay on his lips.
She now looked very closely to discern
If he was breathing, for 'twas not yet clear.
Upon his surcoat were two sable dragons
Sewn there to symbolize the mighty house
Of Pendragon, King Arthur's lineage.
Of this fur now the maiden plucked one tuft
And held it gently underneath his nose,
Observing it intently to detect
If the fur stirred even the slightest breath.
And she discovered that there was still breath!
At once she told her friend to fetch some water,
And this was brought to her with all due haste.
She placed her finger in between his teeth
And gently let some water droplets fall
Into his mouth- not too much. Suddenly,
He opened up his eyes and looked at her.
He thanked the goodly maiden graciously.

"I'm sorry that you had to find me here
In this unseemly fashion," he then said.

"You lie here now adorned in glory sir,"
The kindly maiden answered. "You have gained
Such high renown that you will now grow old,

Rich in goodliness and well content,
For victory, brave soul, is yours today!
Now please assure me that your wounds are such
That we can share with you in this great joy."

"I'm afraid that you will have to give me aid
If you wish me to live, kindhearted friend,"
Gawain said. "But if I must fight again
Then lace my helmet on and leave me here,
For if there's need, I will defend myself."

"You are exempt from fighting further sir,"
Replied the maiden. "No enemy remains.
You've conquered all there is to battle here.
Now let us stay with you, all except one
Who must now be rewarded by four queens
When they bring them the news that you yet live!
They must prepare a bed for you as well
And make it ready for recovery
With ointments and rich salves to heal your wounds
Where you can be restored back to good health."

Thus one of them raced off to bring the news:
"He lives! And in such strength that by God's will
He may bring us abundant happiness!
But he is in great need of swift attention."

"Thank God!" The four queens all said at this news.

Wise old Arnive gave orders for the bed
To be prepared before a fireplace.
For his wounds and bruises she procured unguents[32],
Most rare and most ingeniously concocted.

---

32   Salve or balm for healing wounds.

She then sent four maids to disarm the knight.
They were to take care and use all their skill
To not increase his pain or cause him shame.

So deft were they and thoughtful in their work,
Their patient felt no hint of shame or pain.
They placed a silken cloth around his body
To keep him covered as each plate of steel
Was gently lifted from his wounded frame.
They then assisted him into the room
Where wise Arnive stood waiting by his bed.
He was then carefully laid down to rest,
Supported by their strong and gentle hands.
The old queen then with a soft silken cloth
Took care to gently clean each of his wounds
And bind them with a potent healing salve.
She found some fifty injuries or more.
The crossbow's bolts had pierced him through his mail,
But none of them had pierced to any depth
Since he had slung his shield in front of him.
The lady was relieved to find this so:
The warrior was not hurt mortally.
It took some time to tend to all the wounds.
She worked with calm serenity and care
As she bound every bandage patiently.
So skillful and attentive was this queen
As she meticulously cared for him
That even as his wounds were soothed and bound,
The warrior began to feel revived.
This done, she then attended to his head.
His helmet had been dented by the stones,
And at each point where there had been a dent,
She found a swollen welt raised on his scalp.
She soothed these with both skill and potent salves.

"You will soon feel relief from all your wounds,"
 She said, now speaking gently to Gawain,
"For Cundrie La Suziere oft visits me
 And has instructed me in healing arts.
 When she comes here, she brings me potent salves.
 These salves are used to aid the fisher king,
 And they have helped Anfortas stay alive-
 She brought them here with her from Munsalvaesche."

"Good madam, you have brought my senses back,
 Which had departed ere you lent me aid."
 Now honest Sir Gawain said to the queen,
"My pain too is already lessening.
 The strength and senses that I now possess
 Are all laid at your service humbly."

"We all must do our own part on behalf
 Of serving love and goodness in the world,"
 Replied the gentle queen consolingly.
"You sir bear your part in the world with strength
 As well as courage and gentility.
 If I now offer what help I can lend,
 'Tis but the honor given us by God
 To take part in the doing of His will.
 Now do your part young sir, and do not fret
 Or speak too much, but rest and restore strength,
 For nothing more from you will be required.
 I will now administer this herb
 Which will send you to sleep and do you good.
 You will not then desire food or drink
 Until nightfall. Then I will bring you food
 So that you can hold out until the morn."

She gently placed the herb into his mouth,

And slumber came upon him instantly.
She made sure that he was laid comfortably
And tucked the blankets close around his body.
In this way he lay soft and warm and slept
Throughout the day until the evening came.
With her authority, wise old Arnive
Let it be known that no one raise their voice,
Make sudden movements, or wake him with sounds
As long as their good hero lay asleep.
She also ordered that the door be locked
And that no soul be let into the palace
So that no word of Gawain's victory
Be murmured through the land by anyone
Until Gawain had been restored to strength.
When evening came, the warrior awoke
To find himself in need of food and drink.
Arnive gave orders, and the food was brought.
Gawain sat up and partook cheerfully,
Much to the joy of those attending him.
He looked at all the gentle princesses
Who stood around him joyful as he supped.
He thought of Orgeluse and felt a pang
Of longing once more pull upon his heart,
For never in the past had Sir Gawain
When faced with love, requited or denied,
Been moved by someone as he was by her.
He asked the maidens who attended him
To sit and sup with him for company.
They all requested that he let them stand
And make sure that his every need was met.
He was uncomfortable with this deference,
But Arnive once more told him to forbear
From fretting over those formalities,
For those who waited on him were all glad

To help him to a swift recovery.
When he had had his fill of victuals,
He once more lay down and fell fast asleep.

THE GARLAND TREE

Gawain slept deeply in recovery
From all the hefty toil he'd withstood;
And as the steep night tipped toward the dawn,
He was met by dreams of fair Orgeluse.
So fiercely for the duchess did he yearn
That all his wounds from stones and lethal darts
Seemed pale next to the ache within his heart.
No knight had undergone so treacherous
And fearsome an adventure as had he,
Not even those of Arthur's company,
To win through and attain such high renown.
His name stood tested and unshakable
With such steadfast and stout integrity
That from its perch it could now never budge;
And yet, heartsore Gawain thought not of this,
Nor did he mind the things he had endured.
They all seemed small and insignificant
When placed next to his love for Orgeluse.
If she were ever to return his love,
Though others might exalt his bravery,
His steadfast goodness, and his dauntless strength,
To him, her love would be his greatest prize.
He tossed and turned in his sleep as he dreamed
So that some of the bandages were torn;
And there, he bled as he moved restlessly.

He woke to find the bright day smiling down
Into the chamber where he lay at rest.
So brilliantly the sun beamed through the room
That now the candles which had through the night
Been glowing by the bed looked small and faint.
The warrior sat up and checked his wounds.

His underlinens and his sheets were stained
With blood from where the bandages had torn.
But lying on the bed were some new clothes:
Some buckram[33] hose, a sleeveless robe of fur,
A jerkin, and a pair of summer boots
As well as a rare scarf of silken cloth.
He bound the loosened bandages back on,
Then in this finery he decked himself.
A good repast was set aside for him
Upon a stand beside a bench and chair.
So there he sat and took some sustenance.
These victuals combined with all his rest
Had brought some of his strength back to his limbs.
When he had finished, he rose from his seat
And stepped forth from the room into the hall.

It was magnificent. Ne'er had Gawain
Encountered anything which could compare.
At one end of the room, a spiral stair
Ascended upwards and passed out of sight,
Somewhere beyond the palace's full height.
The staircase wrapped around a massive pillar.
The dark magician, Clinschor, was the one
Who'd brought this masterpiece of craftsmanship
From distant lands ruled by bold Feirefiz-
Brave Parzival's brother whom Cundrie had named.
It had been wrought by cunning artistry.
'Twas round and smooth, made all of burnished wood.
Fair windows into it had craftily
Been fashioned and bedecked with precious gems:

---

33   An archaic usage which was used to describe high quality
cotton or linen fabric.

Sardine stones, amethyst and chrysolite[34],
Topaz, diamonds and emeralds
And garnet stones, all glittered splendidly.
Aloft the ceiling was likewise bedecked
Magnificently with these precious stones.
Gawain went over to the spiral stair
And started upwards 'round the winding steps.
As he proceeded, he saw wondrous things
Such that in all his days he'd ne'er beheld,
For when he gazed into the stunning frames
Of those great windows in the pillar's height,
He felt as though he saw in each a land
Unto itself in its entirety.
These landscapes seemed to be whirling around
With mountains, lakes and quiet forest glens,
And rivers wending through the gentle vales.
Not only this, but he saw people there.
One man was walking while another ran,
And here, he saw a woman standing still,
And there, a child playing by the brook.
Gawain was filled with wonder as he looked.
He sat down in the oriel to watch
And take in all the marvels he could see.
As he gazed at these things, the queen Arnive
Approached him with her daughter named Sangive
As well as Sangive's daughters, Itonje
And Cundrie- who, though she shared the same name
As Cundrie La Suziere of Munsalvaesche,
Did not resemble her in other ways.
Gawain rose to his feet as they approached.

---

34 A kind of olivine which is a grey or greenish brown mineral
used as a precious gemstone.

"You ought to be asleep sir," said Arnive,
"If further trials lie in store for you.
You are too injured in your present state
To undergo them without further rest."

"My kind friend and physician," said Gawain,
"Your help has so restored my strength to me
And brought life back into my limbs and mind
That I am now your glad and humble servant."

Queen Arnive smiled and said to Gawain,
"If you are now indeed my servant sir,
Embrace these three queens who stand here with me,
For they like me shall all be friends to you."

Gawain complied with this and greeted them,
Each gracious empress, gentle as the last.
Once this was done, Gawain then asked Arnive
About the wondrous tower and the scenes
That he had witnessed through the magic frames.

"Since I first came to know it sir," she said,
"The magic stone set loftily atop
This tower shines out over this domain,
A distance of six miles on all sides.
Everything that happens in that range
Can be seen through the windows in the tower."

As she was speaking this, Gawain beheld
Two people through a window in the pillar.
It was a lady and a warrior.
The knight was well armed and prepared for war.
They rode with haste toward the grassy plain,
Which lay upon the river's farther side,
Below the castle by the ferry's quay.

The knight had come to battle with Gawain
And rode forth from the same marsh which Lischois
Had charged ere Gawain had defeated him.
The lady was conducting her knight forth
And by the bridle led his steed along
In a display of curt formality.
Gawain averted his gaze from the scene
And hoped the pillar had deceived his eyes.
A second glance confirmed what he had guessed:
It was indeed the Duchess Orgeluse!
The sight of his beloved stung his heart.

"There is a knight approaching us," he said,
"With upraised lance, apparently intent
On seeking combat. That he shall find here!
If battle is his aim, I'll give it him.
But please confirm for me the lady's name
Who doth attend this warrior I see."

"She is the lovely Duchess of Logroys,"
Replied Arnive to fraught Gawain's appeal.
"Whom doth she now exact her mischief on?
With her is one who is called the Turkoyt.
His name is Florant– he is from Itolac
And is companion to the bold Lischios.
With lance alone he has earned great renown,
Enough to make three lands illustrious.
You must avoid a battle with him sir,
For you have not recovered fully yet
And are still too severely wounded now."

"You say that I am lord of this domain,"
Replied Gawain. "When someone rides so close
In search of combat and requests a joust,

I must give answer, or I am no lord.
Please bring my armor and my weaponry,
For I am set on battling this knight."

The four queens were distressed by his intent.
"If you wish to preserve fame and renown,
You must not fight at all," said Queen Arnive.
"If you were to fall dead before his feet,
Our griefs would plummet to the very depths;
But even if you 'scape death at his hands,
Your wounds encased in all your heavy armor
Could by themselves prove fatal to you sir."

Despite their protestations, Lord Gawain
Was now determined to engage his foe
And gave no further thought as to the cost.
He begged for his equipment to be brought,
And they at last regretfully obliged.
The knight was soon made ready for the joust;
And so, as not to make his presence known
Within the castle's great perimeter,
He tiptoed out to find good Gringuljete
Where he was waiting with the honest huckster.
Gawain was still in great pain from his wounds
Which made it difficult to hold his shield.
This shield showed evidence of all his toils,
For there were dents and holes in many places,
And still the lion's gruesome paw clung there.
He climbed up onto steadfast Gringuljete
And made his way forth from the castle gate
Toward the home of the good ferryman.
His faithful host equipped him with a lance
Which he'd once claimed as ransom from the field.
Gawain then asked his friend to ferry him

Across the river to the jousting ground
Where now his enemy awaited him.
The Turkoyt's reputation was pristine,
For he had thrown down countless warriors
And therefore had acquired great renown.
His fame had spread throughout all Christendom;
Moreover he'd proclaimed a haughty challenge:
To maintain honor only with a lance.
If anyone e'er flung him off his horse,
He would not draw his sword but would submit
Surrender and accept defeat at once.
For this cause he rode solely with a lance
And shield and bore no sword into the fray.
All this Gawain learned from his faithful friend,
The good and loyal-hearted ferryman.
Once they had landed on the farther bank,
Gawain once more climbed onto Gringuljete and
Hauled his battered shield into its place
While readying the stout lance in his grip.
The Turkoyt now rode forth toward Gawain
Like one well seasoned by the blows of war.
At a whisper from Gawain, proud Gringuljete
Wheeled toward the meadow. Gathering in speed
As though gods of storm and hurricanes
Rushed through the great beast's mighty limbs,
The elegant stallion surged toward the foe.
When both opponents galloped at full tilt,
They came together in a deft exchange
Of skill and strength- all in the time it takes
For one bright flash of lightning to appear
And vanish in the vastness of the sky.
Gawain had borne the blow of his opponent
Against his breastplate just above his shield
But held fast in his saddle like a rock

Amid the fierce gusts of a lashing tempest.
The Turkoyt's lance burst in a cloud of chips,
But with such sturdiness Gawain held fast
That through the cloud of splinters his blow struck
With great heft, skill, and expert mastery.
He'd caught the Turkoyt's visor with his lance,
Plucked off the helm, and laid his adversary
Stretched out amid the fresh spring meadow blossoms.
The vanquished warrior's fine accoutrements
And dazzling armor, glinting in the sun,
Vied for brightness with the gentle flowers,
And his fine helm with its impressive crest
Hung dangling from Gawain's lance as he rode.

Gawain turned back and claimed his foe's surrender.
The ferryman as well procured his due:
The Turkoyt's stately stallion- his prize.

"I see you must now flaunt the lion's paw
By carrying it forth everywhere you go,"
Said lovely Orgeluse to vex Gawain
As she rode toward the scene of the exchange.
"Do you think you've distinguished yourself here,
Because some maidens up at yonder fort
Have seen the outcome of this tournament?
I must now leave you to your rhapsodies!
You may dance with delight at your success
For being let off lightly as you were
At Lit Marveile despite the fact
That you quite happily display your shield,
Which has been battered as though you'd been fighting!
I do not doubt you are too badly hurt
To withstand a real rough and tumble fight-
For earnest battles are too much for you!

Add that description to the name of Goose!
You are dismissed! Go cherish your great shield
For giving you sir something to boast of!
It has been punctured with so many holes
That it looks like a large unwieldy sieve!
My guess is that you'll now elect to flee
From further punishment and suffering.
For your reward I thumb my nose at you!
Ride back up to your ladies at the castle,
And do not feign to further contemplate
The undertaking of the mighty feats
That I would set to you were you to seek
Such battles as are undergone for love."

"Madam," replied Gawain, "if I had wounds,
They have now by your presence all been healed.
There is no danger so formidable
That would deter me from continuing
To battle for your love!"
                                        The duchess paused.
"I shall permit you to ride in my presence,"
She then replied, "to fight another battle
In quest of honor if you wish to, sir."

Gawain was overjoyed by this request.
He sent the Turkoyt with the ferryman
Up to the castle with his salutation
To those who dwelt within its stately walls.
Gawain's lance had withstood the hefty clash,
And so he brought it for the next exchange.

The four queens in the castle were distraught
As they watched bold Gawain go riding forth
As were all others of that noble throng:
They feared he'd not survive another joust.

311

But any suffering Gawain had felt,
All heartache and all pain now disappeared:
Banished by the radiance of love.
The softness of the gentle morning came
And draped its blessing o'er them with a kiss
As side by side they rode through grasses tall
And wildflowers bending silently
Beneath the soothing, soft caress of spring.
The melodies of birds rang bright and clear
As though their songs might burst their little hearts
With happiness as onward those two rode
Beside the brooks and through the quiet wood.
It seemed like all else had fallen away
Besides the quiet joy now hovering
Around them in the gentle, fresh spring morn.
And all the challenges which had been faced
And all adventures that were yet to come
Seemed faint and distant like a fading mist;
The trouble seemed to dissipate and lift
Until all that remained was love.
And in that moment, if the truth be told,
Gawain was not alone.

           No word was said
For quite some time. At length the duchess spoke:
"You must fetch me a garland from a branch
That's set upon a certain tree," she said.
"If you can win that garland from the tree
And then bestow the garland unto me,
I will honor your heroic deed,
And then you may ask me for my love."

Gawain's heart swelled unto the very brink
At hearing those words come from Orgeluse,
And he felt such a fiery strength ignite

Within his chest and surge into his limbs
That to Gawain no challenge seemed so great
That it could not be faced and overcome.
All hindrances were insignificant
When placed beside this power most supreme
Which now lit up his spirit with such might
That he felt braver than he had before he'd faced
The battering in bleak Schastel Marveile,
For no force can compare with mighty love:
A love such as that is unstoppable.

"Madam," then said Gawain, "wherever it be
That I may find that tree upon whose branch
The garland sits, I will not ever rest
Until my quest has brought me to that place,
And I have either won the prize for you
Or there encountered death in the attempt."

They had now entered a resplendent forest
With trees of many rare varieties
From far-flung reaches of the world's expanse.
By Clinschor's will had this wood manifest,
For it was he who had reigned o'er that realm.

"I wonder where the tree is with the branch
That I must break," Gawain thought to himself.

"I'll show you where you will need all your strength,
Your valor, and your skill to win the day,"
The Duchess Orgeluse said to Gawain.
They were now riding forth out from the wood
Onto a field, and there they saw the tree.

"Sir," the duchess then said to Gawain,
"That tree is tended by a certain lord

313

Who stole my happiness. If you fetch down
That branch for me, no knight will yet have won
Such glory as thou wilt have from this deed.
I must remain here. If you should ride on,
Then let the outcome rest within God's hands!
There is a river you must vault across
To get to where the tree stands in the field.
With that one leap, the journey is complete,
And what occurs then lies with destiny."

Gawain now recognized the roaring sound
Of a mighty torrent, which had cut a swath
Between where they stood and the garland tree.
So toward this sound the dauntless knight progressed.
When it came into view, he touched the flanks
Of steadfast Gringuljete with his spurred heels.
The mighty charger surged into a gallop.
Not once did the great stallion check its pace
As they rushed toward the flood intrepidly;
And from the bank, the fearless warhorse leapt
Wth a great burst across the churning fiord.
It was indeed a grand vault to behold;
No other steed could have launched with such grace,
Such stately power, and so valiantly;
But when they came down on the other side,
They landed half a stride short of the bank,
For though the stallion's forelegs caught the lip
Of the severe embankment o'er the flood,
His hind legs fell short of the solid ground,
And so the long flight ended in a spill
As man and beast were tumbled o'er themselves
And pitched headlong into the swirling gorge.

The duchess wept when she beheld the fall
And wrung her hands in great anxiety.

She wished with all her heart to rush to them
And help them through the dire circumstance
But knew that for the test to be complete
At all costs, she must never intervene.
The current ran deep and at deadly speed,
Lashing itself fiercely 'round the rocks,
Down cataracts and plunging under cliffs,
Thundering as it cascaded into pools.
Gawain was fighting with all his great strength
To keep afloat but was weighed down by steel
As all his hefty armor pulled at him.
He saw the branch stretched from a mighty tree
Which had spread roots into the river bank
And reached its limbs across the whirling flood.
Around this branch the warrior wrapped his grip.
His lance was floating by him in the froth.
With his free hand he caught his floating spear
And slowly climbed onto the solid ground.
Meanwhile, the faithful Gringuljete fought hard
Against the raging current as he swam,
Now with his head above the churning foam,
Then out of sight submerged into the flood.
The swift flow of the river had pulled him
So far down stream that Sir Gawain was forced
To run, drenched in all his weighty armor,
As compromised and wounded as he was,
In an attempt to save the drowning steed.
Then a whirlpool drove the steadfast beast
Toward Gawain where he stood on the bank,
And with his lance he reached out from a jut
Where heavy rains had carved a rivulet,
Both broad and shallow through the steep embankment.
This breached portion of the riverbank
Was what now saved the worthy stallion's life.

Gawain with patience used his lance to edge
The beast toward land until it was so close
That he could reach out with his hand and grasp
Onto the bridle. Then with all his strength
He hauled the faithful warhorse to the bank,
And up the good beast scrambled, safe and sound,
Then whinnied, snorted, stamped, and shook itself.

Gawain's shield had been flung onto the grass
Where they had struck the bank when they had leapt.
So once the warrior had re-girthed his horse,
They made their way back to collect the shield
And then proceeded onward to the tree.

The tree was not far from the riverbank,
And when they'd come to it, Gawain reached forth
And broke the garland branch from off the tree
Then placed the garland gently on his helm.
As soon as this was done, a handsome knight
Rode up to him without breaking a sweat,
For he rode toward Gawain informally,
Unarmed, and at an ambling pace.
Despite this show of supreme indifference,
He was a fearsome knight to say the least
And dangled his high prowess loftily
Above all others down from a great height:
The tower of his fame and excellence.
The bricks of that spire gleamed forth blindingly
Without so much as one chip, scuff, or smudge;
Not only this, but to accompany
The long-legged and untarnished pole of fame,
His arrogance stretched every inch as tall,
For he'd not fight a solitary knight,
But only would engage if there were two.
He was a king. His name was Gramoflanz.

"Sir," this haughty king said breezily,
"I will allow you to keep the garland branch
And will refrain from battling with you,
But do not think I'm letting you off lightly.
I'd have withheld my greeting from you now
If there were two of you to battle with,
But since you are just one, I shall forbear,
For one contender is beneath my skill."

Gawain, for his part too, was disinclined
To battle since his foe rode forth unarmed
And carried on his wrist a sparrow hawk.
The hawk had been sent as a gift to him,
And by the tight wound threads of destiny,
The giver of this gift lay close to home,
For that fine falcon was a love token
From Itonje, the sister of Gawain.

"Your shield declares that you've been battling,"
Said Gramoflanz, now taking in his foe.
"There is so very little left of it.
So Lit Marveile has fallen to you now.
You have met the adventure meant for me;
But Clinschor has e'er set a precedent
Of peace with me, and I am now at war
With one whose beauty is unparalleled.
Her anger at me remains unabated;
Indeed she has good reason for her wrath.
I am referring to proud Orgeluse.
I slew her husband Cidegast in battle
While he fought in the company of three.
I then abducted the proud Orgeluse
And offered her a crown and all my lands.
Yet all my offers were met by her wrath.

I kept her for the span of one whole year,
Yet still I failed to come within her graces.
I must admit I was dismayed by this.
It's clear that she has offered you her love
Since you've come with intent to end my life.
Now had you brought another with you sir,
You could have had the chance of slaying me,
Or else the two of you would have both died.
That much would you have gotten for your trouble;
But now my heart is set on other love,
For I have lost my taste for Orgeluse.
In fact, if you feel kindly toward me sir,
The love I bear could be saved by your aid.
You are now sovereign there at Terre Marveile;
Your prowess earned this prize of excellence.
Please help me with a lady who lives there;
I yearn for her with pangs of suffering.
She is the lovely daughter of King Lot.
No woman's had such power over me
As now the radiant Itonje does.
I bear her gift of love here on my wrist;
This falcon is a token sent from her.
I now believe she shares my sentiments,
And I have faced fierce battles for her sake,
For after Orgeluse refused my love,
All fame I've won has been for Itonje.
I've not laid eyes on her to my great sorrow,
But if you will console me with your help,
Please give this little ring to my sweet love.
You are exempt from battling with me
That is unless your numbers are increased
To two or more. No credit would I gain
If I should kill you while you fought alone
Or forced you to surrender as you are."

"I am quite able to defend myself
And have been known to give a good account
When things have, in the past, come down to blows,"
The forthright Sir Gawain replied with grace.
"If you have no wish to procure the fame
That you would surely have by slaying me-
For my part, I too would gain little clout
By slaying you unarmed as you are now-
I will then bear your message back with me.
Give me your ring. I'll tell your doleful tale
When I return back to Schastel Marveile."

The king profusely thanked bold Sir Gawain.
Gawain continued by inquiring:
"Since it is so beneath your dignity
To fight me, will you tell me who you are?"

"I will indulge you sir," the king replied,
"But think no less of me for stooping now
So low as to reveal my name to you.
My father was King Irot. He was slain
By King Lot, Lord of Lothian and Orkney.
My name is Gramoflanz, king of this realm.
The integrity of my lofty spirit states
That I must never fight one man alone,
No matter what offense he may have done.
There is but one I'll face in single combat.
He's called Gawain, and I have heard him praised
So highly that I yearn to meet with him
In battle and avenge my father's death.
He is the son of Lot, who slew my father,
And Lot has since died, but now bold Gawain
Has won preeminence and such high fame
That there is no one who can rival him,

Not even those of Arthur's company.
The day when I do battle with this knight
Will come, and until then, I shall not rest."

"If this is how you influence the heart
Of one whom you just named not long ago,
Your friend- assuming that she is your friend,"
Replied the stalwart son of noble Lot,
"Then she does not possess a noble heart,
For if she did, she surely would protest
This negligent behavior on your part:
Accusing her father of this perfidy
And blaming him for such a treacherous act
While stating that you'd gladly kill her brother.
If she had filial and sisterly
Sentiments, she would not now stand by
But would shield both her brother and her father
And seek to wean you from this ill-bred folly-
And from this ill-informed hostility.
How will you reconcile in your heart
The hatred that you bear toward her father
Who may at some time be your father-in-law?
If you've not turned your prideful vengeance sir
Inward and wrought this wrath upon yourself
For having wrongfully assigned this act
Of shame on one no longer in this world,
His son will hold the ground where he once stood
And give an answer which you'll not forget.
Proud Sir, I am Gawain, the son of Lot.
Whatever grievance you claim from my father,
Avenge it on me, for I stand here now
Alive and well, where he no longer can!
To shield the goodness of his dauntless heart,
I stake all honor life has given me

Upon a match between you and myself.
May proof be placed upon the tipping scales
And weighed out by the hand of destiny!"

"If you are he with whom I bear this feud,"
Now coolly answered proud King Gramoflanz,
"Then I am made both glad and melancholy,
For something of you surely pleases me:
Namely that I am to fight with you.
For your part, a great honor is bequeathed
In that I've acquiesced to you alone
To engage with you in a single fight.
It will enhance the fame for both of us
If our encounter is viewed by a host
Of lovely ladies and nobility.
I shall bring fifteen hundred to the match,
And you can bring your host from Terre Marveile;
Additionally, for your compliment,
Invite your Uncle Arther with his host
To see our contest on the dueling ground.
I am 'ware that he and his company
Are now positioned one week's ride from here.
They are camped near the town of Bems-on-korcha.
I shall make my appearance on the field
Close to the river yonder- called Joflanze-
In sixteen days from now to exact pay
From you for having claimed the garland branch
And to avenge my father Irot's death.
Now if you will accompany me sir,
Back through the town that I've just ridden from,
I can then guide you to a pleasant bridge
Which you may cross to get to Terre Marveile."

"I will return the same way that I came,"

Replied Gawain, "and will meet your requests
Regarding our duel sixteen days from now."

The two lords then pledged oaths to meet again
Upon the dueling ground by the Joflanze
In single combat at the time agreed.

Gawain then took leave of that haughty king
And with a light heart gave his horse free rein,
For he had borne away the garland crest
And galloped back toward the rushing gorge;
Nor did he coax or check the mighty steed
In its great pace as it moved toward the brink,
For Gringuljete knew how to leap that flood,
And vault he did with poise and elegance
And such a mighty burst from off the bank
That when they touched down on the farther side,
They landed in mid stride as though the gorge
Were but an average stream to hop across-
Though no one would describe that river thus!
It was a thing of beauty to behold-
So gracefully did they glide o'er the flood.
And on the beast now galloped through the field
Until his master gently drew the reins
And dropped down from the steed's back to the ground
To check his saddle and re-girth the strap.

The duchess rode to meet them where they'd stopped
And leapt down from her mare before Gawain.
And there she stood beside him radiant.
Gawain had never seen her look at him
As she did now with such a gentleness,
For all her proud austerity had softened,
And her great power seemed tempered with kindness.

"Brave soul," she said, "I do not deserve
The hardships you have suffered for my sake
And all that I have asked you to withstand.
You've undergone such pain on my behalf!
I have yearned all this time for you to know
That all your trails have afflicted me
With heartfelt anguish and great suffering-
Such as one feels the pain of a dear friend."

Gawain stood and looked back at Orgeluse
And strove to comprehend what he had heard
And grappled to hold footing in his soul,
Not wishing to be wholly overcome
By what moved in his heart as his love spoke:
The soft strength of her voice quite overcame him.

At length he said to lovely Orgeluse:
"If what you speak is not another trick
And is indeed what lives within your heart,
Then I will not pretend to hide my joy,
For nothing could bring greater happiness.
I was content to bear my love for you
Unanswered, for I've never known a love
That could compare with that which I know now,
But having grown accustomed to its ache,
Which has become the tenant of my heart,
I know not how I would contain myself
Were I to learn this love lives in two hearts.
Is there more mischief lurking in your words?
If I believe them, will they turn to dust
And blow away upon the wind's next breath?
As long as I have known this mighty love,
It seemed too big to fit inside one chest;
Yet though I bear it with me for your sake

And though some others have affirmed my worth,
You have persistently claimed otherwise
And demonstrated your distaste for me."

"Good sir," the duchess said to Sir Gawain,
"If you knew of the sorrows I've endured,
You would not doubt the love I bear for you.
May anyone I've slighted, pardon me!
No loss of happiness could e'er exceed
That which I lost in noble Citigast!
The love I bore for him was torn from me
When he was slain by cruel King Gramoflanz!
So pure and good was my brave Citigast,
And so fast was the bond of our love
That I could not be wed to anyone
Once he, dear and unfortunate, met death
Unless it be one steadfast, bold and pure-
Who'd persevere and prove themselves to be
Unflinchingly his equal on all counts.
I was convinced no such soul could be found
Until you came and I learned otherwise,
For though there can be but one Citigast,
In virtues you are matched abundantly.
If I've misused you in the name of friendship,
I ask you to forgive my cruelty.
It was administered to test your worth;
Not so much for myself, but for the fact
That only someone with a dauntless soul
And a stout heart of pure benevolence
Could stand with me through all my tribulations
And face the onslaught of my destiny.
You have been true and constant as the sun
Which rises each day to illume the world.
You've showed the stalwart goodness of your heart

To such extent that where I once felt grief
And only grief, now grief has moved aside
And offered love a dwelling place in me."

Tears welled up to the eyes of Orgeluse
As she stood strikingly before Gawain
And told him her sad tale unfalteringly.
With such strength did the duchess stand and speak,
Gawain was smitten to his very core.
He was so moved by what she said to him
That though he strove to speak, no voice was heard.

"My lady," he said, once he'd o'er himself
Grasped hold enough for words to sound again,
"Unless death stops me, I shall teach the king,
Who wrought such devastation on your life,
How to accept defeat. I gave my word
That I would meet him in a single fight
In sixteen days from now by the Joflanze.
If God is at my back upon that day,
The arrogance of haughty Gramoflanz,
Which until now seems to have grown to seed,
Will be set right. He will beg for his life
Before the end, if heaven wishes it,
And will become acquainted with surrender.
Dear lady, I forgive all your harsh words
And every slight that you've administered
To test the mettle of my worthiness.
Had I known, I'd have cherished each affront
And worn them all as tokens on my heart,
For now I see that every spurn I've borne
And every hardship that confronted me
Like the oar strokes of a vessel brought
Our toiling voyage to this mooring place

Where we now, in this moment, meet at last-
This day, here on this blessed grassy plain!
In truth dear lady I will not deny,
Though I lament the sorrows you have borne
And feel such poignant ache within my heart,
Until this moment I've ne'er known such joy!"

The beautiful duchess smiled through her tears,
"I've never warmed to arms encased in steel,"
She said, "but if you'll let me ride with you,
I will go with you to Schastel Marveile.
And there, I'll not deny that at some point,
Once care is given to your injuries
And you've commenced in your recovery,
We will partake of our joy together."

Though it was hard to think joy could increase
Beyond that which Gawain already felt,
Increase it did to his astonishment.
It seemed to him that he might be at risk
Of shattering apart with happiness!
He'd battled with a lion and withstood
All manner of distressing incidents,
But none of those adventures made him tremble
And feel so shaky in his knees and limbs
As did this power of Almighty Love.
Good Orgeluse, for her part, also felt
Her heart swell upwards to the heights with love:
A feeling she'd not known since Citigast.

"I am quite able to mount my own steed,"
The lovely Orgeluse said to Gawain,
"But if you wish to, you may help me up."

The ardent lover took her in his arms
And gently lifted her onto her mare.

He followed suit, and they rode from that place.

As they rode side by side, good Orgeluse,
Though their shared joy had not abandoned her,
Was met by all her woes once more and wept.
When her companion saw her bitter tears,
He, overcome by them, joined her in sadness
And begged her to inform him of her grief.

"I will divulge my sorrows to you sir,"
She said. "I wish to tell you more of him
Who slew the good and noble Citigast.
Though I was stricken by grief at his death,
I was not so reduced as not to seek
My vengeance on the man who slew my joy.
I have staged many jousts aimed for his life,
And all of them have failed to bring him down.
In the pursuit of conquering my foe,
I chose the aid of a most noble soul
Who is lord of the world's most precious gift.
This man, a king, is known as Anfortas-
Well known for his great prowess with the shield.
It was Anfortas who sent me the gift
From distant lands, a token of his love:
The riches at the gates of your stronghold.
You would have seen it guarded by the huckster
When you came to endure the perils there.
This mighty and most honorable king
Fought on my behalf to honor me
And win my love with dauntless acts of war.
While serving me, this king met a cruel fate
And suffered a horrific tragedy.
Instead of giving this good man my love,
I was forced to endure yet further grief,

For his wound brought on greater suffering
Than Citigast had power to inflict!
Now how am I to keep a faithful heart
With all these woes that have afflicted me?
Indeed from time to time my mind gives way
When I think of Anfortas lying there
So helpless and in such fraught agony-
The man I chose as comfort for my loss.
Ah, sad and gentle King Anfortas! Woe
That grave misfortune brought you unto me!
Good noble soul! Wounded in my cause!
I am a scourge upon all loyal hearts,
For all I've known have suffered serving me.
Once brave Anfortas, sender of the gift,
Had been forever turned away from love,
I was in dread of what might come to me,
For subtle Clinschor, who then ruled this land
Before you came and lifted the enchantment,
Is practiced at the craft of necromancy
And has the dark arts at his beck and bidding.
He can bind men and women to his will
With conjuring and evil sorcery.
Of all the worthy people of the world
On whom his eye falls, not one does he leave
Unscathed, for all are troubled ever after.
In order that he leave me undisturbed,
I gave him the great wealth sent from Anfortas
To thus appease his sinister desires.
'Twas on these terms the treasure was bestowed:
That I should seek love from one who could win
The kingdom after facing Lit Marveile.
I hoped King Gramoflanz would be brought down
By hazarding the perils in those halls.
Had he attempted he'd have met his end.

But that fate was not ever brought to pass.
Lord Clinschor grasps at opportunity
With shrewdness and invisibility.
For the prestige he permitted me
Deployment of my famous retinue
Throughout the land to seek out fell encounters.
Everyday I have detachments sent
With the intent of harming Gramoflanz.
With such great effort I've planned his defeat.
He has fought many battles with my knights
And always rides away without a scratch!
What is it that shields him from his demise?
From many suitors I've accepted service
Without the promise of anything in return.
There is no man who has laid eyes on me
Who has not offered me his company
Except for one who was armed all in red.
He put my retinue in jeopardy
And laid them all out scattered on the ground,
Which I must say was not much to my liking.
I followed him and offered him my love,
My kingdom, my wealth, and my person too.
He told me he already had a wife
Who was more beautiful. This angered me.
In my annoyance I asked who she was.
He said, 'she who is ever radiant
And is alone the dweller of my heart
Is empress in the land of Belrepeire.
I am known by the name of Parzival.
I do not want your love. I seek the Grail,
Which has endowed me with enough unrest
To keep me occupied without your troubles.'
And with these curt words he rode hence from me."

The duchess paused and looked at her Gawain
As they rode gently side by side and said:
"Now tell me truthfully brave, loyal one,
Was I wrong to give forth my love that way
With the aim of avenging my bereavement?
Has doing so discredited my love?"

They rode on, and Gawain spoke thoughtfully,
"If you had said this of another man,
Though you have done no wrong, I cannot say
What I'd surmise from what you've just told me;
But I know well the knight of whom you speak
And bear a brotherly fondness for him,
For there is no one like him in the world.
Your love has not and certainly would not
Have lessened in its worth for asking him."

They were now looking in each other's eyes,
Which held them in a blissful rhapsody,
Gazing as two hearts were merged to one;
And all their tribulations seemed to fade
Until all that remained with them was love.

CLINSCHOR

There was rejoicing in Schastel Marveile
Upon Gawain's return with Orgeluse.
The four queens and the many noble maidens
And all the entourage of worthy knights
Were overjoyed to see their lord alive.
Gawain had asked the duchess Orgeluse
To forbear from disclosing who he was
In Schastel Marveile, and she acquiesced.
Gawain discovered which of the four queens
Was Itonje his sister, who had sent
The falcon to Gawain's foe, Gramoflanz.
Gawain and Itonje had not seen each other
Since they were children many years before.
Without revealing who he was to her,
He spoke to Itonje of her affair
With Gramoflanz, his mortal enemy,
And saw that she indeed desired him
Though she attempted to conceal this truth,
For she knew of the wrath of Orgeluse
And felt herself to be a prisoner
Entrapped within the bounds of Terre Marveile.
Gawain bestowed the ring from Gramoflanz
To Itonje, and when she saw the ring,
Her cheeks flushed red immediately with shame.
She begged Gawain not to reveal her plight.
Had she known she was speaking to Gawain
Her discomfort would have been even greater.
It was a slim path of morality
Gawain was treading not informing her
Of his identity. He wished to know
What latitude his sister's heart was seeking
Without the influence of their blood's bond.

He trusted in the great design of things-
That with the right touch, all could be made right.
He promised that he would not say a word
Of his sister's affair with Gramoflanz.

Now word to Arthur from Gawain arrived,
And Arthur made haste with his company
To join his nephew on the dueling ground
By the Joflanze at the appointed date.
The great king was displeased that Gramoflanz,
Who was his kinsman, wished to slay Gawain
And was intent to find some thrifty means
To dissuade these two champions from the match.

Gawain and Orgeluse were joyfully
Now met in the fulfillment of their love,
And happily they drew close in their union
Across the days that followed their exchange
Upon the plain beside the garland tree,
For neither ere that time had known such peace,
Such deep contentment, and transcendent joy.

Gawain became acquainted with the land
O'er which he had now assumed rulership,
And all who had been held fast by the spells
Of Clinschor, their dark lord, were free at last.

With hosts of noble ladies and their lords
Filling Schastel Marveile's halls to the brim,
Gawain sought out a quiet place to sit
With the good and wise Arnive in an alcove,
Which overlooked a river far below,
To hear of wondrous tales about the land.

"Dear lady," said Gawain to wise Arnive,
"I do so long to know about those things
Which heretofore have been concealed from me.
I do not wish to impose with my wish
And so do not expect you to oblige,
For it is by your aid alone I live;
But if you think it prudent to relate
All that you know about the magic spells
That have been cast upon this wondrous land,
I would be grateful to now understand
How all these marvels have come into being.
The spells are broken which have taken me
Up to the brink of meeting death,
And you have saved me from that early end
So that I am acquainted with such joy
In love beyond what I knew to be possible.
But there is mystery and magic here
Which lives on since the dark spells have dispersed.
Why is this so? How did it come to pass
That subtle Clinschor cast his wicked spells?"

"My Lord," replied Queen Arnive to Gawain,
"The witchcraft he has cast upon this land
Is like to curiosities compared
With what great spells he's cast in other lands.
Now I shall tell you of dark Clinschor's tale.
The city of his birth was Capua.
His pursuit of high honor was so great
That glory was companion to his name
Until disaster caught up with his fame.
A king named Ibert lived in Sicily
Who unto a queen named Ilbis was wed.
She was fair to behold as one can be.
Lord Clinschor sued to win with servitute

333

The bounty of her sweet affections,
And she in turn gave him what he desired.
The king found Clinschor lying with his wife
While he lay sleeping wrapped in her embrace.
Enraged, he hurled the adulterer from his doors
And banished him far from that kingdom's shores.

It was unto a land called Persida
That Clinschor in disgrace fled from the world.
He was consumed with wrath for the dishonor
That King Ibert had brought against him
And turned to mastering dark sorcery
By which means to pursue his vengeful aims.
He learned to manifest whatever whim
He fancied by means of dark spells and craft.
Such hatred does he hold to those of worth
That nothing else will gratify his heart
Unless it be to rob all happiness
From anyone who bears a noble soul.
There was a king named Irot of Rosche Sabins-
He was the father of King Gramoflanz.
King Irot was fearful of Clinschor's wrath.
And so King Irot offered that dark lord
Whate'er from his possession he desired
In order that he might be left unscathed
By subtle Clinschor's sinister mischief.
Thus Clinschor gained from Irot this fortress,
Famed for its sturdiness, and all the land
Surrounding it in all directions
For the circumference span of eight full miles.
Upon this rock and 'round this mighty castle,
Lord Clinschor wove his ingenuity:
A subtle fabric of witchcraft and spells
Which cloaks the stronghold and spreads through the realm.

Of each and every single precious thing
There is a most abundant plethora.
Should any lay siege to this citadel,
There are provisions to last thirty years.
Lord Clinschor's power holds sway over all
The beings who dwell in the ether's span
Between the earth and the heavenly firmament,
Malign and benign both, saving those
Who are protected by the hand of God.
Since your great peril was averted here
Without it proving fatal to you sir,
The gift of this land is subject to you
Since nevermore will Clinschor dwell again
Within this land, for thus did he proclaim.
He publicly declared it to be so-
And is known to be a man of his word-
That whosoever should pass through this quest
Would thence be free from Clinschor's sorcery
And would receive as the victor Terre Marveile.
You have as your subjects folks of all kinds-
Those he despised who dwelt in Christendom,
Those simply caught beneath his hateful gaze,
And many people brought from Pagandom
Whom he despised for their nobility.
Now sir, do let them all depart from here
And return home from there fraught exile
Where Clinschor cruelly wrenched them in his wrath!
Such exile is a cold frost to the heart.
With cold comes ice but with warmth once again
Is water to its gentle flow returned.
What am I saying now? I know you will
Do as a servant of the hosts above
Would do, for so have you done until now.
I fret with worry from imprisonment

And long endurance held within these walls.
I have been waiting here for many years.
For all that time, not one has ridden here
Or walked in through the gates of this stronghold
To test the stoutness of their bravery
Against the perils in these haunted halls
And win through to obtain our liberty."

"It shall be as your every wish commands,"
Replied steadfast Gawain to wise Arnive.
"And if I live to watch over this realm,
You can be sure that as long as I live,
You may forever count on my protection."

Soon after that King Arthur with his host
Arrived and reunited with Gawain.
Such joy and celebration then ensued
Between the hosts of Arthur and Gawain.
The Lady Guinevere was overjoyed
To find their nephew thus alive and well
Though still weak from the wounds he had received.
Both Arthur and his queen met Orgeluse
And were delighted by the joyful pair.
Gawain then brought King Arthur to Arnive,
And there were tears of joy and celebration
From all eyes as that mother and her son
Were reunited after many years.

King Arthur sent word to King Gramoflanz
With messages of strong disparagement
And disapproval at the Briton's kin
For staging such an uncouth dueling match
With his dear kinsman, noblest of knights,
King Arthur's nephew, steadfast Lord Gawain.

Proud Gramoflanz sent word back to the king
That he was not deterred from his intent
To reap his vengeance upon bold Gawain.
King Arthur was not pleased with this reply.
He was incensed by this king's haughtiness,
His peevish insolence, and disregard.
All this was unbeknownst to Sir Gawain,
Who fastened his heart toward the reckoning
And made himself as ready as he could
Though he still suffered from his mending wounds
And wished he was not plagued by their complaints.
King Arthur kept his nephew's spirits up
With feasting and joy in their company
And reassured him God stood at his back;
But on no terms was Arthur of the mind
To let this match occur while he stood by
And was prepared to go to any means
To stop the senseless duel from taking place.

The night before the battle had arrived
They feasted as the sun sank into dusk.
Once all had had their fill of nourishment
And Arthur and Gawain had bid goodnight,
Steadfast Gawain retired to his tent
Where they had camped nearby the jousting ground.
Long ere the sun had risen, he was up
And armed himself without waking a soul.
He wished to test the stoutness of the bands
That wrapped his wounds inside his suit of steel.
He also wished to exercise his limbs
To make sure he was fit to face his foe.
He stepped forth from his tent in secrecy
And woke a squire quietly nearby.
He told the squire to fetch Gringuljete,

To saddle up the beast, and meet him close
With shield, lance, and his sword upon the field.
The setting moonlight glinted on the steel
Of the beast's trappings as it was brought forth.
The warrior then climbed astride the back
Of the good, faithful steed and sallied forth.
As he rode down toward the dueling ground,
He saw a well-armed knight sat motionless
Beneath the waning moon who surely was
A flintstone of courageousness and might.
May fortune now watch over both of them!

A RECKONING AT DAWN

Gawain now galloped toward a reckoning
That would be sure to test his fortitude.
One could as well be worried for his foe,
But in the end, fear for Gawain's opponent
Would be misplaced, for when it came to war,
He was an army packed inside one man.
His crest had been brought over land and sea
From pagan countries where his quest had ranged.
His surcoat and all his accessories
Including his fine horse's ornaments
Were rich and redder than a ruby's hue.
The hero was in quest of chivalry;
His shield was riddled with holes from great jousts,
And on his helm he wore a garland branch
Clipped from the tree patrolled by Gramoflanz:
He too had claimed a trophy from that place.
Gawain was anxious when he saw the branch,
For he thought it might be that king himself;
And had Gawain encountered Gramoflanz,
A battle could not be avoided then.
And if a chance encounter prompted them
Into this match with no formality,
No witnesses would be there to enforce
The code of honor and govern the match.

The mounts of both knights were from Munsalvaesche,
And urged on by the spur, they galloped
Toward each other, climbing in their speed
Until they were both racing at full tilt.
Across the wide span of the level plain
They sped through grass and clover glistening,
Kissed by the dewy silver of the moon.

It was a battle both would soon regret
Though now they strove at odds 'gainst one another.

Each blow was dealt with such skill and such force
That these two kinsman and companions
Could do no less than bring each other down.
Both steeds and riders were strewn on the grass.
Without a pause, they rose up from the ground
And drew forth their keen blades beneath the moon,
Both set unflinchingly toward the test.
And on they came to meet the fearsome clash
With flashing metal glinting in the dawn
As moonbeams softened into early light,
And faint stars flickered out in the expanse.
And on they battled, neither giving ground
Into the fresh day swiftly burgeoning.
They hacked and battered with such crushing strength
The grass was strewn with chips from both their shields
As each shield was hewn down into a block.
So equally were these two brave knights matched
That they were forced to battle for some time
Without an answer to their reckoning,
For they had started ere the sun was up,
And no one was there to name it a draw.

Now Arthur had arisen and gone forth
To set things right with haughty Gramoflanz.
He'd also roused himself before daybreak,
Intent to stop the match from happening.
Across the river he sent messengers
Who tried all manner of threats and leveraging
To steer the prideful king from his intent,
But all these offers were of no avail.
King Gramoflanz prepared to meet the joust.

When they saw there was no hope of success
In turning Gramoflanz from his intent,
King Arthur's pages hurried back to camp,
And on their way they stumbled on the duel,
Now underway upon the battleground.
Never had these good, truehearted pages
Been more distressed than when they saw them there.
They shouted at the top of their young voices
And bellowed out the name of King Lot's son,
For things had almost reached the tipping point
Where Sir Gawain's opponent could have won.
The latter's strength was so unstoppable
That the unconquerable Lord Gawain
Would have had to be brought to his defeat!
But as the pitch of those young pages' shouts
Pierced through the clang of steel and clashing blades,
Gawain's foe suddenly ceased battling
And flung his sword far away from himself.

"A curse upon my wretched destiny!"
Gawain's contender uttered through his tears,
"For fortune has again abandoned me!
How grossly has this hand of ignominy
Now blunderingly struck at brotherhood!
Fool that I am! I should have known,
For never have I battled 'gainst such strength
And mastery in all my fighting days.
Alack the day when I e'er grasped the sword
Since I have used it so reproachfully.
I may as well have battled with myself!
I will accept and undertake the blame
For this misguided skirmish we have fought.
To think that I've been battling Gawain!
In doing so I have vanquished myself

And will await misfortune's next command-
For fortune fled the instant when I struck."

Gawain bore witness to this heartfelt grief.
"Alas," he said, "who are you sir? You speak
So kindly toward me. If only these things
Had been voiced while I still had some strength left.
I would not then have had to face defeat
Which you have fairly driven me toward.
What is your name that I may seek the glory
Which I've lost from you in future days.
As long as fortune has been at my back,
I've always faced up well against my foes."

"Dear cousin I will tell you who I am
And will be at your service evermore.
I am your friend and kinsman Parzival."

"Then all is well," replied steadfast Gawain.
"All perverse folly has been straightened out.
Two hearts that are one have here shown their strength
In a fierce clash of dire enmity.
Your hand has overcome the both of us.
Regret it as you have for both our sakes.
You spoke the truth. You have subdued yourself."
And having said this, noble Sir Gawain
Could stand no longer. He grew faint and weak
And tottered giddily as his head swam.
The battle had indeed done him some harm.
He fell, stretched to his full length on the grass.
Immediately one of Arthur's pages
Was at his side and pillowed his good head
While others gently unlaced and removed
His helm to fan him softly on his face.

Some water was brought, and he was revived.
Sir Parzival himself knelt by his friend
And helped the pages as they did their work,
For he was sore with wrath against himself
That he had turned his strength upon his friend.

The companies of both hosts had arrived,
Advancing toward positions marked for them
With mighty logs all burnished till they shone.
King Gramoflanz had spared no cost in this
Since he had been the one to call the match.
There were a hundred of these gleaming trunks
With fifty on each side set far apart,
And no one was to set foot in between,
For there, the battle was to be engaged.
Now soldiers from both armies trickled in.
They were all filled with intrigue to behold
Those who had been fighting there so valiantly,
For neither army had brought forth their knight.

'Twas after this exchange of arms had ceased
Upon the fair green of the flowering field
That Gramoflanz arrived in stately pomp,
Impatient to bring vengeance on Gawain.
He heard a sword duel had been fought that morn,
More fierce than anyone had ever seen
Upon that ground, before the hosts were met.
And further, there had been no cause to fight;
But ne'ertheless, two warriors had fought.
King Gramoflanz rode forth from his great host
Toward those battle-wearied warriors,
Deploring their exertions earnestly.
Yet although he was spent in every limb,
Gawain had sprung up from the grassy ground,

343

So both combatants stood together there
As Gramoflanz approached in his chagrin.

The good and gentle Bene rode with him,
For she had been enlisted by Itonje
As messenger and go-between for love
And had arrived that morning in the court
Of Gramoflanz to give the king a gift.
She'd seen the messengers from Arthur's host
But knew not of the duel which had been planned
And so was unperturbed at seeing them.
She knew well of the might of Gramoflanz
And had she known he wished to slay Gawain,
She would have joined King Arthur's messengers
In their goal of deterring Gramoflanz.
But now when she beheld her friend Gawain-
The one she'd chosen as her crowning joy-
Who now stood pale and drained of all his strength,
She leapt down from her mare and ran to him
Then threw her arms around her noble friend
And clasped him tightly with all of her strength.

"A curse upon the one who caused you pain,
For you are the embodiment of strength,
Nobility, and grace, unparalleled!"
She helped him to a seat upon the grass,
Unable to restrain herself from tears,
And wiped the sweat and blood off of his face.

"It grieves me that I find you in this state,
Gawain, except that I wish I myself
Had been the one to inflict pain on you,"
Said prideful Gramoflanz to Sir Gawain.
"If you will come back to this meadow here

Tomorrow morning, I will meet you then,
For in this moment I would rather fight
A person who had never held a sword
Than battle you in your enfeebled state.
Without a better record of your strength,
What honor will I gain from your defeat?
Now rest this night, for you will need your strength
When you face me and answer for King Lot."

Stout-hearted Parzival did not show signs
Of pallor or of weariness in limb.
He'd just unlaced his helmet as the king
Rode up and laid his haughty gaze on him.

"Sir," said Parzival, "let me stand in
For my good cousin in whatever feud
You've engineered as cause to battle him.
I am still fit and in good fighting trim.
If you would vent your anger on this man,
Then I will surely stop you with my sword."

"Sir," replied the lord of Rosche Sabins,
"It will be Lord Gawain alone I fight
Tomorrow morning on this battlefield,
For I must claim my fair price for his prize:
The garland branch he wrested from my tree.
I do not doubt you are a fighting man,
But this duel is not one for you to fight."

"You spineless cur!" sweet Bene now cut in.
"Your heart is in the hands of one you hate!
To whom have you surrendered in love's name?
The woman who must live by this man's favor!
Your senselessness proclaims your own defeat.
This two-faced scheme will lose your right to love,
For it is not love when it's in bad faith!"

King Gramoflanz called her aside at this
And spoke intensely to her in hushed tones.

"Madam," he begged, "do not be testy with me
For fighting this duel! Stay here with your lord,
And tell his sister that I will remain
Her servitor in every way I can."

When Bene heard this confirmation
That her lord was indeed her lady's brother
And was pledged to do battle on that field
Unto the death with prideful Gramoflanz,
Grief's tide washed shiploads of woe through her soul
And mixed with rage in her loyal heart.

"Out with you! You accursed and wretched man!"
She cried out without censoring her voice
Despite the protestations of the king.
"I am acquainted with the blatant fact
That loyalty is something you know not!
Take yourself off, and seek no quarter here!
I will acquaint my lady with the truth-
That your love holds a double countenance.
And we'll gauge if her love for you lives then!
That you should seek her brother's death like this
And still sue unabashedly for love!
Indecency has never been more bold!"

For all his haughtiness, that vengeful king
Was sent off packing by sweet Bene's words.
What could he do? For Bene glared at him
Prepared to spar with such ferocity
While all looked on, he could say no more.
He had no choice but to ride with his band
Hence from that place, before their watchful gaze.

Gawain and Parzival, now reconciled
From the misfortune of their reckoning,
Gave happy greetings, each to one another
With brotherly accord and levity,
For they were joyful in their reunion
And laughed at the strange chance of the encounter-
Albeit somewhat worse for wear and weary.
Their horses were fetched by King Arthur's pages,
And those two champions with good Bene
Rode off the field toward their company.

Now Parzival had with his great exploits
Won such exalted glory on his quest
That his name at that time was on the lips
Of all throughout the span of Christendom
And most especially in King Arthur's host.
For this, there was much joy and much celebration
When he returned with his companion
And dearest friend, the brave and good Gawain.
And so, word flew throughout the mighty ranks
Of Arthur, Orgeluse, and bold Gawain
That Parzival had come and was with them.

"If you should like to meet four noble queens
Who are connected with your lineage,
I'll introduce you to them," said Gawain.

"I do not wish to meet nobility,"
Said Parzival to his most trusted friend,
"For when I was last with this company,
I was so vilified before them all
That they must now detest the sight of me.
I am filled so completely with disgrace
That I am loath to seek their company."

"Well there is nothing for it," said Gawain
And led his friend to meet the four high queens.

The duchess was beset by much distress
To have to welcome one who had spurned her,
Once she had ridden after him so far
And offered both her lands and love to him.
Embarrassment gave her heart much ado.
But like the noble hearted soul she was,
She set by her discomfort for her love
Whom she now trusted without compromise.

Gawain then set to work and artfully
Led all the shame held captive in the heart
Of noble Parzival out from its cell
And showed all doubtful harborage the door
To free his friend from any ill accord.
This having been successfully achieved
By means of Sir Gawain's gentility,
Brave Parzival grew cheerful once again
And acquiesced to sharing in the joy.

Gawain next spoke to his good friend Bene
And asked her not to inform Itonje
About the hatred held by Gramoflanz
Toward her brother and his vengeful aim.

"Please do not speak or show her any sign,"
He urged, "that we will meet tomorrow morn
And fight a battle. Not a word of it,
For I must leave my sister free to choose
Where her heart lies without the fettered bond
Of sisterly duty held on my behalf.
I beg you not to weep on my account,
For she will then detect what you have heard!"

"I have good cause to weep," replied Bene,
"And let my sorrow be seen by the throng.
If either of you fall, you will be mourned.
Itonje will be slain on either side!
What else can I do but lament for you,
For my good lady, myself, and the world?
It will not be a celebration sir
That is held on the morrow at this time
If this foolhardy duel is carried out.
How does it help that you are brother to her
If you with your foe wage war on her heart?"

Their heated conversation was cut short
By all the great hosts marching in to dine.
A mighty feast had been prepared for them,
And it was served with great ceremony.

Itonje did not fail to catch the gaze
Of loyal Bene, who withdrew her glance,
But it was plain that she wept quietly;
And when Itonje saw Bene's distress,
She too took on the countenance of woe
And found she had no stomach for the feast.
"What is she doing here?" Itonje mused,
"Did I not send her to the man I love?
What will it be that I must suffer now?
I bear such pain in loving one who dwells
Outside the bounds of my imprisonment.
This throws me to great turmoil within.
Has Gramoflanz rejected my devotion?
If so, I fear I will die of my grief!"

It was past noon when that great feast had ended,
And Arthur with the Lady Guinevere

Made his way over to greet Parzival
Where he sat 'midst the company of others.

The king paid Parzival all honors due
And thanked him for his exploits earnestly,
Claiming that he'd won such high renown
That by rights, his rank towered above all.

"When last I met you sire," said Parzival,
"My honor underwent a harsh attack.
I was stripped of so much of it I feared
Myself to be almost bankrupt of worth.
But now good King, if what you say is true,
Then in your words I hear the hopeful chance
That there may be some honor left in me
Despite the shame I brought upon myself.
Though I have found it hard to be convinced,
I would still ne'ertheless gladly believe
This to be true if others who were there
And watched me leave disgraced are in accord."

King Arthur and those sitting close agreed
That Parzival had earned such mighty glory
That his name now stood tested and intact.

More knights and ladies had assembled there.
King Arthur, urbane person that he was,
Then sat himself with Lady Guinevere
And his good friend the mighty Parzival
Outside the royal tent of Sir Gawain,
And everyone sat 'round them in a ring
And held discourse in pleasant company.

At length brave Parzival rose to his feet
And then addressed the great throng gathered there:

"May all those present quietly now sit
And help me with a thing which troubles me.
By a strange turn of destiny, my path
Was separated from the Round Table.
I ask those who once knew me as a friend
To help me reunite with this great host!"

King Arthur graciously accorded him
And rose to welcome their friend back again
And then embraced the worthy Parzival.

This done, good Parzival then stepped aside
And found Gawain amid a smaller group
To whom he voiced the following request:
"I shall be happy to await your foe
Tomorrow morning and contend with him.
Before daybreak this morn, I broke a twig
From off the garland tree to challenge him
So that he would attack me, for it was
Expressly to do battle with this king
That I have entered back into this realm.
Dear cousin, I could scarcely have surmised
That it was you who came to meet me there.
I never have regretted something more,
For I imagined it was Gramoflanz
Who'd come to battle with me for the branch.
If his fame is to ever be reduced,
It is I who must bear the brunt of him
And bring his arrogance down from its perch.
My rights have been restored to me again
So that I may once more live as thy comrade.
Remember that we two share lineage.
Restore your strength, and save your dauntless heart
For other battles. Leave this duel to me."

"Dear cousin," said Gawain, "and brothers all,
My kinsmen and my friends who've gathered here,
Not one of you will I allow to fight
In my place against fearsome Gramoflanz.
I am assured by my good cause and hope
That I will attain the victory.
May God reward your offer for my sake,
But I am not so far gone to accept."

Now Arthur overheard their conversation
And came to put an end to this exchange.
He bade them follow him to where he sat
And claim a seat beside him in the ring.

At length the evening drew across the scene,
And Parzival arose to bid goodnight
To his good king and noble company
And gave thought to examining his gear.
If any of the leathers had been snapped,
He made sure that each one had been restored.
He asked a page to bring him a new shield,
For his was holed and whittled to a stump.
His horse, who had been ridden by the Templar
In Terre De Slavaesche before Parzival
Had won it from that knight in their encounter,
Was groomed and dressed till it shone splendidly.
As evening dipped into the quiet night,
Brave Parzival was sleeping restfully.

For his part, Gramoflanz was in a state
Of aggravation that another man
Had battled his opponent earlier.
He was regretful that he'd missed his chance
And was beleaguered by exasperation.

Before first light, the restless king was up
And had himself and his horse fully armed.

Now Parzival too had slipped out unseen
And freed a stout lance of tough angram wood
From its silk pennant, billowing in the dusk,
And was then fully armed to face the charge.
So forth into the dawn, the warrior rode.
As he progressed toward the jousting ground,
Delineated by the burnished logs,
He saw the king whom he sought waiting there.

The two knights paused when they saw one another,
And all was still beneath the silent morn.
Then without any word, they spurred their mounts
And came together in a crushing charge.
Both lances punctured through the other's shield
And burst to splinters in a cloud of chips.
They leapt down from their steeds to meet on foot
And came together in a clash of steel.
Across the span of that wide battleground,
The dew was trampled while their helmets clanged,
And their keen blades bit down with every blow.
The sun rose as they fought on fearlessly
And crushed the grass beneath their armored heels.
The two stout warriors were both enduring
Much hardship from each other without flinching.

And now Gawain arose from where he lay
To make himself prepared to face the duel.
It was midmorning ere it came to them
That mighty Parzival had left their midst.
A bishop had sung mass for Sir Gawain
With many knights and nobles gathered there.

The king himself prayed with gentle Gawain.
The benediction having been enacted,
Gawain departed and armed for the battle.
There were some gathered who began to weep,
Filled with anxiety for their dear lord.
Once all was set the company set forth
Toward the battleground where to their shock,
They heard the sound of sword play in the air,
The crackling of sparks hewn from steel helms,
And mighty blows as they were driven home.

It was the custom of King Gramoflanz
To scorn a battle with one single knight,
But now it seemed to him he battled six
Though Parzival alone was facing him.
The latter was at work with teaching him
A lesson in good fighting qualities.
And truly after he'd met Parzival,
King Gramoflanz remembered his good manners,
For never again did he arrogate
The honor to himself of fighting two.

Meanwhile hosts on both sides had arrived
And were appraising this intrepid match.
The horses of both warriors stood still,
Close by their masters battling on foot.
Time and again the swordsmen tossed their swords
From one hand to the other as they struck
To change the edges of their hefty blades.
King Gramoflanz was clearly worse for wear
And was receiving hefty recompense
For both the garland branches he had lost:
One for Gawain and one for Parzival.
It was for his dear friend and kin, Gawain,

Whose sister his opponent strove to win,
That Parzival administered his strength.
His foe's great fame was swiftly rattling
Toward his first acquaintance with defeat.
Gawain arrived just at the tipping point
When Parzival would surely have attained
A mighty victory against their foe.

Bradelidelin, King of Punterteis,
Who was the uncle of King Gramoflanz,
With two companions rode across the field
And hasted toward King Arthur and Gawain
To speak with them about what should be done.
With swift accord, the five lords were agreed
And brought the confrontation to a close.
The weary Gramoflanz did not oppose
This intervention, for he too agreed
It was the moment to accept defeat
And formally conceded victory
To his indomitable challenger.

"My Lord King," said Gawain to Gramoflanz,
"I shall today do what you yesterday
Did unto me when you asked me to rest.
Now you must rest, for you have need of it.
The warrior who has battled you today
Has sapped the strength you'd have used against me.
I could now with a hand tied to my back
Defeat you in your present feeble state.
Though you insist on fighting two at once,
Tomorrow I will hazard it alone."

Once he had pledged his word to Sir Gawain
That he would join him on the dueling ground

The next morn, Gramoflanz rejoined his host
And with his company rode hence from there.

"Nephew," Arthur said to Parzival,
"Though you requested leave from our Gawain
To stand for him and fight this deadly match,
Permission was not granted for the duel.
And yet without our favor, you have fought
Whether we approved of it or not.
I'd have prevented you had I found out.
Still, I will not be angry with you now,
Nor need you be, Gawain, for it is plain
That though our bidding has been undermined,
Love's supreme order has not been denied;
And therefore, no harm is inflicted here."

"My Lord," Gawain said to his Uncle Arthur,
"The high distinction that my cousin won
In undergoing this encounter here
Does not perturb me. It was in good faith.
To tell you plainly, if I undertake
A duel tomorrow, it is still too soon,
For I have not recovered from my wounds
But can see no way to relinquish it.
If there were any means to be released
From fighting this match that the king can see,
I would receive it as a gracious gift."

King Arthur and his kinsman Parzival
Both quietly rejoiced to hear these words
As they were uttered from their kinsman's lips,
For both of them had independently
Been at pains for a means to help Gawain
And keep him from that dire reckoning.

But knowing that Gawain would never budge
From facing any danger on his path,
Each kinsman had been hard pressed for a way
To stop the fearsome duel from taking place.
King Arthur was resolved within himself
Right then and there to find an argument
To end that conflict unequivocally.

Now while the battle with Sir Parzival
And Gramoflanz was taking place that morn,
Itonje had been questioning Bene
And had learned that her brother and her love
Were set to fight a battle to the death.
With this news, she could not conceal her woe
Which burst forth from the bonds of secrecy
As she gave way to weeping in despair.
She was discovered by the wise Arnive,
Who gathered her granddaughter[35] to her tent,
And with authority bade the young queen
Release the burden from her troubled heart
And there confide the cause of her distress.
Itonje told Arnive the whole of it:
Her love for Gramoflanz, his love for her,
How she feared that the wrath of Orgeluse
Would never rest until her love lay dead,
And further, how if their love were found out,
The vengeful duchess would exact her wrath
Upon Itonje for disloyalty.
And then, on top off her anxieties,
Her brother was to fight for Orgeluse
And battle with her lover to the death!
The only outcome was calamity!

---

35   See page 407 (Character List.)

All hopes of living peacefully were dashed!

"Dear child," said Arnive to Itonje,
"You have held this in secrecy too long!
This situation is too treacherous
To navigate alone as you have done.
Perhaps there is a purpose for your plight.
Where is my son?" Arnive called to the maid,
Who waited by the queen's pavilion.
"Go find him, and bid him come to my tent."

The maiden found the king and gave him word
Sent from Arnive to join her at the tent.
And Arthur went straightway to her pavilion.
Arnive encouraged Itonje to speak
And tell her uncle all that troubled her.
King Arthur listened as Itonje spoke
And told him of her pact with Gramoflanz.

Meanwhile pages sent by Gramoflanz
Had given Bene tokens of affection
Which she was to convey to Itonje.

As Bene came close with the note and ring
Sent for Itonje from King Gramoflanz,
Itonje was still speaking to King Arthur:
"And he who has possession of my heart
Is yet content to slay my noble brother?
What wrong has either done to one another
That has thus forced a battle to the death?
I know the duchess has her grievances,
But will more death bring any peace of mind?
If my love is slain, I will die from grief!
You are my uncle! Settle this dispute!"

King Arthur listened thoughtfully to her
Although the girl spoke vehemently to him.

"Alas, my dear niece," he said when she'd ceased
And sat before him in rage and despair,
"It is a truly loyal love you bear,
Proved by the noble fire of your words.
If only I could put an end to this
And steer your lover from his dire goal.
I have not succeeded in deterring him,
But by your words, I see a narrow path
Which may lead to a peaceful compromise.
Your love is proved by what you have just said.
If I could have proof of his love for you,
This duel, which cannot end well, might be curbed,
For if this king loves you as you love him,
Then you, my niece, may be the only one
Who has the power to redeem his heart.
He is the son of Irot and is made
Of such unflinching courage that this match
Will be fought unless your love can prevail.
Has he on any festive happenstance
Had the good fortune of beholding you
And witnessing your radiance and grace?"

"That has not ever happened," said the girl.
"We loved though we have never seen each other,
But so abundant is the love we share.
In hope of true companionship and joy,
He has sent me many precious gifts
And from me has received what goes with love
To banish any doubt between two hearts.
The king is steadfast in his love for me;
His heart is free of all dishonesty."

At this point, Lady Bene gently spoke
And gave the ring and letter to Itonje.
Itonje read the letter happily
Then kissed it several times and held the ring
Wrapped tightly in her grasp before she said:
"You may read for yourself the proof you seek
Sire, for my lord's love lies on this page."

Respectfully, the king received the note
And read the message over thoughtfully
And found indeed the proof which he required:
That Gramoflanz for all his haughtiness
Knew love when it came to his Itonje.
Each word was written with such faithfulness
That Arthur had not seen more proof of love
With such truth and conviction e'er before:

"To Itonje the guiding principle
And North Star of my quest for happiness:
My love, it is you that I have in mind
Since it is you who solace me with hope.
Our loves must still keep company together-
This is the root of my abounding joy.
Since your heart is as constant as the day,
Your devotion outweighs all other delights.
You are the clasp that holds my steadfastness
And the banisher of my unhappiness.
Your love will help me strive toward the good
With the high aim that no misdeed be found
Within me. To your goodness I ascribe
A constant that does not shift its place.
As the celestial bodies of the heavens
Trace out the courses of their sacred dance,
Revolving in empyrean harmony,

So shall our two hearts orbit one another
Clasped sweetly in love's choreography.
Affection shall stand with faithful loyalty
And never go apart. Now, noble one,
Remember me and how I yearn for you.
Do not be slow to answer me with love.
If any other bears such hatred toward me
That they might wish us to be torn apart,
Hold fast within your heart that mighty love
Possesses such a power to transcend
All hindrances and to requite us both.
Take care, and keep me as your servitor.
I will serve you with all the best in me!"

"You are right, my dear niece!" King Arthur said.
"King Gramoflanz writes with sincerity.
This letter tells me such a mighty tale
That I have never seen so marvelous
An inspiration on the theme of love!
You must put a swift end to suffering!
And he must do the same! Leave this to me.
I will prevent this senseless dueling match
So help me God, and spare us all more tears!
How came it that you found love in each other
With you imprisoned here as you have been?"

"The one who engineered it all is here,"
Itonje said, "and if you think it good,
She will arrange for me to see the man
Whom I have made the keeper of my heart."

"Show her to me," said Arthur. "If I can,
I will see to it for his and your sake
That all your wishes will be so fulfilled

That you may both find peace and happiness."

"It was Bene," replied King Arthur's niece.
"If you care for my life, will you help me
To find out if the king, to whom my joy
Is joined, desires to lay eyes on me?"

Discreet as he was courteous, the king,
Itonje's uncle, took the messengers
Sent from King Gramoflanz aside to speak.
One of these pages then addressed the king:
"Sire," said the boy, "King Gramoflanz
Requests that for the sake of your honor,
You now fulfill the vow pledged by Gawain
And our king to meet upon the field
And settle their account once and for all.
Further, he demands that you must send
Gawain and not another of your knights
To face this reckoning with Gramoflanz."

"I'll clear us of this charge," King Arthur said.
"My nephew has not ever been more grieved
Than when he was not there to fight this morn
In person as was priorly arranged.
As to the knight who fought King Gramoflanz
In place of our Gawain, his victory
Is of his very nature since he is
The mighty son of noble Gahmuret.
All who have joined here in these three great hosts
From all directions have not ever known
A warrior more valiant in the fray.
He is my kinsman known as Parzival.
For now, I will comply with the request
Of Gramoflanz regarding Gawain's oath

And will escort my nephew to the field
Tomorrow morning at the time agreed."

King Arthur rode with Bene and the pages
As they made their way back to Rosche Sabins
Where proud King Gramoflanz awaited them.
King Arthur wished to speak with the two pages:

"Bene, kind friend," he said, "you heard the tale
Of woe told by my dear niece, Itonje?
She was unable to constrain her tears.
Your friends here must assuredly agree
That if King Gramoflanz persists this way,
He will rob our dear niece of wholesomeness,
For such anxiety does not breed health.
Assist me now, you two most nobles pages,
Who do your office so respectably,
And you good friend, Bene, with my design.
Convince King Gramoflanz to meet with me
Midway between our camp and the Joflanze
This afternoon: I'll be there with Gawain.
This will not interfere with their intent
To meet in battle on the dueling ground
Tomorrow morning as they have agreed.
Tell him if he will sojourn to my camp,
He will behold a sight to give him strength.
He will be fired by so great a passion
That his love will be a shield 'gainst his foe.
His adversary will regret indeed
That he agreed to meet him in the duel.
By that, I mean the mettle forged from love
Which wreaks such havoc on one's enemy
When one is facing them in single combat.
Tell him to bring some courtiers along

To be my guest with him among my host.
Between ourselves, I'll tell you of my plan:
To mediate for the good Orgeluse
And your brave king, the noble Gramoflanz.
If you go to this business with discretion,
Bene and pages, you will gain much worth."
The noble pages and Bene the true
Agreed wholeheartedly to this request.

"Since I see by your gentleness and grace
That you are friends with hearts of compassion,"
The king continued as he rode with them,
"I must in confidence make one complaint,
Which I know you will carry gracefully.
What- disgraceful man that I must be-
Have I done to your master Gramoflanz
That he must treat my family carelessly,
To such love and such hatred all at once?
For any fellow king of mine has cause,
And if I may speak plainly, now good cause,
To treat me and my host respectfully.
If he intends with hatred to reward
The brother of the woman whom he loves,
He only need reflect, and he will see
That when his heart instills in him such thoughts,
It has turned traitor to the laws of love."

"If my lord aims at being courteous,
He should refrain from battling Gawain,"
One of the pages said to noble Arthur.
"But sire, you are surely made aware
Of the old blood feud between Orgeluse
And our king? In view of this dispute,
It would be best for our lord to remain

Right where he is instead of coming here
And meeting you as your guest as you've said."

"Come, come, I give my word, he'll not be harmed.
He'll have safe passage as my honored guest!"
Said Arthur. "Let him come with but a few.
While you are gone, I will obtain a truce
From Orgeluse regarding their dispute
And will provide him with a princely guard,
For my good nephew, who is called Beacurs,
Shall meet him halfway and conduct him here.
Assure your lord that he will be protected
And treated with high honor as my guest.
Nor do not let him think it a disgrace,
For in my company he will be met
By a most noble and distinguished host."

The pages took their leave excitedly,
With faithful Bene in their company,
And set forth with this message for their king.

It was a bright day for King Gramoflanz
When Bene and the noble pages came
And told him of King Arthur's invitation.
He felt as though this news was sent to him
Straight from the lips of good fortune itself.

He sent an answer back to Arthur's camp
And said he'd gladly come as Arthur's guest.
A company was chosen for the outing.
Three princes of that realm rode with their king.
And as King Arthur had said to the pages,
The noble Beacurs met them on their way.

King Gramoflanz then whispered to Bene:

"Who is this royal prince escorting us,
Who speaks so kindly and so graciously?"

"He is Lot's son, Beacurs," replied the lady.

"Heart," King Gramoflanz mused to himself,
"Now find the maiden who resembles him,
The one riding beside me with such grace!
She, who sent me tokens of her love,
Is truly this man's beautiful sister!
If she bestows her favor unto me,
I would take her alone above all else,
Above all earthly riches- were the earth
Expanded till it doubled in its size!
I must believe her love to be sincere.
Till now she's given me encouragement
In such a way that I can only hope
She will treat my heart with gentleness
And raise my spirits by returning love!"

Now in the army, it had come about
That Arthur had obtained the truce he sought
From the puissant and kind Duchess Orgeluse.
She now had recompense for Citigast
Whom she had mourned with such intensity.
Gawain's embraces had brought her such joy
That now hostility had ebbed away
And made space for new love and happiness
To blossom where her vengeance once held sway.

King Arthur summoned everyone to join
Within his opulent and spacious tent
And bade them all be seated at their ease,
All but for Gramoflanz who was addressed
By Arthur: "Noble Gramoflanz," he said,

"Before you think of seating yourself here,
Look 'round this tent and see if any lady
Within this circle is the one you love.
Then, if she be here with us in this tent,
I bid you go and greet her with a kiss.
You have my leave to do so in our midst."

Now there was nothing underneath the sun
That could have brought Itonje greater joy
Than when she and her love's eyes came to rest
Within the rapture of each other's gaze.
Nor had that king e'er known such happiness
And gentle peace to settle in his soul.
He went to her and knelt before her feet
Then rose as they reached towards each other's hands
And closed the distance held between their souls,
And their lips came together in a kiss:
A kiss that filled their hearts and all those there
With such a boundless joy it seemed the earth
Had been graced with a touch of paradise.
And all were silent as they stood and looked
And gazed until the world for them dispersed,
And everything fell from them but their love.
It would have been the custom for the queen
To thank her guest for visiting her there
And for him to reply- "the joy was his."
Yet not a word was said. They were content
To simply stand and look at one another.
And there, they, in a blissful rhapsody,
Remained for an extended moment's breath.
At last, they were reminded of the throng
And gently shifted in their reverie
To look with wonder 'round the gathering.
And all those 'round them laughed with merriment

And sweet accord at this delightful tryst.

Then there was happy clamor 'mid the throng
With such a joyful murmuring about
That hummed and babbled like a laughing brook,
Which sings and tumbles over shining stones.
Refreshments were brought in for everyone
As all the joyous hosts were mingling
And celebrating in the festive mood.

King Arthur cordially clapped his mighty hand
Against the back of King Brandelidelin,
The uncle of the noble Gramoflanz,
Who had accompanied his nephew there.
"Come sit with me good king," Lord Arthur said
And affably escorted his fine guest
Toward a small pavilion pitched close by
The great tent where the throng was mingling.

"My fellow king," Lord Arthur then continued,
Once they had greeted and both sat at ease,
"Suppose now that our nephews meet to duel
And that your nephew, worthy Gramoflanz,
Were then to slay my nephew, Sir Gawain.
If he then wished to woo my lovely niece,
Who is now sitting in yon tent with him,
She would not then incline toward his intentions,
For she would be grief-stricken by the loss
Of her dear brother, noble Sir Gawain.
She would be hostile toward your Gramoflanz
If he expected anything from her.
Where love is tinged with hatred, happiness
Is denied entry to the constant heart."

"Wise king," replied the Lord of Punurteis,

"These two nephews of ours who seek a duel
Must be dissuaded from their foolishness.
No other outcome must they be allowed
Than that they learn to live in brotherhood
And love each other with all of their hearts.
If my young Gramoflanz would seek her love,
Your niece Itonje must command my nephew
To turn from folly and embrace Gawain,
Lay by his hatred and forgo the duel.
When he sees this match is a threat to love,
It will be dropped without a second thought.
And if you can, please help my reckless nephew
Toward the favor of good Orgeluse.
I will accept your generosity
In good faith and with humble gratitude."

"That I shall do," said Arthur to the king.
"I have already learned from Orgeluse
That she is ready to lay by the feud,
And I suspect the radiant Itonje
Is at work while we two sit and speak,
For if she has not by this moment moved
The worthy son of Irot's heart from hate
To love and toward friendly fellowship,
Then she will have done ere we find our seats."

The two great kings, both mighty warriors,
Then rose and met the other's hearty grip,
And headed back toward the happy throng.

King Arthur found Gawain and Orgeluse
And drew them both aside to speak with them.
The duchess was prepared to reconcile
With Gramoflanz should he accept her terms:

369

If her beloved Gawain would renounce
The duel for her sake, she would offer peace
But only if her enemy withdraw
The accusation 'gainst her father-in-law
King Lot. This she asked Arthur to convey,
And he, most gracious of all lords, agreed.

King Gramoflanz did not even protest,
For love had done its work entirely.
What could he do? Now happiness and peace
Were governing the kingdom of his heart,
And any malice he had entertained
For good King Lot had melted like the snow
In sunshine for lovely Itonje's sake;
No patch of trouble or resentment stayed.
This came about while he sat at her side:
He happily agreed to all they asked.

He rose without a hint of hesitation
And sealed their fellowship upon the spot,
Embracing Sir Gawain and kissing him,
Much to the joyful wonder of them all.

"Brother," he said, "I know no greater prize
Than to be granted brotherhood to thee.
Nor do I know what spell was cast on me
To cloud my sight till I could see no love
But only hatred when I thought of you.
Methinks 'twas love hid by hate's countenance.
I wished to battle with nobility,
To know and understand nobility.
But now by grace, I see nobility
When met in love is mightier than war.
Never have I known a greater strength

Than that which lives since light-filled Itonje
Hath granted me the power of her love,
To whose force I surrender happily-
For such a strength must surely conquer all."

It is not possible to shape with words
The level of exalted happiness
And blissful peace that was encountered there
By everyone who stood in company
With Sir Gawain, the Duchess Orgeluse,
Itonje, Gramoflanz, Queen Guinevere,
King Arthur, Sir Beacurs, Bold Parzival,
Sweet Bene, and the noble ferryman,
Wise Arnive, and all others of that host.
It was as though a blessing had been placed
By love's true hand, deep into every heart,
And over all that mighty gathering,
Uniting them in blissful peace and joy.

Now over the expanse of those few weeks
That had transpired since Gawain had come
To Terre Marveile and freed Schastel Marveil
And won the love of mighty Orgeluse,
The other sister of Gawain, named Cundrie,
Had joined in love with the renowned Lischios
While King Lot's widow, the fair Queen Sangive,
And the great Turkoyt were likewise engaged.

King Arthur ordered that a marriage feast
Be readied for a mighty celebration
That would be held for all those who had met
And found love in their meeting to be wed.

That night brave Parzival sat in his tent,
Once all the celebrating had died down,

And slumber lay draped over that great camp
Of Arthur, Sir Gawain, and Orgeluse.

Now Parzival was thinking of his wife
Condwiramurs while all those lovers met.
"How has love treated me," he to himself
Now pondered, "since I first encountered love?
I am born from a lineage of love.
How then have I been taken from my love?
 If I am to strive for the Holy Grail,
Desire for the sweet and pure embrace
Of one whom I left many years ago
Must ever wrangle my heart on my quest.
No one could ever be high-spirited
While bearing such opposing aspirations.
May I be guided to do what is best
For me to do, for I've ne'er yet found peace!"

His gaze was resting softly on his armor
Which lay close by as he mused to himself.
"Since I lack what the happy ones enjoy-
I mean love- that cheers sad thoughts to delight-
Since I'm cut off from taking part in this-
I do not care what happens to me now.
God does not wish me to have happiness.
If our love, that is my love and her love,
Were such that doubt and gloom preyed on our minds,
Then I could easily attain another.
But as things are, the love that she inspires
Has taken from my heart all other love
And any other hope of happiness;
Thus, I find no release from suffering.
May grace give joy to those deserving it,
A lasting joy both final and complete.

May God grant joy to all these companies
Who've gathered here in these festivities!
As for myself, I must ride from their joys."

He reached and took his armor in his hands,
Which he had often put on without aid,
And had soon cased his body all in steel.
He was prepared to face whatever trials
Where held in store upon his lonesome path.
This done, he girthed and saddled up his horse,
Then lifted up his hefty lance and shield,
And set forth, heading into early dawn.

THE PAGAN EMPEROR

Now Parzival rode briskly through a field
Toward a wood and toward his destiny.
Once he had entered the forest, he held his course
Through the hilly woodland toward the sea.

Not far away, along that rugged coast,
With cliffs and rocky outcrops interspersed
By sands and shallow coves with gentle surf,
A powerful emperor had moored his ships
And ordered that he with his horse be rowed
Ashore. He was a high born pagan king
Of vast renown and undefeated strength.
This pagan stranger was magnificent.
No other word depicts his personage
With more precision, though it still falls short,
For anyone who e'er encountered him
Would be left at a loss to speak of him.
He was endowed with every quality
That could be wished for in an emperor.
Not only this but he possessed vast wealth.
If one were to recount his mighty riches
Until one's listeners grew faint with boredom,
One still would not have told the half of it.

In keeping with his power and his wealth,
The pagan lord ruled twenty-five great hosts,
Not one of whom could speak the other's tongue,
For many lands sought out his governance,
His statesman's craft, and skill in leadership.
He was a master of diplomacy
And was admired for both strength and wit
And ease with many cultures and customs.

He left his escort and rode forth alone
To stretch his limbs, restless from voyaging,
In search of glory, fame, and adventure.
It was this most impressive warrior
Whom Parzival encountered on his path.

The eyes of each lit up when they beheld
The other as they moved toward the exchange.
The hearts of each rejoiced, yet sorrow lurked,
For each knight bore the other's heart within–
There was an intimate strangeness indeed!

Both shortened rein and urged their mounts to charge,
Accelerating from a gentle canter
And climbing smoothly in pace to full tilt.
No point of their routine was overlooked.
They took a firm grip on their stallions' backs
And braced their armored frames to meet the shock.
Both lances shattered with a deafening crack
As they met in that masterful exchange,
But neither warrior gave up their seat;
They held fast through the cloud of splintering.
The pagan was incensed that his stout foe
Had not been unhorsed, for brave Parzival
Was the first to withstand that king's boundless strength.
They wheeled their chargers 'round and drew their swords
And came together in a flash of blades,
Both striking fiercely from their stallions' backs.
They lunged and ducked and struck with hefting blows.
The sparks shot from their blades and off their helms
While mighty hooves smote down upon the earth
And churned the ground up underneath the fray.
It was a battle of such mastery,
Of boundless courage, and such crushing strength

That there were only two souls in the world
Who could withstand the onslaught of the match:
Those two contenders who were battling.

The horses grew too weary to fight on,
And so, both knights then vaulted to the earth
To battle one another on the ground.
And now the fight climbed to a fevered pitch
As both contestants strove with all their worth
To conquer their opponent by sheer strength,
For neither were familiar with defeat,
And neither warrior was giving ground.
But this fierce pagan king possessed such strength
That for the first time in the Parzival's life,
He was hard pressed to keep up with his foe.
It would be more than great strength alone
That he would need to summon from within
If he desired to hold off defeat.
The pagan now roared out his battle cry,
Which added power to his fierce attack.

If only Parzival could call to mind
Those pure, exalted principles to which
He'd given all his courage and his strength:
The love he bore for his wife Condwiramurs
And his unyielding quest to serve the Grail.
Why did he not reach down into the depths
Of his brave soul and call upon the strength
Of his ideals, the pillars of his being?

The pagan emperor raised up his sword,
Unleashing a barrage of battering,
Which forced brave Parzival onto his knees.

This fearsome pagan king's great might and skill,
Which were at work upon brave Parzival,

Were unrelenting as a hurricane.
It was a test of spiritual strength
Which far surpassed what Parzival had known,
For any battling he'd undergone
Up to that point was child's play compared
To the relentless reckoning at hand.

"Come Parzival, seek in your heart!
Remember who you are and why you live:
Your blessed queen, your subjects and the Grail,
Gawain, King Arthur, all of that company.
There are two children whom you are to meet,
And you will come to know of fatherhood!
Rally thy stout heart back into the fray!"

So might the silent call have given voice
Around the steadfast warrior as he fought
Had there been words and if one could have heard
The graceful presence of angelic hosts
At work to fortify the brave knight's heart
And grapple his soul back into its place.

He must have heard or somehow understood
Some whisper or faint echo of that call,
For as these two great lion-like warriors
Locked in a deadly impasse, blade 'gainst blade,
One beaten to his knees, one bearing down
With such a crushing strength no average soul
Could ever have avoided buckling,
The good and ever steadfast Parzival
Dug down into the deepness of his being,
And there, upon the brink of nothingness,
The vast might of the heavens touched his soul
And merged into the center of his heart,

Condensing from the great periphery
Down to a flame, ignited at his core.
And suddenly, the Red Knight hurled his foe
With such a powerful burst of boundless strength
The mighty pagan was flung several paces
Back from the grappling point of the impasse.
And Parzival fought upward from his knees
Relentlessly with great blow upon blow,
Each stronger than the one preceding it,
Until he'd gained his footing under him.

Once more the sparks flew from their blades and helms,
And sword strokes whined and hissed against the air
As they swung forcefully and clashed and rang.

The Christian was remembering his love,
And as she entered back into his heart,
It was as though a door was opening
Within his breast from which a fire leapt
And surged out from his chest into his limbs
And down into the great blade in his hands.
And now he was remembering the Grail
To which he had surrendered everything,
And heaven's fire surged within his chest.
Now there was nothing that could conquer him!
Each blow struck home with such unequaled strength
That the pagan king was slowly giving ground.
Never had that emperor met blows
So powerful and in such quick succession.

Chips of the value of a thousand marks
Were flying from the pagan king's great shield,
But neither of these two unflinching hearts
Were near surrender, so they battled on!

How would this fearsome contest ever end?
But suddenly, the blade gripped by the hand
Of mighty Parzival broke at the hilt
As he smote with the mightiness of heaven
Against the helm of that fierce pagan lord.
The blow had brought the stranger to his knees,
But God no longer wished for Parzival
To hold the blade he'd pilfered from the corps
Of Noble Ither, King of Cumberland.
A stolen sword could not withstand the strength
Of spiritual purity, which now
Bold Parzival was wielding as he fought.

The pagan king, who'd never once gone down
Beneath a sword, leapt to his feet again,
And now the verdict lay within the hands
Of Him on high. The two knights faced each other—
Parzival was weaponless, his foe,
Still gripping the mighty pagan blade in hand.
And all was still for one taut moment's breath.

Into the silence spoke the emperor
Of pagan lands with magnanimity
And graciousness: "it is quite plain to me,
Good warlike knight, that you would now fight on
Without your sword. But what would come of that?
What honor would I gain from you that way?
Refrain most valiant knight, and speak with me.
I've never battled 'gainst such mastery
And such great strength. Who are you, mighty one?
I must allow that had your sword not snapped,
You surely would have won my fame from me.
Come, let there be a truce between us now
Until we've rested and recovered."

They sat down on the grass not far apart.

"Believe me knight," the warrior went on,
"In all my days I've never met a one
More worthy of the fame that battle wins.
I wish to know your name and lineage.
If you will tell me that, my voyaging
And toiling will have been worthwhile."

"Since I am at the disadvantage
Now being reft of sword and weaponless,"
Replied the son of Herzeloyde to this,
"You need not trouble yourself asking me
To inform you of my name and heritage.
I will not by duress grant your request."

"Then I will name myself," replied the pagan,
"And will accept the slight of speaking first.
I am Feirefiz Angevin and a king."

At hearing these words, Parzival replied,
"By what law hast thou leave to use that name
Angevin? Anjou, with its fortresses,
Its lands, and towns are my inheritance.
I pray you sir, adopt a different style.
If I must lose my lands in this exchange,
Then you will have done me an injustice.
If either of us is an Angevin,
I claim by true descent that I am he
Unless it be by some strange circumstance
That you are one of whom I have been told,
The fearless warrior from pagan lands
Who has won love and fame beyond compare
With feats of arms, for that man is my brother.
All who have mentioned him have sung his praise.

Now sir, will you reveal your features unto me
That I may recognize if you indeed
Could be the man of glory who is praised?
I have been told that he is beautiful,
And further, that his beauty is most rare.
It is distinct and unlike any other.
If you will go that far with me and trust
To bare your head, you have my solemn oath
That I will not attack you thus unhelmed."

"I have small fear of any harm from you,"
Replied the splendid pagan warrior,
"For if I were to now remove my armor
And battle you with nothing but my sword,
All your skill in war would not avail you
Unless I chose to spare you from defeat."

The warrior then showed his bravery:
"This sword shall not be used by anyone.
Not you, nor me," he said and flung the blade
With all his might so that it whirled and flew
A lengthy distance from where they were seated.
"If there is any fighting to be had,"
The pagan stranger then continued,
"It shall be undergone on even ground.
Now, sir, you've told me that you have a brother.
Describe his face to me the way you've heard-
Tell me the complexion that they have named."

"His skin is dark and light, all intermixed,"
Said Parzival, "that's how it is described
Each time someone tells me of that great man."

"Then I am he," said mighty Feirefiz.

They wasted no time but removed their helms
And drew the chain mail coifs off of their heads.
Both found a treasure trove in brotherhood
More precious than all riches in the world,
For when their eyes met, they knew one another,
The courageous sons of mighty Gahmuret.
And in each heart, the word "brother" resounded
As though they were one soul placed in two bodies.
And Feirefiz was recognizable
By his complexion without any doubt.

The brothers ended their strife with a kiss,
Amid laughter and tears of exuberance,
Embracing with unbounded happiness:
It was more fitting to be friends than enemies.

"Happy I, to see the noble son
 Of mighty Gahmuret!" said Feirefiz.
"The gods have been exalted by this chance!
My goddess Juno has been glorified.
All gods and goddesses, I praise your power!
May that star's light be praised which casts its beam
Upon the path that led me on this quest
To you, most valiant and noble warrior!
Praise be the breeze and praise the gentle dew,
Awakening this morning of our meeting!"

"You speak well," answered noble Parzival.
"I would speak better if I knew the way,
And with affection. But I am not versed
To thus exalt with words your reputation.
Alas, God knows I do not lack the will.
Whatever skill my heart and eyes command,
I can say nothing else but that thy glory

Is the leader, I and my eyes the chorus.
I know for certain that I've not ere now
Been ever better matched by any knight."

They sat down for a second time in peace
And spoke of many things together there:
Their lineage, the death of Gahmuret,
The many years that had led both their steps
Toward the very ground where they had met.
And there were tears of joy and poignant sorrow
And such a mighty lionhearted love
That was shared by those two souls born of one.

At last, they rose from where they had been sitting,
Embracing once again in brotherhood
Before they rode from there to Arthur's camp.

Bold Feirefiz gave orders for his host
To pitch their camp upon those gentle shores
And wait for him until he should return.

THE RETURN

The morning slowly dawned in Arthur's camp,
And many gathered there were sorrowful
When they awoke to find that Parzival
Had once again departed from their midst.
King Arthur vowed to stay positioned there
For one whole week in hope of his return.
But as the sun ascended in its arc
Toward the midpoint of that gleaming day,
There was a message from Schastel Marveile
That there had been a battle by the shore,
Seen through the windows in the magic tower,
More mighty and more fierce than anyone
Had ever heard of or witnessed before.
The messengers were at pains to describe
What they had glimpsed through the enchanted glass.
Nor did they recognize the warriors
Who strove against each other with such might.

"I know who fights on one side," Arthur said,
"But who might it be who opposes him?
There are not many to withstand his strength."

Not long thereafter word was sent again
That two great warriors, the same that fought,
Were making their way toward King Arthur's camp.

Gawain was first to meet them in the field,
And when he learned who had accompanied
His dear friend Parzival into their midst,
He was delighted to meet that great king.
He made them welcome in his royal tent
Where they disarmed and were given fresh clothes
Which they put on before they journeyed onward

Toward Arthur's tent where he awaited them.

King Arthur was o'erjoyed when Feirefiz
Was brought before him with brave Parzival.
He sat them down and put them at their ease,
And those three spoke for many happy hours.
Both kings had great respect for one another
And had long wished for such a happenstance
As that which now grace had bestowed on them:
To meet and sit and speak with one another.

Arthur gave word that a festivity
Be held upon the meadow in the morn
And had a special table for the day
Be built, symbolic of their brotherhood,
To welcome Feirefiz into his host.
And Arthur among the troup himself was seen
With active fervor, busily engaged
In making ready the magnificent
Round table. By the moonlight clear, they made
A ring of seats upon the dewy green.
And when the sun's first rays touched o'er the hills,
The waking field shone in the dazzling splendor.

When morning on its climb into the day
Attained its midmost point, there, all the knights
And ladies had assembled in the ring.

Once all were seated, they beheld a maiden
Approaching them from far across the field.
Her clothes were fine and costly and well cut.
Her cloak was of rich samite, black as jet stones[36],
And on it gleamed a flock of turtledoves,

---

36   Black gemstones.

Wrought finely with Arabian gold, whose style
The insignia of the Grail did symbolize.
Her wimple high and white hid from their view
Her face with many folds as she with grace
Rode smoothly o'er the field to where they sat
With Parzival, placed close at Arthur's hand.
Down from her palfrey and with courtesy,
She leapt to kneel before Lord Parzival.
Then to her feet she rose and flung her hood
And wimple with its ribbons into the ring
As Cundrie the sorceress was recognized
By those who knew her well assembled there.
She spoke at once, addressing Parzival,
"Be modest now, and yet let all rejoice!
The writing of the Grail has testified
Now vouched by Trevrizent: 'you are to be
The King and Lord protector of the Grail.'
You must address Anfortas with your question
And end his suffering. He will be healed.
The prophecy will be fulfilled at last.
You fostered sorrows in your youthful plight,
But gladness comes now toward your destiny.
You have outlived your grief, won through to joy,
And purified your heart to serve its most
Exalted promise on behalf of God."

The wellspring of a heart's foundation true
Poured forth as tears streamed down the noble face
Of kingly Parzival, sprung from a source
Within a light eternal, vast, and good.

And thus spoke Parzival to mighty Cundrie:
"If I have been found worthy in God's eyes
Of what you name for me, then God has been

386

Benevolent and truly kind to me.
But tell me how or when I am to start
Upon my long sought road to happiness.
I do not wish to stall or put it off."

"My dearest lord," the sorceress replied,
"I shall show you the way to Munsalvaesche.
But you must not delay, nor put it off,
Because the help you bring has urgent need
Of those who wait, and lingering would be
To waste the time that could be lived redeemed."

And so, good Parzival set off next morn
With his bold brother, noble Feirefiz,
And- under guidance of wise Cundrie- thence
Did make his way toward his destiny.

THE GRAIL CASTLE

For all this time Anfortas and his people
Still suffered in great agony and grief.
From loyal love they left him in his plight,
For oft he asked they let him die and would
Indeed have done so shortly, had they not
As regularly brought the potent Grail
Before his eyes. They would have let him die,
Allowing his release, but for the hope,
Voiced by his honest brother, Trevrizent
The hermit, that with time a second chance
Would come for Parzival to fulfill his quest.
And so, with expectation in their hearts,
They waited for the day when Parzival
Would ride again to hopeful Munsalvaesche.

He was riding toward an outpost on that day
When a host of Templars, fully armed, rode out
To greet him on the field and bring him back
To the mighty fortress of the sacred Grail.
Once there, he straight sought out the wounded king
And found Anfortas lying on a bed,
Unable to sit up, held down with pain,
Who greeted Parzival kindly but with signs
Of anguish too.
                    "The many weary years
Of torment I have suffered- wondering
If ever you would come again to end
My heartache and my ceaseless agony-
Have spanned into an endless sea of woe
From which I've lost all hope of any return.
When last you came to these unhappy halls,
Your stay brought only more bereavement on.

Your parting in such fashion doth foretell
That if you are a warrior of grace
And reputation, you'll now show remorse.
Is your name truly Parzival? I'm told
It is. If so, please ask these knights and ladies
To let me die and so end all my grief.
If you are Parzival, tell them to keep
The Grail out of my sight for seven days
And eight nights, then all my travail shall end.
I dare not urge you any other way.
How gladly would your name be sung if you
Were known to be the one who brought me peace
By aiding thus my long awaited death."

Parzival wept, and to this he replied:
"Where is the Grail that we may now behold
Its hallowed presence as I speak the words?
If God in me is now to work today,
This company shall all be witnesses."

The Grail was brought before him. Thrice did he
In its direction kneel to glorify
The holy trinity in reverence.
Then rising to his fullest height, he spoke
What long awaiting years had potentized:
"Dear uncle, who does the Grail serve?"

The One that weaves through everything with grace
And loving power then helped Anfortas
To be well and whole, for his strength returned.
As doth the flower from bud to blossom bloom,
So color into his complexion poured.
His eyes, whose gaze for many years had been
The harbingers of pain by sorrow wracked,

Were changed into deep pools of gentle peace
As noble luster shone in them once more,
And warmth to his extremities was spread.

God's power to redeem and resurrect,
Applying divine artistry in acts
Of healing as the promise is fulfilled-
That power as the truest life to seek
Was made apparent to that company.

United by this healing act were all,
And Parzival was recognized as king-
Anointed the protector of the Grail.

So dies the winter into spring, and borne
With upward lift into the holy sun,
The heart with spreading petals through the warmth
Within the Godhead's light aligns itself.
Asleep before, awakes the holy spark
And knows itself within the mighty flame:
A love benevolent, omnipotent,
All powerful and ever born anew.

Condwiramurs, united with this shift,
Though separate from her love by outward space,
In spirit was joined with Parzival
And felt the distance close between their hearts
As all the trials of the earthly world,
The many years of loneliness and ache,
The longing chasm stretched between their souls,
Began to melt away. And messengers
Sent from the Grail arrived to speak the words
That she had heard already sound within:
The Grail had summoned her to join her love
And serve its holy name. So forth she rode
To Munsalvaesche to reunite with him.

Now Parzival rode to where Trevrizent
The faithful holy man dwelt humbly
Within the wilds of Terre De Salvaesche.
The wise old hermit's heart rejoiced to hear
The blissful news of this great miracle
Which had by grace at long last taken place.

"High God has many mysteries," he said
When Parzival had given him the news,
"There's no way to comprehend His power.
Not all of the angelic hosts above
Will ever understand the whole of it.
God is Man and is His Father's Word.
God is both the Father and the Son
And Holy Spirit, which has such a power
As to bestow great succor for our pain."

Good Parzival spoke to the holy man
And told him of his longing for his wife,
How he'd received word of her joining him,
And that he planned to meet her on her way.
The wise old man commended him to God
And sent him forth with blessings on his way.

The steadfast Parzival rode through the night
Toward daybreak, and as dawn's first light broke,
He saw pavilions pitched some distance off.
The sun had risen when he reached the camp
Of his beloved queen Condwiramurs.
There was a radiance, that day they met,
That seemed to shine out brighter than the sun.
Perhaps the sun itself increased its light;
In any case, some beacon shone out bright
Upon the crowd assembled there with them.

For many had come unto that meeting place
To gather on the meadow where at last,
They closed the distance held so long between
Their loyal hearts.
                  And there our story rests.
There was a love once in an age gone by
That hovered o'er two noble souls that lived
And found itself fulfilled within its source,
Awoken through the suffering travail
Of questing life as all who truly seek
Shall find the true spark, born within the flame.
So freedom dawns, so love fulfills its aim.

EPILOGUE

Here lies a brief account of those events
Which took place after noble Parzival
And his beloved queen Condwiramurs
Had reunited on their joyful day
Of celebration after Parzival
Had asked the fateful question of his uncle,
The kind Anfortas, to restore his strength
And free him from his ceaseless agony.

Now it was not known to good Parzival
That when he'd set forth many years before
From Belrepeire and left Condwiramurs,
She had discovered that she was with child
Soon after Parzival's departure thence.
Within that same year, she gave birth to twins:
Lohengrin and Kardiez were their names.
Across the long years of their father's quest,
They had grown up to be two noble princes,
And they were beautiful and radiant
As blossoms on the breath of early May.

When Parzival and his Condwiramurs
Had come together on the fateful day
Of their reunion, Parzival beheld
Kardeis and Lohengrin standing behind
Their mother with her lords and attendants
As she stepped forward to embrace her love.
She then turned and led Parzival to them-
His noble sons who stood awaiting him.

King Parzival could not believe his eyes.
He stood with tears upwelling filled with wonder
And gazed with love and awe at his two sons.

Then slowly and with gentleness, he reached
And placed his palms against each of their cheeks.
"My sons," he said, "my beautiful princes,"
Then wrapped them in his arms and kissed them both.

Kardeiz became the prince of all those lands,
Which Gahmuret, with his exploits of the shield,
Had won before he crossed out of this world,
And Lohengrin became prince of the Grail.

There was great joy and celebration there
Upon the field for one whole day and night.

The next day they returned to Munsalvaesche.
Before they rode from there, Lord Parzival
Requested to be brought unto that place
Where he had come upon his cousin's cell,
Sigune the woeful in that wilderness.
He was conducted to the rustic chamber
Through which the little stream still ran its course.
And there, they found the maiden where she knelt
Upon her knees beside her lover's tomb
Where death had come and brought her from this world.
They broke in through the wall to find her there,
And Parzival bade them raise the great stone slab
Off from the tomb for his dear cousin's sake,
Revealing Schionatlunder where he lay
Embalmed and left untarnished by decay.
Close by his side, they laid steadfast Sigune,
Who'd loved him faithfully until her death.
And over those true souls, they placed the stone
To close the tomb in which they lay together.

Now shall I tell you of bold Feirefiz,
The noble brother of the Grail's protector?

When they had journeyed back to Munsalvaesche,
The Grail was brought forth by Repanse De Schoye,
The keeper of the Grail of whom you've heard,
And all the great abundance of the Grail
Was there bestowed upon that company,
And though bold Feirefiz beheld the gifts
Bestowed upon them by the potent Grail,
He could not see the Grail before his eyes.
He only saw the cushion in the hands
Of the magnificent Repanse De Schoye
On which the Grail was placed, he saw no Grail.
He was most intrigued to behold the feast
Appear upon their plates before his eyes
And all the fine elixirs in the cups,
Which had not been poured though they shimmered there.
But more than anything he saw the queen,
The radiant Repanse, and was by love
So smitten that he was in agony
And yearned for her with all his mighty heart.
No longer did he care for all his wealth
Or all the exploits he had won with strength.
He only longed for beautiful Repanse.
Now kind Anfortas sat close by to him
And had observed this brave knight's suffering
And noticed that he was perplexed to see
The great abundance that was manifest.
He questioned Feirefiz and ascertained
That he could not behold the potent Grail
But only that which had been manifest.
He also learned from speaking with this lord
That he was in great torment for Repanse,
The sister of Anfortas. Now the Lord
Anfortas was of a most kindly nature
And wished to bring aid to the suffering
Of the magnificent and bold King Feirefiz,

So he spoke with his nephew Parzival
About the suffering of Feirefiz.
It came to them, both servants of the Grail,
That those who had not sworn to serving it
Would not be able to behold the Grail.
The Grail King then sat down with Feirefiz
And told his brother of the Son of God,
The path of love, forged by the flames of freedom,
Of giving up all one's ambition
And placing it in service of the Grail.
They spoke that night of many things together,
Of brotherhood and spirit and of God.

"It is a baptism of holy fire
That one must undergo to serve the Grail,"
Said noble Parzival to Feirefiz,
"And one must be prepared to give up all
For love and for the workings of the Grail.
You are a mighty king of many lands
And are free to choose any path you wish,
But if you yearn to see the Holy Grail
And for the love of fair Repanse De Schoye,
You must swear unto the path of love
And baptise yourself in the name of freedom."

"If baptism will bring me to Repanse,"
Said noble Feirefiz, "let it be done!"

Good Parzival laughed heartily at this
As did Anfortas who had joined them there.

"My dear and honest, valiant hearted brother,"
Replied the Grail King, "if it be your love
That guides your steps to Christianity,
Then it is love who will await you there
When you stand with all of your mightiness

Upon the path of true benevolence.
Your gods that you have worshiped until now
Will also be there when you have arrived,
For they too are the servants of the one
Who is supreme and master over all.
It is to serve the highest principle
That Templars of the Grail must ever strive."

The next day, noble Feirefiz Angevin
Was baptized with joy and solemnity
And gladly swore to serve the path of love
And place all of his might before the feet
Of freedom and the mission of the Grail.

That night as they sat, he beheld the Grail
And was filled with such awe and reverence
That tears were seen to glisten on his face.

Repanse De Schoye and he were met in love
And joined in marriage not long afterwards.
He was a mighty Templar of the Grail
With his pure queen, the radiant Repanse.
They traveled far and dwelt in distant lands
For many years as servants of the Grail
And helped the brotherhood of Munsalvaesche
Extend the power of the Holy Grail
Across the reaches of the world's expanse
Through Christendom and pagandom alike.

Anfortas lived on as a Templar knight
And rode great jousts to serve the mighty Grail.
Lohengrin, the young prince of the Grail,
Was known thereafter as Knight of the Swan.
His story you may hear if God allows
When fortune and time in accord may vouch.

APPENDICES

Appendix A- List of Characters
In Order of Appearance

Gahmuret- King of Anjou, Zazamanc, and Wales. Father of Pazival. Husband of Herzeloyde. Father of Feirfiz. Brother of Galoes. Lover of Belecane.

Belecane- Queen of Zazamanc. Mother of Feirefiz. Lover of Gahmuret.

Herzeloyde- Queen of Wales and Norgals. Wife of Gahmuret. Parzival's mother. Sister of Anfortas, Trevrizent, Schoysiane, and Repanse de Schoye. Daughter of the king and protector of the Grail (Frimutel), granddaughter of the first King and protector of the Grail (Titurel).

Gawain- A knight of the Round Table. Nephew of Arthur. Son of King Lot and Sangive. Brother of Beacurs, Cundrie, and Itonje. Husband to Orgeluse. Cousin of Parzival.

Lot- King of Norway. Husband of Sangive. Father of Gawain, Beacurs, Cundrie, and Itonje.

Parzival- The king and protector of the Grail. Descendant of the Grail family through his mother, Herzeloyde. Son of Gahmuret. Brother of Feirefiz. Father of Loherangrin and Kardeiz. Husband of Condwiramurs.

Jeschute- Duchess of Lalant. Wife of Duke Orilus.

Orilus- Duke of Lalander. Brother of Lahelin and Cunneware. Husband of Jeschute.

Sigune- A duchess. Daughter of Kyot and Schoysiane. Parzival's cousin. Lover of Schionatulander.

Schionatlunder- A prince. Son of Gurzgri and Mahaute. Grandson of Gurnemanz. Beloved of Sigune.

Ither of Gaheviez- King of Cumberland. Nephew of Uther Pendragon. Cousin of Parzival. The Red Knight. Slain by Parzival.

Iwanet- A page of King Arthur's court. Nephew of Queen Guinevere.

Arthur- King of Britain. Son of Uther Pendragon and Queen Arnive. Brother of Queen Sangive. Maternal uncle of Gawain. Brother of Sangive. Husband of Guinevere.

Guinevere- Queen of Britain. Cousin of Sir Segramors. Aunt of Iwanet. Wife of Arthur.

Sir Kay- The seneschal of Arthur's company. Stepbrother of Arthur.

Lady Cunnaware- Duchess of Lalant. Sister of Orilus and Lahelin. Friend of Parzival.

Gurnemanz- King of Graharz. Parzival's first mentor. Father of Schenteflurs, Lascoyt, Gurzgri, and Liaze. Uncle of Condwiramurs. Grandfather of Schionatulander.

Liaze- A princess. Daughter of Gurnemanz. Cousin of Condwiramurs.

Schenteflurs- A prince. Son of Gurnemanz. Brother of Lascoyt, Gurzgri, and Liaze. Cousin of Condwiramurs.

Lascoyt- A count. Son of Gurnemanz. Brother of Schenteflurs, Gurzgri, and Liaze.

Gurzgri- A prince. Son of Gurnemanz. Brother of Schenteflurs, Lascoyt, and Liaze. Husband of Mahaute.

Mabonagrin- Cousin to Clamide.

Mahaute- Sister of Ehkunat. Wife of Gurzgri.

Condwiramurs- Queen of Brobarz. Cousin to Sigune. Niece of Gurnemanz. Wife of Parzival.

Kyot- A duke. Brother of Manpfilyot. Father of Condwiramurs. Father of Sigune. Paternal uncle of Condwiramurs. Husband of Schoysiane.

Manpfilyot- A duke. Brother of Kyot. Paternal uncle of Condwiramurs.

Clamide- A king who tries to conquer the kingdom of Belrepeire in order to wed Condwiramurs. He is conquered by Parzival.

Kingrun- The seneschal to King Clamide.

Anfortas- The king and protector of the Grail. The Fisher King. Brother of Herzeloyde, Trevrizent, Schoysiane, and Repanse de Schoye. Son of Fromutel. Grandson of Tirurel. Suitor of Orgeluse.

Segramores- A knight of Arthur's company. Cousin of Guinevere.

Cundrie La Suziere- A sorceress. A messenger of the Grail. Sister of Malcreatiure.

Kingrimusel- Landgrave of Ascalun. Cousin of King Vergulate.

Beacurs- A knight of the Round Table. Son of King Lot and Sangive. Brother of Gawain, Itonje, and Cundrie.

The Turkoyt- A knight. Also known by the name of Florant of Itolac. Servant of Orgeluse.

Gringuljete- Gawain's horse. A warhorse from the company of the Grail given to Gawain by Duke Orilus as a token of friendship. Orilus received Gringuljete from his brother, Lahelin, after Lahelin slew one of the Grail Templars in a joust.

Vergulate- King of Ascalun. Brother of Antikonie. Kinsman of Kingrimursel. Distantly related to Parzival.

Antikonie- A princess. Sister of King Vergulaht.

Ehkunat- A lord. Brother of Gurzgri's wife, Mahaute. The king of Ascalun is slain by Ehkunat.

Liddamus- A member of Vergulaht's court and council.

Gabenis- A lord of the kingdom of Punterteis.

Trevrizent- A holy man. Brother of Anfortas, Herzeloyde, Schoysiane, and Repanse de Schoye. Son of Frimutel. Grandson of Titurel. Uncle of Parzival.

Schoysiane- A duchess. Sister of Anfortas, Trevrizent, Herzeloyde, and Repanse de Schoye. Wife of Kyot. Died giving birth to Sigune. Daughter of Frimutel. Granddaughter of Titurel.

Repanse de Schoye- Queen of the Grail. Sister of Anfortas, Trevrizent, Herzeloyde, Repanse de Schoye, and Schoysiane. Son of Frimutel. Grandson of Titurel.

Frimutel- Prior king and protector of the Grail. Son of Titurel. Father of Anfortas, Trevrizent, Schoysiane, Herzeloyde, and Repanse de Schoye.

Titurel- First King of the Grail. Father of Frimutel. Grandfather of Anforta, Trevrizent, Herzeloyde, Repanse de Schoye, and Schoysiane. Great-grandfather of Parzival.

Orgeluse- Duchess of Logroys. Widowed by Citigast. Loved by Anfortas. Wife of Gawain.

Ujurns- A knight of Puntereis who violates the knightly code and steals Gawain's horse, Gringuljete.

Malcreatiure- Brother of Cundrie la Surziere. The page of Orgeluse.

Lischois Gwelljus- Duke in the service of Orgeluse. Companion to the Turkoyt. Husband of Cundrie, Gawain's sister.

The Ferryman- Also called Plippalinot. Knight-ferryman near Schastel Marveile. Father of Bene.

Clinschor- Sorcerer. Duke of Terre de Labur. Enchanter of Terre Marveile. Lover of Iblis.

Bene- Daughter of the ferryman. Servant of Intoje and Gramoflanz. Friend of Gawain.

Arnive- Queen of Briton. Held captive in Schastel Marveile. Mother of Arthur and Sangive. Grandmother of Gawain, Itonje, Cundrie, and Beacurs. Wife of Uther Pendragon.

Sangive- A queen. Held captive in Schastel Marveile. Daughter of Uther Pendragon and Arnive. Sister of Arthur. Mother of Gawain, Itonje, Beacurs, and Cundrie.

Itonje- A queen. Held captive in Schastel Marveile. Daughter of Sangive. Granddaughter of Arnive. Sister of Gawain, Cundrie, and Beacurs.

Cundrie- A queen. Held captive in Schastel Marveile. Daughter of Sangive. Granddaughter of Arnive. Sister of Gawain, Itonje, and Beacurs.

Gramoflanz- King of Rosche Sabins. Son of Irot. Nephew of Brandelidelin. Husband to Itonje.

Irot- King of Rosch Sabins. Father of Gramoflanz. Brother-in-law of Brandelidelin.

Brandelidelin- King of Punterties. Uncle of Gramoflanz.

Feirefiz- King of Azagouc, Zazamanc, and Tribonit. Son of Gahmuret and Belecane. Brother of Parzival. Husband of Repanse de Schoye.

Kardeiz- Prince of Norgals and Anjou. Son of Condwiramurs and Parzival. Twin brother of Lohengrin.

Lohengrin- Prince of the Grail. Also known as the Knight of the Swan. Son of Condwiramurs and Parzival. Twin brother of Kardeiz.

Appendix B- Extended Prologue

Across is an example of an alternate prologue that I wrote when first developing the piece for various communities. The first stanza of this version is identical to the prologue at the beginning of the story in this book. From there it endeavors to address some of the social issues of our time in a way that is supportive to telling this story. I invite teachers, parents, students, and community members to create their own extended prologue for their version or telling of Parzival- A Journey of Initiation. You may find addressing specific social themes of the current time and events can help create a supportive beginning to your community's experience of your work with this story. You are of course also welcome to use the version below if you find that it is helpful.

EXTENDED PROLOGUE

Into our age, beings of eternity
Now manifest and herald forth this tale.
May primal wisdom, written in the stars,
Inscribed, safeguarded, be a healing balm
For ailments of the world's extremity.
Into the hands of honesty and truth,
Let fall these pictures of thy mighty works
And thunder forth your epic messengers.
Begin now where a tale is best begun,
At its beginning; though were we to trace
All true things to their truest origin,
We'd find all roads lead to their truest source.
But getting there is how we learn to love,
Which is the worthiest of all the arts,
For journeying unfolds our humanness.
Thus, let us hear this epic tale of quest
And perseverance for the highest goal
Toward which a human life can ever strive-
As though it were the tale of each of us.
It's clothed in garments of another time,
Attired outwardly in foreign style,
Which might to some seem far from modern ways;
But, nonetheless, behind its ancient cloak
Resounds the very essence of our times.
May primal costumes make perspectives new,
Now hearing how the future sings its way
Through the characters of old into the present.

To those who've gathered here, take no offense
At what you hear recounted in this tale,
For there are many references to God.
If there be those of you who have been wronged

411

By others who have slandered that word's meaning,
Please hear me out before you close the door
On hearing this account of Parzival.
His essence is so true it transcends creeds,
And though this story's steeped in Christian symbols,
Its universality speaks for itself,
For all religions at their origin
Are universal till they are corrupt.
I know of this as I myself for years
Have fought 'gainst dogma with distrust of creeds-
Torn in conceptual paralysis
Between love for this tale and my unrest,
Allergic to the lies of religion,
And indoctrinated by that very thing.
But in the end, love for the tale won out.
I stand here now before you undeterred
And vouch in confidence that if you reach
Into this story's core, you'll without doubt
Come to its revelation as I've done
And do continually, for its depth,
And breadth and height are infinite.

There is a secret that a friend once told me
That I'll now share before continuing-
Which is a doorway to the heart of things.
It is to contemplate for one's own self alone,
One's highest ideal. Not someone else's-
For only one's own ideal will turn the lock
And open the door to see things as they are.
It is a human trait to have ideals,
To strive for something greater than ourselves.
This may fill us with reverence, wonder, awe
And teach us to surrender unto grace.
Such wonder-filled experiences, if missed,

Can leave a heart reft of its nourishment.
The cynicism of our day oft robs
A person from connection with the depths
By which a soul derives its understanding.
For some it's God, for others Buddha, Christ,
Still others find divinity in nature,
The arts, peace, scholarship, or love,
Mohammed, Vishnu, Krishna; it for some
May be the case that their highest ideal
Lives in the practice of religion,
Indeed perhaps the very one to which
They have been born and raised up in to date:
Judaism, Christianity,
Islam, Buddhism, or Hinduism;
The list continues of religious names,
But finding one in freedom differs greatly
From living out old ways unconsciously.
Whatever it is, once one has conjured it,
It's possible to ponder further still:
What aspect is it of this high ideal
That turns your heart? What virtue calls it up?
Love? Reverence? Courtesy? Compassion?
What is it that instructs the soul to strive
Without the dictates of an outer creed?
Whatever that may be contains the key
To one's own unindoctrinated door
And higher understanding of true freedom.
One may from there find universality
And meaning in all things that bear a truth.
Now Parzival himself grappled these things
Until he understood them in his way.
And it took years of toil for his path
To be traversed in fullness to its end.
And so it is we set out on this quest,

And by the story's end with every hope,
We'll find its revelation as he did.
So when you hear the word God spoken here-
For Parzival again holds Christian symbols-
If such a word repels you from the story,
Try this suggestion ere you run from it-
That's if you wish to, if not, suit yourself,
For no one will arrest you if you go.
But if you wish to stay and hear the yarn
Despite the challenge of conflicting thoughts,
Replace whatever words have tripped your trigger
With your highest ideal, whate'er it be,
And see if that allows you to attend
More freely to this tale of all our lives.

And lastly, though it's said: "write what you know,"
One might in equal turn reply this way:
"Know what you write," for the events of life
Tell only of our own experience,
And there are greater things to come to know
Than only that which we have known till now.
And thus I say that though I've lived my life
Which may have seasoned me up to this point
To some degree, the actions of this tale
Are far from autobiographical.
You'd think the swords and jousts would make this plain,
But one might still assume they're but a foil,
A costume for one's own biography.
It's not my own life, but all of our lives
Whatever place we come from in the world,
Whatever race, sex, gender we may be,
Whatever the complexion of our skin,
For Parzival is a story of everyone;
However, I'll admit it comes from Europe;

What's more from western Europe to be precise.
We western civilizations both historically
And presently have shown ourselves to be
No less than a bunch of cultured barbarians
Who've given small thought to human dignity,
Love for our siblings here upon the earth,
Or recognition of more than ourselves.
To such extreme is this made evident,
I hardly dare to put this story forward;
And in some ways I probably should not.
I do not have an answer to that problem
And know that on this theme I'm poorly versed,
For I've been born to privileged ignorance
And cannot speak to my nearsightedness.
The only thing that I will venture forth
Concerns the nature of all tales good and true:
Their essence transcends their outward regard
And is united by our humanness,
For from the same source have they all arisen
And speak beneath their outward character
To that which we all share in siblinghood.
The scenes in this tale are not literal,
Nor are the characters made separate.
They are all aspects of a person's soul.
Each of us has both a king and queen
Within our individuality.
The sorceress, the ladies, and the knights,
The hero and the villain, royalty
And poverty, all live in each of us,
No matter how our lives look outwardly.
But this cannot be gleaned by reasoning,
It must be felt in our experience.
Though this will not repair the tragedies
That have been played out in our social constructs

By listening beneath these outward things,
We may find something that unites us all.

So we begin. Invoke the blessing now.
Call forth from thunder and the grace of kings
That power written from those lofted heights:
The warrior of spiritual strength
And boundless courage, he whose mighty soul
Withstood the test of time, relentless toil,
Fraught loneliness, and longing for his goal.

Raise from the depths again, you gods of grace,
His song to echo in our times once more.
Let it resound through us into the world.

Appendix C- Notes on Iambic Pentameter

Iambic pentameter is a poetic form that has five iambic feet in each line of text. An iambic foot is an unstressed syllable followed by a stressed syllable. One can notate this by using a small curved line for the unstressed syllables and a small straight line for the stressed syllables.

> ˘   _ ˘   _   ˘   _ ˘   _ ˘   _
> There is a love that hovers o'er our souls

While this story can be read and studied within a literary context, it was also written so that it could be spoken, made into short (or longer) plays, or told by a storyteller. To these and other ends, there are places in the text where the iambic pentameter is irregular or interrupted or shares the iambic verse with the previous line of text.

Here are some examples:

Shared lines: when the line is split in two parts, then the second half of the line is in the next line of text continuing the iambic pentameter.

Example:

And sluggishness!"
>   Then Kay lunged at him hard,

Exceptions:

When a second speaker interrupts the first speaker, the interruption is placed below the word that it is interrupting (this at times requires hearing the iambic rhythm in order to experience the interruption).

Example:

And honor, chivalry and courtesy."

>   "Be silent!"
Snapped Clamide angrily when he heard this,

Short lines: When a line does not complete the full iambic pentameter due to a style or character choice.

Example:

"Here lies Ither, king of Cumberland,
Slain by a javelin"

There are many ways to work within the artform of poetry to try and convey what one wishes to express. Still in other places in the text, you will find longer lines (an extra iambic foot), an extra unstressed syllable (also known as a feminine ending), or places where there are a couple unstressed (or stressed) syllables that happen next to each other, thereby disrupting the iambic rhythm.

These were placed there with intention - breaking the form can also allow for something else to be revealed. In these moments the reader can consider and investigate what could perhaps be stirring in the inner life of the character in that moment or what is happening in the scene of the story that would bring that disruption into the text.

About the Author

Séamus Maynard is an actor, writer and musician. He completed his degree in acting at *The Guildhall School of Music and Drama* in London. While there, he studied speech, classical acting and Shakespeare with Patsy Rodenburg. Prior to that he trained intensively in the Michael Chekhov Technique for several years studying and performing with Ted Pugh and Fern Sloan who founded *The Actor's Ensemble* based in Hudson, NY. Séamus co-founded a two year acting training entitled *Shakespeare Alive!* which was based on the teachings of Michael Chekhov and Rudolf Steiner's indications for speech and drama. Alongside *Shakespeare Alive!* Séamus studied speech formation with speech artist Christy MacKaye Barnes. He then attended *Artemis School of Speech and Drama* in West Sussex, England where he studied speech formation with Christopher Garvey. Currently, Séamus teaches the art of speech at *Inner Work Path* workshops and retreats (www.innerworkpath.com). He is a primary author of the *EduCareDo Speech and Drama as Living Arts* subject course (www.educaredo.org). Séamus also supports and facilitates the arts program on behalf of *Developing the Self Developing The World* (www.developingtheself.org). Séamus has taught acting, speech and movement at Emerson College in England, Stephens College Missouri, California State University's Summer Arts program, The New School NYC, Saint John's College in Istanbul Turkey and is a faculty member for *The Michael Chekhov School Hudson*, as well as MICHA (*the Michael Chekhov Association*). He currently teaches acting, movement and speech to young people of all ages.

As an actor and musician Séamus has worked with *Improbable Theatre* (London), The Belgian National Theater, Triple Shadow (La Mama NYC), *Heads Theater Company* (NYC) and *The Actors Ensemble* (NYC & Hudson, NY). Séamus is a co-founding member of Third Wheel Collective – a collaboration based theater company.

As a musician, Séamus studied classical guitar and composition with classical guitarist and composer Ed Flower. Séamus composes for and co-founded *Quiet In The Head*, a music group that composes original, instrumental music for violin and classical guitar. He also writes and performs with an acoustic folk group called *Living Roots*. He is the author of the book *Parzival A Journey of Initiation*.

About the Illustrations

Ella Manor Lapointe is a visual artist and children's illustrator. She trained in the *Neue Kunst Schule* (*New Art School*) in Basel, Switzerland. Since 2007 Ella has worked as a freelance artist and illustrator with work featured in various publications, including *Stella Natura*, a biodynamic planting calendar, *Das Goetheanum*, a weekly magazine based in Dornach, Switzerland, with international distribution, and has fulfilled commissions for postcards, art prints, and illustrated stickers around seasonal themes for children, for *Waldorfshop.EU*, based in Germany. In 2020 Ella created illustrations for the children's book *Tiny Tin Elf* by Eric G Müller (Alkion Press).

The graphite drawings in this book came into being while listening to recordings of Séamus speaking the text. Each picture attempts to resonate with the whole episode's unfolding.

To see more of Ella's work you can visit her website: http://ellapointe.com.

9 780648 578949